Printed in Great Britain
by Amazon

68536145R00253

The Sins of Jack Branson

A Novel

David Schulze

David Schulze Books | davidschulzebooks.com

Copyright © 2021 David Schulze
All rights reserved
Cover designed by Michael Star
Published in the United States of America

ISBN-13
eBook: 978-1-7370378-1-1
Paperback: 978-1-7370378-0-4

This book is based on a true story. Certain characters and incidents are inspired by real people and events, with intentional name changes, creative liberties, civil liberties, statue of liberties, fictionalizations, dramatizations, contextualizations, memorizations, amalgamations, salutations, salivations, heart palpitations, esophageal gestations, composite characters, characters who composite, compositions of said compositable characters, historical anachronisms, linguistic anachronisms, accidental anachronisms, blatant anachronisms, characters with a knack for isms, knick-knack-patty-whackronisms, and good ol'fashioned Hollywood inspiration-bastardization added for emotional, thematic, and/or artistic purposes. In short, any similarity to any real persons, living or dead, is completely coincidental and does not represent the intentions of the author.

Real London addresses are assigned to fictional Victorian businesses and residences for immersive purposes. Any similarity between a fictional business or residence depicted in this book and any business or residence at the same address is completely coincidental and does not represent the intentions of the author. For example, if your Varden Street flat is covered in mould, I had no idea. Also, holy crap get that taken care of.

No part of this book may be reproduced, or stored in a retrieval system, or transmitted in any form or by any means, electronic, mechanical, photocopying, recording, or otherwise, without express written permission of the author and a damn good reason.

There is nothing in the world more gratifying, more powerful, more indispensable than the love of a mother.

For Deb Stehman

PART I

The Sins of an Irishman in London

CHAPTER ONE

Full of Dandies

I.

Nothing is more powerful than the written word. Here's the proof: you have absolutely no idea who I am.

You don't, do you? I could just be one of those modern narrators, a Mark Twain type. Common. Aggressive. Sarcastic to pique your interest, but with just enough courtesy to avoid impertinence. That's how I get you to buy this book. Me being nice. Isn't it funny how that works? Even Shakespeare's Iago, a monster most wicked, treats you like a friend so you don't jump out of your seat and stop him. Of course you wouldn't, why would you? He lets you in on the plan. Respects your discretion. He ruins every life he touches, but you're okay with that. Because he's such a gentleman.

How is that not odd to you people? Where do you draw the line?

Iago and I have something in common; we are not who we appear to be. When I pass you on the street, when you serve me food, when I enter your shop, you say to yourself, 'What an upstanding young man, so fit and charming, not like those disgusting Frenchmen or Negros. A good old-fashioned Londoner.' But I am not one of you. You tell me so, the moment you hear my voice.

Unlike Iago, I won't pretend to be your friend. Friends know when to stop. When to change the subject at dinner parties. They look out for you when you need a place to stay. They have your back. They let you finish your story before judging you. They speak highly of you after you go.

Don't get me wrong, I'd love to be your friend. (I wouldn't be wasting my time writing a novel if there wasn't a chance.) You don't want to be mine. Why? Because of a book. The first book you've ever read. The only one you'd memorise. Its significance so assumed, you call it 'The Book' to save time. I admit, even I admire its power. It's why I'm writing this book. Men like me need all the help we can get.

I am a real human being. Not a fictional folk hero, or a cautionary tale, or the figurehead of some political manifesto. I'm not writing this for the money, and it's not an advertisement. What I have to say will shock you, and my frankness might offend some of you, but for good reason.

You see, I'm one of those homosexuals they told you about. Yes, those perverts that make you sick. The ones you blame for the ills of the world.

Have you caught your breath yet? Good. I have another special secret. I'm also a prostitute. Yes, you can be both.

Before you get too revolted and toss this book in the bin, let me make something clear. I never chose to be like this. I only became a prostitute when I came to London, which I never would've done if I wasn't exiled from my homeland.

The reason? Something happened in April of 1881, an incident I'd rather not get into. Just know that my parents disinherited me

three weeks later, banishing me across the sea and forbidding me to return. I was only twenty-four.

There. You know my sins now. If you want to cast this book aside, fine. I wouldn't blame you. I have no right to speak of such things, but stay, please, just a moment more. I'll only ask once.

There was a time when I refused to write such damning secrets, when I was afraid you'd use them to hurt me. But I'm writing this novel in September 1888, seven-and-a-half years into my exile, and I'm not afraid anymore. The Incident was my fault, yes, but it wasn't why I was banished from my homeland. My parents, otherwise decent people who made me the man I am today, believed exiling their homosexual son was honourable. That we were meant to be forgotten.

It's wrong, of course, but that's the way it is.

I'm writing this novel so you know what it's like to be a man like me. We suffer because you refuse to understand us. We are not evil. You are the evil ones, destroying our lives and calling it justice.

To the homosexuals reading this in hiding, you are not strange and you are not alone. Please, learn from my story. Write your own. By putting our lives on paper, we finally have an equal say. It's the only way we can prove we exist.

II.

I was blessed with life on 15 March 1857 among the beautiful hills of Ireland, in a charming rustic village you've never heard of.

It's not Dublin.

It's nowhere near Dublin.

Yes, you should still care about it.

Just as I loved my parents and younger brother, I loved my hometown. Everyone knew my name. My mates in school were the mates I drank with. When I graduated, I worked with Father in the fields. It was all to be mine, you see. I wanted that life, the same life as my Father, and his father. It was hard work, but I was good at it.

It wasn't always crops and livestock for me. Mother collected books. Homer, of course. Some Dickens. Verne and Dumas with bad translations. A large Shakespeare with full colour illustrations. I can still remember her favourite chair by the window where she read new releases and reread the classics. As I grew, Mother taught me to read with her. It's because of that dedication, that commitment, that I was able to evolve from reader to writer.

If you think it's unusual that a prostitute can both read and write, it is. I'm one of the few with a mind. Whores don't plan to write great classics of literature, just like I didn't plan on becoming a common slut. It was never supposed to be this way. My home. My family. My friends. My plans. My dreams. They were all taken away from me.

Normal people have the freedom and resources to develop into great men. Thanks to my exile, I was a finished product at twenty-four. I was all I would ever be. I had no real skills. My interests were my friends' interests. My future was my Father's future. My hometown was my whole world. The only part that was truly mine was my homosexuality. That's all I carried with me to London.

I don't regret loving men, but for some time I despised earning money with it. It's gross. There were fickle girls in my school days

who'd fling from one boy to another, always to fill some void in their lives. Just a phase of course. Once a man treated them like a diamond tiara, they enjoyed life properly. Not me. My world is one of secrets. Guilt. Lies. Panic. Both a sin and a crime, the associated fears in abundance.

I ultimately chose a whore's life for two reasons: it pays well, and I finally had a chance to feel complete in my own skin.

When the shame reached its peak, I bought a diary to pour my stories into. Every client is in that book. Their name. How we met. Where we did it. What they looked like. What it felt like. What I thought of them. Entire encounters in real time. It wasn't for blackmail. I'm not that clever, let alone cruel. I only told that book what burly farmers talk about in the pubs. What gentleman of the Empire tell each other in their clubs over cigars and brandy. What all men think about. I was on my own. No friends to boast to. No work associates who shared my life. Putting what I did into words meant something, like my days weren't wasted, and describing the sex in structured paragraphs made it seem normal.

Contrary to what you people believe, sodomites don't seduce random streetwalkers. It is a crime after all. We have to be sneaky about it. The men in the pubs back home talked on and on about the British, how soft you all are, how queer. They told me London was full of dandies, but I couldn't find any when I first came here. I honestly thought I missed them.

Did they tell you how to spot one? How they walk? What company they keep? You probably think you've never met one, but you have. We're everywhere, not just the working class. Gentlemen.

Lords. Heirs. Hundreds throughout the aristocracy. 'Impossible' you say, but it's true. And if you've met a peer who's secretly homosexual, chances are good I've already slept with him.

You might be wondering how someone like me even becomes a prostitute. It's a bit complicated, so let me formally regress to the beginning of my story, the first day of my exile, and I'll tell you how it all started.

III.

28 April 1881

Not an hour off the train, I bought a bundle of parchment, some ink, wax, and a pack of envelopes to write Mother a letter. I apologised for the Incident and begged to be let back. I grew antsy the next day, so I sent another, telling her how scared I was, that I forgave her for banishing me. The next day another letter, and the next, until I found myself writing one every morning.

And I still do.

I don't ask to come home anymore. I just give updates on my London life, nothing specific. A newspaper headline. A book I was reading. A memory from my youth. A joke. My weekend plans. Never the men, that wouldn't help. In the end, I treat her with respect. Even after everything, she will always be my Mother.

I conclude every letter with 'I love you' and attach a £5 note; a son must provide, after all. She hasn't thanked me for the money yet, though she doesn't have to. Matter of fact, she hasn't responded at all.

I'm sure there's a logical explanation. More than three hundred a year? She has to have gotten one by now.

I stayed in a public house those first few weeks. I had no savings for a flat, and I needed a job before I ran out of money. I roamed the streets every day looking for work, but so did everyone else. There's just too many damn people here. Thanks.

Fortunately, I acquired the one job no one wanted: courier for the Cherry Street Post Office in Camden Town. Its sole proprietor was one Mr Munce, a foul-tempered git who burnt through three pupils the month before. He claimed they never cared about the job and moved on to better things, but I sensed spite in his voice. I think Mr Munce verbally abused those boys until they quit. He had that way about him. Gin in his morning coffee. Enough cynicism to spoil a dinner party. Was it because his tiny spectacles hurt his glassy eyes? Did the lack of hair on his melon head make him insecure? What could explain his consistent lack of decency towards the only other employee in that joke of a post office? Such answers elude mortal men.

I organised Mr Munce's files until four, after which I delivered telegrams. It was all dreadfully dull, but Munce paid well for small jobs. He even gave me a raise a few weeks later. (No doubt a bribe to keep me on; couldn't be anything else, since he never thanked me for the hours I spent on him.)

Mr Munce didn't have a bicycle for me to use, so I bought my own at a church bazaar. It was scratched and a bit rusted, but it still had life left. I didn't know how to ride one until I was twelve. My kid brother knew before I did. Mother didn't shame me for waiting so

long. She was good like that. Now I can ride across the whole city.

How far I've come.

IV.

18 June 1881

Once I had enough saved, I moved into the first flat I could find, a one-room on Varden Street, Whitechapel. I had the space to myself, a blessing from what I'd heard of London tenements, but it was still too small for one man. Water stains and mould swirled across the ceiling like a perverted Sistine. Dirt clawed its way up the walls. No bed frame, just a mattress on the floor. (I borrowed the landlord's blanket my first night; never gave it back.) The cooker was broken, which made the kitchen worthless. I never used the table or chair, except to write my letters.

One of my few possessions was a cigar box I salvaged from the rubbish, an ornate little thing, perhaps once belonging to a Czar or a Sultan. I used it to store my savings and writing supplies. I hid it in the hole under my mattress, and not just from potential burglars, the flat itself. I didn't trust it. Everything was sickly, even the light. My window was crusted in a rust-coloured film, some ancient stain of questionable origin that tainted the morning light a filthy amber hue. I dreaded returning there at night. Some evenings I stayed in The Regent's Park and prayed for God to destroy that abysmal place.

He wasn't too far, turned out. On Waver Street, twenty minutes from my flat, is a tearoom called Dubeau Frères. Don't let the name discourage you. Heaven is French. Try a Délice de Mousse if you don't believe me. It's impossible to describe without sounding

sexual. The wet, runny chill of perfectly balanced vanilla ice cream. The ephemeral, soft pillow of chocolate mousse. The super sweet kicker of classic whipped cream. Strips of dark chocolate on top like a crown.

Even such a basic description fails to capture its magic. It makes a philosopher stop thinking. A politician question his platform. A Shakespeare actor of fifty years forget his lines. An exiled homosexual feel like he's back home.

V.

3 October 1881

I was celibate for six months before my carnal urges spiked. It was the smell that did it. Brandy and cigars, a natural musk for gentlemen. Nothing else like it in the world. I counted the hours until my telegram deliveries, eager just to be in the room with them. Their scruff with slight twinges of grey. Their nods of recognition. Their soft smiles. Their envy of my youth.

I touched myself dreaming of men like them, but not because of their looks. They were too old. Big guts from decades of fatty meals. Misty eyes from clouds of smoke every night. All of them were quite angry as well. No, it certainly wasn't their looks, nor their status either. I loathed their huffs of disappointment as they read my telegrams in their vast libraries, surrounded by books they never read and expensive handmade furniture they never used. They had nothing to sigh about. They never spent two weeks in a public house. They never begged for work door to door.

In the end, I was a man lost at sea, ravenous enough to eat my

own arm. Such desperation got me exiled, but to deny it is inhuman. I had not lost my sense of reason, not yet, so I bided my time and waited for a natural solution to present itself.

You can find anything in a city of four million people, especially in places with alcohol. Drunk men are fascinating creatures. They shamelessly confess foul, personal secrets in crowded pubs, and anyone close enough to listen would be too drunk to remember any of it. What a strangely harmonious ecosystem. A sober bobby could arrest half of London in a place like that. I was there, amid the wretches, when I found my answer. I overheard an old dandy, cheeks red as his port, boasting to a friend that he sodomised a boy in his own house under the guise of a telegram delivery.

It was so simple it made me angry. Risky, degrading, but with incredible potential. I couldn't ignore such a perfect setup. The biggest immediate problem was Mr Munce. He wasn't smart, but he wasn't stupid either. I had to cut him in to keep him quiet, which meant I had to tell him what I was.

I should've been more careful, looking back. I was naive. I underestimated how dangerous it was to tell an employer, let alone someone I barely knew, and I was incredibly lucky. My revelation made Munce sick of course, and any respect he had for me (if any!) instantly vanished, but I chose the right man. Mr Munce hated the Post Office. I was a gateway to a fortune of untaxed income, and he exploited me with vengeance.

He started with an advertisement in the window: *Special Services for Esteemed Customers, £2/hour*. A mere trifle, of course. Mr Munce didn't quite understand what he was doing. He assumed

sodomites were exclusively working class, but chimney sweeps and dockers don't send telegrams. Didn't take long for him to receive enquiries from Honourables, Barons, even Earls and Viscounts. It was difficult for Munce to accept that his great nation rewarded depravity, but once the shock subsided, he made a slight adjustment: *£12/hour*.

Mr Munce and I shared the profits fifty-fifty. It sounds steep, but Mr Munce took the enquiries, managed the books, and stayed silent to the police. My risk matched his workload, and I depended on his reliability over the years.

We never talked about our personal lives or met outside work, but we didn't need to be friends. It was bad enough being accomplices. He hated being in debt to a sodomite, often mocking my manhood, insinuating I had sluttier tendencies than I did, constantly making assumptions about how I lived, sometimes using nicknames like 'Princess', 'freak', or 'Mary-Ann'. When I left to deliver my telegrams, he wished me luck before adding a degrading comment about women, children, or dogs.

Everything Munce said was in jest, so the insults were never a real problem. He was only occasionally heartless.

VI.

15 March 1882

On my first birthday in exile, I was convinced Mother wasn't receiving my letters. I wanted Mr Munce to gently alleviate my fears, but he had a different tone in mind.

'Do you have any idea how the post works, Princess?' Munce

scolded over his gin and coffee. 'We don't stuff the boats with letters until they overflow into the sea, we're organised. Do you have any idea how unrealistic it is for daily letters to disappear?'

'But what if she moved?' I whispered. 'Or if she refused them?'

'Then they'd come back here with a big red Undeliverable stamp.'

'And you're sure—?'

'Hasn't happened.'

I looked down at my shoes and started sobbing.

Mr Munce crossed his arms. 'You really are a freak, Freak. Why do you care so much? They banished you.'

'They're still my family!' I cried. 'They need to know I forgive them, that I want to go back!' I blotted my tears with a knuckle.

Mr Munce lowered his eyes. He tenderly approached me, hesitant to touch else I'd explode. He settled for rubbing my back.

'It's okay, kid, just... Don't cry, okay?'

'I'll be fine.' I cleared my throat. 'I get over it eventually. This happens all the time.'

'Why am I not surprised?'

'It's just... I put so much time into each one. And don't get me started on the five quid.'

'What five quid?'

I chuckled cynically. 'Exactly.'

Mr Munce blinked. 'Not every day.'

'Course not,' I muttered. 'Mondays I send ten.'

Munce softened. 'Why?'

I snorted. 'No post on Sunday, Beefeater.'

'Why in general, Cock-eater?' Munce jeered back.

I shrugged. 'I love them.'

Mr Munce looked at me in an unusual way, a gentler way. Fast as it came, he cleared his throat and returned to normal.

'Listen. Kid. If it happens, I'll make sure you're the first to know.' Then a miracle happened: Munce smiled. 'I'm in this too deep.'

I nodded with gratitude, and we hugged it out.

That's how Mr Munce was. He could be a bit condescending, but his sympathy was sincere.

Munce stopped calling me Freak by birthday number three, settling for just the girly ones. He didn't bake a cake, but he did buy me a present: a silver pocketwatch.

Things weren't so bad between us. For a time.

VII.

Judge me if you must, but I know there's a part of you deep inside that wants to know what sodomy is like. You've come this far, haven't you?

I won't give my clients' true names (I am still in business after all), but trust me, they are established men of all shapes and sizes, and not just in London. Many times I met an Earl named Reggie in his country manor. I'd bike to the Servants' Entrance and interrupt Reggie at dinner with an urgent telegram in front of his wife and daughters. We'd sneak off to the library, where he'd shag me over his writing desk, finishing just in time to avoid suspicion. Other Lords liked to show me off at society gatherings where I'd be their escort. Opera premieres. Art galas. Fabulous dinner parties. Some might've suspected our real relationship, but no one dared to accuse

a Lord. Some clients bought me clothes. Others were too ashamed to talk. I'm not surprised. When I walked through their houses, every hall filled with gorgeous paintings and statues, I'd remember how painful it was for them. None of them bought those things. Their kind always inherits. Every room reminded them what they would lose if they spoke the truth. That's why they like me, I suppose. I'm the only one who understands what it's like to have the whole world against them. I let them be their true selves, and in exchange they protect me from my oppressive society.

Do you see the irony? They sure don't.

Physically we do everything. I suck them, they lick my arse, shag me backwards, upwards, whatever the mood calls for. Some sip brandy or smoke cigars while we do it. Many prefer theatrics, scenarios we'd perform, like a headmaster punishing a delinquent... *with his cock!*

We never talk about our lives. Well, they do. Mostly how their wicked wives drive them mad. They don't want to hear about me. I don't blame them, of course. I'm a handsome and young companion. I'm flattered that they can't hold a conversation in my presence.

They're busy people, I understand that. I shouldn't expect them to talk about trivial matters like my feelings.

But truly, is it so inhuman to want respect? Am I not a person? I dunno, is it too much to ask? Doesn't have to be every time. I don't even care that much. I'm not desperate or needy.

Just once in a while.

Anal penetration is far from painless, but there's pleasure there too. I don't know why. With the right angle and enough lubrication,

it's phenomenal.

I'm sure you people envy whores, male or female, for having adventurous, lust-filled lives. Who wouldn't want to shag multiple times a day? To be entirely truthful, I haven't enjoyed sex in a while. There are special exceptions of course, but I fake my enjoyment most of the time. My clients are old and fat. Do you really expect them to do any work for my pleasure? After they finish, do you think they stay behind and help me off? Just like their wives, I'm on my own. They make the money, they get what they pay for.

I earn on my back, but it's far from easy work. I have to read my clients' bodies to figure out what I need to do for them to finish as fast as possible, while also keeping watch to make sure we don't get caught. (One of us has to. Might as well be me.) That's more instinctual, though. I pass the time by doing maths in my head. Rent. Food budget. Other expenses. I don't have time otherwise, and separating my brain from my body does wonders for my stamina.

When it gets to the point of the maths hurting more than their cocks, I like to turn off and admire my surroundings. Oh, those houses! I'll never be able to live in those places. What a world. Entire rooms dedicated to menial tasks, like the Brandy Room or the Bridge Room. Duplicates differentiated by their sizes, like the Small Library, the Large Smoking Room, or the Intimate Dining Room. Each adorned to the nines with large paintings of their ancestors, revered Lords of old. I love making eye contact with them. They see it all. They know. Nothing they can do but watch their kin, a great man burdened with the legacy of their dynasty, shag an Irish sodomite in front of them.

I made a fortune with my scheme but not enough to justify the risk of capture. Just being in their houses made me vulnerable, even though I was invited. Telegram boys don't stay long anywhere. People would ask questions if they saw me. I wouldn't be surprised if their wives and butlers already know about me, who I really am.

One time I left my messenger bag in Reggie's library, my diary inside, and I had to sneak past servants just to retrieve it. I wouldn't have much protection if I were caught. The telegrams themselves were just nonsense translated into Latin, a natural deterrent, but if a bobby was bold enough to translate a Lord's private message, my only safeguard was to claim that the message was in code. There was no alibi for the act itself. Just one accidental witness could start a scandal.

You must think I'm mad. Why would I willingly put myself in danger? If it wasn't for the sex or the thrill of escape, was it worth the money? I already told you, I didn't have a choice. If I did, I'd be home right now. Reading books with Mother. Working with Father in the fields. Helping my brother with his homework. Drinking with my mates. Roaming those beautiful green hills. Taking holidays with my family.

I miss it so much.

I kept telling myself how lucky I was. I knew it wasn't ideal. I was past hope, fraternising with adulterers, with liars. But I was so proud of it all. I salvaged my entire life, built it back up on my own. I was finally me. And I could make a decent living while staying me. That was never possible back home. If the Incident hadn't occurred, I'd still have to lie every day, filled with shame, filled with hate.

Coming here taught me that. That's what strengthened me the most. I was always destined for a rotten life; I learnt it hard, but thank God I learnt it young.

That's what I told myself every day for three years. Three bloody years. Then nothing. Gone, all of it. My happiness, my gratitude, my pride in my London life, all in the span of a single night. Because they weren't real. They never existed in the first place. Just delusions of a madman, a sailor so afraid of drowning, so grateful for a boat that he ignores the cracks in the hull. How obvious it is to me now, what I fool I used to be. So unhappy. So scared. A goddamn liar.

And all because of that night. The night I woke up. The night that ruined everything.

The best night of my life.

The night I met Oliver.

CHAPTER TWO

Homosexual Too

I.

9 November 1884

Oliver Hawkett and nothing else. No Sir. No Lord. No acronym tacked on. I wasn't raised in a society that focused on such trivial matters, but three years in London was enough for me to understand: if you hadn't a title or an estate, you're nothing.

'Who is he?' I asked, as if I was mistaken.

'No idea,' Munce replied. 'Doesn't matter anyway. He paid in advance.'

I reread the name again in Munce's ledger. Impossible. 'How can he afford me if he's not a Lord?'

Munce shrugged.

'Shouldn't we be concerned?' I asked.

'Not everyone's a bobby, kid. Quit being so soft.' Mr Munce cleaned his glasses with trembling hands.

I furrowed my brow. 'Mr Munce, are you okay?'

Munce sipped his Beefeater & Coffee. 'Should be asking you that.'

'Are you still upset about yesterday?'

Munce closed the ledger. 'Don't be daft.'

'I wouldn't blame you. That man with the beard—'

'Nothing happened!' Munce snapped.

I held my tongue. 'Okay. If you say so.' I wetted my lips. 'You just look unhappy.'

Mr Munce scrubbed a hand over his face. 'I work for the Post Office. I have a headache. The weather is dreadful every day. And to top it off, my sodomite telegram boy prostitutes himself to upper class perverts, and not only is there a market for such services, it's expanding. So what in God's name makes you think I was ever happy?'

We stared at each other with mirroring frowns.

Munce cocked his head back. 'You should go.'

I nodded uneasily and ambled away.

'And don't worry about Hawkett,' Munce added. 'He looked harmless.'

I half-smiled. 'Just surprised, is all.'

Munce took another sip of his spiked coffee. 'Not too long ago, rich blokes came here to send actual telegrams. Now they want you to wear a bonnet and knickers for a Sunday stroll down Piccadilly.'

I chuckled. Munce didn't. He turned away, letting out a long sigh. 'Nothing surprises me anymore.'

II.

The rest of the day crawled. When Munce handed me Oliver's telegram of nothing, I found myself obsessing over the address.

A layman with a flat on Audley Street? In bloody Mayfair? Where did he get the money? How could someone earn that much

on their own? Besides me?

Not like me to be paranoid. Just an unusual case, nothing more.

Still. Doesn't add up.

My mind was still preoccupied by eight o'clock, and since it was unseasonably fair for an Autumn evening, I decided to walk to Mayfair. I tried to pace myself at first, but my curiosity over the mysterious Mr Hawkett got the better of me. I jogged down Hampstead Road, cut across Grosvenor Square, and arrived at 5 Audley Street ten minutes early.

After double-checking the address, I rang the bell. Footsteps raced down the stairs. Before I had time to react, the door whipped open.

The mysterious Oliver Hawkett was the opposite of what I imagined, which only bothered me more. Not just young; practically a kid, looking eighteen despite being twenty-three. Curled auburn hair. Big green eyes. Dimples that made his freckles stand out. Shorter than me. Thin. Youthful build. His dress suit was clean but noticeably haphazard. Jacket three sizes too big. Tie askew. Waistcoat buttons misaligned by one. Shirt half-tucked in. No belt. The only part that didn't match were his shoes, a pair of brown loafers caked with scuffs.

Oliver was out of breath, grinning at the sight of me. There was something unusual about it, and not just because his front teeth stuck out like a beaver. It wasn't a smile of lust or simple courtesy. It was friendly. He was genuinely glad to see me.

'Telegram for Oliver Hawkett,' I blurted with stupid formality.

'Oh wow!' Oliver cried, looking me up and down.

I glanced down at my clothes. 'What? What's wrong?'

'I didn't know what to expect. I hoped you were cute, but I didn't think...' Oliver chuckled. 'Wow!'

I forced a smile, slowly closing my jacket. 'I don't—'

'Oh, how rude of me.' Oliver held the door open, and I plodded in. The lobby was small and warm, soothing green paper on the walls and a large staircase that spiralled up.

Oliver stuck out his hand. 'Oliver.'

I shook it. 'Nice to meet you.'

Oliver gasped. 'You're Irish! That's great, I didn't know that.'

I clenched my jaw, nodding awkwardly as I removed my paddy cap.

Oliver frowned. 'Did I say something wrong?'

'No,' I mumbled, drifting toward the staircase. 'Shall we go up?'

Oliver didn't move. He simply stared at me with glossy eyes.

'Are you okay?' I asked, blushing a bit.

Oliver laughed spontaneously. 'You're the most beautiful man I've ever seen.'

My heart skipped a beat. I stuffed my cap into my pocket. 'Thanks.'

'I love your eyes.'

I blinked. 'My eyes?'

'They're so blue. I could get lost in them.'

I smiled bashfully. 'That's very sweet of you.'

'I'm sure you get that a lot.'

'No, that... That's a new one.'

Oliver cocked his head to the stairs. 'Race you to the top?'

I snorted. 'Race me?'

Oliver nodded excitedly.

I smirked. 'Alright.'

Oliver dashed up, skipping steps. I darted after him. Oliver laughed as he rounded the corners. Flight after flight, we raced like schoolboys. Oliver made it to the top first and waited outside the door.

'Not far behind,' Oliver said, impressed. 'Good stamina.'

I stopped, trying to slow my breathing. 'You have no idea.'

Oliver unlocked the door and held it open. I took two steps into the drawing room before halting with wonder. Such extravagance! A chandelier of crystal and gold. Beautiful paintings on every wall. A flat built for a king. Never knew luxury could be so concise. Perfectly sized Persian rugs. Hand-carved furniture custom made for two. Porcelain both beautiful and practical. Nothing was wasted. Everything had value.

Oliver locked the door and stood next me, gazing at his possessions like he never truly saw them before.

'This is amazing,' I said.

'It is, isn't it? Took a lot of effort.' Oliver undid his tie. 'I'm sorry about my state. Don't have a man for this sort of thing.'

'It's okay, I don't mind.'

'I could change. Should I change? Something more comfortable?'

I smiled at the implication. 'If you want. Need help taking it off?'

'No thanks. You can wait on the sofa.'

I lifted my brows. 'Oh. If you prefer.'

'Actually, can you open the Merlot? I'll be back in a moment.'

Before I could respond, Oliver ran into the bedroom and closed the door. I looked at the windowsill. He wasn't joking about the Merlot.

I slowly uncorked the bottle. *What's happening right now? He doesn't want me drunk, not with wine. Does he want to talk? Everyone else would have me naked by now.*

The front door suddenly unlocked. A Postal Boy moseyed in with a ring of keys and a parcel under his arm, stopping short at the sight of me.

I stared back. What a strange moment. It felt wrong, like neither one of us was supposed to be there.

'Can I help you?' I murmured.

The Postal Boy slowly placed the parcel on the door-side table. 'I'm sorry. I thought no one was home.'

Just then, Oliver made a thud inside the bedroom. The Postal Boy whipped his head toward the door like a meercat.

'Is that all?' I asked.

The Postal Boy squinted at me, slowly stepping out to the hall. He closed the door with a loud click.

'What was that?' Oliver called from the bedroom.

My muscles relaxed. I poured the Merlot into two gold-leaf glasses. 'You got a parcel.'

I pussyfooted to the door-side table, a glass in each hand, to inspect the parcel. No name on the label. Correct address. Customs stamp from Bombay.

Oliver strolled out of the bedroom in an entirely different suit, one that fitted better and matched the shoes. It was more charming,

but incredibly common. Matter of fact, it looked downright cheap.

'I'm not really a tails person. Hope you don't mind.'

Oliver stopped at the door, furrowing his brow. He reached over and slowly turned the lock.

I studied his behaviour with concern. 'What is it?'

Oliver smiled at me and took a glass from my hand. 'Something I bought in India. Took a while to get here, as you can imagine.'

I faked a smile and sipped the Merlot. Good stuff. 'You went to India?'

'Just for a visit.' Oliver sauntered to the sofa and sat down, his green eyes inviting me over.

After a deep breath, I joined him, sitting at the opposite end.

Oliver immediately slid closer. 'Tell me about yourself,' he said, sipping his wine.

'What do you mean?'

'Not a very complicated question.'

I blew my cheeks out, exhaling softly. 'Not much to tell.'

'Of course there is.'

I smirked. 'You say that as if you're sure.'

'Everyone has a story. What's it like being a prostitute?'

I pointed to the parcel. 'Tell me about India.'

'I asked you first.' Oliver smiled. 'Relax.'

'Funny, you telling me to relax.'

'Why do you say that?'

'You talk fast and say nothing.' I blinked, surprised by my wit.

Oliver raised his brow. 'That was good.'

I chuckled sharply. 'It was, wasn't it?'

Oliver refilled our glasses. 'Is this unusual?'

'No, I've had Merlot before.'

'Not with your clients, I take it.'

'Some feed me first, but we don't talk. About me, at least.' I flashed Oliver a resolute look.

Oliver rubbed the back of his head. 'I understand if you don't want to— '

'I don't understand why you do.'

Oliver stared into his glass. 'Would you believe me if I told you I don't have many friends?'

I examined the expression on his face. 'I don't see how that's possible.'

'It's okay to say it. Just a fact. I have acquaintances, sure, but not someone like you.'

'Like me?'

'I dunno. Confident.'

I snorted. 'What makes you think I'm confident?'

'You seem like you have everything figured out.'

I sipped my glass with a frumpy frown. 'That's the magic of confidence. Makes insecurity look like pride.'

'Aren't you?'

'Aren't I what?'

'Proud?'

'Of what? Being a whore?'

Oliver shrugged. 'Everything.'

I looked away, rolling my tongue across my teeth. 'I'm glad I'm still here.'

'What about being Irish?'

I pursed my lips. 'If I ever implied I wasn't proud to be Irish, you're mistaken.'

'No!' Oliver exclaimed apologetically, 'I just... You acted strange when I mentioned your accent.'

I shook my head. 'That's nothing. Just me being peevish.'

'Why?'

I studied Oliver's posture. His body was facing me, eyes unblinking. He actually wanted to listen.

I swallowed. 'I don't belong here. When people hear my accent, they ask, "Are you from Dublin?" It's always Dublin. If not that, it's "Did you leave because of the famine?" or "Why don't you have red hair?" They don't even care about the answers, they just need to say something. That's all I am to you people. A bloody topic of conversation.'

Oliver lowered his head. 'I shouldn't have asked.'

'I'm glad you did. No one does.'

Oliver smiled, relieved. 'Where are you from?'

'Dunderrow, in County Cork.'

'What's it like there?'

'Lots of farms, really. Potatoes, barley, cows, sheep, pigs.'

'Sounds nice.'

I sighed wistfully. 'It really was.' I took a big sip of wine.

'Something happened,' Oliver whispered, 'Didn't it?'

I shook my head. 'I don't talk about it. Neither did my parents. If we did, we just called it the Incident. That didn't happen much.'

'You don't want to tell me?'

'It's not hard to guess,' I mumbled, shifting in my seat. 'I haven't seen my family in three years.'

Oliver rubbed my back. 'That must've been awful.'

I sat up. 'It was for the best, really. I get to be myself out here and all, so... What about you? What's your story?'

Oliver waved a dismissive hand. 'Don't worry about me. I want to know more about you.'

'What's there to know?'

'This is what you do, all the time? Sleep with Lords for money?'

'And you. Speaking of, how can you afford a place like this?'

'Almost exclusively Lords, correct?'

I sighed. 'Yeah.'

'And always with the telegram charade?'

'Yeah.'

'It's brilliant.'

'I can't take credit for it, but yes. Quite brilliant.'

'Why the Post Office?'

'I work there, actually work there. Used to be all I did at one point.'

'And that man who took my appointment, the bald one with the speech impediment...?'

I laughed sharply. 'Mr Munce? No, he talks fine. He was probably drunk.'

'He knows you're homosexual?'

'Hence the drinking.'

'And he's comfortable working with you?'

'He doesn't approve if that's what you mean. He's in it for the

money.' I chuckled. 'He said he'd turn me in if I tried to leave.'

Oliver frowned. 'Why would you work for a man like that?'

I shook my head rapidly. 'No, no, he wouldn't really do that. He's quite sarcastic. More ally than enemy.'

Oliver shifted in his seat, not quite convinced. 'He seemed angry when I paid for you.'

'When was this?'

'Yesterday.'

'What time? After four?'

'Perhaps.'

I nodded. 'That explains it, he... Well, he got into a nasty row with a customer. He's still raw about it.'

'What happened?'

I hunched over, biting my lower lip. 'It's quite strange, actually. After lunch yesterday, I was washing the window outside when a growler pulled up. An angry young man with a beard stepped out. And I mean a long, ugly... like he grew it out *because* he was angry, you know? He raced in, and I noticed there was a woman inside the growler, a beautiful blond with a worried look. I heard raised voices behind me, and through the window I could see the man with the beard screaming at Mr Munce. His face was all red, spittle flying out, but I couldn't understand what he was saying because Mr Munce was screaming over him. They kept interrupting each other. I tell you, I've known the man three years, but I've never seen him that angry. Gave me chills. After a while, the man with the beard stormed out the door, spun around, and screamed, "DROP DEAD!"'

Oliver flinched.

'Sorry,' I whispered. 'He jumped back into the growler with the blond and drove away, just like that. Couldn't have been five minutes.'

Oliver and I shared a puzzled silence.

'Who was he?' Oliver asked.

'I have no idea. When I came back in, Munce didn't say anything. He acted like nothing happened. I had an appointment at five, and I came back to Cherry Street really late, around eleven, to write about it in this diary of mine, and I keep it in Munce's office to avoid incrimination, you know? He's usually gone by then, but last night Munce was still there, sitting on the floor with a bottle of gin, blind drunk, mumbling to himself. I got him a chair and asked who the man with the beard was. He got angry and threw the bottle at my head, just barely missing. It hit the wall, shattered, glass and gin flying everywhere, and Munce mumbled something like, "Don't ye pity me, Tommy." Then he passed out, right there on the chair.'

Oliver squinted. 'Who's Tommy? The man with the beard?'

'Could be.' I shook my head. 'Strange, isn't it?'

Oliver forced a cheery grin. 'Explains why he wasn't in good spirits, pardon the pun.'

I furrowed my brow, suddenly realising something. 'How do you know about me?'

Oliver blinked. 'Pardon?'

'We used to have a card in the window, but now it's just aristos gossiping in their clubs. Did someone tell you about me?'

Oliver rubbed the back of his head. 'Not exactly.'

'What does that mean?'

'Well...' Oliver hesitated. 'I was in a pub a couple nights ago. The Black Sheep on Greenland Road.'

'I know the Black Sheep.'

'So I've heard.'

I cocked my head, puzzled.

Oliver smirked. 'A couple of blokes were talking about you in the booth behind me.'

'Really? What did they look like?'

'Fit. Handsome. Wearing blazers, I think. One of them was named Kip.'

I grinned. 'Blond?'

'Yes.'

'Did his mate have black hair? Manny?'

'Yeah, that's it. They were bragging to a friend of theirs.'

I looked down, blushing. 'Did they say what we did?'

Oliver gasped. 'Then it's true? The three of you in the back alley?'

I smirked devilishly.

Oliver pushed my shoulder. 'You're mad! What if you were caught?'

'They took shifts. One kept watch while the other...'

'How racy!' Oliver paused. 'Why blazers? Are they students?'

I nodded. 'Oxford. Sons of Yorkshire Barons. Strong, dashing, and reckless.' Memories of that night flashed into my brain, my arse twitching with nostalgia.

Oliver laughed. 'What else have you done?'

I started with a small anecdote, which led to another, and another after that. By the end of the second bottle, we were having a

gay old time. His reactions made me laugh. I felt no need to censor anything, and he never showed a hint of judgement.

During a lull in our conversation, Oliver leaned back with a sigh. 'I can't tell you how nice it is having a friend who's homosexual too.'

I melted in my seat at 'friend.' Even more amazing were those last two words: homosexual too. Someone else who happens to share a trait, like two Irishmen, or two blonds, two men. Not something up for interpretation. A fact. Something real. I never heard it legitimised like that before. They called us sodomites. We were charged with gross indecency.

Homosexual sounded good. Academic. Clean. Something to be proud of.

III.

I looked at the clock. Two hours had passed. I didn't want to stop talking, but I felt compelled to remind Oliver what he paid for.

Oliver cleared his throat. 'I apologise. Didn't mean for it to go this long.'

'No, I loved it.'

Oliver looked at me with a slight frown, breath quickening.

'What?' I asked.

Oliver looked away. He huffed bitterly and crossed his arms.

I sat up and placed a hand on Oliver's shoulder. 'It's okay. Tell me.'

Oliver shook his head slowly. 'I've never done this before.'

'That's nothing to be ashamed of.' I forced a light chuckle. 'I never hired a prostitute either.'

Oliver frowned. 'That's not what I meant.' He grabbed our empty glasses and carried them to the sink.

I raised my brows. 'Not once?'

Oliver whipped around. 'Have a laugh, why don't ya?!'

'I'm not.'

Oliver softened. 'I'm so sorry.'

'Don't be.' I smiled slightly. 'Take as long as you like.' I patted the seat next to me, calling him over like a puppy. Oliver sat next to me, his body still rigid. I moved in for a hug.

Oliver sharply leaned away. 'Not yet. I...'

I blinked, not understanding what he wanted from me. I don't think he did either. He simply stared into my eyes. I never truly looked at another man's eyes before. It was amazing how his pupils grew and shrank in tune with the flickering candlelight. How green they were. Reminded me of the Cliffs of Moher.

Oliver's harmless glance froze my body and silenced my mind. I couldn't remember where that parcel was from. What kind of wine we drank. How long I had been at the flat. What Oliver's old suit looked like. How many storeys up we were. Only his eyes. Everything I felt at that moment, he did too. Oliver and I connected. We both fit.

Oliver leaned in first. I expected a kiss, but he simply touched me. Not the same way my clients touched me, or my parents, or my brother, or my mates back home. It was strangely foreign to me. The tips of his fingers softly brushed my arm and travelled to my chest, over my nipples and down my abdomen, back and forth. It was like a medical exam except his search was aimless.

He's never touched a man before, I realised.

The more he roamed, the more pressure he used. His graze became a caress. He felt the smoothness of my skin. The light fabric of my shirt. The muscles of my arms. The reaction of my nipples. The brush of my arm hair. He touched my face with his other hand, felt my cheeks, ran through my hair, slow and tender. I never felt that way before. It wasn't lust, closer to comfort, but not the usual tranquil kind. It was much warmer.

Care. He made me feel safe.

His squeezes were compliments, parts of me he liked. He pinched my nipples when they perked, gripped my bicep as if to say, 'Good job there.' He stroked my hair because he knew I liked it and wanted to give me that feeling again. My erection pressed against my trousers, but I didn't want to touch it. I savoured it. My mind raced with the senses. I closed my eyes without meaning to.

That's when Oliver kissed me.

The perfect signature. He gave as much as he took. Might've been his first kiss. He squeezed his eyes, as if he were ready to cry, but he only kissed deeper. Our lips together, I exhaled into him. He inhaled my breath and gave it right back. We let go, spittle hanging between our lips. Our heads were fuzzy, and we smiled like dumb fools.

BANG! BANG! BANG!

Oliver and I shot up, ripped back to reality.

'WHO'S IN THERE?' an aggressive voice yelled from the hall, paralysing me.

'There's a light on!' cried a different man.

I looked at Oliver, quaking in my boots. He put a steady finger to

his lips. Pointed toward the bedroom.

'They're inside,' the first man realised. 'Open it!' Footsteps hurried to the door, a ring of keys jangling.

We raced into the bedroom. Oliver closed the door. It was completely dark, save for the moonlight. Oliver's dress suit was folded in a neat pile on the four-post bed.

Oliver, calm and collected, beelined to the window. Unlatched it.

I stayed where I was, unable to move. *I've been had! Did they follow me? Was it Munce? What did I do wrong? What will I do now?*

BANG! Four pairs of boots marched into the drawing room.

'Away from the door!' Oliver hissed, a foot out the window.

I couldn't move. *This is all wrong. Like something out of a penny dreadful.*

'How did they find me?' I whispered, in a daze.

'They're not after you,' Oliver answered.

I looked up at him, brow furrowed.

Oliver flashed a cocky smirk. 'This isn't my flat.'

And just like that, everything made sense.

'Check the bedroom,' a bobby ordered.

Oliver jumped onto the slanted roof and waited for me. In the heat of panic, I grabbed Oliver's dress suit and leapt out the window.

'What're you doing?!' Oliver cried.

'It looked like evidence.'

'That's not my suit! Now we look even more suspicious!'

'Well, it's too late now.' I peered over the roof's edge at the large hedgerow below. 'How's that?'

Oliver glanced down. 'After you.'

I took a deep breath and jumped. The hedge was farther down than I realised. A branch stabbed my ankle, enough to bruise, but I was cushioned nonetheless. I rolled over, using the suit to brace the impact. I hit the ground hard. My ankle throbbed.

Branches crunched above me. Oliver landed on his feet. 'Are you alright?'

'Help me up,' I croaked.

Oliver grabbed my hand and lifted me to my feet. 'Can you still walk?'

'Yeah, I'll be fine.'

A whistle shrieked above us. I don't know if they saw us, but we assumed the worst and ran away.

IV.

The two of us sprinted for a full minute through Mayfair when my ankle started to strain. We scurried into an alley to catch our breath.

'Oh hell,' Oliver moaned, a hand pressed to his chest. 'Cramp.'

'What are you, a burglar?'

Oliver smirked. 'Burglar. Pickpocket. Thief.'

'Virgin?'

Oliver groaned. 'After all those bloody hours it took to get in. You have no idea how disappointed I am.'

I half-smiled. 'I have some idea.'

Oliver chuckled abruptly.

'Do you even know who's flat that was?' I asked.

Oliver shook his head. 'Just that he's in Bombay for the next six weeks.'

I extended my leg and rotated my foot. 'Why did you do it?'

'You only worked with Lords. I was gonna tell you eventually.'

'You should've told me when the boy dropped off the parcel.'

'I thought you answered the door! If I knew he had a key, I would've told you. Honest.'

I studied Oliver's doe-eyes, barely shining in the moonlight.

'Strange as that is,' I murmured, 'I actually believe you.'

A whistle screeched through the air.

'Bloody hell,' Oliver breathed. 'They're on top of us.'

I looked down at the dress suit in my arms, an idea in my head. 'Help me put this on.' I kicked off my shoes and slid the trousers over my own.

Oliver grabbed the tails and dressed me like a proper valet. 'What about me?'

'The boy didn't see you. They're looking for someone with my description and an accomplice.' The whistle screeched again, much closer this time. 'All good?'

Oliver stammered, his hands trembling in a panic. 'I don't know!'

I looked down. The studs weren't perfect, the jacket was scuffed from the hedge, but the tie was perfect.

'Good enough.' I looked out at the street, at the fork. I gave Oliver my paddy cap. 'Stay close and let me do the talking.'

Oliver donned my cap with a worried look. 'You're not going toward them?!'

I strode out of the alley.

Oliver grabbed my arm. 'Stop! This is a bad idea.'

'You wanna get out of this? Say nothing.' I kept walking at a confident pace. Oliver followed nervously.

The whistles shrieked louder as we approached the fork. Our paths were about cross.

'They're coming,' Oliver whispered.

'Be quiet.'

Oliver squirmed. 'It's not gonna work.'

I looked back at him with soft eyes. 'Trust me.'

Oliver nodded, raising his chin and erecting his back.

The ease of it made me double take, but I couldn't say I was surprised. After the night we had, I would've done the same for him.

I took a deep breath and crossed the fork.

'HALT!' Four bobbies ran toward us, a Sergeant and three deputies.

I stopped where I was. *Tell the truth. My name is Sir Martin Cavendish.*

I gave the Sergeant a pompous scowl. 'Whatever's the problem?'

Oliver's eyes bugged at my flawless British accent.

The Sergeant, primed to accuse, suddenly softened. 'Oh, uh...' He drew his brows together. 'What are your names? And why are you walking so late?'

'Sir Martin Cavendish,' I whined. 'My carriage wasn't at the station. My man and I were walking home. Is that a crime?!'

'No sir, uh...' The Sergeant glanced down at my dress suit. 'We've had a burglary in the neighbourhood.'

I tsked, shaking my head. 'Such a shame.' I looked at Oliver with

knowing eyes. 'Isn't it, Al?'

Oliver hesitated. Nodded a bit too roughly.

The Sergeant squinted, his suspicion resurrected. 'Did you see anyone run by in the last few minutes?'

I stared at the Sergeant. 'No.'

The Sergeant studied my face, trying to read me. 'What did you say your name was?'

'Sir Martin Cavendish.'

The Sergeant hesitated. At long last, he bowed his head. 'My apologies, Sir Martin.'

I nodded respectfully.

The Sergeant blew his obnoxious whistle and led the deputies down the street. Oliver and I fled in the opposite direction.

V.

After tossing the tails, I took Oliver to the Masons Arms on Devonshire Street, Marylebone for a pint.

'That was unbelievable!' Oliver gushed. 'That accent, the cover story. You were so convincing!'

I bobbed my head, my eyes on the menu. 'Do you want food?'

'And you made it look so easy!'

I looked up. 'What?'

Oliver chuckled. 'Lying to that policeman! How did you do it?'

I shrugged. 'Comes with the business.'

'What do you mean?'

I took a big swig of beer and sat there a moment. Oliver's eyes begged for an answer.

'My clients are rich, married, and unhappy. I might be expensive, but I am the only way they can be who they really are. If their wives ask too many questions, or word gets out, they'd lose their money, their friends, their power, their reputation. They're risking their entire world to be with me, but they can't just stop. A conflict like that changes them. It splits their mind. They imagine they're someone else, just like they're putting on a mask. They tell themselves, "I'm not sodomising this boy, Martin Cavendish is." Because it's the only way they can lie. It's more than confidence. They're broken in two. And the more they do it, the easier it is.' I paused, looking off with a heavy heart. 'They're the best liars in the world because of me.'

Oliver frowned.

I forced a smile. 'I guess I picked up the basics.' I returned to the menu. 'Are you sure you don't want food?'

Oliver shook his head imperceptibly.

I looked up. 'What's the matter?'

'How can you be so numb to it all?' Oliver whispered.

I blinked. 'I know it's sad.'

'It's a tragedy! Being forced to lie to the people you love? To yourself?'

'I know it is.'

'Then why do you act like it's the facts of life?'

I hardened my face. 'Because it is.'

Oliver smirked bitterly. 'They're not the only ones wearing masks.'

'Don't compare me to them!' I snarled. 'I hate lying, it's pathetic!

I didn't want to be good at it! I didn't want any of this!'

Oliver softened and looked away.

I cleared my throat. 'I'm sorry.'

'It's okay.'

I felt my face sulk. 'Everything I told you was true. I never told anyone else.'

'I know.'

'That's why I started doing this, you know? I don't want to lie anymore. I made the best of what I could, and I'm happy. I get to be with men all the time, and they look out for me in return.'

'But are you sure they'll—?' Oliver suddenly stopped himself.

I hesitated. 'What?'

Oliver looked into my eyes. 'Are you sure you're happy?'

I smiled softly. 'I don't think I knew what that was before to-night.'

Oliver smiled back. My heart fluttered.

I checked my pocketwatch. 'It's later than I thought.'

Oliver stretched his arms, moaning. 'My back's gonna hurt in the morning.' He hunched over the table, his head resting on folded arms. His fringe fell out of place as he looked up at me.

I smiled. *How cute he is!* 'You wanna come back to my flat?' I asked, hiding my desperation. 'It's dreadful, but there's a mattress.'

Oliver whined indecisively. 'I'm still a bit shook up. Maybe an-other time.'

My stomach hardened. *A no would've been better. Final.* I forced a smile.

After I paid the bill, we stood outside the pub and donned our coats.

'I want to explain myself,' Oliver said, buttoning his jacket. 'If that's alright.'

I put on my paddy cap. 'Go ahead.'

Oliver stuck his hands in his pockets. 'I'm staying with a friend tonight. He won't mind, he's still up.' He hesitated. 'Can you walk me over? It's not far.'

I smirked. 'Quite the explanation.'

Oliver looked around. 'I can't say here. But I can show you.'

VI.

Oliver led me down Montgomery Street to a large house hiding in the dark, a residential silhouette. He pulled out a ring of keys and unlocked the front door. I tiptoed in, shivering from a sudden draught.

We stood in the Great Hall. A huge staircase ran along the right-hand side to a balcony, continuing as a hallway. It was difficult to see in the dark, but I could make out a smoking room to the left and dining room to the right. The silence was ominous but not frightening. Everything was covered in cobwebs and dust, but it was nothing more than an empty house.

'What is this place?' I marvelled, my voice echoing.

Oliver looked up at the balcony with a warm smile. 'My friend inherited it, the one I'm staying with tonight. We're gonna fix it up. New furniture. Fully functional kitchen. Loaded bar. Fresh paint. New roof. The works. It's gonna take a few years.'

Dust got in my throat. I coughed. 'A lot of work for just a house.'

'We're turning it into a brothel.'

I pointed at the balcony. 'Good place for it.'

'For homosexuals.'

I looked at him, flabbergasted. Oliver chuckled.

'Why would you do that?' I asked.

Oliver stepped closer to me. 'Can I ask you something?'

'Of course.'

'You don't do it for the sex, right? You just want to be the real you."

I nodded slowly.

'And it's dangerous,' Oliver continued, 'but you tolerate it because it's your only option?'

I cleared my throat. 'I suppose.'

Oliver smirked. 'What if I told you there was a way we could be just like them? Free to love whoever we want? Only worrying about things normal people worry about?'

I stared at him. 'I'd say you're wrong.'

'Why?'

I chuckled. 'Are we really having this conversation?'

'Tell me.'

'Because sodomy's a crime!'

Oliver crossed his arms. 'Wasn't always.'

'Always what?'

'A crime. King Henry VIII made it one, three hundred years ago. In fact, they used to hang us until they stopped twenty-three years ago. Did you know that?'

I shook my head.

'It's true,' Oliver insisted. 'They decided murder was worse and changed the punishment to prison. Just like that. Who's to say it'll still be a crime in a hundred years?'

I hesitated saying the obvious. 'God.'

'God hates divorce too, but that didn't stop King Henry, did it?'

I rolled my tongue around my mouth. 'Prostitution's a crime too.'

'We passed four brothels on the way here. They're doing something right.'

I blinked. 'But how's a brothel for homosexuals gonna change how they treat us?'

'If it works, others just like it will show up in other cities. Then there'll be other businesses, normal ones, for homosexuals, by homosexuals, until the world gets so used to us that they toss those wicked laws and let us live as equals. We have the power to make that happen. They just need to know we're not afraid anymore.'

I looked down at my feet, struggling to find the right words. 'I don't mean to sound rude, but... What does this have to do with me?'

Oliver kicked aimlessly. 'I overheard Kip and Manny talk about you and wanted to know more. What you're like. How you work. Like an audition.'

'I thought it was because you were a virgin.'

Oliver shrugged. 'Two birds, one stone.'

I grinned. 'Are you offering me a job?'

Oliver smirked. 'It's not too different from what you're used to.'

I gazed at the staircase, tentatively touching the banister. Everything was suddenly real.

'I'm a bit expensive.'

'You're a professional with experience. I only have amateurs. You can train them. Train me for that matter. I don't know how to run a brothel, none of us do.'

'I'm not that experienced.'

'You already proved otherwise. Stamina in good form. Attractive. Sociable. Stable client base. Hundreds of encounters. Reliable under pressure. Strong leadership in case there's a raid. I was already excited to meet you, but you've far exceeded my expectations.'

A million questions swirled my brain. I looked at Oliver. 'Do you really think I can do this?' I asked softly.

Oliver placed a comforting hand on my shoulder. 'Kip and Manny were bragging about you at the Black Sheep.'

I shook my head. 'I don't—'

'They never talk about us.' Oliver smiled sweetly. 'But they talked about you.'

I couldn't help but grin back.

Oliver patted my shoulder and wandered onto the porch. I looked up at the balcony with a wistful smile and followed.

Oliver locked the front door. 'My friend is at his office down the road, where it turns into Newman Street. You don't have to walk me back.'

'I can't give you an answer now.'

Oliver pocketed his keys. 'I'm not asking for one. I'll stop by Cherry Street the day after tomorrow. We'll get lunch.'

I smiled. 'I'd like that very much.'

We stared at each other, his green into my blue. The wind was

frigid but neither one of us wanted to leave. I wanted to kiss him, or at least hug him, but I foolishly offered a handshake.

'It was nice meeting you, Oliver Hawkett.'

Oliver shook my hand, squeezing tightly. 'My pleasure.' He lifted my hand to his lips and kissed it. I wanted to hold on just a bit more, but he let go. With a nod, Oliver stepped off the porch and trekked down Montgomery Street.

'Oliver!' I called.

Oliver about-faced, his eyes already thanking me.

I chuckled, my mind suddenly blank. 'I know the real reason you hired me.'

'Oh, you do?'

'Virgins can't run brothels.'

Oliver smirked. 'I can't sell what I don't understand. And why not start with the best?'

The air left my lungs, my brain turning to mush.

Oliver winked and went on his merry way.

'Oh wow,' I breathed.

On my way back to Whitechapel, I realised the fake telegram was still in my pocket. I pulled it out. Traced Oliver's name with my fingers.

Smiled.

CHAPTER THREE

Fire Everyone Wants to Kill

I.

10 November 1884

I couldn't stop thinking about Oliver. I wanted to see him smile again, to have him sitting next to me while I wrote to Mother. It was difficult for me not to tell her about Oliver. His sex aside, nothing I could say would do him justice. Even at Cherry Street, when I wrote *Oliver Hawkett* into my diary, I couldn't put what happened into words. I didn't have the skill, and I refused to demystify such magic. Oliver was to be special, the only encounter I didn't write about.

I pondered Oliver's offer at lunch. *He's quite persuasive. A world where we can be just like them? What can I lose? Why would I want to stay with Munce anyway? He's still bitter about that row with Tommy. I'm done being insulted for what I am. I want to be with Oliver. He listens to me. He sees potential in my abilities. He's my friend. I trust him.*

I carried a resolute smile on my way back to the Post Office. Only twenty-four hours until Oliver's visit. I couldn't wait to see his face when I said yes. I could hear his laugh in my mind. I spoke for him in entire conversations. I could see him walking next to me, his

auburn fringe parted just enough, that friendly, flirtatious smile. Suddenly we were back in that Mayfair flat. Candles and Indian trinkets left and right. Glasses of wine in our hands. My heart fluttering at his wit. His skin close enough to touch. I felt warm everywhere, like I was wrapped in a blanket by a hearth.

Mr Munce obliterated my trance at my return. He was angry, of course, going on and on about something I forgot to do before lunch. I was standing there, tuning out his insults, waiting for him to run out of steam, when I realised what I felt in my heart, an insurmountable thought I finally decided to climb.

I was falling in love with Oliver Hawkett.

Can't be that simple. How have I become so careless, so loose with my caution? Should I allow such feelings? None of this makes sense, but isn't that what love is? Isn't it inhuman to snuff such a force? Why should I forbid myself of anything? Oliver wanted his world his way, why not me? I want to be equal to everyone. I don't deserve abuse, I deserve to be loved.

II.

I met one of my regulars that afternoon, Sergeant Marty Williams of the Metropolitan Police. The perfect client. Strong. Hairy. Incredibly masculine. One of the few who actually wanted me to enjoy myself. Adventurous too. He loved shagging me in his office at Scotland Yard, and this time was no exception.

At half four, I walked into the office and found Marty leaning against his desk, thrilled to see me. I kept forgetting how attractive his smile was, even with a moustache the size of a new-born puppy.

The way it curved when he smiled was strangely adorable. The top half of his shirt was unbuttoned, his hairy chest exposed. Brown eyes staring me down with direct lust.

My cock throbbed as I approached. Marty wrapped his big arms around me. Held me tight as he kissed me. His moustache pricked my upper lip as his tongue slowly made its way into my mouth. Breath quickening with pent up aggression. Coarse hands roaming down my back. He needed my body with a carnal desire that never seemed to leave. He thought about me during his meetings. Fantasised about me before bed.

Marty spun me around, pinning me against the wall with natural dominance. Forced me to my knees. Pushed my head down as I sucked him to control the pace. The only thing between us and exposure was a locked door, yet I felt completely safe at his command.

I lost myself in that moment, my senses finally returning a half-hour later. I was sprawled out on the floor, my arse burning from his needlepoint moustache, aching and wet in all the right places. Marty looked down at me as he dressed, admiring my spent naked body. I gulped up the air, too stunned to move.

So that's how he made Sergeant.

With a sloppy kiss and an affirmative spank, Marty dismissed me from his office. I floated back to the lobby.

The security guard was the same one who checked me in thirty minutes ago. I didn't want to draw attention to myself, so I sat on a bench in the lobby and waited for the guard to be relieved. I had time and needed the rest.

What would he think of a man like Marty? I smiled. *Amazing. My body's still quivering but I keep coasting back to Oliver.*

I heard voices coming in from outside, and I looked out the window with blasé curiosity. Two Inspectors were on a fag break, a fat one named Pete and another with a crescent scar on his cheek.

'Yer makin too much of it,' Pete complained.

'Wish I was,' the scarred one insisted with a gravelly voice. 'Tellin ya, I can't go. Too in the hole as it is.'

'Even for a pint? C'mon, Vic, can't be that bad.'

'Nah, Big Man got me good. Owe him at least a couple months.'

'How's that?'

'Lost me nightstick.'

Pete grumbled. 'Bullocks, that is! Deputies lose em all the time. No one pays for em.'

'This is different. Lost it on a case.'

'Which?'

'Member two weeks ago, when me and Jeffy raided that warehouse in Stepney?'

'Remind me.'

'Coupla squatters. Orphans they said, except they weren't just. Turned out, we found ourselves a pair of fairy Marys.'

Pete's chuckle turned my blood cold. 'Ya don't say!'

Vic gagged. 'Makes me sick thinkin bout it. Anyway, Jeffy and I burst in, poofs get scared, right? One of em starts runnin, I go chase it. Jeffy pins the other queer down, and that bitch is screamin, cryin, its eyes all droopy...'

Pete cackled. 'Bloody freaks.'

'I ram me poof, and I mean hard. It's on its back, fightin me, screechin like a cat, and I didn't want that. Already in a bad mood fightin Alice that mornin, and I couldn't stand hearin it, so I hit it wit me stick, right?'

'Right.'

'And I hit it a coupla times, but it kept on screamin. And I wasn't angry or nothin, I just wanted to shut the freak up for a bloody minute. So I hit it a little harder. Its face gets all bloody, and I heard it chokin and such, but I tell ya, that bitch would not stop screamin! So I give it one good whack, right in the forehead, right? And I was expecting the thing to twitch or lurch or somethin, but nothin. Like it didn't hurt.'

Pete squinted. 'Wot?'

'See, turned out, it wasn't the one screamin. It was the other poof, Jeffy's!'

Pete gasped. 'No!'

Vic chuckled. 'Right? So I look down... Head's bashed in.' He took a drag, shaking his head softly. 'Didn't even know me own strength, I guess.'

'Big Man didn't like the killin, did he?'

Vic blew out smoke, disappointed. 'Nah, he let me have it. But we got the other one on sodomy and resistin arrest, so he said, "Don't matter." No family to row bout it, ya know?'

'Good thing. What bout the nightstick?'

Vic's face softened. 'That's what's strange. We get the boys down there to clean, the poof's in the waggon, cryin its eyes out, and...' He slowly shook his head. 'I couldn't find it anywhere. As if it just... '

Pete furrowed his brow.

Vic resumed his theatrical smirk. 'Five quid they cost, canya believe it?'

Pete tsked. 'Rubbish, that is.'

'Big Man says I lost it, I buy the next one.'

Pete clapped Vic's back. 'Hey, at least it was worth it.'

'Aye. If it had to go, better over God's work.'

I didn't hear the rest. I ran. Hopped on my bike and raced away. Didn't care if the guard saw me. Needed to get far away from Vic. Didn't feel my body until I fell off a mile away. Hit the ground hard. Wasn't hurt, but I didn't want to get up. Couldn't stop shaking.

I couldn't sleep that night. Noises in the hall made me flinch. Could've been Vic lurking in the dark, ready to pounce.

That poor kid. Could've been anyone.

III.

11 November 1884

The terror of Vic's lynching lessened by the morning, but it never truly ceased. Even black coffee couldn't stop the buzzing. I don't remember how I got to work. Wasn't until half eleven when I remembered Oliver was stopping by for lunch, with that offer I was so eager to accept.

How could I have been so sure? Nothing in life is certain.

I was swimming in a sea of files when Munce poked his head into the office. 'Sorting the papers now. Man the counter, will ya?'

I licked my cracked lips. 'I'd like to stay back here if you don't mind. I'm not feeling too well.'

'Quit whining,' Munce slurred. 'You're already worthless to society. Can't you at least pretend to be decent for the customers?'

Noon. All quiet on the front. I hunched over the counter, my anxiety flowing in waves.

I don't want to hurt him. I just hope he understands.

The bell above the door rang. DING DING DING!

Oliver. In the flesh. Just how I remembered him. 'Didn't think you actually did anything here,' he teased.

I grinned. 'I'm a postal worker. I do nothing all day long.'

Oliver seductively rubbed the finish of the counter, flashing those green eyes I loved so much. 'I missed you,' he whispered.

My lip trembled. 'Me too.'

'Oi! Perverts!' Mr Munce stormed in with a stack of papers. 'No flirting in my lobby. Take it outside.'

'Right away, Mr Munce!' I beelined to the door and held it open. DING DING DING!

Oliver grimaced at Munce. 'Perverts?!'

My stomach dropped. 'Oliver, let's go.'

Oliver gave me a bewildered scowl.

'Princess!' Munce snapped his fingers. 'Get your bitch outta here!'

'Oliver!' I begged. 'Please!'

Oliver recognised my desperation and softened. He headed for the door.

'That's right,' Munce egged. 'Go home to Mummy.'

Oliver stopped short, clenching his jaw.

'Oliver, c'mon!' I cried.

Oliver turned around. 'You take that back,' he growled.

Munce cackled. 'Or what?! You're gonna hit me?'

'Oliver!' I grunted.

Oliver glared at Munce before storming out the door with rigid humiliation. I raced after him, struggling to keep up. 'He isn't like this all the time.'

'How can you let him talk to you like that?' Oliver muttered.

'I don't want to give him a reason to turn me over to the police. Insults come with the territory.'

'Keep telling yourself that.' Oliver stopped abruptly at the fork, looking around randomly. 'I don't know where I'm going. Take me somewhere.'

I patted his shoulder. 'I know a good place.'

IV.

We shared a booth in the back of Dubeau Frères, a ghost town as usual. Oliver settled down over tea and biscuits.

'How's business?' he asked.

'Good.'

'Anyone since me?'

I smirked. 'Maybe.'

Oliver cooed like a schoolboy. 'Who is he? A Lord, no doubt.'

'A Sergeant, actually.'

'Ooh! Army, Navy?'

'Scotland Yard.'

Oliver crunched into a biscuit. 'Heavens. How did you manage that?'

I sipped my Darjeeling. Damn good stuff. 'He hired me last summer. His mates in the department gave him some money as a promotion gift.'

'For what, a prostitute?'

'He's the only one unmarried. There was lots of winking, I'm sure.'

'They must've known.'

'They wouldn't have made him Sergeant if they knew.'

Oliver leaned back. 'Fascinating. They practically gave a Sergeant permission to hire a whore, but he still has to hide that it's a man.'

I nodded. 'Strange world.'

'Must be nice having a bobby client. An ally on the inside.'

'Not likely. Marty wants to be a good policeman more than anything. Problem is, the higher up he goes, the fewer chances he'll have to be himself.' I let out a hefty sigh. 'That's the worst part, I think. Too many hard choices.'

Oliver inhaled sharply, folding his hands. 'Speaking of...' He smiled. 'What'll it be?'

I looked down. Scraped a crumb off my cup.

Oliver deflated. 'It's a no, isn't it?'

I flashed a crooked smile. 'I want to believe you, Oliver, I do. I hope you know that.'

Oliver huffed with disappointment.

'It's a nice dream,' I whispered. 'But yesterday, I...' I stopped, pausing longer than I intended.

Oliver raised a brow.

I cleared my throat. 'Exposing ourselves won't change anything.

They don't listen to us. They don't care about us. They can kill us and get away with it.'

Oliver audibly sighed. 'I thought you'd be better than that.'

'Better than what?'

Oliver shrugged. 'A coward.'

I tightened my face. 'You're a businessman, Oliver. Take rejection like a professional.'

'You think you're better off where you are now?'

'I've done well so far.'

'If they get caught, they'll turn you in to save themselves. You know that, right?'

'They wouldn't do that to me.'

'Of course they would.'

'They need me.'

Oliver laughed. 'You trust them over your own people?'

I scrunched my face. 'You don't know them!'

'You sneak into their homes, they use you, then they pay your rent so you feel like you're part of the club. They're not your friends! You're their dog!'

'They're just like us, Oliver. Their status doesn't change that.'

'Yes, it does!' Oliver snarled. 'They might want to be with you, but they'll do anything not to be you! And if you don't know that by now, it's only a matter of time.

'Of course I know that!' I snapped. 'Do you think I want to keep doing this? This wasn't easy for me. I wanted to say yes!'

'Then say yes, please!' Oliver softened. 'I can't do this without you.'

I wanted to hug him. Tell him it was gonna be alright. That I had changed my mind. But Vic was still out there.

'What you want...' I started, my voice scratching. 'It's impossible.'

'But that's what they want you to think! That's not power, that's fear! That's what the brothel is for. We'll show them we're not afraid. That we're proud to be what we are!'

I scowled. 'What I am got me banished. My family forced me out of my home to live in a country I grew up hating, in a city just a filthy as I imagined, and the only way I can feel like a normal person is when I sell my body to fat, spoiled codgers, and I'm still afraid of losing everything. But that's the best I can do. That's what we get. We have no rights. No culture. No community. We're dead-ends. We can't get married. We can't have children. And once our parents find out, they disown us. Banish us. Remove us from family trees. Inheritances. Conversations. Diaries. And anything we do. Anything we create. Any legacy at all would be destroyed the second they learn what we are. They *want* to forget us, Oliver, don't you understand? Once we die, we're gone. And they did that to us. That's their power. And it *terrifies* me.'

Oliver stared blankly. After a moment, he looked away and scratched his cheek. 'I know you hate lying, but...' He paused. 'There are virtues to discretion.'

'I'm saving your life. The world is a dark place. The sooner you know that, the easier it'll be to live in it.'

Oliver shook his head. 'You've been in the dark too long. You think you've done something to deserve it.'

I closed my eyes, huffing with annoyance. 'I know it's difficult to

accept. I was young too. We all want to believe in a brighter world because we're afraid of the dark. But the fire's going out, Oliver. It always does.'

Oliver leaned in, close enough for a secret. 'It doesn't go out on its own. That's why the world's a dark place. Everyone keeps killing it.'

I stared into his hauntingly bold eyes, a wave of sadness rushing through me. 'Well, we'll just wait and see who's right, won't we?'

Oliver took my hand, rubbing it slowly yet desperately. 'Please,' he whispered. 'Do the right thing.'

My heart pounded. I clenched my lips together. 'I am.'

I tossed a shilling for the bill, donned my cap, and swaggered away. I wanted Oliver to rush up and stop me, but he never did. It was over and I knew it.

Back at Cherry Street, I ripped Oliver's name from my diary and tore it to shreds.

V.

When I returned to my flat, I saw Oliver's telegram sitting above my bed. My stomach turned. I snatched it up. Wrenched a good grip on one side. Tense fingers cracking into the envelope, ready to tear the memory of Oliver Hawkett in twain.

The moment came and went.

I released the telegram. Smoothed the cracks. Propped it above my bed like an idol. It watched me sleep. I felt safe. Oliver protected me.

I dreamt of beauty. A bedroom of pure white. The hush of ocean waves crashing outside. Windows wide open. Whole room filled with

morning light. Ephemeral white curtains floating on the warm breeze. Sheets of ivory satin. I'm naked. Full of the peace and warmth of a thousand calm summers. I open my eyes. Oliver sleeps next to me. His green eyes peak open like a baby bird. He recognises my face. Smiles. I kiss his lips. Move my body closer. We intertwine our limbs. Hold each other tenderly. His skin so warm and smooth. Protected in each other's embrace. Just him and me. Purer than lovers. Partners. Together until the end of time.

I woke with a start. My eyes were wet. The moonlight had vanished. Not yet dawn. I had no idea where I was.

Then I recognised the mould above me. The lifeless furniture surrounding me.

The air was cold. Quilt rough. Mattress too small.

I was alone.

CHAPTER FOUR

Miraculous Punishment

I.

12 November 1884

The adults who peopled my youth, teachers, family-friends, grocers, clergymen, they all tried to warn me: 'You just wait, boyo. Life is full of difficult choices and you won't have any help.' I heard variations of that statement for twenty years, but I never considered it wisdom. Sounded more like the cautionary tale they never had, a desperate attempt to prevent their mistakes repeating in the next generation. I nodded every time and said, 'I know,' and I did, but only in theory. That's the scariest part of adulthood. No matter how many times you try to warn someone, they'll never truly understand until it happens to them.

Refusing Oliver's offer was the hardest decision I ever made. It didn't feel good, even though it made perfect sense. I had to actively convince myself that I did the right thing.

Oliver returned to Cherry Street the next day. I stayed where I was in the office so Munce would act as my proxy refuser, a role he was too good at. They two of them got into a row, Munce threw a broom at him, and Oliver left in a rage.

The next day, I stayed in bed with a bad cold. I learnt later that Oliver had reappeared around lunchtime, asking for me again.

Next time, I told myself. *He'll be back. When he does, I'll reconsider.* But that time never came. That's what they don't warn you about. You seldom get the closure you want.

Two weeks later, I awoke in a panic. *What am I doing with my life? Had I grown so numb? A whore with delusions of grandeur. No friends. A silent mother. Pathetic! Three years and no reply? She's moved on. Why can't I accept it? Twenty-seven and still a damn child!*

The wave of dread passed after an hour, and I continued my life with a queer sense of determination. *I need advice. I'm getting it.*

In that morning's letter, following a monotonous paragraph on pigeons and their mysterious babies (Seriously though, *where are they*?), I gave Mother an update on my personal life:

> A man offered me a job a couple weeks ago. I turned it down. He meant well, and I admire him plenty. He made me happy, confident, even optimistic. I trusted him, but the job wasn't right, or at least it didn't make sense. I hurt him by saying no. He doesn't want to speak to me anymore.
>
> I want to stay close to him, but I don't know how to move forward. What should I do? Please write back. I know I've never asked for advice, but he's important. More important than anything actually. I don't want to spoil what we had. I forgive you for

> everything, and I love you. I just want a reply. I need help. I'll be all alone if I lose him.
>
> Hope all is well. Miss you all.

I know I rushed the conclusion, but it was enough.

Every day for three weeks I asked Munce if he received a reply, even if it got on his nerves. Nothing. My anxiety went away again.

They're not going to Dunderrow, I told myself. *I'm tossing them into a void. A pagan lifeless abyss.*

What a frightening thought.

II.

1 January 1885

I escorted a Scottish Viscount (whom I'll call Matthew) to a dinner party at the Marquess of Huntly's castle in the Highlands. Such grand people were there, the best of society stuffed into every room. Matthew was such a simpleton; he introduced me as his nephew. He had no idea how many of those men I knew. He didn't fool anyone.

A man made eyes with me at dinner, a naval officer in his sixties with a scruffy grey beard and youthful smile. His seduction was quite aggressive, and when Matthew left me in the Drawing Room to get champagne, he took the opportunity to introduce himself to me.

Commodore Archie Collins of the Royal Navy. Now that's a title!

He leaned in when he talked, his strong body trapping me in the corner of the room, which made me both worried and incredibly hard. Archie rarely blinked, and I actually heard him sniff my cologne. His pleasantries (who I was, whom I was with) were

noticeably artificial. He knew. Somehow he knew. I bet he would've dropped his coy façade if his mate hadn't called him away, just in time for Matthew to return with two glasses and his brainless smile.

Ten minutes passed. Archie approached Matthew and I as if by accident, introducing himself to me as if he hadn't already. I played along with the charade, and that unspoken understanding made our reintroduction quite taboo. Matthew knew Archie well, as it happened, and they spent some time reminiscing their glory days at Cambridge. Every so often Archie locked eyes with me, his gaze both hypnotic and predatory, and I devilishly smirked back. He then asked to speak with Matthew in private, to which I nodded knowingly and strolled away, convinced a recommendation was in progress.

And I was right. Three days later, Archie visited the Cherry Street Post Office to enquire Munce of my services. He wasn't a typical client, and he certainly didn't have a typical appointment. In three weeks, Commodore Collins and his crew of thirty well-bodied seamen were to stay at Kensington, Admiral Edward Harrison's castle up North. Archie's men had been at sea for quite some time, and they had specific taste.

Has your blood chilled yet? Sounds awfully like the Collins Affair, doesn't it? Impossible, I know, just aliases in an elaborate homage. I couldn't have met the actual Commodore Collins, right? If I was at the real Kensington, you would've heard of me when it happened. But here's the thing: I was there. I saw everything. If you're one of the few who hasn't heard of the Collins Affair, I won't spoil the surprise. Even if you have, *The Times* didn't tell the whole story.

Being there was quite... different.

Collins had hosted orgies many times before. He was very methodical and very secretive. Thankfully, I wasn't the only boy invited. Three other 'couriers' were to accompany me. I never met my competition before, but safe to say I wasn't excited to meet them. Wasn't excited for the orgy either. I didn't know what to expect. It was difficult managing three at once, let alone thirty. I suppose that's why the money was there. Archie paid a fortune.

III.

23 January 1885

Commodore Collins told Mr Munce he was sending a coach to collect me outside the Post Office at eight o'clock. I sat on the ground. Back against the wall. Waited. No wind. Everything was quiet.

I looked at my bike, leaning peacefully against the window. *A cheap has-been*, I said to myself. *Belonging to a child before it was donated to the church, no idea of its future. No hope he was to be saved. Which metaphor is more suitable? Oliver the child disposing me? Or Oliver the second owner, giving rubbish a new purpose?*

I sighed. *Either way I lost.*

I heard the coach before I saw it, harsh clops on the stone, old timber creaking behind it, swaying like a ship, a metronome of rotted wood over the rumble of big wheels. I stood, eager for it to find me. Wasted enthusiasm, since no one else was around, but I didn't care. I couldn't miss it. I needed a distraction. Thirty of them.

I saw the coach at last, a massive ornate box driven by four white

horses. The Driver cracked his whip, steering in my direction, the horses slowing just in time for the door to stop perfectly in front of me.

Damn good driver! I saluted the man. He nodded back.

The others were already inside. I hopped up and squeezed into the last seat. The man sitting across from me, pale as the moon, pounded the roof two times.

The Driver cracked his whip. The coach shoved forward.

No one spoke. The Pale Man vacantly looked out the window. The Sleeping Man next him snored softly. The Droopy-Eyed Man to my right, the only one alert, stared forward.

My excitement faded in increments. I extended my hand to the Pale Man. 'Nice to meet you.'

The Pale Man scoffed and looked away.

The Droopy-Eyed Man shook his head. 'Don't bother. They don't talk much.' He shook my hand. 'Tucker.' He was about my age, with stubbled cheeks and a friendly smile. 'You're new to this, aren't you?'

I blinked. 'Aren't you?'

'We've done a few of these together. Not used to fresh faces.'

'Only found out about you a couple hours ago,' the Pale Man grumbled. 'And of course you're Irish. Insult to injury.'

Tucker cocked his head. 'Nasty one's Wyatt.'

Wyatt gave me a once-over. 'I see what the fuss is about.'

I looked at Tucker. 'Fuss?'

Tucker pursed his lips, dancing around his words. 'It's unusual. Collins never adds strangers.'

I shifted uncomfortably. 'Why did he?'

Wyatt rolled his eyes.

'That's what we've been discussing,' Tucker mumbled.

'It's cause he's sick of us!' Wyatt snapped.

'Wyatt—'

'No, don't do that! Stop defending him!'

'I wasn't!'

'He'll toss us aside, you'll see!' Wyatt sniffed, on the verge of tears. 'Look at me! Christ, Tucker, look at him! One look was enough for that fickle old bastard—!'

'Wyatt!'

'You'll see! He'll throw us out, and then what're we gonna do, huh? Huh?!'

Tucker lowered his head.

Wyatt frowned out the window. Moonlight shone into the coach, giving me a better view of what he looked like. Premature wrinkles. Red burns around his nostrils. Bloodshot eyes. Bony shoulders. He was visibly malnourished but most of all sweaty, his entire body covered in a moist dew.

The Sleeping Man yelped, twitching in his seat. I caught a glimpse of his face as he tossed over. He was just a boy. Young. *Really* young.

Wyatt's anger shifted to pity. He placed a calming hand on the boy's back. 'Poor thing. Must be another nightmare.'

'Little late for a nap, isn't it?' I asked.

'That's what Henry does,' Tucker explained. 'Sleep and work. Doesn't say anything. He just wakes up and does his thing.'

Henry yelped again, his face contorted in fear. My blood chilled.

'He doesn't have anyone!' Wyatt cried at Tucker. 'He can't do this without me! And if that damn pig takes him from me, I swear I'll—!'

'Get it together!' Tucker snarled, face to face with Wyatt, their noses almost touching. 'We've got a job to do! Stop acting like a bloody child!'

Wyatt let out a strange noise, the combination of a sigh, a whimper, and a bitter laugh. 'You see it, don't you?! He's done with you too, so don't bother—!'

Tucker smacked Wyatt across the face. 'SHUT YOUR DAMN MOUTH!'

Wyatt nursed his cheek, petrified.

Tucker forced his eyes closed, exhaling uneasily. After a moment, he whipped his eyes open and smiled at me. 'What's Ireland like?'

I smiled awkwardly. 'Beautiful. Haven't been there in years.'

'Because of the famine.' Not a question.

I pursed my lips. 'No. That happened before I was born.'

'Are you sure about that?'

I squinted. 'Quite.'

Tucker pursed his lips sceptically. 'I don't know—'

'Just take my word for it, okay?'

'Oh,' Tucker mumbled, suddenly embarrassed. 'Okay.'

No one talked for twenty minutes. I grew tired of the dour mood and decided to add some light. 'What's it like? The orgy, I mean.'

Wyatt rummaged through his coat pocket. 'There's thirty of em.'

'Is that a lot for you guys?'

Wyatt pulled out a silver snuffbox. 'It's enough.'

I nodded uneasily and returned Tucker, who suddenly didn't seem so bad to talk to. 'Do you enjoy it?'

Tucker blinked and looked at me. 'What?'

'The sex. Is it enjoyable with all those men?'

Tucker hesitated. 'I dunno.'

Wyatt opened the snuffbox with a pleasant click. He scooped a teaspoon of white powder, snorted it with his left nostril, and again with his right. He clapped the box shut and pocketed it.

I furrowed my brow. 'What was that?'

'I'm not sharing!' Wyatt growled, rubbing his nose.

I looked at Tucker with concern.

Tucker shook his head. 'We do this a lot. It pays well, but it's bloody brutal. We're just not made to do this. Everyone has a way of making it easier.'

'I don't.'

Tucker gave me a patronising smile. 'I know you're new at this, but you should find something that works soon.' He widened his eyes. 'It doesn't stop.' He abruptly faced forward, his breath wavering.

My skin crawled just looking at him. I kept staring at his eyes, expecting him to tell me to look away, but he didn't notice. He didn't even blink.

I glanced down at his forearms. Across his wrists were long red scars, deep frenzied slashes. 'What happened to you?'

Tucker yanked his sleeves down, eyes frozen in fear. 'I don't talk about that.'

A chill ran up my spine. I forced myself to look out the window.

This coach will stop eventually. When it does, I'll get far away from Tucker. I don't need him to enjoy myself. Plenty for all of us.

I looked up at the moon, marvelling the way it stayed still as the trees raced by. *Wish Oliver was here. Forgot how smart he was.*

IV.

After two more dreadful hours of silence, we finally arrived at Kensington. I audibly gasped at the sight of it. It wasn't just a castle. It was a bloody compound. Acres of land in every direction. Stable the size of a house. Full cricket pitch. Lake with Venetian gondolas. Huge garden. And finally the castle itself, enough to fit thirty families.

The Driver stopped outside the Officers' entrance, the door ajar, beckoning us like something out of a fairy story.

Wyatt slapped Henry's leg. 'Wake up.'

Henry jolted awake, and Wyatt helped him out of the coach. Tucker motioned for me to leave first. I gladly obliged. Tucker closed the door behind him. The Driver cracked his whip and drove the coach toward the stable.

Tucker nodded at Wyatt.

Wyatt nodded back with a sniff. He pushed in and led the way.

The Entrance Hall was grand, but not as impressive as the others I'd seen. Sterile. Functional. No heirlooms, just a few paintings (of course) and some trophies. Queerest of all was the silence. No servants. No sounds coming from other rooms. Not a single soul to receive us.

I followed Wyatt up the grand staircase, the carpet muting my

footsteps. Wyatt reached the top and turned right; he obviously knew where he was going. The four of us strolled down the hall, passing dozens of bedroom doors. Another turn. As we approached the door at the end, I could hear muffled voices two rooms away, a great many of them.

Wyatt opened the door and led us into a Parlour. He beelined to the bookcase, reached in, and turned a hidden knob. A secret door swept open. I felt a sudden wave of heat and cigar smoke. The miasma of voices, now unfiltered, hushed themselves as we marched in. We stood in a row and marvelled the sight before us.

Scattered around the room were thirty handsome, strong, shirtless sailors. Some leaned against the wall. Others stood around the fireplace. A couple loitered by the balcony door. Smiles all around. The only man fully dressed was Commodore Collins himself, sitting in a big leather chair by the fireplace with a snifter of brandy.

The potent smell of lust made me fully erect.

Collins stood. Strolled toward us. Stopped in front of Wyatt. Ran a tender hand through his hair. Wyatt grinned with near-orgasmic joy. Collins ripped off Wyatt's shirt. Then everything else. The Sailors chuckled eagerly.

My turn. Archie gave me a nod of recognition. I smiled back, flattered. He leaned in. Inhaled deeply. Smiled. Let out a masculine chuckle. He pulled me in. Kissed me. Sharp beard scratching my face. Leathery tongue forcing its way into my mouth. I could taste brandy. His breath reeked of tobacco. He was aggressive. Dominating. I didn't realise I was kissing him back.

Archie abruptly pulled away. Winked. I winked back. He removed

my shirt. Undid my trousers. Exposed me to the audience. My head must've been fuzzy already; Henry and Tucker were naked before I knew it. The Sailors ogled, panting in heat. Months at sea had driven them mad, but they remained obedient dogs.

Collins returned to his chair. Swirled his snifter. Savoured the anticipation in the room. Took a sip of brandy. Looked at his men.

'Dig in, boys.'

The Sailors laughed heartily. Tossed off their trousers. Cocks fully erect. They descended on us fast. One grabbed me. Pulled me in. Kissed me. Many others touched me. A hundred fingers grazed. Pinched. Penetrated. Explored everywhere. They passed me around. My body kissed by many mouths. I stopped thinking. Lots of hands. Licks. Warm breaths. Some blond. Some dark haired. Their faces the same. Boyish. Clean shaven. Bodies like demigods.

I was barely aware of what was happening to the others. Wyatt getting tossed, one man to another. Henry already on his knees in the centre of a Sailor circle. Moans. Taunts. Cheers. I couldn't see Tucker from my vantage point. Good riddance.

A tray of white powder appeared. 'Sniff this.'

I obeyed without hesitation. Whatever it was made me feel strange. A sudden burst of energy. Sharp eyes. Horrible metallic aftertaste. My throat went numb. Something was in my nose I couldn't snort out.

I was sucking on a cock before I knew it. Someone else penetrated me from behind. First time I ever had both at once. I thought it would feel different, a combined pleasure of sorts, but it was more like two separate jobs.

The Sailor from behind slammed sharply. Made me wince. The tray of powder reappeared. I snorted another.

Everything went numb.

V.

I can't say how much time passed. Hours. Many men entered me. Lost count. No break at all. One pulled out. Another slid in. A queue stretched behind me. Wyatt was in a similar position, a queue of his own, both of his hands occupied as he snorted that powder off a Sailor's abdomen. Henry moaned rapidly behind me, no doubt from aggressive slamming. That little guy had so much energy.

Commodore Collins stayed in his chair, watching the chaos with a regal smile.

I had trouble breathing. Felt pain again. Needed a break. Struggled to my feet. The queue didn't care. They moved on fast.

I was disoriented. Vision blurred. Smoke everywhere. Puddles of whisky on the carpet. Stumbled toward the balcony. Arse burning with each step. Whole body aching. Cum dripping down my leg. Possibly blood as well.

I stepped onto the balcony, my senses clearing fast. I gulped up the cold air. The moon was clear as ever. I gazed out at the grounds, admiring how beautiful Kensington was. As I caught my breath, my body cooling down, I suddenly remembered what was happening inside. I smiled, ready for more. *What a night. Can't wait to tell Oliver.*

I heard a soft rumble down at the treeline. Looked over the balcony.

Fifty policemen charged out of the woods, rifles and nightsticks in their hands.

My stomach dropped so hard I stopped breathing. Panic ripped through my veins.

I ran back inside. Whipped the door open. BOOM!

'Stop!' I croaked. No one heard me. My knees buckled before the fireplace. I collapsed onto the carpet. A man walked over to me, panting heavily. I looked up.

Commodore Collins. White powder all over his face. Drool from his lips. Vacant stare. 'My turn, boy,' he slurred. He grabbed me by the wrist. Dragged me across the floor.

'No!' I screamed. I yanked my arm, trying to resist, but that only hurt my shoulder. I felt the floor vibrate. They were close.

'Stop!' I shouted. 'They're here!'

BANG!

Dozens of bobbies swarmed in, whistles shrieking. The Sailors screamed, stampeding on top of each other in a pointless flight. Everything happened so fast. Policemen hitting Sailors with their nightsticks. Wrestling the unruly ones to the ground. Slamming even more against the wall. Three bobbies struggled to subdue Wyatt, his face contorted in a silent scream, tears streaking white powder on his face.

Archie dropped me and fled. Naked as a new-born. Leathery skin from top to bottom. Grunting like a warthog. A selfish, disgraceful dash. Four bobbies chased him around the room. Archie senselessly climbed over furniture. A fifth jumped out from behind a pillar, knocking Archie down. He almost escaped before three more piled

on, pinning his arms down. Collins writhed on the ground. Flailing his legs. Roaring like a monster.

I could only watch. My heart beating too fast. Cold in the wrong places. Senses overwhelmed. That drug distorted everything. Nothing felt real.

CLICK! A bobby pressed a rifle to my head. A second helped me up. Wrapped me in a sheet. Ushered me out of the room. I joined the queue. They led us down the hall like cattle. Down the stairs. Front doors wide open. Everything felt real the moment I saw the metal waggons. I was caught. Finished. Off to jail.

A Superintendent and a Sergeant were talking to a man on the sidelines. They didn't look at me as I passed. The bobbies shepherded my queue into one of the waggons. The Sailor in front of me hopped in, his tear-drenched face shining in the moonlight.

My turn. I jumped in. Sat down. Scanned the rest of the queue behind me. Henry was four or five spots back. Eyes down. Strangely calm. No idea what was happening. His soul sucked out long ago.

My eyes continued down the queue, stopping at the officers. My blood chilled. I recognised the man they were talking to.

Tucker. Fully dressed. Smiling. Shaking the officers' hands. Other bobbies patting him on the back.

I kept staring. *Look at me, you bastard.*

By chance he did. Tucker's eyes found me. Held my gaze. His faced softened. No joy. No frown. Plain recognition. After a moment, he turned back to the officers. Resumed his smile.

Last man in the waggon. A bobby grabbed the door. SLAM!

Darkness.

VI.

25 January 1885

All of us (sans Collins) were ushered into a holding cell when we arrived at Scotland Yard. Every hour or so a deputy walked in, read a few names off a manifest, and took them away. None of us talked. We just sat there, waiting in agony.

Two days passed. I was the last one and I didn't know why. *Who will save me? Collins? The other clients?* Bile hit my throat. *No. This is it. The end. Nothing more to do.*

The door opened, an exhausted deputy waving me out. 'Come with me.' He led across the hall to an interrogation room with an iron table and two chairs. 'Inspector Wainwright will be here in a moment,' the Deputy mumbled, not wasting any time. He stepped out and locked the door.

I looked at the table and started trembling. *This can't be it. There must be something I can do.*

Desperate, I dropped to my knees.

> *Dear God,*
>
> *I'm sorry I don't pray anymore. I don't worship you. I don't go to church. I'm lost. I understand if you don't want me, but I beg you for mercy. Please, I want to see the sun again. I want to be safe. It won't happen again, I promise. Get me out of this mess. Please save me, just this once.*
>
> *Amen*

CLANG!

I jumped onto a chair. Inspector Wainwright wandered in, a crescent scar on his face and a file under his arm.

'Sorry bout the delay,' Vic grumbled, plopping across from me. 'We weren't sure what to do wit ya.'

'OH GOD!' I screamed, recoiling in terror.

Vic winced, covering an ear. 'Shut up!'

'Yes, sir,' I breathed.

Vic furrowed his brow, cold eyes studying my face. 'Have we—?'

I shook my head immediately.

Vic stared, murmuring to himself. After a moment, he looked down at the file. 'We interrogated Collins's men. They were quite intoxicated, but we could understand—'

'Just tell me, please.'

Vic peered up. 'What're ya on bout?'

'Prison. How long?'

Vic rolled his throat. 'Ugh...' He massaged his temple with both hands. 'You're not goin to prison. We're lettin ya go.'

My lungs evaporated. 'What? Why?'

'Don't start!' Vic groaned. 'I've been up all night arguin bout this. Let's just get it over wit.'

I squinted. *A trick. Has to be.*

Vic withdrew a piece of paper from the file. 'You'll have to pay a fine, but just sign this discharge and—'

'I don't understand.'

'Fine!' Vic slammed the file shut. 'Collins confirmed everythin Tucker gave us on Wyatt and Henry. Two dozen charges of sodomy

and prostitution. Big Man's puttin em away. But we don't have enough on ya. No one knows where you came from. Collins can't member where he met ya, where he hired ya, not even when he hired ya. Only that yer Irish.'

'Figures,' I mumbled.

'Queerer than that, none of the Sailors membered doin anythin wit ya either. Not one.'

My face went numb.

'Don't take it personally,' Vic added. 'In their state, I'd be surprised if they could remember the Queen.'

My lips fluttered. 'How is that—?'

'Listen, Mick! Big Man don't care bout ya. He's happy wit Collins and the two dandies. If he wanted to investigate, I'm sure he'd find somethin. But *The Times* wants a story now, so... We're closing the case.'

I let out a long, wavering sigh.

Vic shook his head. 'Big Man might be the Superintendent, but he's wrong. I know what ya are and I know why ya were there.'

I froze.

Vic leaned closer. 'Pay the fine,' he hissed. 'And dig deep. Some of us need new nightsticks.'

The hairs on the back of my neck stood up. 'I don't have anything on me.'

'Where do ya live?'

I shook my head desperately. 'No! Please!'

'Answer me, freak!'

Tears rolled down my cheeks. 'Whitechapel. A flat.'

'Ya got some there?'

I lowered my head.

Vic grinned, his yellow teeth shining. 'Pay the fine and yer free.' He stood and headed for the door.

I glared up at him. 'You didn't say how much.'

Vic smirked and opened the door. Pete bumbled in with a devilish smile.

'It wants to know how much the fine is,' Vic said, his eyes on me.

Pete chuckled. 'I'll decide when I get there.'

'Be right back, poof.' Vic and Pete walked out and shut the door.

I closed my eyes. Exhausted. Ashamed. God heard my prayer, but He didn't save me. He gave me a second chance. A miraculous punishment. A test disguised as salvation.

Won't happen again? God asked. *Prove it.*

VII.

Pete led me into a growler and smiled the entire ride to Varden Street.

I was never so thrilled to see that awful flat in my life. Pete closed the door and pulled out his revolver. 'I don't want to use this.' He laid the gun on the table and sat down. 'Where is it?'

I pointed to the mattress across the room. 'Under there, in a cigar box.'

'Get it.'

I inched toward the mattress, my eyes fixed on Pete as I crouched down. I slid the mattress aside, pulled the cigar box from its hole, and lifted the lid to peek inside. £2,000 in neat little rolls.

'How much?' I asked.

Pete chortled. 'Hand it over.'

'No, Please! It's all I have!'

Pete cocked the revolver. 'Now.'

My lip trembled. I placed the box on the floor and slid it over.

Pete flipped the lid. 'Bloody hell!' He chuckled. 'You're a busy little whore! How long did it take to earn this?'

I stared at the floor, trembling on my feet. 'Three years.'

Pete fingered through a roll, shaking his head in disbelief.

'I need to eat,' I begged. 'Please, don't take everything.'

Pete's face hardened. 'I'm not a monster. You're quite lucky, you know. Someone else would've killed you by now.'

'I know.'

Pete snickered. He pulled five rolls from the box and stuffed them into his pockets. 'I'll come back when it's full.'

I closed my eyes, my lip trembling.

Pete laughed. He tossed the box on the floor. Holstered his gun. Stomped into the hallway. 'Keep up the good work, slut.' He tipped his hat and breezed away.

I raced to the door. Slammed it. Locked it. Collapsed. Sobbed mercilessly. I looked over at the cigar box. Grabbed it. Looked inside. £75. A fortune down to nothing.

Need to get back to work. Munce still has my share of Collins's fee, three hundred pounds. That'll carry me over for a few months.

VIII.

I changed into new clothes and started my four-mile trek toward

Cherry Street. *Stupid, stupid idiot! Why'd you leave your bike over there? Do you have any bloody foresight at all?*

As I entered Westminster, I couldn't stop replaying the raid in my head. *Tucker. That bastard. Oliver was right, I couldn't trust them. Collins would've given me up if he could. None of this would've happened if I said yes.*

I roamed into Camden Town, rambled down Cherry Street, and stopped outside the Post Office. My bike was gone. Stolen perhaps, because of course it was!

Don't want to think about that now. I'll get a new one.

DING DING DING! I pussyfooted inside. Newspapers all over the place. On the counter. All over the floor. A total mess. I could hear Munce shuffling about his office.

'Morning, Mr Munce,' I said timidly.

Mr Munce clumped out, dropping a stack of papers on the counter. He avoided eye contact with me.

'We were raided,' I whispered, inching closer. 'They got Collins and the others, but they let me go. They have nothing on us. Thank God for that.'

Munce sorted the pile of papers with a frown.

I rubbed the back of my head. 'They got me on the fine, though.' I forced a self-deprecating chuckle. 'Almost all I had.'

Mr Munce treaded into his office. He re-emerged moments later with another stack.

'I could use some more work,' I said. 'Until I get back on my feet.'

Munce finally looked at me, his breath wavering.

I smiled softly. 'Please say something, Mr Munce.'

Munce grimaced, his face turning red. 'YOU'RE FIRED!'

My head pounded. 'But it wasn't my fault,' I whined. 'One of the others tipped the police. They don't know anything about us, I...' I started hyperventilating, too tired to cry. 'I-I-I know you're angry, but we can get through this!'

Munce threw a newspaper at me. 'They named you as a suspect!'

My hands trembled as I skimmed the front page of *The Times*:

INDECENCY AT KENSINGTON: COMMODORE DISGRACED

A perfect sketch of Commodore Collins. My name in the third paragraph. Next to it:

Courier for the Cherry Street Post Office.

A fate worse than death. In ink, no less.

'This doesn't mean anything!' I lied. 'They didn't name you!'

'Everyone pulled out!' Munce snarled. 'All of em! No more appointments! They don't want anything to do with you, and neither do I. Get out!'

'Please, Mr Munce!'

'And I'm keeping Collins's money! Lost a lot of business thanks to you!'

'YOU CAN'T DO THAT!' I screamed.

'YES, I CAN!' Mr Munce's lip trembled. He looked away. 'Dunno what I was thinking. I should've done this at the start.' He grabbed a bottle of gin and lumbered into his office.

I stayed put, crying like a child. *My life is crumbling! WHY WON'T IT STOP?!*

'Please,' I breathed.

Munce stopped short, his back to me.

My body trembled with anticipation.

Munce lowered his head. 'If you don't leave,' he whispered slowly, 'I'll tell the police everything.'

'I don't have anything left!' I blubbed. 'I'm sorry I hurt you! I'll make it up, I promise! I need to work! I can't pay my rent! I won't be able to get a job because of this! I'll go hungry! I need you, Mr Munce! Please! HELP ME!'

Mr Munce covered his eyes, his hands shaking. 'You're not my problem anymore.'

I gasped, suddenly very dizzy.

Mr Munce closed the office door.

I stood still, too shocked to breathe. Wandered over to the cupboard. Pulled out my messenger bag. Checked to see if the diary was still inside. Left.

I don't remember the walk back.

As soon as I entered the flat, I started packing.

Need to leave London, I told myself. *The scandal will only get worse. Can't be here when it does. Vic knows where I live.*

I didn't have enough to get to the Continent. My only choice was to go back to Ireland and lay low until it was safe to return.

I had one foot out the door when I suddenly remembered Oliver's telegram above my bed. I raced back and grabbed it.

That's what I'll do. When this is all over, I'll come back. We'll be together.

With a hefty sigh, I closed the door and gave the keys to the Landlord.

XI.

The Times called 'The Collins Affair' the nastiest sodomy scandal in two hundred years. What a ghastly ordeal. Archie Collins dishonourably discharged. Scotland Yard launching an investigation into the Royal Navy. Admiral Harrison accused of covering up Archie's behaviour for years. Queen Victoria herself delivering an official statement from Buckingham Palace. Every Sailor discharged, their names in the papers.

Collins got all the jail time. Abandoned by his allies, his reputation tarnished, and not a penny to his name, he hanged himself a week into his sentence. The scandal buried the news of his suicide.

Henry was too young for prison, so they institutionalised him. Scientists wanted to understand his mind, something regarding sexual studies and trauma therapy. They prodded and poked. Put him through weeks of tests. Gave him drugs. Treated him like an animal. I never learnt what happened to him.

The Judge gave Wyatt a choice, prison or castration, and he chose the latter. Horrible. He had no education or skills, so they threw him to the workhouses. Everyone knew what he was. They gave him hell for it. He was nothing more than a harmless eunuch, but they still targeted him.

And me? I was the lucky one, but it didn't matter. I left London

with my tail between my legs. Couldn't even afford one last Délice de Mousse. A leper on the brink of poverty. Everything lost but my life. Starting over. Again.

As the train shoved away from King's Cross, I traced Oliver's name on the telegram envelope. *I have unfinished business,* I reminded myself. *Just a few weeks and I'll be back.*

I didn't return to London for two years, four months, and twenty-six days.

CHAPTER FIVE

A Neutered Mutt

I.

26 January 1885

I never expected Ireland to feel foreign. The world changed me.

I stepped off the ship at Dublin, shivering from the cold air. A gaggle of dockers leered up at me, salty generational types, old enough to remember the Great Famine. I could tell what they were thinking: *Londoner. Too soft for the gales.* But when I asked them for directions to the nearest post office, their faces lit up. My accent might've soothed their suspicions, but I didn't belong. Not anymore.

There was to be no homecoming for me. I was a fugitive in both lands.

I tentatively stepped into the Dublin Port Post Office. Its clerk, a hairy man with a pale eye, slouched over the counter with a vacant expression. 'You'll have to wait. I'm breaking for lunch.'

I awkwardly removed my paddy cap. 'It'll just be a moment.'

The Clerk smiled instantly, just like the dockers. 'I can wait. What'll it be, laddo?'

I dropped my bags and approached the counter. 'A few enquiries, please. Some addresses.'

'Family?'

'Friends. Is that possible?'

'Tell me the names. I'll look.'

I tapped my fingers on the counter. 'Kerrigan Mullaly. He might go by Kerry.'

The Clerk scribbled on a piece of paper. 'Okay.'

'Bayrd Walsh.'

'Next?'

I half-smiled. 'Seamus Costigan.'

The Clerk scribbled some more. 'Anyone else?'

'Yes, and...' I stopped myself in time. 'No, actually. That'll be all.'

'They your mates?'

I pursed my lips. 'Used to be.'

'When were they born?'

'Same as me, '57. Maybe '58.'

The Clerk smiled warmly. 'Mates from school.'

'Aye. They were in Dunderrow when I saw them last, four years ago. Suppose that's a start.'

The Clerk flipped the paper and jotted some more. 'Gimmie a few minutes.' He lumbered into his office.

I rubbed my eyes. *I haven't said their names in so long. Kerry and his stupid cricket teams. Bayrd and that laugh of his. And Seamus, oh!* My mind wandered off. *But not Greg O'Brien. Not anymore.* I swallowed, a deep pain growing inside my chest. *I don't wanna know what happened to him.*

The Clerk came back with three cards. 'All checked out. Kerrigan Mullaly moved to Tralee a year ago, occupation unknown.'

'You got the right Kerry.'

The Clerk smiled. 'Bayrd Walsh is still in Dunderrow with his parents on Oak Ridge Farm.'

I pursed my lips. *That's a shame.*

'And Seamus Costigan lives in Mulhussey, First Footman to Lord Barrington.' The Clerk handed me the cards. 'Very impressive.'

I reached into my pockets. 'How much?'

'No need.'

I froze. 'What?'

The Clerk pointed to my overstuffed messenger bag. 'One run-away to another? You'll need every penny.'

I smiled, genuinely moved. 'Thank you.'

The Clerk nodded. 'Be safe, laddo.'

I rambled to the station with my head slightly higher. *I picked the right place.*

II.

27 January 1885

Seamus worked in a big house and Bayrd was literally too close to home. That made Kerry the only good option.

I slept on the train and stepped off at Tralee around half twelve. After grabbing a quick bite at the station, I trekked down the road to Kerry's cottage and knocked.

I almost didn't recognise Kerry when he answered the door. No beard. Fit. Only partially resembling that rowdy boy in the muddy pitch. He half-smiled as if expecting someone else before softening with recognition.

'Hello Kerry,' I said with a weak smile.

'What are you doing here?' Kerry whispered, each word carefully selected.

'I'm in some trouble. I need a place to stay.'

Kerry craned his head around the corner. 'I shouldn't be talking to you.'

'Nothing's changed, Kerry. I'm still me.'

'I don't want people to think I'm...' Kerry bobbed his head. 'You know.'

'No one could think that of you.'

'I know!' Kerry snapped. After a moment, he added, 'But you know how they are.'

'If no one knew I was here, would that make a difference?'

Kerry took a deep breath. 'Believe me, mate, I wish I could, but...' He rubbed the back of his head. 'Suppose you do something.'

I scrunched my face. 'How could you think that of me? After all this time?'

Kerry looked at his feet. 'I know what they say about you people.'

'I don't want you, Kerry. I promise you that.'

'But you're all liars. Father Dominic said so.'

'I never lied to you.'

'You kept it from me, didn't you? All those trips to the pubs, blabbing about girls and families. Weren't they lies?'

'It wasn't a secret I could tell. My folks would cast me out. And I was right, wasn't I?'

Kerry lowered his head.

'I'd do the same for you, mate,' I said. 'And it won't be for long.

Just until I get a job.'

Kerry softened. 'I really do wanna help. Wasn't right what they did.'

I sighed. 'I know.'

Kerry licked his lips. 'But I need to know something.'

'Name it.'

'What they said you did with O'Brien. Was that true?'

My eyes swelled with shame. 'Yeah,' I croaked. 'Yeah, it's true.'

Kerry nodded apologetically. He tenderly stepped inside and locked the door.

I missed the last train out of Tralee. I didn't have enough for a night at the pub, so I waited at the station and planned my next move.

What'll it be? Mulhussey or Dunderrow? Seamus would say yes, but what could he do? Hide me in the Servants' Quarters? Don't want him to lose his job over me. Bayrd might be able to hide me on the farm but not the house. Mrs Walsh is quite the gossip. It would only be a matter of time before Mother heard about me. I don't wanna know why she isn't writing back. I'm not ready.

I pulled Oliver's telegram from my breast pocket. *What would he do, besides break into expensive flats*? I laughed out loud. *It's like he's travelling with me. All this walking's making him tired. I need to get it right so he can rest.*

I caressed the envelope. *Oliver would be cautious. After he lost the flat, he stayed with a friend.* I smiled. *Seamus it is.*

I curled up on the waiting room bench and fell asleep.

III.

28 January 1885

The trip to Mulhussey was long, all the way back to Dublin and then some. Slept as much as I could between transfers.

Barrington Place was easy to find, being obnoxious in size. I'd heard of Lord Barrington from my former clients; an Englishman, of course, and an Earl. (Or was he a Count? Don't think I know the difference.)

I rang the bell at the Servants' Entrance. An old valet named Travers answered. 'May I help you?'

'I'm a friend of Seamus Costigan. Is he in?'

'He's in the boot room, I believe. I'll tell him you're here.' Travers closed the door and skittered away.

I paced the courtyard. *Please don't despise me, Seamus. Anyone but you.*

'I don't believe it!' Seamus ran out, ecstatic to see me. How handsome he was still, and all grown up. His livery was stiff, apron stained with shoe polish, but I could still see his muscles.

We embraced tightly, my smile just as big as his. I felt myself getting hard. I pulled away before he noticed.

'What are you doing back?' Seamus asked.

'That's what I wanted to talk about. You free for a pint?'

'Sorry, mate. Not until after dinner.'

'I'll wait at the pub then.'

'Are you sure?'

'Yeah, I'll be fine. Finish your work.'

Seamus smiled. 'Barrington Arms, half eight. See you there?'

'See you there, buddy.'

Seamus waved a small farewell and ambled back in.

I lingered a moment more, my head fuzzy with emotion. *Thank God for you.*

IV.

Seamus treated me to a pint. There's nothing quite like Irish beer. Strong and bitter like my people.

'I'm sure you heard why I haven't been back home.'

Seamus nodded uneasily. 'I did.'

'Does it bother you?'

'It's not the worst thing in the world.'

I couldn't feel my face. 'Really?'

Seamus shrugged. 'Father made me shoot a horse when I was twelve. Blokes shagging isn't quite as disgusting.'

I smirked. 'Depends on the blokes.'

Seamus laughed.

I took a deep breath. 'Did you hear about Archie Collins?'

Seamus cocked his head back. 'How do you know about that?'

I chuckled nervously. 'What do you mean? It's all over London!'

'Really?'

I studied Seamus's naive expression. 'You're serious? No one knows about it out here?'

'Oh, they're definitely covering it up. They don't want us to think we're being ruled by a bunch of dandies.'

'Jokes on them. We know they're dandies.'

Seamus raised his glass. 'Amen to that.'

'Sláinte.'

We toasted our pints.

'If it's so secret out here, how do you know about it?' I asked.

'Lady Barrington knows the mum of one of the Sailors.' Seamus chuckled. 'Messy business, eh?'

'Yeah.' I looked away nervously.

'What's wrong?'

I scratched my nose. 'I can tell you anything, right?'

'Of course.'

'And you won't tell a soul?'

'Promise.'

I took a deep breath. 'I was there.' I looked at Seamus, waiting for him to respond.

Seamus rolled his tongue around his mouth. 'Don't say any more.'

My stomach dropped. 'Oh, I... I thought you said—'

'Why would you do that?' he asked, disgusted. 'For the money?'

'What else could I do, Seamus? Marry a woman? Live a lie?'

'Anything's better than letting strangers violate your body.'

I laughed bitterly. 'That's bold, coming from you! What were you up to when I left? Two a week? Did you know any of them?'

Seamus glared at me. 'You know that's different.'

'Do you?'

Seamus looked away.

I snorted. 'I didn't get a chance to sneak behind the bike shed like the other boys. Try pretending you're someone else for twenty-four

years. See how desperate you get.'

Seamus huffed, embarrassed.

'Doesn't matter anyway,' I grumbled. 'I can't do it anymore. They printed my name. I lost everything. Happy?'

Seamus frowned shamefully. He put an arm around my shoulder. 'I'm sorry.'

'It's okay. I don't blame you.'

'What can I do?'

'I need a place to stay until I get a job. A room here would be enough. I'll pay you back, don't worry.'

Seamus thought silently for a moment. 'Do you wanna work at the big house?'

I furrowed my brow. 'As what?'

'A footman.'

'They have an opening?'

'They will when I leave.'

I gasped, shaking my head. 'Oh, Seamus, don't—!'

'Steady on,' Seamus said with a smirk. 'I was already leaving. I'll put you in as my replacement tomorrow.'

'Why are you leaving?'

'To get married.'

I almost spit my beer. Seamus chuckled.

'Why didn't you say, cheeky devil?!' I embraced Seamus, startling him. 'Congratulations!'

Seamus laughed and hugged back.

'I can't believe it!' I exclaimed. 'Who is she?'

A sly smile grew on Seamus's lips. 'Annabelle Feeny.'

I gaped. 'No!'

'I know. Can you believe it?'

'How did that happen?!'

'I was in Dublin running an errand for His Lordship and we bumped into each other. Her father gave his blessing and everything.'

'So he knows you shagged her behind the playground?'

Seamus snorted. 'Naturally.'

The two of us cracked up. We settled down. Shared a comfortable silence.

'I'm so happy for you,' I whispered, beaming.

Seamus smiled back with warm, vulnerable gratitude. 'Thanks, buddy.'

Seamus booked me a room at the pub before he left. I slept like a baby. The chaos of the past few days melted away.

I dreamt of beauty again. That same white, windy room by the sea. I'm dressing myself next to the bed. Oliver naked on the satin sheets. Pawing at me. Making me laugh. Trying to get me to stay. I dodge his hand. He gets up. Lifts me. Tosses me on the bed. Jumps on top. We laugh. He kisses me. I hold him tight.

I woke with a start. Couldn't remember where I was.

Looked above my bed. Oliver's telegram looked back. *Forgot I put it there.*

V.

29 January 1885

Mr Huxley studied me with restrained approval. A large fellow,

eyes too small, brows too big, appropriately compensated by a booming baritone voice. 'What experience do you have?'

I looked at Seamus. He smiled back with encouragement.

'I worked on my family's farm in Dunderrow,' I answered. 'Lots of heavy lifting. And I was a postal courier when I lived in London.'

Mr Huxley nodded cautiously. 'And why were you dismissed without a reference?'

I hesitated.

'I've known him since we were kids, Mr Huxley,' Seamus interjected. 'He's a hard worker and a fast learner.'

Mr Huxley harrumphed, a classic butler tone.

'I'm very keen, sir,' I insisted. 'Always wanted to work in a big house. I'll prove myself.'

'I'm sure you will.' Mr Huxley stood. 'I'll take your word, Seamus. You can train him until you go.'

I eagerly shook his hand, a huge weight off from my shoulders. 'Thank you, Mr Huxley!'

Mr Huxley smiled. 'And between you and me, I'm glad I could find a reliable replacement before giving Chester more work.'

'Chester?'

'The Second Footman,' Seamus explained. 'Selfish as they come.'

'I'll have none of that from you, Seamus,' Mr Huxley scolded. 'Chester deserves his place here, just like you do.'

Seamus lowered his head. 'I apologise, Mr Huxley.'

Mr Huxley flashed me a smile. 'He does, however, have a propensity to whine.'

'I suppose he's First Footman now,' I said. 'With Seamus gone, that is.'

Mr Huxley took a deep breath. 'The position of First Footman will go to the man who deserves its prestige. I'll make my decision after your training is complete.'

I furrowed my brow.

Seamus opened the office door. 'Better get started. Lots to do.'

I shrugged off my confusion and followed Seamus out.

VI.

23 February 1885

'*What's* it called?' I asked.

'System of operations,' Seamus repeated with an amused smile. He extended his arm. 'Take note of the shape of the rooms. You see how the path flows out of the Great Hall, past the Painted Room, all the way down to the Drawing Room?'

I squinted. 'I think so. It gets bigger, right?'

'The rooms do. The path is the same.'

'Never thought posh people had actual rationale in their way of life.'

'They're a lot smarter than you think.'

I snorted. 'Yeah. Sure.'

Seamus hesitated. 'Alright.' He cleared his throat. 'In a standard system of operations, when a guest arrives, you take their coat and lead them to the pool.'

'That's what it's called? The pool?'

'I call it the pool. It's like a lobby or a cafeteria. A place for gathering.'

'And what's so standard about the standard system of operations?'

'The walk.' Seamus took my hand and waltzed me into the Painted Room. 'You have to be slow. Gradual. Respectful.' He about-faced and led me back to the Great Hall. 'Not too fast. Not too slow. A comfortable pace.'

'Interesting,' I said, reluctantly letting go.

'Other systems involve announcing the guests or dance cards, but the walk never changes.'

'They can't walk themselves?' I asked, only half in jest. 'I've been in a lot of these places, you know, and if you've seen one, you've seen them all.'

'Even if they've been here before, the guests feel like they're intruding. If there isn't someone waiting at the door for them to follow, they'll leave.'

'No, they don't.'

'I've seen it.'

I tilted my head playfully. 'Just seen?'

Seamus smirked. 'Never you mind.'

We laughed hard, a hearty display quite inappropriate for a Footman. In the silence that followed, I suddenly realised how close we were to Seamus's departure. I could tell by his expression that he was thinking the same thing.

'I can't tell you how fun it's been,' I said. 'Being here with you.'

Seamus nodded softly. 'Me too. It's like... we've always been friends, you know?'

I nodded, my stomach hardening.

'It's funny,' Seamus said. 'I haven't spoken to Kerry or Bayrd in years, but I don't miss them at all. I think the only reason we spent so much time together was because there was nothing else to do.' He smiled at me. 'You're the only one who truly understood me.'

'What about Greg?' I mumbled. 'You liked him.'

'Yeah, well...' Seamus chuckled.

I swallowed and looked away.

Seamus softened. 'I didn't mean to make it awkward.'

'I'm fine.'

Seamus looked around the hall. 'Sit down for a moment.' He led me to the window and sat on the sill next to me. 'I want you to know that I haven't been avoiding anything. I respect you too much to talk about... what happened.'

I bowed my head. 'Thank you.'

'Because I know it was ghastly for you.'

'Thank you, I...' I cleared my throat. 'I-I can't talk about it anyway, it's still...'

'Yeah,' Seamus murmured. 'Maybe you will one day.'

My breath suddenly wavered. 'I'm gonna miss you so much.'

'I'm sure,' Seamus whispered, his eyes meeting mine.

I stared back. 'What?'

Seamus shrugged casually. 'I know.'

My throat went dry. 'How?'

'I know a panting dog when I see one.' Seamus chuckled. 'And you know I can tell when I'm being flirted with.'

I shook my head. 'No, Seamus, I—'

'I'm not upset, really,' Seamus insisted. 'Honestly, I'm flattered. I never thought I had anything to offer, you know? But Annie, she...' A warm smile crept onto his face. 'Remember all those single birds back home? The ones who burped a lot and didn't wash their hair and snapped at everything?'

'Your prey of choice.'

Seamus sighed. 'Don't remind me.' He paused. 'I used to think they were the only ones left because the good ones were taken. Truth is, the good ones are good because they're taken. Annie's become a real lady, and I'm... Well, I like to think I'm a gent.'

'You are,' I whispered. 'You really are.'

Seamus beamed. 'Moves me for you to say so. And I know I came down on you hard for what you've been doing, but—'

'But I'm a bad bird.'

'No,' Seamus insisted. 'No, you're not.'

I smiled.

'Love is a special thing,' Seamus said. 'It's more than just sex. More than marriage even, or children. It's the only way we can be the men we were born to be.' He chuckled. 'I mean, a life without love? That's like being naked in a rainstorm.'

I took a deep breath. 'It's funny you say that...'

'Oh-ho!' Seamus teased. 'Everyone has their thing, I suppose.'

'That's not what I...' I stopped myself. 'I never told anyone this.'

'I'm here.'

'I... One of my, um... He's not really a client, but...' I looked into Seamus's eyes. My lip started trembling. 'I love him. I truly, deeply love him.'

Seamus shifted his posture. 'Okay. What's his name?'

'Oliver. Oliver Hawkett.'

Seamus forced a nod. 'Tell me about him.'

I raised my brows. 'Really?'

Seamus half-shrugged. 'Really.' He smirked. 'Why not.'

I exhaled nervously. 'Okay. He's younger than me. And he's brilliant and funny.' My eyes drooped. 'And so bloody beautiful!'

Seamus smiled warmly. 'I'm glad.'

I shook my head, a dumb grin on my face. 'And you know what's strange? He makes me glad everything happened the way it did. Because I wouldn't have met him.'

'Where is he now?'

My smile slowly faded. I lowered my head. 'Back in London.'

Seamus frowned. He gently rubbed my back. 'I'm sorry.'

'I'm going back when this is all over, of course, but...'

I didn't speak for a long time. Seamus never stopped caressing me.

'I feel broken without him,' I whispered.

Seamus sighed. 'He probably feels the same about you.'

'You don't know that.'

'Did he love you before... whatever split you apart?'

I hesitated. 'I think so.'

Seamus smiled. 'Then he feels the same about you.'

I studied Seamus's encouraging expression and softened. 'Annie?'

Seamus nodded. 'Annie.'

I reached over and gave him a big hug.

Seamus patted my back and pulled away. 'Anyway.'

I cleared my throat. 'Yeah. Where were we?'

'Do you remember the three Nevers of service?'

'I think so.'

'Go on then.'

I held up one finger. 'Never leave a guest unattended.'

'Right.'

I held up another. 'Never lead a guest somewhere they'd soon grow tired of.'

'Good.'

I tentatively raised a third finger. 'And...?'

Seamus smirked. 'Never wing it. Ever.'

VII.

28 February 1885

I stood in the Servants' Pantry and watched Seamus follow Mr Huxley into the Dining Room with a tray of salmon mousse. Lord Barrington, a portly man using his dress suit like a corset, scooped a serving from the tray and laid it onto his plate. The rest of the family followed suit: Lady Barrington, the vapid shell of a once beautiful debutante; buck-toothed son Lord Roger; eldest daughter Lady Catherine, dolled like a tart; dreadfully plain younger sister Lady Victoria; and finally the Dowager Countess Barrington, a melting wax figure with a deviated septum.

Chester almost crashed into me with a crystal decanter. 'Out of the way!'

'Sorry,' I whispered, stepping away from the door. Chester minced into the Dining Room and started refilling the wine glasses.

'I need the carriage tomorrow, Papa,' Lady Catherine mumbled gracefully. 'I'll be back before the gong.'

'I have to be in Drogheda in the morning,' Lord Barrington grumbled.

'I'll join you then. It's only to the station.'

'What's this?' the Dowager Countess asked.

'Nothing, Granny,' Lady Catherine replied. 'I'm meeting some friends in Dublin.'

'Anyone we know?' Lady Barrington asked.

Lady Catherine hesitated, her poise unwavering. 'Just the usuals. Rosie. Caroline. Audria—'

'Audria Penberthy?' Lady Victoria interrupted, intent on causing trouble. 'Lord Aberforth's daughter?'

Lady Catherine rolled her eyes. 'We came out together. What of it?'

'Wasn't she the one who was caught slumming in London last Season?'

'Slumming?!' the Dowager Countess whined. 'That sounds quite unsuitable for a Lady.'

'Nonsense,' Lady Catherine insisted. 'It's quite chic. Everyone's doing it.'

'What is it?' Lord Barrington asked, suddenly remembering he was in the middle of a conversation.

'Charlie Blackworth told me about it, Papa,' Lord Roger answered, the gap between his teeth whistling. 'People dress in rags and roam through Whitechapel.'

My blood went cold.

'But why would anyone *want* to go there?' asked the Dowager Countess.

'To see how the other lives, I suppose,' Lord Roger replied.

'They're quite silly, those people,' Lady Catherine said, cutting into her salmon mousse. 'Begging on the street, no money for decent clothes.' She chuckled. 'I wouldn't last a week!'

I grimaced, my face muscles tightening.

'It sounds dangerous,' Lady Barrington said. 'What if you were recognised?'

'It's quite safe, Mama,' Lady Catherine insisted. 'Audria has an entire wardrobe of costumes. She even puts this funny black stuff on her face that looks like soot.'

'How do you expect to fit into her clothes?' Lady Victoria taunted. 'Isn't she half your size?'

Lady Catherine pursed her lips. 'Mm. Good point. Lend me your frock when you're done with it.'

Lady Victoria scowled.

Lady Barrington, desperate to change the subject, looked over at Seamus. 'When are you leaving, Seamus?'

Seamus smiled politely. 'Tomorrow morning, Your Ladyship.'

'Lord Barrington and I wish you the best of luck with your wedding.'

'Thank you, Your Ladyship. It's been an honour serving you these past two years.

I snorted. *Bootlicker.*

After dinner, Seamus, Chester, and I stayed behind to clean the Dining Room. I watched Chester extinguish the candles. The infamous Second Footman wasn't as nasty looking as I expected. He was actually quite handsome. Clean shaven jaw. Combed back hair.

'Catherine's so pompous, isn't she?' I muttered, folding the tablecloth. 'How could anyone do something like that for fun? It's disgusting!'

Seamus glanced around for witnesses. 'She might be a spit-fire, but she's not heartless.'

'How can you defend her? What if she was slumming through Dunderrow?'

'You don't know what her world is like, just like she doesn't know yours.'

I scrunched my face. 'Mine?! Seamus, what's the matter with you?'

Chester pointed at me. 'You better cut that talk before Huxley hears you.'

'What's it to you?!' Seamus snapped.

Chester glared at Seamus and returned to his snuffing.

'Seamus, what's wrong?' I asked.

'He needs to mind his bloody business,' Seamus whispered.

'I'm on your side, bastard!' Chester growled. 'Why'd you pick him, anyway? He's got quite a mouth.'

'You don't know anything about him!' Seamus retorted. 'He has good reason to hate them!'

My lungs evaporated.

Seamus realised what he said and looked down at the table.

Chester studied our expressions. 'What was that?'

I forced a smile. 'I was a postal courier in London. Nothing is lower than that.'

Chester stared at me for a moment. He grabbed a candelabra and carried it into the Servant's Pantry.

I elbowed Seamus. 'What the hell?!' I hissed.

'I'm sorry!' he whispered back. 'He just—!'

Chester returned with a basket of dirty silver and a dry rag.

'I'm glad to finally get out of that pub,' I spoke up, smiling at Chester. 'Seamus told me you snore, but I don't mind. I can sleep through anything.'

Chester held a fork to the light and scraped off a crumb. 'What else did Seamus say about me?'

'Only the truth,' Seamus mumbled.

'Good riddance to you!' Chester spat. 'Though I daresay, Guy Fawkes over there's the perfect replacement!'

'Shut your damn mouth!' Seamus snarled.

Chester threw the fork across the room and stormed away.

'Wait!' I called after him. 'You still have to—' Chester slammed the door. I sighed. 'Dammit.'

'He's not worth it,' Seamus said.

'You're not being fair with him,' I said, picking the fork off the ground. 'He's not that bad.'

'Just wait. The prick never asks off, ever. He can spend twenty minutes on his hair, but if Huxley gives him extra duties, he'll complain your head off.'

'Why?'

'Why what?'

'Why does he complain?'

'Because it's beneath him. Because he's lazy.'

I furrowed my brow. 'But he never takes a day off.'

'So?'

'So how could he be lazy?'

'I dunno. He finds a way.'

I shrugged. 'What does that even mean?!'

Seamus laughed. 'Why are we still talking about him?'

'He gets the job done, doesn't he? Not everyone whistles while they work.'

'Hand me a tray, will you?'

I grabbed a wooden carrier from the Servant's Pantry and laid it on the table.

Seamus piled the dishes on. 'You need to watch what you say. Won't last long as First Footman if Mr Huxley catches you bad-mouthing the Family like that.'

'I'm not gonna be First Footman, Seamus,' I insisted. 'And I don't care. They don't respect me, I don't respect them.' I paused. 'Don't see why you do.'

Seamus took a deep breath. 'This place is strange, buddy. Every day's the same, we never leave. One day you'll wake up and forget there's even a world out there.'

'Good!' I said with a laugh.

Seamus frowned at me with pity. 'Just remember, I warned you.' He lifted the tray and carried it off.

'It's just for a few weeks,' I called after him.

'That's what I said,' Seamus called back.

VIII.

While Seamus was serving tea in the Drawing Room, I made my way to the Men's Quarters and knocked on the third door on the left.

'Chester, it's me.'

Silence. The door opened a bit. Chester peered out. 'What do you want?'

'I'm sorry to disturb you, I just... I want to make something clear. You don't have to say anything.'

Chester furrowed his brow.

'I know Mr Huxley doesn't like you,' I said. 'And I love Seamus, but I won't defend him. He's quite unjust when it comes to you. You and I will be spending a lot of time together the next few weeks, so I wanted you to know that I understand what you're going through. I do, truly. I am not Seamus, I don't know you, and I don't have anything against you.'

Chester didn't react.

I swallowed. 'We don't have to be best mates or anything, but... I want to have a go at us being friends. I noticed, pardon me for saying, that you're not so great at making friends. And that's fine. I understand. I'm not so great at keeping them.'

Chester lowered his head.

I bobbed my head. 'That's it, so... I'll see you tomorrow?'

Chester nodded softly. 'Yeah. See you then.' He closed the door. I smiled, quite proud of myself, and returned to the Servant's Hall.

IX.

1 March 1885

I gaped, struggling to find the words. 'Sir, I don't think I should.'

'Nonsense,' Mr Huxley insisted. 'Seamus taught you well.'

'I know he has, but—'

'And you have a natural talent for it. Why shouldn't you be First Footman?'

I pursed my lips. 'I don't think Chester should be stepped over.'

Mr Huxley furrowed his massive brows. 'What do you mean?'

'He's a Second Footman in his mid-thirties. Is that fair?'

'Chester was the Second Footman long before Seamus was taken on. If he wanted the post, he would've tried harder to earn it.'

'But that's the thing, Mr Huxley, Chester isn't lazy. He could be more personable, sure, but don't you think he's earned it from loyalty alone?'

'Isn't his lack of cooperation a bad thing?'

'I just think he's at the point in his life when he doesn't like being told what to do anymore. He's put years into his work, grunt work, I know, but...' I scoffed. 'He wants you to trust him, Mr Huxley, and you're throwing him aside again?! Why?! Because he's not perfect?! Because of some minor thing you personally dislike?!' My blood chilled. I wasn't talking about Chester anymore.

Mr Huxley tapped his fingers on the desk, restraining his dis-

approval in my outburst. 'How are you sure he feels this way?'

I hesitated. 'Personal experience.'

Mr Huxley hesitated. 'It moves me to hear you defend Chester with such passion, but I'm afraid the decision has already been made. Someone has to be First Footman, and I chose you.'

I nodded reluctantly. 'Thank you, Mr Huxley.'

Twenty minutes later, while we were eating our breakfast, Mr Huxley summoned Chester into his office. The other servants, two dozen valets, maids, and hallboys, chattered pleasantly with each other, but I couldn't stop staring at the door.

'It's not right,' I whispered.

'Don't worry about it,' Seamus said, sipping his coffee. 'The waggon will be here at noon. There's not much to bring down. What about you? Do you need help with your bags?'

'THAT'S RUBBISH!' Chester screamed from inside Mr Huxley's office.

The entire Servants' Hall went silent. My heart started pounding.

'No, I WON'T keep my voice down!' Chester whipped the door open, his eyes ablaze with fury. 'YOU'RE ALL GARBAGE!' He slammed the door behind him and stomped upstairs. The other servants whispered to each other in soft gossipy hushes.

I stared off. A familiar pain hit my chest.

Seamus chuckled. 'Surprise he cared.' He looked at me. 'Well?'

I rubbed my neck. 'No, I'm good.'

X.

Outside the Servants' Entrance, I tied Seamus's bag onto the

waggon and gave him one last hug.

'Good luck with the wedding. Wish I could be there.'

Seamus nodded, a lump in his throat. 'If things were different, I'd make you my best man.'

'I'd say the same.'

Seamus flashed a bittersweet smirk. 'Oliver's a lucky bloke.'

I sighed, moved almost to the point of tears.

The Driver whistled impatiently. Seamus hopped up, his feet dangling over the edge of the waggon. He smiled and waved goodbye as it shoved away.

I never saw Seamus again.

I still think of him from time to time. Sitting by a fireplace with a big beard, maybe a gut. Annie on his arm, children at his feet. A Dunderrow lad moving up in the world, living the life I should've had. A career greater than that of a Footman. A legacy history actually wanted to remember.

I don't resent his happiness. I'm glad, actually. Seamus Costigan deserves such peace.

I carried my bag upstairs and stepped into my new bedroom. Chester was lying on his bed, staring at the ceiling with a strange calmness.

I glanced at him, waiting for him to speak first. After a moment of silence, I plopped the bag on my bed. 'I'm sorry, Chester. I didn't want—'

'We won't be friends,' Chester whispered.

I froze, too stunned to reply.

Chester silently stood and left the room.

XI.

2 March 1885

Life at Barrington Place was quite the opposite of the one I had in London. A warm, clean bedroom. Three hot meals for free. Plenty of work to keep me occupied. The pleasantries stopped there.

Chester was a tiresome roommate. He loathed my very existence after the promotion and, just like Seamus said, never took a holiday. I rarely had a moment of privacy. Every room had a maid, hallboy, or Barrington.

I was safe from the police in those walls, but the cost of my freedom was celibacy. How humiliating it was to lie again, just like I did in Dunderrow. The other servants freely expressed their risqué desires (so long as Mr Huxley was out of earshot), and I didn't want to appear antisocial, so I played along, cracking bawdy jokes of fictional female conquests. It worked too well. They kept inviting me to pubs on our weekends off. I forced myself to flirt with women, innocent maids from other houses, the ones who wanted a handsome man to treat them properly. It was difficult for me to be convincing, but even more difficult to avoid hurting their feelings with my indifference. I became a common tease. Makes me sick thinking about it, even now.

I didn't have time for pleasure, anyway. It was hard enough setting time aside for Mother's letters (£5/day, like always). I didn't tell her about my return or the new job, and I kept using my old Whitechapel address. It was better that way.

Oliver's telegram stayed above my bed. I couldn't sleep without it.

I needed a friend after Seamus, someone who knew my story, who understood me. It was something to work for. The lying had to be worth it.

Every First Footman in history had the same duties I did. Lay the table for each meal. Serve the family breakfast on trays. Take shifts with the Second Footman watching the front door whenever the Butler was busy. Rub the silver every day. Clean them once a week. Brush the dinner table. Lay out the silver. Sweep the floor every Saturday before breakfast.

Nothing was difficult. Just the same thing every day.

The repetition of Barrington Place fascinated me. Posh people follow the same routines they've had for thousands of years, even in their own homes. No wonder they are slow to change. One unexpected guest made the whole house panic.

Unlike Chester, I never complained, not once. I did my time. Outside, I was the perfect employee. Inside, I continued my stubborn disdain to preserve my sanity.

How strange they are, how fragile. Such a dull existence. Cut off from the rest of the world. Days filled with vain charities. Silly gossip. Petty squabbles. Extravagant parties they took for granted. Whining about the Liberals in Parliament and the immorality in London.

I loved mocking them. It gave me power over them. Something they couldn't take away.

Weeks of hard work went on.

Criticising the aristos stopped being fun after a while.

Then it became counterproductive.

So my defiance dwindled...

...a little bit at a time...

...until one day...

...when I wasn't looking...

...the candle burnt out.

XII.

15 June 1887

Where did it all go?

I barely remembered Mother's voice. Had to use maths to remember my brother's age. Almost forgot Munce's name. Oliver's telegram was the only thing keeping me grounded. I could never forget him. I dreamt of him every night, always the same room, that beautiful bed of white satin.

The envelope wasn't as crisp and one of its corners had torn. The Mayfair address had rubbed off long ago. Only his name remained.

Oliver Hawkett. Something to go back for.

If I still wanted to.

I had become numb to posh life. I understood its appeal. It wasn't soft or weak. It was predictable. Dependable. Comforting. It wasn't for me at first, but what was I now? I hadn't shagged a man in two years. I was their creature. A neutered mutt.

I paged through my old diary, filled to the brim with erotic, graphically detailed exploits. What adventures I used to have! What variety! I couldn't believe that man was me.

I rolled out of bed. Looked at myself in the glass. I had muscles. Clean hair. More handsome than ever. Thirty years old. The prime

of my youth wasted in service, hiding from a scandal no one cared about anymore.

I could've gone back. I had the money. Had it for a long time. But what was the point? What had changed? I was just as smart, just as cautious as I was at Kensington. My mistakes didn't ruin me. Forces out of my control did. It could easily happen again. I'd be on my own, no Seamus to save me next time.

Everything's normal here. Why would I want anything else?

Excitement was in the air at breakfast. It was Lord Barrington's birthday. 'The party will begin half-past six,' Mr Huxley told us. 'Lady Mary Parksley, His Lordship's sister, is staying the night, as well as His Lordship's cousin, Lord Westley Barrington. Lady Parksley's maid stayed behind, so Ms Smithers will dress her.'

Ms Smithers (Her Ladyship's maid) nodded. 'Yes, Mr Huxley.'

'What about Lord Westley?' I asked.

'I want you to dress him.' Huxley answered.

Chester crunched into a biscuit, eyes wide with shock.

I gaped. 'Me, Mr Huxley?'

Mr Huxley nodded. 'His man was taken ill just before he left.'

'But he's never been a valet before,' Chester interjected.

I glared at Chester.

'There's a first time for everything, Chester,' Mr Huxley said with understated scorn. He smiled at me. 'Ask Mr Travers what to do. I'm sure you'll get the hang of it.'

I beamed. 'I'll do my best, Mr Huxley!'

'See that you do. Who knows? We might not need to hire a new valet for His Lordship after all.'

'Now wait just a minute!' Chester cried. 'You said I was to dress His Lordship when Travers retired!'

Mr Huxley pursed his lips. 'That was before Seamus left.'

'But, Mr Hux—!'

'That'll be all.' Mr Huxley stood. The rest of us stood in unison. 'Get to work, everyone.'

I sighed, stunned. *His Lordship's Valet? What an honour!*

Chester scowled at me and stormed out of the Servants' Hall.

Mr Travers spent the afternoon reminding me the basics of valeting. If there was one thing I was already proficient in, it was undressing Lords. I just had to reverse the process.

'Have you met Lord Westley?' I asked.

'Only once,' Travers replied. 'He came up for the grouse a couple years ago.'

'Nice, I hope.'

'Oh yes. He's very polite.'

I smiled. *Good to know I won't be shamed if I screw up.*

Huxley rang the gong at six. I waited for Westley Barrington in the dressing room, fantasising my future as Lord Barrington's valet.

A position of confidence! Why would I want to scrape through London when I could be dressing an Earl?

The door opened. My jaw dropped.

'Good evening,' Lord Westley said in a deep, masculine voice. He was young and dashing, a long throw from the bald, brandy-gutted Lord Barrington.

'Good...' I swallowed. 'Good evening, m'lord.'

Lord Westley flashed an attractive smirk. 'Shall we get started?'

'Of course.' I removed his shirt and almost fainted. Broad chest. Muscled arms covered in thick, black hair. Cologne. I couldn't stop staring as I dressed him.

'Very attentive, aren't you?' Westley murmured.

I chuckled nervously. 'I'm new to this, m'lord.'

'Wes, please.'

I sighed. 'Wes.'

I knotted his tie, our faces close enough for me to sneak a kiss. A yearning awakened inside me. I realised how hungry I was, filled with an urge that disobeyed common sense. I imagined the two of us sneaking into the Study during the party, his instincts the same as mine. He'd take me. Penetrate me hard. Release his fluids deep inside me.

'How do I look?' Wes asked. 'Presentable?'

I smiled with cracked lips. 'Yes. Very presentable.'

Wes chuckled. 'Good to know.' He bowed his head and left the room. I was a quivering, lustful mess.

An hour later, I carried the entrees around the dinner table. My eyes never left Wes for long.

I know what I must do. I need a man. Don't care who he is. Don't want to know. Just someone I can use. How long it's been!

After dressing Wes down for bed, I returned to my room in the grip of madness.

'Look who's here,' Chester grumbled. 'The interloper.'

'Stop your whining,' I whined. 'You'll be First Footman now.'

'I never wanted to be a footman. I've been vying for Head Valet since I started.'

'Then stop being so lazy and earn it!'

Chester grimaced. 'Huxley won't pick you. You didn't even have a reference!'

I cackled. 'And yet I'm still miles ahead of you!'

Chester softened, visibly hurt.

I slipped into my pyjamas. 'Don't worry, though. I'll make sure His Lordship considers you when I retire.' I chuckled. 'In thirty years!'

Chester's upper lip trembled viciously.

I chuckled and went to bed.

XIII.

16 June 1887

'Chester's taking off Friday. You'll be on your own for dinner.'

I stared at Mr Huxley, completely flabbergasted. 'But... he never asks off.'

Mr Huxley shrugged. 'I couldn't believe it myself, but I suppose he is entitled.'

I struggled to suppress my jubilation. 'Did he say why?'

'Something about his family in London. Nothing serious, I believe. Just an impromptu holiday.'

'And when is he coming back?'

'Saturday morning. Perhaps a break will mend his spirits.'

I nodded. 'Well said, Mr Huxley.'

I went back to work, my mind ablaze with anticipation. *The room all to myself the day after tomorrow? What timing! Fate must be*

on my side. I better act fast. God knows I won't get this chance again.

I found an advertisement in *County Meath Weekly*:

Beautiful Ones! Whenever and Wherever You Prefer!

That might not seem like much to you people, but homosexuals know: 'Beautiful ones' are always men. If they were girls, it would say 'girls'.

I posted an enquiry alongside my Thursday letter to Mother (first time I ever sent more than one), asking to meet my man before the day's end. I received a reply in the evening post:

Sheep's Head Pub, Eleven o'clock.

Davie

XIV.

I crept out the Servants' Entrance and raced to the Sheep's Head. I was ten minutes late, but Davie was still there. He looked fairly normal, not another drug fiend like Wyatt or that lunatic Tucker. He wasn't handsome, and I could tell he was a bit slow, but under the circumstances I was relieved.

Davie, on the other hand, wasn't so subtle with his assessment.

'Bloody Hell!' he exclaimed with wide eyes. 'Where have *you* been?!'

I blushed. 'Nice to meet you too.'

'Didn't think anyone decent lived around here.'

'They can't be that bad.'

'But they are!' Davie insisted childishly. 'Fat ones. Ugly ones. The only ones who look like you are the whores!'

I chuckled. 'Are you saying I should become a whore?'

'You'd probably be good at it.'

I smiled. His naivety was endearing.

'Of course, I didn't mean to offend,' Davie added. 'It's just...' He squinted. 'You really aren't a whore?'

I pursed my lips and reluctantly shook my head. 'No. Never was.'

I can tell a girl I'm attracted to her while she smiles back. I can look a bobby in the eye and say I'm Sir Martin Cavendish on my way home from the station. I can convince my friends after three beers that I shagged a bird the night before. I've lied so many times to so many people. That one bloody hurt. Being a whore was the only thing I was ever good at.

I reached into my pocket and handed Davie his fee. 'Okay, here's the plan. Friday night, quarter eleven, I'll hide a key outside the Servants' Entrance. Everyone should be in bed by midnight but wait until one just in case. There's a set of stairs on the left. Two flights up are the Men's Quarters. I'm the third door on the left. Don't pick the wrong one.'

'I won't. Third on the left.'

I nodded. 'The boards creak in the hall, so be careful, but we'll be fine in the room. I checked.'

'You put a lot of thought into this, handsome.'

I smiled. 'Got nothing but time, apparently.'

XV.

18 June 1887

Chester left before the morning post. I never saw someone so eager to get to London.

The day flew by without him. I hid the key at quarter eleven, like I promised, and retreated to my room. My heart raced as one o'clock inched closer.

Ten minutes to showtime. No noise in the hallway for over an hour. Everyone was asleep. I was excited. Just the thought of shagging again made my body quiver, but there was fear as well.

Just echoes of the raid. That was the last time. I looked over at Oliver's telegram. It callously leaned against the window, judging me.

Why does this feel wrong? It shouldn't be. I want it. I bloody need it. It's the only way I can. How is that fair? I can't bear living like this. A shell of myself, desperate for scraps. Even if it gets me sacked.

Oliver wasn't brash. He never gave into urges. A virgin at twenty-three yet always calm and collected. He was smart. He was cautious.

How's this different from Kensington? If I couldn't trust Collins, I can't trust anyone. It's not worth the risk. I squeezed my eyes shut. My blood ran cold. *I'm making a huge mistake.*

I checked my pocketwatch. Five to one.

I rushed out of the room. Crept down the hall. Raced down the stairs. Poked my head out the Servants' Entrance.

'Davie,' I whispered into the night. 'Davie!'

Twigs cracked. Davie stepped out from behind a hedge. 'What? What's wrong?'

'I'm sorry. I changed my mind.'

Davie groaned with brutal disappointment. 'Are you sure?'

'I am, sadly.'

Davie rummaged through his pockets with a frown. 'I still have your money.'

'Keep it. I insist.'

Davie smiled weakly. 'Thanks.'

We silently looked at each other, sharing our lonely frustration.

'I'm sorry I couldn't be more helpful,' Davie mumbled.

'You were amazingly helpful.'

Davie kicked a pebble. 'I wish it worked out, you know? Don't get blokes like you. I was looking forward to it.'

I felt bad for the poor guy. After checking for witnesses, I leaned in and kissed Davie, slow and deep, before abruptly pulling away. 'There. Something to remember me by.'

Davie smirked. 'Thank you.'

'Good luck, Davie.'

'Same to you, handsome.' Davie turned and rambled on.

I bit my lip curiously. 'What door was my bedroom?'

Davie stopped, struggling for a moment. 'Third on the right.'

A chill raced up my arms. I forced a smile.

Davie sighed. 'I was wrong, wasn't I?'

'No,' I murmured. 'You said the right thing.'

Davie grinned triumphantly and carried on into the night.

I swiped the spare key and raced back to my room.

I touched myself many times that night, fantasies of Oliver ripping through my mind, until the lust finally evaporated from my brain. Everything was suddenly clear. I made the right choice.

I don't want to be their creature anymore. It's time to return to the real me. No more lying and misery. I'll stay on for a month and return to London with a fantastic reference. If something goes wrong, I'll be safe this time.

I slept with a huge smile on my face.

XVI.

19 June 1887

Chester was back when I woke. He didn't say a word. He just stared at me, a nasty grin on his face.

Mr Huxley stopped me in the hall before breakfast. 'I need to speak with you.'

'Of course, Mr Huxley.'

Mr Huxley led me to his office, closed the door, and sat behind his desk. 'There's been a situation.'

I blinked. 'What do you mean, sir?'

Mr Huxley looked at me directly. 'Chester doesn't have family in London.'

I swallowed, confused. 'Then why did he go?'

Mr Huxley opened his desk drawer. 'I can't say I'm surprised. Twice passed over as First Footman, then again as Lord Barrington's valet...'

I grinned. 'I'm going to be His Lordship's valet?!'

Mr Huxley peered up. 'You *were*.' He held out a newspaper.

My stomach dropped. I didn't need to read the headline. Recognised the sketch of Commodore Collins.

'That bastard!' I hissed.

Mr Huxley grimaced. 'I'll have none of that talk from someone like you.'

I snatched the paper from his hands and threw it against the wall. 'This is wrong, Mr Huxley! You can't let Chester cheat his way into a promotion!'

'I admit, Chester's motives were duplicitous. But that doesn't make his actions less honourable.'

'Honourable?!' I shook my head. 'I can't believe this.'

'You'll be dismissed at once, without a reference.'

I scowled. 'No reference?!'

'You're lucky I don't report you to the authorities.'

'FOR WHAT?!' I screamed. 'I WAS ONLY A SUSPECT!'

Mr Huxley stood, staring me down like a cross headmaster. 'There is no place for a sodomite in a great house like—'

'Please, Mr Huxley—!'

'DON'T interrupt me,' Mr Huxley growled with bulging eyes.

I clenched my jaw.

Mr Huxley shook his head. 'You are a depraved, indecent creature that degrades the very history of these walls. You do not deserve the respect of a reference, good or bad, because you do not have God's respect. You are everything unnatural about this world, the very reason He smote Sodom and Gomorrah with fire and brimstone.'

Bile hit my throat. I looked away.

Mr Huxley gritted his teeth. 'I'm. Not. Finished.'

I glared back.

'I pity you!' Mr Huxley spat. 'You are on the path of your own destruction with no hope of redemption. Even if you beg the Lord for mercy, you will still burn for your sins. Life is not about lust or perversion. It is about right and wrong, and you will get what you deserve.'

We glowered at each other for a few moments.

Mr Huxley sat. 'I have one question before you go.'

I huffed. 'What?'

Mr Huxley folded his hands. 'Did Seamus know?'

'No,' I lied.

Mr Huxley hummed, almost surprised. 'Door's over there.'

I closed my eyes, lip trembling with shame.

Mr Huxley harrumphed impatiently.

I opened the door. Looked back. 'I served Lord Barrington for two years, Mr Huxley. I was the perfect Footman.' I took a deep breath. 'Can you please give me a reference?'

Mr Huxley shook his head with defiant contempt.

I chuckled from the shock. 'Well... I might be a monster in the eyes of God, but so are you.'

I slammed the door on my way out.

CHAPTER SIX

Ships that Pass

I.

28 April 1881

I wandered out of King's Cross with nowhere to go. Red eyes. Cheeks coated with dry tears. Head throbbing from dehydration. I was scared. Never saw so many people in my life.

Twelve hours had passed since that final row, yet it lingered. Ringing through my head like a gunshot. The toxic details refluxing themselves. The all-encompassing ache of betrayal. The colourless miasma of humiliation. My pathetic naivety. Father's cracked voice. My desperate pleas to Mother. Those horrible things we said to each other. Burnt my heart to recall such dread, but I couldn't think of anything else. I was starving. Penniless. Carrying a bag of meaningless possessions into the worst city in the world.

They can't be serious, I kept telling myself. *They love me. I'll be alright. I'll just stay at a pub and wait for them to calm down. Even better, I'll write to them. Yes. That's what I'll do. I'll write to Mother and go from there.*

One day at a time.

II.

19 June 1887

I stood outside King's Cross and sighed with relief. Nothing had changed. The same cross people. Same wet overcast. The rotten heart of the Empire. Oh, how I missed it!

What can they do to me now? My skin's tougher. My back's straighter. I know where I'm going. To Marylebone. To that old mansion on Montgomery Street. To Oliver.

It was finally happening. To see him again after so long... I wasn't nervous, just bewildered. So much had happened since that lunch at Dubeau Frères. I believed him now. Even if his dream was impossible, I knew it was better to hope than to give up. That was going to be music to his ears.

I hoofed through Westminster, nostalgia hitting me left and right. Christopher Street with that bakery with the cream pasties. Victoria Street with that wonky cheese shop with the cute name. The Regent's Park with my favourite bench. Edward Avenue with their quaint bookshops. I was close to Cherry Street, and only four miles from that revolting flat I used to have in Whitechapel. Amazing how distance makes everything a treasure.

I crossed into Marylebone, finally turning on Montgomery Street. Didn't take long to spot that old house, no longer hiding in the shadows. Clean façade. Banisters draped with garlands, like the ones in New Orleans. A fresh coat of rosy paint. No more cobwebs. The house was breathing again. Waking up.

Standing on the porch was the most peculiar creature I've ever

met. Very tall. Unusually thin. Skin black as soot. Puffy lips smoking a fag with strange urgency. Posture unashamedly ladylike. Hand resting on jutted hip. Even the slightest mannerisms flamboyant. A big red ribbon wrapped around his hairless skull and tied into a bow. Tight shorts. Sleeveless shirt tied at midriff, like a tart. An offence to common decency, yet immovably fierce. No passer-by dared to start a fight. They'd lose.

His name? François Brion.

His eyes were on me before I saw him, more from security than suspicion.

'You're lost, boy.' The most feminine voice I ever heard from a man. An unusual tone, both flirtatious and patronising. His French accent only the third queerest part.

'Do you live here?' I asked.

François blew out smoke, studying me up and down. He smirked. 'Really are lost.'

'What?'

'Thought you people had red hair.'

I rolled my throat. *Took Ireland for granted.*

'Not many where I'm from.'

François smiled slyly. 'You run out of them too? Or just the potatoes?' He put the fag back in his mouth, dragging with teasing eyes.

I clenched my jaw. 'Shouldn't you be on a plantation somewhere?'

François raised a long, thin eyebrow. 'Take a joke, darling,' he whined with deadpan sass. 'The tone doesn't suit you.' He paused. 'Neither does the wool.'

I looked down at my jacket. It was a bit patchy.

'Ever the gentleman,' I mumbled.

'Honesty, honey. Truth ain't graceful.'

I huffed impatiently. 'Does Oliver Hawkett live here?'

All levity vanished from François's face. 'You know Oliver?'

'I want to speak with him.'

'About?' He emphasised the t as a third syllable.

'He offered me a job couple of years back.'

Recognition hardened François's face like a stone. 'Hmm. Thought you'd be taller.'

'You know who I am?'

François tossed his fag on the ground, extinguishing it with his shoe. 'Unfortunately.' He strutted to the door and held it open. 'C'mon then.'

III.

What a beautiful entrance! Well-lit. Grand paintings. Balcony and railings polished a bold mahogany. I could hear chattering voices in another room. A hammer slammed upstairs.

François didn't wait for me. I followed him up the staircase and down the hall. He stopped at a door and knocked.

Silence.

François furrowed his brow. He reluctantly opened the door and peeked in. 'He's not in his office,' he murmured with genuine surprise. 'Must be downstairs.'

As if on cue, a row erupted downstairs.

'Follow me,' François muttered.

He led me downstairs and stopped just outside the Barroom, raising a hand for me to wait. I couldn't see the arguers, but I could distinguish three voices: one feminine, one masculine, and one androgynous.

'I asked Louise for the can on the right.' Feminine.

'He said left!' Androgynous.

'I don't care what you told him, Mary.' Masculine. 'You put the maroon on the wall. It's your responsibility.'

Mary strained his voice. 'How was I supposed to know Louise picked the wrong can? Why are two shades open anyway?!'

'Stop making excuses!' barked the masculine voice. 'You set us back a whole day. Once the maroon dries, you have to paint the whole room over. Both of you!'

'Why me?' whined Louise.

'I trusted the two of you to keep organised. He painted the wrong colour, but you gave him the wrong can. Get it done.'

'But he—'

'ENOUGH! Quit pointing fingers and do what I say! And if I hear you messed up again, Mary, you'll be on bathroom duty. Understand?'

A pair of mumbles.

'Mary! Louise! Do you understand?!'

'Yes, Oliver!' they cried in unison.

My stomach dropped. *Couldn't be.*

'What is it, François?' the masculine voice asked, inches from me.

I looked up. Our eyes collided like a boxer's punch. His green into my blue. So hard it silenced us both.

Oliver. Bags under his eyes. Auburn hair cut short, no more curls. Scruff under his neck. Broad shoulders. He was a man now.

Neither of us blinked.

François awkwardly cleared his throat. 'Oliver—'

'Help Denny with the cabinet,' Oliver ordered.

François snorted. 'I'm on break.'

Oliver raised his brows.

François huffed. He glared at me and strutted away.

Oliver and I stayed where we were, our discomfort thick enough to slice. There was so much we wanted to say. So much missing. And he was just as scared as I was.

All we did was stare, softening every second, until smiles grew on our faces.

IV.

Oliver led me into his office. His desk was haphazardly coated with papers, treaties, and bills. I spotted coffee stains and biscuit crumbs between his typewriter keys.

'Sorry about the mess,' Oliver said. 'Been meaning to fix it up.'

'It's okay.' I sat down.

Oliver hopped on his desk, his beautiful bum crushing a mound of papers. 'It's really you,' he whispered.

I smiled. 'You look good.'

'You too.'

I definitely blushed. I looked around the room, admiring the decor. 'You did a good job fixing the place up.'

Oliver groaned. 'I dunno. We're way behind schedule.'

'Believe me, it's fantastic.'

Oliver raised his brows with relief. 'Truly?'

'Truly.'

Oliver smiled. 'I forgot how far we've come. There's always something going wrong, you have no idea. Permits. Ledgers. Maths. All for something that can easily buckle opening night.'

'I'm sure it'll be successful.'

'You don't know that. None of this has been easy.' Oliver huffed. 'Wish I knew more going in.'

'Like what?'

Oliver scratched his ear. 'Advertising, for instance. How are we supposed to mass-market something illegal? And what if no one shows up? There's so much overhead in this place. Even Charlie's getting desperate. He has touts handing out cards in Piccadilly, can you believe that?' Oliver rolled his eyes. 'I guess we're a carnival now.'

I furrowed my brow. 'Charlie?'

Oliver looked at me quizzically. 'I told you about Charlie.'

'I don't think so.'

'He's the one who inherited this place.' Oliver snapped his fingers. 'I did tell you about him! I stayed with him the night we met, remember? After they raided the flat in Mayfair?'

'You never said his name.'

Oliver mused. 'Oh. Suppose I didn't.'

'He's has the office on Newman Street, right?'

'Yeah. The publishing house on the corner.'

I froze. 'Not the Charlie Smith Publishing House?'

Oliver chuckled. 'As opposed to what, the other publishing house on the corner?'

I held up a hand. 'You're friends with Charlie Smith?!'

Oliver blinked. 'You know him?'

I grinned. 'Are you kidding?! His books are all over the city! I have three in my bag!'

Oliver smirked. 'I had no idea you were such an admirer.'

I laughed. 'I can't believe it! This is his house?!'

'It was his mum's first. She never lived here, though. A distant relative bequeathed it to her, I think.'

'I'm sure she wishes she lived here now.'

Oliver frowned. 'She died seven years ago.

I gasped. 'Oh no. That's so sad.'

'Yeah, well... He didn't really know her.'

I frowned solemnly. 'Still. Must've been so tough for him, losing a mum so young.'

Oliver shrugged. 'It's what it is.' He cleared his throat. 'Getting the house was difficult. Rightfully his, yet his grandmother refused to give him his inheritance. Odious woman.'

'Why was it difficult?' I gasped. 'Charlie's a homosexual?!'

'He is, but that wasn't the reason.'

'Oh. What then?'

Oliver held up his hands. 'Does it matter? He has it now.'

I hesitated. Forced a smile. 'Well, it looks great.'

Oliver rolled his eyes. 'I suppose.'

'Wish I could've been here.'

Oliver stared at me, crossing his arms. 'What happened to you? I

went back to Cherry Street, and your boss threw a broom at me.'

'Who...? Oh. *Him.*' I sighed. 'I was still around, but, uh...' I scratched my nose. 'I'm sure you heard about Kensington.'

Oliver nodded. 'I did.'

'Yeah, well... Munce fired me after he saw my name in *The Times*.'

Oliver softened with genuine concern. 'Christ. That's terrible.'

I frowned. 'Who needs him.'

'Where did you go?'

'Back to Ireland. An old friend from home got me a job in Mulhussey. First Footman for some Earl.'

Oliver forced a smile. 'I had a feeling you turned out okay.'

I licked the inside of my mouth. 'I got sacked this morning.'

Oliver's smile faded. 'What happened?'

'The Second Footman heard about Collins, told the butler. That was it.'

Oliver's face hardened. He slid off the desk. 'So, what's the plan?' he asked, a bit too cheery. 'What'll you do now?'

'That's why I'm here.'

'What do you mean?'

I looked him in the eye. 'I want to take the job after all.'

Oliver inhaled sharply.

'You were right,' I told him. 'I was stupid. I should've listened to you. I know better now. Whatever you want me to do, I'll—'

'No.'

I lost my breath for a moment. 'What?'

Oliver shrugged definitively. 'No.'

'Woah, wait, I-I don't understand.'

Oliver paused. 'You don't? Truly?'

I stammered a bit. 'I-I-I thought—'

Oliver flashed a quizzical smile. 'You don't care about this place. What we're fighting for. You made that very clear.'

'I do now.'

Oliver nodded generously. 'Of course you do. You got sacked this morning.'

My stomach dropped. 'No, that's not—'

Oliver beelined to the door. 'I don't have time for this, I really don't.'

'Oliver, please!'

Oliver held the door open. 'Get out.'

My voice caught in my throat. 'Stop! No, just—!'

'Get the hell out of my office!'

'I was wrong, alright?! About everything. I'm sorry I didn't go to you after Munce sacked me, I'm sorry I didn't write, I'm sorry for so many things! I know I hurt you, but I learnt my lesson. I'm here now. I'll take the job. You need me!'

'I don't need you!' Oliver roared. 'I needed you two years ago! You abandoned me! You don't get to take your time and waltz back in! I did everything on my own. I didn't miss you! You know what I said after I heard about Kensington? Good riddance! You don't believe in anything. You don't value anyone. Just yourself. You always have.'

My lip quivered. 'No.'

'The offer's rescinded. Get out of my office.'

Can't end like this. 'Wait.'

Oliver huffed impatiently.

I stood, my legs wobbling. 'I'll do it.'

'Do what?'

'You said it yourself. You can't sell what you don't understand.'

A revolted scowl grew on Oliver's face. 'You're pathetic, you really are.'

I rubbed the back of my head. 'You paid in advance.'

'I'm not a virgin anymore.'

I froze. My whole body turned cold.

Oliver sighed dismissively. 'I found someone else.'

I sat back down, waves of dread filling my veins. 'Who was he?'

'Nothing special.' Oliver chuckled. 'Cheaper than you, that's for sure.'

Don't cry. Don't you dare cry. It shouldn't matter to you. He doesn't deserve to see you like this, saying those horrible things. He's not worth crying over. That Oliver doesn't exist anymore. All those years you spent trying to be like him were just a waste of time.

Grow up, you sissy! Be a man! That's life! You had your chance, but NO! You were too scared! Too stupid! You waited too long and missed it! It's over! Move on! He doesn't love you! He NEVER loved you! And he was never going to!

The dyke broke. Tears rushed out of my eyes. I was a complete babbling mess. Wailing into my hands. Snot dribbling on my fingers. I tried to hide my face.

Oliver wasn't stupid. He saw everything. Eyes frozen in horror. Cheeks twitching with helplessness. A realisation dawning. He knew

me. More than he thought he did. The reason I came back. Why his words affected me so.

Oliver pulled a handkerchief from his pocket, cautiously approached me, and handed it to me. I sobbed into it. He crouched and rubbed my back. 'I'm so sorry,' he whispered. 'I didn't know.'

I reached into my pocket and showed him the fake telegram. 'I still have it. You were with me everywhere I went.'

Oliver held the telegram with delicate care. Studied every stain. Every wrinkle. Every smudge it had acquired over the years. The address was gone. His name perfectly legible. A strange expression flashed across Oliver's face, far deeper than flattery. I had immortalised a special part of who he was. One he jettisoned long ago.

Oliver gently laid the telegram on his desk and embraced me tightly. I hugged back, sobbing into his shoulder.

Oliver suddenly pulled away. He looked to the floor with an apologetic frown.

We stayed silent for a few moments, digesting everything.

'I'm running a business,' Oliver murmured with a dry throat. 'I'd be your employer, but that's all.'

'Oliver—'

'I don't...' Oliver stopped himself, clearing his throat. 'I can't be anything more.'

My lip trembled.

Oliver held out the fake telegram. 'Please.'

I looked into his beautiful green eyes. With a heavy heart, I took the telegram back.

Oliver helped me to my feet and walked me to the door. 'Second

door on the left. Dinner's every night at six. Don't be late.'

We stood in the hall. Voices floated up, a cloud of mutters, gossip, and bickering.

'They won't trust me, will they?' I whispered.

'Probably not.' Oliver looked at me, a soft expression on his face. 'But you're one of them. And that means more than you think.'

He winked. Just like the night we met.

That made me smile.

CHAPTER SEVEN

Not Alone

I.

My new bedroom was decently sized. Fresh polish on the mahogany walls. Furniture that had never been used, still smelling of sawdust. Mattress twice as big as the one I had at Barrington Place, with good support and soft sheets.

I unpacked my bag and put everything where it belonged. Clothes in the cabinet. Cigar box on the corner shelf. Diary on the desk. Oliver's telegram propped above my bed.

I sat down and took it all in. *A bedroom all to myself. Personal and for work. Strange. They'll come to me for once. I can be on all fours, arse raised, blindfolded, and they'd walk in, take their time.*

I smiled. *Maybe brothel life won't be so bad after all.*

Quarter to six, I minced my way downstairs. The Great Hall was quiet. The setting sun gave the wood a golden glow. I wandered into the Smoking Room, its walls half-painted and stripped of decoration. Tarps covered the ground, the infamous maroon and crimson paint cans sitting side by side.

The Barroom was after that. A well-furnished cabinet against the wall with every liquor and cordial, the proper tools stocked and

organised. The counter had been recently polished, a second coat by the look of it. It was long enough for ten stools. I stared at the shelves. *A drink, a drink. My kingdom for a drink.*

I made my way into the Dining Room, which circled back to the Great Hall. Red ornate paper on the walls. Small gas-lamp chandelier. Eight-man oak table. In the corner was a swinging door with a porthole. The Kitchen lights were on, and I could hear François singing a French aria over bubbling water. The smell was heavenly.

I sat at the table. Checked my pocketwatch. Five minutes early. I sighed and waited.

II.

Fifteen minutes passed. The table was still empty.

How embarrassing. This isn't Barrington Place, stupid. Mealtimes aren't punctual anymore. I'll look like a fool.

Footsteps pattered down the stairs. Two voices quarrelled like hens.

'You're absolutely mad,' Mary cried. 'You know very well that's my damn dress.'

'The fact that it fits me means it's mine, bitch,' Louise retorted. 'I know you've been sneaking pudding when no one's looking.'

'You look like you could use a few extra servings, strutting around like a twig. *In my dress*!'

'Then leave some for the rest of us, you slutty cow.'

'Oh, hush up!'

Mary walked in, stopping abruptly with a surprised squeak. Louise bumped into him, almost falling over.

I gasped. *What the hell was I expecting?*

Mary was in his mid-twenties, short, pale, and pudgy with a large wig of small red curls atop his head and enough rouge on his cheeks to impersonate a painted doll. The frills of his bright pink debutante gown rustled as he walked, quite the bombastic choice for such a low-drum affair. At least he made his tissue-paper bosoms small enough for good taste.

Louise's emerald dress was far more casual, perfect for a soiree or a barbeque. His blond wig was short, yet elegant, and he used enough powder on his face to achieve a perpetual colourlessness one could only describe as Ghost Chic. His height, age, and feminine mannerisms were identical to Mary's, his muscled arms and toned thighs providing a healthy contrast. He hadn't stuffed his chest, but his pectorals compensated enough.

'Hel-lo!' Mary cooed. 'And who might you be?'

Louise pushed past Mary. 'C'mon, move!'

Mary slapped Louise's arm. 'Don't touch me, pig! I'm not that kind of woman.'

'Not any kind of woman, you fat wall.'

'Yeah, made of the finest marble.'

'Sure. White and heavy as hell.'

'Shut your mouth, you...' Mary strained. 'Foul... heap of rubbish!'

Louise stared at Mary. 'That is such a bad comeback, I'm actually concerned about your wellbeing.'

My eyes volleyed back and forth. *Men. In dresses. Men. Dresses. Men in dresses.*

'Well?' Mary asked me.

I blinked. 'What was the question?'

'Wonderful,' Louise whined. 'A Guinness boy.'

Mary gasped, long and deep. 'You're that telegram boy Oliver told us about!'

'The one who got caught,' Louise murmured.

I shifted in my seat, embarrassed.

'That's not very nice, Louise,' Mary whispered. 'It wasn't his fault they found him at that orgy.' He smiled at me. 'Are you staying with us?'

'*Times* said Collins had a tiny pecker,' Louise blurted. 'That true?'

'Lou-ISE!' Mary squealed, on the verge of tears. 'My God, I know he's dead, but you shouldn't mock his pecker! He was a Commodore. And you're just a tramp.'

'Oi, Four-Leaf Clover!' Louise barked. 'Small or not?'

I shrugged. 'Not that small, I guess.'

Mary gave Louise a smug grin. 'See?'

Louise sat next to me. 'Doesn't mean anything. I don't know his point of reference.'

'Then why'd you ask?' Mary grumbled, sitting across from us. 'Nosey bitch.'

Louise leaned over to me and whispered, 'And his nose is bigger than mine.'

'What was that?!'

'Nothing!'

I couldn't stop staring at Mary's dress. *How does it stay on?*

Mary caught my eye and looked down. 'Is there something on my chest?'

'He's staring at you, Mary,' Louise whined.

I gaped. 'Oh, no, I wasn't—'

'There's nothing wrong with staring, Louise,' Mary insisted. 'Not everyone's seen a cross-dresser before.'

'If he's staring, you're not doing it right,' Louise retorted.

'WILL YOU HUSH UP?!' Mary screeched, on the verge of tears again. It was difficult not to laugh at his melodrama.

A young man waddled in on a wooden crutch. He had a boyish face, soft chestnut hair combed over perfectly, and huge smile. 'Pay no attention,' he said to me with a strong Welsh accent. 'They can go on for hours.' He held out his hand. 'Denny Evans. Glad you could finally join us.'

I shook Denny's hand, smiling at his chivalry. 'Everyone seems to know who I am.'

'We've heard a lot about you.'

'You and all of London.'

Denny flapped his hand. 'Ehh, we can take em. Anglo bitches.'

I chuckled. 'I keep forgetting I'm not the only Celt behind enemy lines.'

'Then we better stick together.'

I smirked. As Denny waddled away, I realised his left leg had been amputated at the knee.

François pushed in from the kitchen, a heavy stock pot in his arms. He took one look at me and stopped short. Stew almost flew out. 'Why's he still here?'

'I think he's working with us,' Mary said.

'Good thing,' Denny added cheerfully. 'We've been needing an expert.'

'Speak for yourself,' Louise groaned.

François laid the stock pot on the table. 'Denny, get the rouille and toast from the counter.'

'I can do it,' I said, standing up.

'Denny's quite capable of getting things himself.'

Denny nodded at me and waddled into the kitchen with ease.

François stirred the stew with a ladle.

I took a big whiff. 'Ooh! What is that?'

'Bouillabaisse.'

'It smells wonderful.'

'I know.'

I frowned at his tone.

Denny hobbled back with a tray of grilled bread topped with spiced mayonnaise. 'Want something to drink?' he asked me. 'I can make a mean martini.'

I grinned. 'Oh, thank—!'

'Not now, Denny,' François muttered, spooning out the servings. 'Eat it while it's hot.'

I blinked. 'No, I wouldn't mind—'

'Bon appetit, everyone.'

I huffed. Denny flashed me an apologetic frown.

We ate silently. The bouillabaisse was sublime. Red rascasse. Sea robin. Some kind of eel. Velvet crab. The rouille was made with olive oil, garlic, saffron, and cayenne pepper. I couldn't believe what I was eating.

Halfway through the meal, as I scanned the faces of that motley crew, I realised someone was missing.

'Where's Oliver?' I asked.

'He doesn't eat with us,' Mary answered dryly.

I deflated with disappointment. 'Why not?'

'What's it to you?' François grumbled.

I chuckled bitterly. 'Why don't you like me, François?'

The others suddenly stopped eating. They looked up with worried faces.

'Oh dear,' François whined. 'Thought I was being subtle.'

I wiped my mouth with a napkin. 'Don't you think I deserve to know why?'

François stared at me. 'I think you should eat.'

'No. Tell me.'

François put down his spoon, wiped his mouth, and folded his hands. 'You were found naked among thirty Sailors and Collins himself—'

('I don't think he knows what subtle means,' Louise whispered to Mary.

'At least he could spell it,' Mary whispered back.)

'—But they didn't arrest you. They just... let you go.' François crinkled his face. 'Ain't that a bit strange?'

Everyone looked at me. I shrugged with a nervous smile. 'Guess I got lucky.'

'No one's that lucky.' François squinted. 'What did you do? Who'd you give em?'

'No one.'

'C'mon, you can tell us. Why'd they let you go? You slept with them, didn't you?'

'No, I didn't!'

'What then?'

I wiped my mouth again. 'They couldn't prove I did anything while I was there.'

François chuckled. 'Oh please!'

I stared at François. 'I don't understand it either. That's just what they told me.'

François pursed his lips. 'So you say.'

'It's the truth.'

François smirked. 'Tell us about the fine.'

My stomach dropped.

'What fine?' Denny asked.

'He gave them nineteen hundred pounds,' François answered. 'Nineteen hundred twenty-five to be exact.'

Mary blew a long whistle. 'Your highness!'

'A bit steep, isn't it?' François raised his brows at me. 'Sounds more like a bribe to—'

'How do you know about that?!' I snapped.

François flapped a hand. 'It was all over the papers, but I understand. You were probably long gone by that point.'

I smashed my lips together. 'It wasn't a bribe. An Inspector robbed me at gunpoint.'

François nodded. 'Of course he did.'

'And I know how that sounds—'

'Don't waste your breath! Oliver told us what a great liar you are. You actually turned us down because you trusted them MORE!'

'And that was a mistake!' I cried. 'Obviously, I learnt my lesson.'

François shook his head. 'Fleeing a scandal ain't learning your lesson, sweetie. It's just as reckless and self-serving as before.'

I inhaled sharply. 'Well, it's in the past, so... Oliver trusts me now.'

François's face hardened. 'I don't know how you could've changed his mind, but believe me. He doesn't trust you.'

Bile hit my throat.

'That's enough, François!' Louise scolded. 'He's been through enough today. Let him eat.' He gave me a respectful nod. I nodded back and returned to my stew.

The rest of the conversation was a dance, an unspoken waltz around the Great Matter. Mary and Louise talked about a man they shared, and Denny queried me for intimate details of my former clients.

François didn't say anything else. He didn't have to. The seed had already been planted.

III.

21 June 1887

I posted Mother's letter in the Penny Post box outside the brothel (since I was avoiding Cherry Street like the plague) and returned to Dubeau Frères for my first Délice de Mousse in two years. Somehow it tasted even better. *A recipe change?* I wondered. *How can someone improve perfection?*

Everyone at the brothel was in a tizzy. They were supposed to open 1 June, but furnishing delays forced Oliver to push the big night to 15 July. One more delay and they'd miss the busy season. I spent my days slaving on that house, but it wasn't the work that was difficult. It was everyone else.

I wasn't a novice. I knew how to stain wood. And hang pictures. And clean floors. And install oil lamps. And make lunch. I did it all on my farm. But the others didn't trust my knowledge. They kept trying to teach me everything, so naturally I resisted. I didn't want to be talked down to. Before I knew it, I had an unfair reputation: loathsome collaborator. Even Denny thought it was better if I worked alone.

I didn't mean to offend! François set the tone on day one, calling me reckless and self-serving. I felt the need to redeem myself and show my strengths. Any mistake just proved François right. I tried too hard to be perfect and lost a different fight in the process.

Dinner felt like a stage show, all of us actors waiting to speak our lines. If you miss your chance to talk, you're skipped. I didn't feel I had anything worth contributing. The others talked about small things, inside jokes, continuations of prior conversations. I felt added on. I couldn't ask them what I wanted to know. How Denny lost his leg. Why Mary and Louise dressed like women. What a French Negro was doing in England. Why Oliver never ate with us. That was old news. Their conversations went forward, not backward, so I stayed silent.

IV.

22 June 1887

Working alone, I had plenty of opportunity to study the others' personalities and work styles. I could grasp the hierarchy of power within two days.

Oliver made the rules and gave the orders, but he stayed in his office the whole time, leaving only to use the bathroom and get food. His absence made everything strange. There was no structure to anything, yet it was all too strict. No direction, no feedback, no encouragement. Only scoldings and lectures. The others talked negatively about him, especially Mary and Louise. 'Nasty,' they said. 'Lazy.' 'Sadistic.' It broke my heart to hear such slander, but I couldn't contradict them. I didn't want to stand out more than I already did. But even if I dared to defend Oliver, I wouldn't know how. He wasn't a good leader. And it was all my fault.

François was the closest we had to a supervisor. Denny called him 'Oliver's watchdog.' He followed the rules verbatim, like that kid everyone hated in school. We could scrub an entire floor and François would only notice the spots we missed. Any word of resistance was a waste of time. Nothing could sway him. Even if everything was perfect the first time, an entire cabinet dusted, a room meticulously painted, a chaise placed in the ideal orientation, François created something wrong, an extra step we missed, no matter how stupid. He'd be useless otherwise. He couldn't lift anything. Took too many fag breaks. I think knew he didn't deserve to be in charge. It would explain his fanatical loyalty to Oliver, even

when Oliver blatantly contradicted him. If François wasn't perfect, his authority could easily be taken away.

Denny was cooperative to the point of bootlicking. He did everything with gusto, hobbling fast and climbing high. The others took advantage of his selflessness by giving their extra work to him, but he never complained. He always smiled.

Mary might've been a dainty thing, but he was much smarter than he looked. He knew everything about homes and construction. Plumbing systems. Heat. Nails. Screws. Paint. Saws. Cleaning solutions. Dusting techniques. A seemingly endless encyclopaedia, yet easily overwhelmed. He'd panic if a job wasn't finished fast enough. Never saw someone cry so much.

Louise, on the other hand, was a rock. Incredibly strong, but a complete waste in a pinch. Like Chester, Louise never volunteered for extra work, no matter how simple, and Denny enabled him by always picking up his slack. Louise's day was done two hours before the rest of us. I'm not even exaggerating. He'd literally drop whatever he was holding, sit on the side, and watch us finish the job.

Fascinating how such different personalities and work styles intertwined so seamlessly. A perfectly efficient collective two years in the making. A puzzle I didn't fit in.

V.

1 July 1887

I dreamt of beauty again. Oliver and I make love in that white, windy room. Cuddle on the bed. Nothing to do. No places to go. Nothing to tear us apart. I hold him close. Gaze into his beautiful

green eyes. He's special. Happy. All mine. Oliver caresses my cheek with a smile. Leans in. Kisses me.

That's when I woke up. Remembered where I was. Which Oliver was the real one.

At half four, the five of us worked together to hang a chandelier in the Great Hall, an absolutely jaw-dropping fixture we converted to work on gas. Mary and I stood at the top of the ladder; he screwed in the bolts while I held up the damn thing. Denny spotted the ladder, François stood by to coach us through it, and Louise (already done for the day) sat on the last rung and sighed.

'I'm losing my grip,' I strained.

'Al-most there,' Mary said, tightening the last bolt.

'Get the one on the right,' François called up. 'Looks a bit loose.'

Mary smirked at me. 'What do you think? A loose woman joke or a loose arsehole joke?'

My arms buckled under the weight. 'Screw the damn bolts.'

'I'm trying, okay?!' Mary cried.

'Louise!' I called down. 'Can you help me out?!'

Louise chomped into an apple. 'Just a bit more, you'll be fine.'

Mary tightened the last bolt. 'There. All good.'

I released the chandelier, my whole body spent, and rushed down the ladder. Louise didn't see me come down. I crashed into him and lost my balance.

'Woah, careful!' François cried.

On my way down, I knocked a beautiful white and gold vase off its pedestal. SMASH! It shattered into a thousand porcelain pieces.

'Oh God,' I whispered.

'Ohhh boy,' Denny murmured. 'I think that belonged to Charlie's mum.'

Louise rubbed his shoulder. 'Bloody hell! Take it easy next time.'

'Why were you sitting there?!' I hollered. 'I could've gotten hurt!'

'You should've looked where you were going!'

I closed my eyes and forced myself to calm down. 'Are you okay, Louise?'

'Yeah. I'm fine.'

STOMP-STOMP-STOMP-STOMP! Oliver raced down the stairs. 'What the hell happened?!'

François pointed at me. 'He broke Charlie's vase.'

I gaped angrily. 'Woah! Wait a minute! It wasn't my fault! Louise was in the way!'

'Do you have any idea what you just did?!' Oliver shouted. 'How could you be so STUPID?!'

'I wasn't! Louise was sitting on the ladder and—'

'You broke the vase! Don't blame him!'

'It's just a vase! No one got hurt!'

Oliver grimaced. 'Just a vase?! It was an heirloom of Charlie's! He can't just buy another!'

I looked at the others, suddenly embarrassed. 'Can we...?'

Oliver widened his eyes. 'I'm sorry, what?!'

I swallowed. 'Can we go somewhere else and talk?'

'NO!' Oliver roared. 'I wouldn't have to yell at you if you were more careful! Stop acting like a baby!'

'I'm sure Charlie will understand—'

'How would you know?! You never met him! I have to be the one

to tell him you shattered his mother's priceless vase because you didn't care about his property!'

'I'll tell him then! Just stop yelling at me!'

'No! You screw up, you get yelled at!'

'I almost got hurt! What about Louise?'

'You broke the vase! Own up to it!'

'I know I broke the vase, but it wasn't my fault! You weren't here! You didn't see what happened!'

'François saw it!'

'Yeah, but François doesn't like—'

'ONE MORE WORD AND YOU'RE FIRED!' Oliver snarled.

I looked down, holding back tears.

'You're only here because I let you be here,' Oliver scolded. 'You are not the only one who matters anymore, so stop WHINING and do your bloody job. I will not let this place go under because of your carelessness.' He paused. 'Do you understand me?'

I nodded slightly.

'DO YOU UNDER—?!'

'Yes, Oliver,' I whispered.

Oliver studied my face and nodded. He leaned down to Louise, 'Are you okay?'

Louise shrugged, incredibly uncomfortable. 'Yeah, I'm fine.'

Oliver looked up at Mary. 'You okay up there?'

'Yes, Oliver,' Mary mumbled.

Oliver looked at Denny.

'Always am,' Denny said with a soft smile.

Oliver gave François a sharp frown. 'Everything better be secure

next time. I don't want this happening again.'

'Yes sir,' François whispered.

Oliver nodded. He breezed up the stairs and slammed his office door.

I rubbed my eyes, my breath shaking.

François inched toward me with an apologetic frown. 'I didn't know he was going to say all—'

'Get the hell away from me,' I grumbled, on the edge of sobbing.

François lowered his head. 'Do you want to go to your room?' he whispered.

I hesitated. 'Yeah.'

François nodded. 'Go.'

I wandered up to my room, collapsed on the bed, and wept into my pillow.

VI.

I stayed in bed and read a book, trying to forget what happened. At half seven, Denny knocked on my door. 'Are you okay?'

'Yeah.'

'Can I come in? I brought you something.'

I hesitated for a moment. With a hefty sigh, I slid off the bed and opened the door.

Denny held up two glasses and a frosted cocktail shaker. 'Thought you could use one of my mean martinis.'

I gasped. 'Oh, Denny. You didn't have to.'

'Nonsense.' Denny hobbled in. Sat on a chair. 'Oliver dug into you bad. Worst I ever saw.'

He poured my martini, and we toasted. It really was delightful, a scratch getting itched.

'You didn't come down for dinner,' Denny whispered. 'We were wondering what happened to you.'

'I'm sure François was pleased.'

'Don't worry about him. He might be a bitch, but he's our bitch.' Denny chuckled.

I looked off with a frown.

'What's the matter?' Denny asked.

'Nothing.'

'Nothing?'

'Yeah, nothing.'

Denny snorted. 'C'mon, let's not play that game.'

'Don't take this the wrong way, Denny, but I don't know you.'

'Hey, I'm here to help. Don't be afraid to talk about yourself.'

'I'm not afraid! It's just...' I sighed, gently mussing my hair. 'You wouldn't understand what I'm going through.'

'Oh, I wouldn't?'

'No.'

'Try me.'

I looked away. Denny waited patiently.

I took a sip of my martini. 'I don't belong here.'

Denny rolled his eyes. 'Christ, stop listening to François! He's like that with everyone. Me, Mary, Louise, we like you. You're a nice guy. And meaning well goes a long way.'

'It's not François,' I whispered. 'I don't deserve to be here, at the brothel.'

'Because of the scandal?'

'No, it's...' I hesitated. 'I don't think it's gonna work.'

Denny frowned. 'Don't you want it to work?'

'Of course I do, but...' I struggled to phrase it properly. 'I was so sure that...' I stopped myself again.

Denny sipped his martini, eager to hear.

I shook my head. 'You're all so proud to be like this. I didn't think that was possible growing up. When I found out, I thought I had to settle to be happy. Sure, I could get married and have kids. It's what my family wanted. But it would've been a lie. I'd have to keep a secret my whole life. But if I didn't do that, I'd be living on the street. No family. No friends. Working as a whore. Addicted to drugs. I knew those were my only options, I knew it my whole life, until...' I stared into my martini.

'Until you met Oliver,' Denny murmured.

I scratched my nose. 'Is it that obvious?'

'It certainly explains a lot.'

My face hardened. 'I couldn't believe it. He was so unashamed, and he listened to me, and he made me feel loved, and...' I cleared my throat. 'He kept talking the brothel, and the cause, and a future where we can be normal. But I knew better. Because no one talked like that. I thought he was naive, or in denial, or...'

Denny lowered his head.

Tears formed in my eyes. 'I could've been here from the beginning!' I whined. 'But I said no. And I really wanted to believe it, but I didn't want to be wrong.' My lip quivered. 'And I lost everything anyway! My money. My job. My name in the papers. I had to run

away, Denny! Two years of my life gone because I'm too bloody STUPID!'

I took a big swig of my martini. *Beefeater. Munce's favourite.*

Denny silently digested my speech with a strangely serious expression. 'The only amputees I ever saw were those old veterans sitting outside the market in Cardiff. They were dirty. Hair too long in the wrong places, too short in the right ones. And they smelt awful. Just rancid. Begging for halfpennies, scraps of food. And it made me really sad. But Mum didn't give them anything. When I asked her why, she told me, "No one gives them anything."'

Denny shrugged. 'Then I lost my leg. I was only ten. I spent a long time in that hospital. Sitting. Thinking about those men, those veteran amputees. And I realised I never saw a young one.' He chuckled. 'So naturally, I assumed they didn't exist.'

I smirked.

Denny sighed. 'Six months later, I was still there. I couldn't use a crutch. And there were some bad days. Terrible days. I kept praying to go back to how I used to be. Anything would've been better. Amputees don't get into Parliament, or take to the stage, or see the world. And I figured... Sooner or later, they grow the hell up, accept their inferiority, and go where they belong: outside the market, on the ground, begging. And anyone who disagreed, like those young amputees I never saw, were just in denial like I was.'

A strange feeling grew inside my chest. I couldn't believe what I was hearing.

Denny downed his martini, wiping a drop off his chin. 'One of the nurses found me crying in my room. She gave me ice cream and

asked why I was upset. I told her about those men. That I didn't want that life. The Nurse looked at me, nodded, and said she was taking me on a little trip. She put me on a waggon, took me to the market in Cardiff, and walked up to every amputee, one by one, and asked them, "Why are you begging?"

'And they gave different excuses. "I don't have a job." "I don't have any money."

'So the Nurse asked, "Why aren't you looking for a job? Why are you giving up?"

'And they said, "I'm nothing without both legs."

'So she asked, "Why do you think that?"

'And every single one said the same thing. "That's what I've always been told."'

I lowered my head.

'Hey,' Denny said, taking my hand. 'Look at me.'

I cleared my throat. Looked up.

Denny pointed at me. 'You are not stupid. You were just misled, we all were. But it's not too late. You're here now.' He smiled. 'You're not alone anymore.'

Tears fell from my eyes. Denny cooed and gave me a big hug.

I sighed into his shoulder. 'That was quite a speech.'

Denny laughed. 'Sorry.'

'No. No, it was good.' I sat up and wiped my eyes.

Denny grabbed his crutch. 'François left your dinner in the oven. I'll bring it up.'

'You don't have to.'

'It's okay. I'll be back.' Denny waddled out to the hallway.

I looked up. 'Denny.'

Denny stopped and turned.

I smiled. 'If that nurse were here, she'd be very proud of you.'

'Stop now or you'll make *me* cry.' Denny chuckled as he hobbled away.

Denny Evans changed my life. I worked harder than ever. Opened my mind to feedback. Helped Denny with the extra tasks no one wanted. Even offered to help François make dinner. That surprised him, and my calm obedience impressed him, but I didn't do it for his approval. I did it for us.

What did I have to worry about, really? I wasted so much time trying to stand out, to be perfect, because I always had to make up for being homosexual. But in that house, it was the norm. I was an equal for the first time in my life. I didn't even have to explain my sudden shift in attitude. They already knew.

It happened to them too.

CHAPTER EIGHT

Achieving Forgiveness

I.

13 July 1887

We made tremendous progress over the next two weeks thanks to my newfound confidence. The last couple days were set aside for inspections and formalities, giving us a much needed reprieve. I was excited for opening night. The house looked great, and I was more than ready to get back to work.

I stood before the Montgomery Street Penny Post box, Mother's letter in my hand, when I had a strange impulse. *I need to resolve what happened with Mr Munce. Nothing spiteful, just a mature conversation between two adults. I'm not afraid of him anymore.*

I marched into Camden Town after lunch, but as I approached the Cherry Street Post Office, I slowed to a crawl. *He'll call the police if I'm not careful.* I stopped inches from the door, my nose almost touching, and took a deep breath. I pushed in.

DING DING DING!

Mr Munce handed a parcel to a customer, a housewife by the looks of her. His face had more wrinkles and a few spots, but his eyes were noticeably clear.

'Just sign here,' he said, handing her a receipt.

The Housewife opened her pocketbook and pulled out a pen.

Mr Munce craned his head to the door. 'I'll help you in just—' His eyes met mine.

I removed my paddy cap with a melancholic frown.

Munce's jaw slacked, his face softening with recognition.

'Here you go.' The Housewife handed back the receipt.

Mr Munce left his trance and smiled. 'Thank you. Have a nice day.'

The Housewife nodded politely and walked out. DING DING DING!

I pocketed my cap, already uncomfortable. Munce rubbed the back of his head.

I stepped up to the counter and held out my letter.

'Haven't seen one of these in a while,' Munce murmured, taking it gently. 'Assumed you stopped.'

'Took my business elsewhere.'

Mr Munce laid the letter on top of the outbox. 'Anything?'

I shook my head.

Munce let out a long sigh. 'Wow.'

I stuck my hand in my pockets, nodding gently.

Munce looked up at me. 'Where did you go?'

I rolled my lips. 'Home.'

'Just not... *home*.'

I shrugged. 'I'm not their problem either.'

Mr Munce's eyes drooped. 'Kid, look...' He removed his spectacles. 'I'm sorry about everything. What I said. What I did.'

I held up a hand. 'Please, Mr Munce—'

'I was bitter in those days, and I drank too much, and I hurt my wife—'

'I don't want to...' I blinked. 'What.'

Mr Munce smirked. 'I didn't tell you about her, did I? I'm not surprised. She left me a long time ago. We didn't have much money, and we were just kids when Tommy came along, and, well...' Munce snorted. 'He doesn't like me either.'

'Tommy?' I gasped. 'That was your son?!'

'You didn't see the family resemblance?' Munce chuckled. 'Red face. Sharp lip.' He dangled his finger above his forehead. 'Little vein up here that...' Munce frowned, dropping his hand with a sigh. 'I didn't want him to be like me. He could've been so much better, but he just wouldn't stop causing trouble! Getting into fights at school, and then the gambling started and the whores, and I tried to...' Munce shook his head. 'He could've been perfect, I know he had it in him.' Munce sighed. 'But I went too far. He thought I hated him.'

I looked down, my stomach hardening.

'Tommy needed my help,' Mr Munce whispered. 'He got a tart pregnant, in debt up to his ears, and he just needed some money. That's all. And he hadn't seen me in so long, but he still tried to...' Munce's face tightened. 'But I said no. And I kept saying no, no, over and over, and... And he told me to...'

My breath wavered. Painful memories flashed across my face.

Mr Munce smiled weakly. 'We got along, didn't we? Much as people like us could, I suppose.'

I nodded reluctantly.

Mr Munce swallowed. 'It wasn't right what I did. Not a day's gone by when I didn't worry about you.'

I looked to the floor.

'I don't drink anymore,' Munce said. 'And I'm eating better. I went back to church.' He paused. 'I'm ashamed. And I really hope you can forgive me.'

I stayed silent for a long time.

'Make sure she gets it, okay?' I whispered.

Munce lowered his eyes. Nodded.

I donned my cap and turned to leave.

'They still ask about you,' Mr Munce called.

I stopped at the door. Hesitated. About-faced.

Mr Munce donned his spectacles. 'Once everyone forgot about Collins, they came back.' He pulled out an address book. 'Where should I send them?'

I crossed my arms. 'What makes you think I still do that?'

Munce peered over his glasses. '*Please*.'

I struggled to suppress a smirk.

Munce grabbed a pen. 'Where should I send them?'

I hesitated. 'I thought you didn't want to be a part of this anymore.'

'I can't stop you from being you. But I can make sure you'll be well off this time.'

I sighed. After a few reluctant moments, I told Mr Munce the address and that we were opening in two days.

Mr Munce wrote everything down. 'I'll let em know.'

I opened the door and looked back. 'Thank you, Mr Munce.'

Munce smiled with doting eyes. 'No problem, kid.'

II.

I turned onto Montgomery Street, my mind still buzzing from my reunion with Munce, when I noticed a handsome stranger walking in the same direction I was on the opposite side of the road. He was about age, very tall, with dark brown hair and a custom-fitted dress suit.

The Stranger noticed me staring from across the street and tipped his top hat. I nodded back. Awkwardly faced forward. We stayed in each other peripheral vision the entire walk, and it was obvious he was just as uncomfortable as I was.

I veered to the left, convinced the Stranger would keep on walking, but he followed me towards the brothel. Our paths converged on the porch steps. We looked at each other with equally perplexed expressions.

'Afternoon,' I murmured cautiously.

The Stranger softened with a charismatic smile. 'Thank God. I sure hoped it was you.'

I blinked. 'Pardon?'

The Stranger removed his top hat. 'Forgive me, I must've left my manners at the office.' He held out his hand. 'Charlie Smith.'

I almost fainted. 'Oh, Mr Smith!' I clapped his hand and eagerly shook, a childlike grin on my face. 'You have no idea—!'

'Charlie, please.'

I whipped off my paddy cap. 'I can't believe this is the first time we're meeting, I... I dunno. There was so much I wanted to say.'

'Good things, I hope.'

'I'm such a great admirer of your books, Mr—' I stopped myself. 'Charlie.'

Charlie chuckled. 'I'm glad to hear it.'

'I love your Gold-Cover Edition of Homer's *Odyssey*.' I puffed out my lips. 'Beautiful! It's like a work of art.'

'I love the classics. Matter of fact, we released a new Gold-Cover just yesterday—'

'*The Collected Edgar Allen Poe*, I know. Already have one upstairs.'

Charlie stared at me in wonder. 'Do you really?'

I nodded eagerly.

'I have to say, I'm...' Charlie beamed, almost uncomfortably. 'Very impressed by your enthusiasm. I hope you're not just saying it for my sake.'

'No, sir. I've been reading your books for years.'

Charlie looked away, overwhelmed with flattery. 'You're too kind.'

'It's the least I can do. You have such a great house.'

Charlie rolled his eyes with a chuckle. 'Not if you see the bills.'

Oliver whipped the front door open, glaring at me. 'What the hell are you—?'

'My fault!' Charlie cheerfully interrupted, stepping onto the porch. 'I didn't mean to loiter.'

Oliver instantly grinned. 'Oh, I didn't see you there!' He looked at me with a soft smile. 'Sorry about that.'

'What was I doing wrong?' I challenged playfully.

Oliver looked at Charlie then back at me. 'Doesn't matter.' His

posture was noticeably looser, his mannerisms bubblier, the good humour I fell in love with fully restored.

My own Dr Jekyll, I mused.

The three of us stared at each other in an awkward silence.

'Oh, I'm sorry,' Oliver interjected. 'Charlie, have you met—?'

'I have!' Charlie teased, a coy grin on his face. 'You certainly were right about him.'

Oliver's face suddenly hardened. 'Stop.'

Charlie raised his brows. 'What?'

'You know what. Get inside before someone sees you.'

Charlie winked at me and walked inside.

I gave Oliver an amused look. 'What did he mean by that?'

'Never you mind,' Oliver whispered with an ambiguous smile. He held the door open and we walked in.

'I can't believe it,' Charlie whispered, marvelling the chandelier. 'It's fantastic.'

'They did a good job,' Oliver said, giving me a knowing look.

I smiled. *What the hell is going on?*

Charlie's eyes checked the rest of the hall. 'That reminds me, Oliver, we need to talk about the gas bill and how we could cut back on the—' He stopped on a lone pedestal. 'Where's Mum's vase?'

My stomach dropped hard. 'What?'

'My mother's white and gold vase, the one her mother gave her on her twentieth birthday in Geneva.' Charlie looked at me. 'Did something happen to it?'

I stammered. 'Oh, I-I thought—'

'We don't know where it is,' Oliver answered casually.

I furrowed my brow.

Charlie frowned at Oliver. 'Did you miss a box?'

Oliver shook his head. 'We checked them all,' he said with unwavering sincerity. 'Maybe they didn't pack it.'

Charlie studied Oliver's expression. Nodded. He touched the pedestal solemnly. 'What a shame. It was such a beautiful piece.'

I softened with amazement.

Oliver's eyes met my mine before returning to Charlie. 'We really should get started on the tour.'

Charlie resumed his golden smile. 'Oh yes. I can't wait to see the rest of it.'

'Is that Charlie?' Mary pitter-pattered up to the balcony's edge and gasped. 'Charlie!' He raced down the steps.

Charlie laughed, arms open wide. 'Mary! Beautiful as always.'

Mary hugged Charlie. He turned his head and screeched, 'LOUISE! GET YOUR UGLY FACE DOWN HERE!'

Louise descended the steps with a smile. 'Personality goes a long way, you horse-faced banshee.'

'Hush up!'

Charlie chuckled. 'Play nice, children. Where's François and Denny?'

Louise hugged Charlie. 'Making dinner. I'll tell them you're here.'

'No, don't disturb them. I'll see them on the tour.'

'Are you staying for dinner?' Mary asked. 'We're having duck.'

'Is there enough for me?' Charlie asked Oliver.

'There's always enough for you,' Oliver answered. 'We'll eat in my office.'

Louise unhooked Mary from Charlie's waist. 'C'mon, let him inspect.' They shuffled into the Dining Room.

I awkwardly thumbed behind me. 'I should follow them, so...' I smiled at Charlie. 'I'm glad I can finally put a face to the name.'

Charlie smirked at Oliver. 'Likewise.'

Oliver slapped Charlie's shoulder and led him upstairs.

III.

The inspection was a rousing success. Charlie's approval radiated throughout the house. The air felt warmer. Our smiles were bigger. A truly observable phenomenon one could gauge with the proper instruments.

François, Mary, Louise, Denny and I ate dinner early, half six, easily the best duck I ever tasted. I still think about it.

'I really like Charlie,' I said.

François sipped his Bordeaux. 'He's easy to like.'

Mary sliced his breast with sharp two-handed slashes. 'Did you see Oliver smile?' he grumbled. 'A unicorn, if ever there was one.'

'He was practically floating around Charlie,' Louise said, taking the tiniest bites possible. 'He can be quite the bootlicker when he wants to be.'

'He wasn't faking,' I said.

Louise snorted. 'Don't be daft.'

'No, I could tell. Oliver genuinely admires him.'

Mary giggled. 'François must've put something in your duck!'

'Why would I?' François mumbled. 'I agree with him.'

Denny pointed at François with his knife. 'Now *that's* a unicorn.'

I reached for the orange jam. 'It's understandable. Oliver's dream wouldn't be possible without Charlie's investment.'

Denny coughed on his wine.

Mary raised his brows at me. 'His what?'

I froze, taken aback. 'Charlie's our patron, isn't he?'

Louise laughed sharply. 'Oh, you sweet Irish boy!'

'What?'

'This is Charlie's brothel, not Oliver's.'

I shrugged. 'I know it's his house, but—'

'No, everything,' Denny said. 'Charlie's the reason we're here. The cause was his brainchild.'

I blinked. 'Oh, I didn't...' I wiped the jam off my fingers. 'He's never here, so I just assumed that Oliver—'

'Charlie's our legitimate front,' Mary explained. 'On paper, we're just an offshoot of his Publishing House. Naturally, he can't be here every day, so Oliver acts as his foreman.'

'How do they know each other?' I asked.

'I dunno,' François answered. 'But Oliver was the first. There'd be no cause without him.'

I smiled. 'Charlie must be really brave, putting his career at risk to fight for a better world.' I shook my head. 'I couldn't do that.'

François rolled his eyes. 'We know.'

I stared at François.

François flashed a smug grin.

'I can't believe it's finally here,' Mary whispered. 'Years of prep and now... Day after tomorrow, rain or shine.'

I nodded. 'I know, I'm actually getting nervous.'

Denny chuckled. 'You're nervous?! God help us all.'

'I never did anything like this before.' I topped off my wine glass. 'What are we supposed to do anyway? What's the system of operations?'

Louise squinted. 'Our what?'

'What are we supposed to do when the guests arrive? Oliver never told us.'

Everyone stopped eating at the same time.

I looked around, realising. 'Are you serious?'

'We thought you knew,' Mary murmured.

I huffed. 'No. Why am I always the last to know everything?'

'Tactical discretion,' François muttered under his breath.

'What was that, François?!'

'I'm sure he just forgot,' Denny interjected calmly.

'Sure,' François whined. 'And Brutus forgot to warn Caesar.'

I scowled.

'It's not complicated,' Denny told me, 'We wait in the Great Hall and greet the guests as they come in.'

'What does that mean?'

'You know. Introduce yourself. Compliments, jokes.'

'Okay, what else?'

'What do you mean?'

'What happens next? Where do we take them?'

Denny hesitated. 'The bedroom?'

I chuckled sharply. 'There has to be more than that.'

'What do you mean?' Mary asked.

I glanced at Mary, Louise, and François's serious expressions.

'They can't just pick out who they want and go upstairs. That sounds like a human soup kitchen.'

'Meet-and-greet,' François corrected.

'What?'

'That's what Oliver calls it, meet-and-greet.'

I cringed. 'That's so dull! Why would anyone want to stay?'

'Because we're shagging them?' François chuckled.

I took a deep breath and folded my hands. 'Someone please tell me we're dimming the lights.'

Louise looked at François.

François looked at Denny.

Denny looked at Mary.

Mary looked at me, his mouth full of duck. 'Don't we want them to see us?'

I snorted. 'They had two years and that's the best they came up with?'

'Oliver said most of the work was in the bedroom,' Denny said.

'Then he doesn't know what he's doing.'

'Go and tell him that,' François mumbled.

I stared back. 'I will.'

François furrowed his brow.

I flashed a smug grin.

IV.

My heart raced as I climbed the stairs. Charlie strolled past the balcony, a dirty plate and spoon in his hand. 'Hello again.'

'Is Oliver up there?'

'He's all yours.' Charlie clip-clopped down the stairs, passing me.

'Where are you going now?' I asked, turning.

Charlie stopped and looked up. 'I want to catchup with the others before I head out.'

'Oh. You're not staying over?'

'I can't. Lots to do.'

I sighed. *Guess Mr Hyde's coming back.*

Charlie stared at me. 'Are you okay?'

'Yeah, I'm just...' I swallowed. 'I think I ate too much duck. I'm a bit bloated.'

'No, you're not.'

I blinked. 'What?'

Charlie gave me a strange smile. 'Don't give up. You're still special to him. He'll come around.'

My face hardened. 'You have no idea what you're talking about.'

'You're actually right,' Charlie said with a chuckle. 'He doesn't tell me anything anymore.' He raised his brows mischievously. 'But you didn't know that.'

I forced a definitive look. 'Yes, I did.'

Charlie snorted. 'Liar.'

I swallowed nervously. 'Am I supposed to be impressed?'

Charlie squinted. 'Did you phrase it like that because saying "I'm not impressed" would've been a lie? And I'd be able to tell?'

I hesitated.

Charlie flashed a pleasant smirk. 'Don't worry, it's not just you. And it certainly isn't everyone.' He raced down the steps and into the Dining Room.

I watched him go, an envious smile on my face. *How the hell did he do that?*

V.

I was so preoccupied rehearsing what I wanted to say that I entered Oliver's office without knocking.

Oliver was at his desk, head bowed, lips fluttering in a soft whisper. Soon as I opened the door, he jolted up. 'What is it?'

I stared, processing what I just witnessed. 'Were you just—?'

'No.'

I hesitated. 'Is everything okay?'

'I was resting. What do you want?'

I closed the door behind me. 'Why didn't you tell me about the system of operations?'

'The what?'

'The meet-and-greet,' I said with an eye roll. 'I only just found out from Denny.'

Oliver rubbed his temple. 'What about it?'

I snorted. 'Alarming as it is that you intentionally kept it from me—'

'Hold on!' Oliver snapped. 'I've had a really rough month, doing shit ten times more important than that. I forgot.'

'The way Brutus forgot to warn Caesar?'

Oliver stared at me. 'Is that how you think of me now?'

My face dropped. 'No, it's... Just something stupid François said.'

Oliver studied my eyes with silent scepticism before looking away.

I regained my bearings and powered through it. 'I understand, Oliver. You're so focused on getting the business started that you've overlooked the execution—'

'I haven't overlooked anything.'

'You certainly didn't think it through.'

'What's there to think through? You can't read a room? Ever heard of improvising?'

'Ever heard of writing a script?'

Oliver rubbed his eyes. 'I'm too busy for this. Get out.'

'No.'

Oliver looked up at me, too stunned to emote.

I forced myself to stare back. 'We have two days. It's not too late to salvage this.'

'Salvage?!' Oliver exclaimed. 'You've got some nerve.'

'Why are you fighting me on this? This why you hired me.'

'That offer was rescinded.'

'I'm not blaming you! You never ran a brothel before.'

'I don't need a consultant.'

'You know you do! I just walked in on you praying!'

'I was...' Oliver stopped himself. 'I can do this myself.'

'You're in over your head!'

'Stop!'

'And if this place fails, it will fail because of you!'

Oliver's nostrils flared. 'Since when do you care about the cause? You never believed it!'

'I DO NOW!' I roared.

Oliver stared at me, speechless.

I shrugged helplessly. 'You don't want to be with me? Fine. That doesn't matter anymore.'

Oliver's gaze softened.

I hesitated, stunned by my own words. 'This place, this is what matters now. I didn't see it before, but you've got something here, Oliver. Something great. And I don't even think you know how great it can be.'

Oliver lowered his head.

'We want the same thing,' I muttered. 'I know what I said before, but I've been through a sodomy scandal, and poverty, and forced celibacy since then.' I inhaled sharply. 'I spent the last two years of my life grovelling to a family of posh English idiots, and I can't prove it even HAPPENED! I have trudged through a river of shit, not to mention your rotten attitude, to get back here, and I am NOT throwing it away because you don't have the balls to admit you need professional help!'

'*I* need professional help?!' Oliver interjected.

I scowled.

Oliver diverted his eyes with instant regret.

I shook my head. 'What happened to you, Oliver?'

'I don't know,' Oliver whispered with startling honesty. 'I don't bloody know.'

My heart broke. I stepped forward to hug him.

Oliver abruptly stood. 'Charlie's leaving soon, so... I should see him off.' He squeezed past me and opened the door.

'Thank you,' I said, turning my head. 'For not telling Charlie I broke the vase.'

Oliver's green met my blue, a gentle gaze that made me feel warm inside. 'I would never do that to you,' he whispered with a hint of offence.

'You said you would.'

'You said things too.'

I looked to the floor, my stomach hardening. I lifted my head to apologise but Oliver was gone.

VI.

I hunched over the balcony and watched Charlie make his goodbyes in the Great Hall. Mary and Louise hugged him. François waved from afar.

'When will we see you again?' Denny asked, kissing his cheek.

'Not until next week,' Charlie answered.

'But you'll be at the office if we need you, right?' Oliver asked.

Charlie stared back, a serious expression on his face. 'Are you sure you can handle this?'

Oliver chuckled sharply. 'Of course. Why wouldn't I be?'

Charlie shook his head, an air of sadness surrounding him.

Oliver's smile faded. 'What?'

'That's the first time you ever lied to me,' Charlie whispered.

I furrowed my brow.

Oliver frowned, a flash of fear in his eyes.

Charlie pursed his lips with disapproval. 'God, I sure hope it was.'

Oliver turned away, his head bowed in silent introspection. After a moment, he lifted his head and matched eyes with mine. 'Go on. Tell him.'

Louise, Mary, Denny, and François looked at each other with mutual confusion.

I hesitated. 'Really?'

Oliver nodded. 'You're the professional.'

Charlie gave Oliver a patriarchal grin.

Nothing's more disquieting than entering a room with six silent men. By the time I touched the ground floor, standing before them like a substitute teacher, my heart was beating in my ears. I don't know which made me more nervous: the blank, expectant faces staring at me or the two hundred pound crystal chandelier hanging above me like a guillotine.

I cleared my throat. 'I want to start by saying...'

Charlie stared at me, expectant.

He'll know if you're lying. What do you have to lose? I looked at Oliver.

Oliver smiled back with encouragement.

I took a deep breath. 'I understand what you're doing. You're approaching the brothel like it's a business, or a charity, or... whatever the simile is. You're thinking of partnerships, supply and demand, product and service, and that's all important, but a good system transcends logic. You need to think like an artist.'

Charlie raised an eyebrow.

'Take my old system for example,' I continued, my nerves gradually flying away. 'The reason it worked wasn't because I was selling me. I was selling the idea of me. Hearing of me through word of mouth. Going to the post office. A fake telegram delivery. Sneaking around the house. It's an erotic fantasy. That's why they kept coming

back. I wasn't great in bed, they did all the work, but the *fantasy*! That was something they couldn't get anywhere else. If we're all standing here at the start, they'll see an Irishman, a French Negro, two cross-dressers, and a Welsh amputee. That's it. There's no desire, no mystery, and sex is about atmosphere. Without it, they can easily say no and leave.'

Louise leaned towards Mary. 'Especially if you're the first one they see.'

'Trash!' Mary hissed.

My eyes met Denny's for a brief moment. That's all it took. Half a second at most. That's when I got the idea. The great idea. The one that changed our lives forever.

'Wow,' I whispered. 'Oh, WOW!'

'What?' Denny asked.

I grinned. 'We're cutting ourselves short! We're missing a huge opportunity here! It's not about the sex at all, it is about the cause, right? It has to be more than a brothel!'

Oliver's smile vanished. 'What?'

I smiled. 'A club for homosexuals. Think about it! After a long day pretending to be someone they're not, they can come here and be who they really are, surrounded by others just like them. They can drink, they can have fun, they can have sex, but we're really selling them the best atmosphere of all: validation.'

Mary and Louise gasped simultaneously.

'Holy shit,' Denny whispered.

Charlie furrowed his brow. 'How could we even pull that off?'

'That's the thing, we almost have!' I cried. 'We already have the

space, the bar, the whores. We just need a bit more. Places to sit. Cigars. Music. Anything, as long as they stay all night. The longer they're here, the more they're in the atmosphere. More atmosphere, more regulars. More regulars, better reputation.'

'What about the meet-and-greet?' Mary asked. 'What are we supposed to do instead?'

I studied the shape of the Great Hall. 'We had a standard system of operations for dinner parties when I was a footman. We can use that instead.'

'Great,' Louise muttered. 'More shit to learn.'

'It's not complicated. But we're gonna need one more for...' I looked at Charlie. 'Can you be here?'

Charlie hesitated. 'Only if you really need me.'

'Someone needs to guard the register. I'll be the footman. I'll answer the door and escort them to bar. Denny, you'll make them whatever they want. Everyone else will take shifts serving hors d'oeuvres. Nothing fancy. They don't even have to be hot, just something to keep them busy. The waiters will be fully clothed, tight fits, sensual. We want to tease the merchandise, something for them to look forward to when they get drunk and frivolous.' I paused. 'We need music too. Can anyone play?'

Silence.

François let out a long sigh. 'Okay, I play the trumpet.'

'Great. We'll put you at the bar.' I turned to Charlie. 'And the best part? Because it won't look like a brothel, we'll have insurance in case we're raided.'

Charlie pensively stroked his chin.

'Well, that's all I got,' I murmured. 'What do you think?'

Charlie pursed his lips. 'To be honest...' He crossed his arms. 'It's good, but on two days' notice? That's not what we spent years planning for.'

My stomach dropped. 'I know it's a bit much, but—'

'That's quite the understatement. Hors d'oeuvres, waiters, guests staying all night. The price tag alone makes me wary, not to mention the logistical nightmare it's gonna cause.'

I took a deep breath. 'Then let's try it the first night, just to see if it works. If it doesn't, we can go back to the meet-and-greet and cut our losses. But at least we tried.'

Charlie sighed. He looked at Oliver. 'What do you think?'

My heart started racing.

Oliver licked his lips. 'We can be a human soup kitchen two years in the making... or a homosexual utopia two *days* in the making.' He looked at me.

I stared back, pleading.

Oliver raised his brows subtly. He looked at Charlie. 'I think it's worth the risk.'

Denny, Mary, and Louise cheered. I almost collapsed from light-headedness.

'Are you sure?' Charlie asked.

Oliver sighed. 'If it works, we'll make a fortune that'll keep this place running for years.' And if we fail...' He flashed me a knowing look. 'At least it won't be because of me.'

I smirked.

VII.

15 July 1887

François arranged the hors d'oeuvres on four silver platters. Denny cut the garnishes and stocked the bar. Charlie dimmed the lights. Mary and Louise slipped into their nicer dresses. Oliver rummaged through the attic for sheet music. I spent the day running through the standard system of operations with everyone. Louise gave me some resistance, but Oliver took him aside and insisted the changes were mandatory. Everything went so much smoother thanks to him.

I dressed at sunset, studying myself in the glass. Skin clean. Hair styled perfectly. Muscles looked good. Cock and arse in peak shape. Then I looked into my eyes, a steady gaze.

Everything's working out.

I covered my face with both hands. Took a deep breath. Massaged up and down. Dropped my hands. Stared back at my blue eyes. Smirked.

Don't screw it up.

I sauntered downstairs. 'It's almost time,' I muttered to Charlie. 'Is the lantern lit?'

Charlie looked out the porch window at the old red lamp hanging above the door, the beacon to announce when we were open. 'Not yet. Get François, he's at the bar.'

I nodded and wandered toward the Barroom. I could hear François and Oliver talking as I approached. I slowed to listen.

'I don't like this.' François.

'He wants this place to work, same as us.' Oliver.

'But what if we get raided?'

'We'll see what happens, François.'

'Do you think he'll turn us in?'

Silence.

'Oliver?' François asked.

'I don't want to know.'

'What does that mean? You think he will?'

'It means I'm giving him the benefit of the doubt.'

'But he's a liar. That's what you told me.'

'I know, but—'

'But what? He's sorry? And you believed him?'

'You don't know him like I do, François. He's been through so much.'

'And I haven't?'

Oliver sighed.

'Trust isn't supposed to be complicated,' François murmured. 'If something happens, I can trust you. Can you trust me?'

'Yes, of course.'

'Would you trust him?'

After a long pause, Oliver whispered, 'I wish I could.'

My heart skipped a beat. I poked my head into the Barroom. 'François, it's time to light the lantern.'

François gave a knowing look to Oliver and strutted toward the Great Hall, passing me without acknowledgement.

Oliver wandered up to me with an awkward smile. 'I'm suddenly nervous.'

I frowned. 'Me too.'

Oliver opened his mouth, as if he wanted to say something. He settled for touching my arm. 'Good luck.'

I nodded, my eyes to the floor. 'Thanks.'

Oliver stared at me, lips pursed with concern. He reluctantly turned and made his way to the Dining Room. I watched him go with a heavy heart.

Perhaps some things are too late.

VIII.

Five past eight. I sat on the steps, jaw slacked, eyes fixed on the front door. My mind wandered back to my days at Cherry Street. Waiting for Oliver so I could reject his offer. Wanting him to show up. Secretly hoping he didn't.

BOOM! BOOM! BOOM!

I took a deep breath. Stood. Stepped up to the door. Opened it. At that moment, a homosexual brothel was born on Montgomery Street. We were officially breaking the law.

We had only a handful of guests those first couple hours, which wasn't surprising, but it wasn't great either. I took their coats and led them to the bar, where François was tooting a standard. Denny poured their brandies and I sat on their laps. They were old, of course, but I could smell their lust. I loved the attention. Their envious devotion to my beauty. My worries about the success of the night, about opening myself up to police attention, about Oliver, they all went away with a touch of a wrinkled hand on my young skin.

Another knock at the door. I made my way to the Great Hall and looked out the porch window. I gasped sharply.

Charlie sidled up to me. 'What's wrong?'

I looked at him with a massive grin. 'We're gonna need more hors d'oeuvres!' I opened the door and six gentlemen walked in, grinning of recognition. 'Boys!' I cried, kissing them one by one. 'It's been too long!'

Mr Munce called them, just like he said. The clients are coming!

The house was full by eleven o'clock. Oliver stayed in the kitchen and rushed out the hors d'oeuvres. Charlie left the register at the door and took over as footman. Denny was a surprise powerhouse, making drinks for everyone while still having time to flirt with his own guests. Our resident cross-dressers were surprisingly popular. Many peers discovered a new fetish that night.

And me? I was on top of the world. Dozens of old favourites let me know just how much they missed me. Kip and Manny took me upstairs for a group job, and I spent a good forty-five minutes on my knees in the Smoking Room, passed from one cigar-smoker to another. Do you remember Reggie, the country Earl I mentioned in Chapter One, the one who liked to shag me in his library while his wife and daughters ate dinner? Guess who made a surprise visit.

'I missed you, boy,' Reggie whispered in my ear.

'So did everyone else.'

'They're all for you?'

'Most, not all. I've been busy all night.'

Reggie smirked. 'I bet you have.'

He led me through the crowd, pinned me against the wall, and

stripped me down. His strong hands roamed all over my body, and I lost myself. Dozens of randy faces watched Reggie take advantage of me, easily one of the most erotic moments of my life. The spell broke once I caught a glimpse of Charlie rushing out the front door, Oliver right behind him. Reggie kissed my neck as I looked out the porch window.

A coach parked out front. Six bobbies standing in front of it.

My eyes bugged.

I managed to soothe Reggie and get my clothes back on. 'Don't get too excited now,' I whispered. 'Get a drink. I'll be right back.'

I didn't waste any time. I donned my cap, bolted out the door, and crept up behind Charlie and Oliver.

'How about I go to your house and call it gross and indecent?!' Oliver taunted the Inspector from the porch.

'Not the house, you imbecile!' the Inspector groaned. 'Gross indecency. Sodomy. Perverted activity.'

'Lotta big words, chum. You have to look em up?'

The Inspector rolled his eyes. 'Step aside and let us investigate.'

Oliver blocked the porch entrance with his arm.

Charlie moved it away. 'On what grounds, Inspector?' he asked politely.

'We received an anonymous complaint from one of your neighbours,' the Inspector replied. 'And they believe such indecency is still in progress. That's more than enough probable cause.'

'And if we refuse to let you in?' Oliver challenged.

'Then we'll raid!' the Inspector jeered. 'And I'll arrest you for obstruction of justice!'

Oliver blew raspberries.

'What's going on?' I whispered to Charlie.

Charlie shushed and waved me off.

'Under whose authority?' Oliver retorted to the Inspector.

'Superintendent Williams.'

I froze. 'Marty Williams?'

Oliver whipped his around, shocked to see me there.

I looked at Oliver then back to the Inspector. 'Bald? Muscular? Huge moustache?'

The Inspector cocked his head back. 'You know him?'

My world stopped at that moment. A million thoughts raced around my head.

I'll be damned. Superintendent in two years. Bravo Marty!

What if they raid? All those Lords in one place, in the company of sodomites. We'd be ruined. No reference from Barrington. I won't survive another scandal, so doing nothing isn't an option.

But I have a Superintendent on my side now. That could be a way out. No more hiding. No more being afraid. No more begging and scraping for François's approval. I'd get plenty of money if I gave him the brothel. What could I lose? Besides their respect?

No! I won't be like Tucker. He was alone, I'm not. Not anymore.

But why should I stay here? Oliver? I should be honest with my-self. He'll never trust me again. I apologised, I grovelled, and yet...?

Maybe he's right to move on. Life's too short to waste on a one-sided love.

There must be hope. Denny said it wasn't too late. Look what happened with Mr Munce. He abandoned me, just like I abandoned

Oliver, but I don't resent him anymore. Why? It wasn't his apology. No, it was what he did! He redirected the clients. He made this night a success. In a single action, he removed all my doubts.

That's the answer. Words have no stakes, no sacrifice. They're just as meaningless as these thoughts. Actions are real, an extra step, certifiable proof. What reputations are made of.

It worked for me, but will it work for Oliver? What if I save the brothel and he still doesn't trust me? What will I do then? Stay for the cause? Is this place even worth saving?

I can't predict the future. Only one way to know for sure.

'May I speak to the Superintendent?' I asked.

The Inspector studied my face. He turned to his deputies and whispered.

'Stop,' Oliver hissed at me. 'What are you doing?'

'I know him,' I whispered back. 'He's that bobby I told you about, the one I had as a client. I can get us out of this.'

Oliver's breath quickened with fear. 'No, please don't do this.'

'Trust me.'

Oliver stared into my eyes, green to blue, and we connected. We were suddenly back in Mayfair, marching toward those bobbies.

I smiled softly. 'Trust me.'

Oliver took a deep breath. Nodded.

The Inspector turned back to us. 'I'll leave two men on the street.' He hopped into the coach. Three deputies followed.

I sat at the window seat. Looked out at Oliver. Winked.

Oliver smiled back. The Driver cracked his whip and we drove off.

IX.

The Inspector knocked on Superintendent Williams's office and escorted me inside.

Marty looked up from his desk, almost fainting at the sight of me.

'I'm sorry to disturb you, sir,' the Inspector started, 'but this man says he knows—'

'Leave us!' Marty snarled.

The Inspector raised an eyebrow. He awkwardly bowed his head and left.

Marty raced to the door, locked it, and scowled at me. 'Why are you here? What have you done?'

'They don't know anything, Marty,' I whispered. 'I need a favour.'

Marty softened. He slowly made his way back to the desk. 'I thought I'd never see you again.'

'I only just got back.' I squinted. 'Was Mr Munce the one who told you about the brothel?'

Marty furrowed his brow. 'What brothel?'

I chuckled. 'He really isn't stupid.'

'Pardon?'

I sat across from Marty. 'Your men were just about to raid a house on Montgomery Street, a brothel for homosexuals.'

Marty's face went numb. 'A what?'

'At least, it was going to be. A nosey neighbour decided to ruin our fun.'

Marty leaned in cautiously. 'And you want to make a deal? You give us the brothel and we give you immunity?'

'Not exactly.'

'What then?'

I pursed my lips. 'We'll give you five per cent. Anytime someone gives you a tip or complains about something suspicious going on in that house, you'll ignore it. That means no raids.'

Marty shook his head. 'I'm not that kind of policeman, you know that.'

'Well, this ain't that kind of bribe.'

Marty scratched his moustache. 'You have to understand my position in all this. I'm glad you're safe.' He smirked. 'In many ways.'

'I'm sure.'

'But I worked hard to get here. As much as I'd love to help you...' Marty shrugged. 'I'm not losing my career over a brothel.'

I strolled over and sat on Marty's knee. His breath quickened.

'I worked as a Footman in a big house for the last two years,' I murmured sadly. 'I understand it now, the way it hurts. What we have to give up to be successful.' I caressed Marty's cheek. 'Everyone gets both, but not us. We have to choose.'

Marty smiled, his bushy moustache curling at the ends.

'You were always special to me, Marty,' I whispered. 'You're the only one who isn't pretending to be one of us.'

Marty took my hand and kissed it. 'I missed you so much.'

'It's not too late, you know. We can still make up for lost time.'

Marty snorted, pointing to his Superintendent star. 'Not likely.'

'That's why it needs to be protected.' I smiled. 'It's different. I've seen what it can do first-hand.'

Marty frowned and looked away.

I guided his chin back to me. 'You're a good man, Marty. I don't

want to take advantage of you.'

Marty smiled weakly. 'I appreciate that.'

I gently rubbed the back of his head. 'What can I do, besides throw myself into the bargain?'

'I assumed you already were.'

I chuckled. 'Of course I am. You're the Big Man now.'

Marty rolled his eyes. 'You sound like an Inspector I know.'

My smile vanished, my blood turning cold. 'Is he here?'

Marty sat up, concerned. 'Who?'

'Vic.' I shook my head in a mad panic. 'Christ, Marty, tell me he isn't here!'

'No, no, he's gone. He's gone.'

I swallowed. 'Are you sure?'

'Yeah.' Marty paused. 'Yeah, I'm sure.'

I exhaled uneasily. 'What about that friend of his, Pete?'

'I dunno. He ran off, same time you did.'

I closed my eyes and sighed with relief.

Marty stared at me. 'Did Vic...?' He licked his lips. 'Did he do something to you?'

I shook my head. 'But you know what he's like.'

Marty nodded uncomfortably. 'Yeah. I-I do.'

We shared an uneasy silence.

'What happened to him?' I whispered.

'Discharged.'

'For what?'

'I don't know why, but he punched Commissioner Monro in the jaw.'

I burst out laughing. 'What a bastard!'

Marty laughed along. 'You should've seen his face when he sacked him!'

I giggled, rubbing my face with both hands. 'Damn, I needed that.'

Marty smiled warmly. 'Me too.'

I rested my head against Marty's chest, and he held me in peaceful silence.

'I don't want you to be afraid of anything,' Marty whispered.

'The way I see it, I could've gone to anyone. They'd take the bribe, but they wouldn't do a good job. It means nothing to them. It's for us, Marty. A place where we don't have to choose.'

Marty frowned slightly. 'I can't move mountains, even for you.'

'I know. But you'll do the right thing.'

Marty petted the back of my head with a sweet smile. 'You could've given me up after Kensington, but you didn't.'

'That's right.'

Marty's eyes softened. 'And I'll be able to see you?'

'Anytime.' I slid off Marty's lap and returned to my chair. 'Just tell me how we can make it work.'

Marty thought carefully. 'If something happens I can't contain, another scandal or God forbid the Commissioner finds out, you're on your own. I'll turn you in for bribery. I'm not losing my job.'

'If you don't hold up your end, we'll make sure you do.'

Marty raised his brows. 'Are you threatening me, boy?' he teased.

'Motivating, sir.'

Marty nodded. 'Okay. Twenty per cent.'

'No way.'

Marty smirked. 'Do you even know how much twenty per cent is?'

I hesitated. 'No. But you wouldn't open with it unless it was your ceiling.'

'Per cent of profits only works if you actually make money.'

'We will.'

'How can you be sure of that?'

'You're not my only client.'

Marty raised his brows, ala *touché.*

'Ten per cent,' I countered, 'plus one hundred pounds a month.'

Marty cocked his head. 'One hundred?'

'In notes.'

Marty smiled, impressed. He held out his hand. I shook it.

I stood to leave. Marty jumped up, wrapped an arm around my chest, and pulled me towards him. He slowly kissed my neck, sliding a hand all the way down the front of my body. I could feel his erection poke my arse through his trousers.

'Can't wait to see you again, boy,' Marty whispered in my ear.

I grinned. 'Me too, Superintendent.'

Marty gave me a deep kiss, his moustache scratching my upper lip. His tongue roamed around my mouth and suddenly stopped. He pulled away, squinting inquisitively. 'Why do I taste brandy?'

I shrugged. 'Gotta get back.'

Marty smiled. He gave me another whiskery kiss before dismissing me with a spank. The Inspector (completely oblivious to everything that happened in Marty's office) led me to the coach and sent me back to Montgomery Street alone.

The two deputies were still waiting outside the brothel. Oliver and Charlie were nowhere to be seen. I hopped out of the coach, the bobbies hopped in, and the Driver took them away.

I looked up at the house. Opening night was still in progress, and I could see a pack of Lords laughing in joyful conversation through the porch window.

I half-smiled. *They'll never know how close they were.*

X.

I circled the house to the backdoor, and I could hear raised voices coming out the kitchen window.

'I'm not worried,' Denny said. 'We knew a raid was inevitable. He knows what to do.'

'He'll be back any minute,' Oliver muttered, 'so let's just remain calm—'

'We're done for!' François cried.

'What did I just say?!'

'You let a self-serving LIAR negotiate our fate! How could you do that?!'

'BECAUSE I TRUST HIM!' Oliver roared.

I grinned widely.

'Well...' François murmured. 'What if I don't?'

Silence.

'Then you better get out there and shag while you still can,' Oliver answered.

Satisfied, I knocked on the backdoor. Charlie scurried over and let me inside.

Everyone was in the Kitchen. Mary and Louise sitting in the corner, François smoking a fag by the cooker, Denny wrangling liquor bottles from the pantry, Oliver standing in the centre of the room with a defiant scowl. As soon as I walked in, they hounded me with anxious anticipation.

'Well?' Denny blurted. 'What happened?'

I gently removed my cap with a glum frown.

Mary gasped out of nowhere.

I looked at Charlie. 'Ten per cent and an extra hundred a month. Can we do it?'

Charlie paused for mental maths. 'That could work.'

My lungs evaporated with relief. With a grin, I hollered, 'I BOUGHT US IMMUNITY!'

Everyone cheered at once. What followed was a surreal bombardment of pats on the back, hugs, and happy faces.

'You're mad!' Denny cried, wringing me like a sponge. 'Absolutely mad!'

I chuckled. 'Guess I am.'

Charlie shook my hand firmly. 'Great work. I couldn't have done better.'

I must've blushed. 'That means so much, sir. Thank you.'

François puffed his fag on the sidelines. 'Ten per cent's too high.'

I snorted. 'Nothing impresses you, does it?'

François smiled slightly. 'I suppose you did your best.'

Mary kissed my cheek. 'You're so brave, honey!'

Louise kissed my other cheek. 'You lucky bloody leprechaun!'

Oliver stayed where he was in the centre of the room, watching the celebration with restrained grace. 'They've been asking for you. Better get out there.'

I dropped my smile. Nodded. Headed for the door.

Oliver bit his lip. 'Wait.'

I looked back, my heart pounding.

Oliver opened his mouth a few times, trying to find the right thing to say. He stared into my eyes. Gave me a vulnerable smile. 'Thank you.'

I raced over and hugged Oliver. He squeezed back nice and tight. I almost kissed him on the lips, redirecting at the last second for his cheek. Oliver chuckled and waved me away. With a cocky grin, I dashed out of the kitchen and rejoined the party.

I had the night of my life, dozens of clients in a lustful frenzy, no break until sunrise. I made more in one night than I ever did in a month. The best part wasn't my deal with Marty, or François's change of heart, or Mr Munce calling the calvary, or the fantastic sex, or all that money. It wasn't even regaining Oliver's trust.

When I first learnt I was homosexual, I was scared. I couldn't see the path before me, and I made many missteps. The Incident. My parents banishing me. Refusing Oliver's offer. The Collins Affair. Munce sacking me. Kerry rejecting me. Almost hiring Davie at Barrington Place. Mr Huxley sacking me without a reference. My rough start at Montgomery Street. I was forced to start over every time, years of my life wasted in a constant realignment. But not anymore.

As I conclude this novel, fourteen months after that fateful night,

I'm proud to say I'm on the right path for the first time. I'm safe, surrounded by men like me, my naysayers now my supporters. It's been a long time coming, but I found the place that accepts me.

I'm finally home.

CHAPTER NINE

Knowledge and Silence

Introduction: Why I Wrote a Novel

Since the Montgomery Street Brothel opened sixteen months ago, we've been thriving like magic. We have different personalities and come from all walks of life, yet we're united by common ground to make something wonderful. How are we so different from King Arthur's Round Table? George Washington's Continental Congress? The East India Company?

Think of us as a locomotive. Charlie (our financier and legitimate front) is the steam, and Marty (our police protection) the steel track. The two of them keep the balance. Charlie makes sure we don't move too fast. Marty clears our path of obstructions. By my suggestion, Charlie hired Mr Munce as his personal courier. Munce delivers Marty's monthly payments for an equal share of the house profits, as well as our own post.

Oliver (our bookkeeper and overall manager) is the locomotive's wheels, the keystone of the entire system. He and I became great friends after I bought the immunity. I even convinced him to eat dinner downstairs with the rest of us. He thinks it spoils the mood, but I disagree. It makes him more of a person to the others. The last

thing we need is disloyalty in our commander.

Mary, Louise, Denny, François, and I are the crew, entertaining the passengers and fulfilling their needs. Brothel life is tough work. It requires a lot of sleep and plenty of food and water. We're already fatigued with the sex. Our clients aren't just old and fat. Some have personal problems, strange requests, or God forbid small cocks, but we power through.

We love exchanging stories with each other, like that time Denny was carried upstairs on the shoulders of three men, or when Mary and Louise dressed alike and kept swapping rooms until someone noticed. François had the best anecdotes, thanks to his new talent: abuse. Most of his regulars have a role-reverse fetish, a slave whipping and penetrating his own master. How perverse our minds are! How mysterious our desires!

Our first year was a blur, one I recollect only through its holidays. We had a traditional English Christmas, complete with paper hats and brandy pudding. We welcomed the New Year together with champagne, hugs, and kisses. Even Oliver and I kissed, nothing more than a polite formality. I sensed he wanted more, just like I did, but nothing came of it. In March, I was thirty-one for the first time. My friends surprised me with a party, full of gifts and men, the first birthday I enjoyed in exile.

During our second busy season, I felt a strange wave of familiarity. After so many years changing places and fighting for more, I found myself coasting into dormancy. I didn't want to end up like Mr Munce in that post office. I yearned to do something more while I had the energy.

On 17 August 1888, Oliver and Charlie were standing in the Great Hall, debating how to reattach a crystal to the chandelier, when a young man with short blond hair and big eyes moseyed in without knocking.

'Hello,' Charlie murmured uncomfortably. 'Can I help you?'

'I'm looking for Charlie Smith,' the man said in an American accent.

Charlie hesitated. 'Who are you?'

'My name is Andy. I want to work here.'

Charlie and Oliver froze.

Andy blinked. 'Your secretary said I'd find you here.'

Charlie furrowed his brow sternly. 'This is my house.'

Andy smiled up at the chandelier. 'It's very nice.'

'Thank you, but you should leave. Give your application to my secretary and I'll get back to you.'

Andy stared at Charlie. He burst out laughing. 'Okay, I'm confused!'

'So are we,' Oliver mumbled.

Charlie rubbed the bridge of nose. 'What position are you applying for? Secretary? Courier?'

Andy squinted. 'Nooo...?' His eyes shifted between the men, back and forth. 'This is the homosexual brothel, right?'

Oliver coughed from shock.

Charlie burst out laughing. 'How ridiculous!' He paused. 'Who told you such a thing?'

'Your secretary.'

Charlie feigned a moment of understanding. 'Ah. He's quite the

prankster, I'm afraid. Such a place doesn't exist.'

Andy flashed a knowing smirk. 'He said that too. Until I showed him this.' He pulled a magazine from his waistband and held it out.

The newest edition of *The North London Press*, opened to a full-page advertisement:

Meet the Beautiful Ones on Montgomery Street!
Only the Best for Your Needs!

Oliver frowned, looking at Charlie with concern.

Charlie didn't look at the magazine. He kept staring at Andy. 'What did you say your name was?'

'Andy.'

Charlie nodded. 'You're in the right place.'

A few hours later, Andy waited in the Dining Room while Charlie, Oliver, Louise, Denny, Mary, François, and I huddled in the kitchen.

'Were you advertising for a job?' I asked Charlie.

Louise smirked. 'He finally decided to replace Mary.'

'The advertisement is for clients,' Charlie corrected. 'I have no intention of replacing anyone.

'But what if *The North London Press* starts asking questions?' I asked.

'They won't. I bought them last year.'

'What do you...?' I raised my brows. 'The whole paper?!'

'They're obscure. Political. Way too radical for their sponsors. It almost bankrupted them. I offered them carte blanche in what they could print in exchange for complete control of their advertising. It's the best way to market the brothel.'

'What about the touts in Piccadilly?'

'We haven't used them since the deal with Marty. Anything too public might jeopardise the immunity.'

Oliver waved Charlie aside. 'What are we doing with him?' he whispered.

Charlie sighed. 'I don't know. I certainly didn't expect this.'

François watched Andy through the porthole. 'An American boy, all the way out here. Poor thing.'

I stood next to him. 'Why don't you accuse him of being in cahoots with the police? Isn't that how you normally greet strangers?'

'Only the ugly ones, honey.'

Twenty minutes later, we crowded around an end of the table, studying the American elephant in the room.

Andy stared back with mousy eyes. 'Is someone gonna talk?'

'Where are you from, Andy?' François asked.

Andy hesitated. 'Chicago. Ran away last year, hopped a boat. I had an apartment in Liverpool until I ran out of money.'

I held up *The North London Press*. 'Where did you find this?'

'The men's room at King's Cross.'

'Have you ever done something like this before?' Charlie asked.

'No, sir. There's nothing like this back home.'

'Your folks threw you out cause you like blokes?' Mary asked.

'Yes, ma'am.'

'Sir.'

'What?'

'I'm a man.'

Andy furrowed his brow. 'Really?'

Oliver smirked. 'Andy.'

'Yeah?'

'I talked it over with Charlie. We're letting you stay.'

Andy grinned. 'I got the job?!'

'You got the job.'

'Oh, thank you!' Andy frantically shook Oliver's hand. 'Thank you so much!'

'On one condition,' Charlie added cryptically.

Andy's grin dropped. 'Oh no. What?'

'You start tonight.'

A few hours later, after a particularly exhausting session with the overzealous Lord Cavrenon, I wiped myself off and (completely naked) walked down the hall to use the bathroom. On my way back, an old man wandered out of François's room, nursing his arse with a dumb smile on his face.

François stepped out, his bare black body shining from sweat. 'Au revoir, Bertie!'

'Au revoir,' the old man slurred, inching down the hall.

I rested my shoulder against wall and crossed my arms. 'I hope you weren't too hard on him.'

François laughed. 'Bertie? Not enough. It's his third day in a row.'

'Who is he? I never saw him before.'

'I think he's the Duke of Middleborough.'

My jaw dropped. 'A Duke?!'

'*Maybe*. I don't care for their titles. Everyone's equal after I sic Hercules on them.'

'What's Hercules?'

François chuckled. 'Even you couldn't take it.' He wiped himself with a towel. 'You done for the night?'

'I think so.' I looked down the hall. 'I haven't seen Andy since we started. Do you think he's okay?'

'He's still in his room, last I heard.'

I hummed. 'I should go check on him.'

François nodded. 'Okay. I'm heading to bed. Blow the lantern out, will ya?'

'Sure. Good night.'

'Night.' François shut the door.

As I walked down the hall, I could hear a loud, irate voice coming from Andy's room. I started to worry, convinced an aggressive client was being too rough on our newest resident.

Then I recognised the accent.

'Harder!' Andy cried. 'Yeah, c'mon, you can do better than that! Harder!'

The door was wide open. I stopped at the threshold and gasped. Andy was lying on his back, covered in sweat, arse hanging off the side of the bed, both legs in the air, surrounded by five muscled young men. A blond rammed Andy in the arse, two with brown hair held up his legs, and two others, one black-haired and one red, stood by and watched. Andy had the biggest grin I'd ever seen as he stroked the two brown-haired men, one cock per hand.

'Harder!' Andy yelled at the blond. 'Harder! Yeah, boy, c'mon! You like that ass?! Fuck that ass! It's your ass now!'

I couldn't help but stare. *What happened to the mouse from this morning?*

Like a magnet, Andy's eyes found me. 'Hey,' he muttered, exhaling with each thrust. 'Wanna jump in?'

I tried not to laugh. 'No, I—'

'I don't think there's any space left on the bed.' Andy turned his head to check. 'You can stand in the corner.'

'No thanks, I—'

'Let me introduce the boys. Black hair's Manny, red hair's Eddie, Henry and Mitch are the browns.' Andy beamed at the blond penetrating him. 'And this big boy is Kip!'

I chuckled. 'I know.' I waved. 'Hey, Kip.'

Kip looked at me and smirked. 'Hey there.'

'Don't look at him!' Andy ordered. 'You're not fucking him, you're fucking me, so fuck me!' Kip faced forward and pounded away. 'There you go! Yeah!'

I awkwardly scratched my head. 'I didn't want to disturb you, Andy. I just wanted to see if you were alright.'

'This ain't my first rodeo,' Andy stated plainly.

Kip groaned, slamming into Andy with a couple of big, rough thrusts. He slid out, gasping for air.

'C'mon! Who's next?' Andy barked.

Manny stepped up and slid right in.

'You want some more, huh?' Andy egged. 'Yeah! C'mon, don't stop!'

Kip wiped the sweat off his forehead and headed for the door.

'Where are you going?' Andy called after him. 'Get back here. I'm not done. I can keep going if you can.'

Kip smirked and reluctantly rejoined the group.

'You're right,' I mumbled. 'How silly of me to worry.'

Andy grinned at me. 'This place is great! We do this every day?'

'Except Sundays.'

Andy laughed. 'A sense of humor! Hell yeah!' He scowled at Manny. 'No, no, no, don't slow down! Keep going, c'mon! Fuck me! Yeah!'

Andy turned his head to me and smiled (a natural transition, as if he *wasn't* getting penetrated while stroking two cocks at the same time). 'How many are still in line?'

I blinked. 'What?'

'In the hallway. How many are lined up?'

I looked down the hall in both directions. 'I don't—?'

'Oh, right, how many are in the...' Andy huffed, turning his head. 'Kip, what do you call it over here?'

'Queue,' Kip replied.

'Queue, that's it.' Andy looked back at me. 'How many are in the *queue* outside?'

I checked again. 'No one.'

'What?' Andy cried, flabbergasted. 'What time is it?'

'At least two.'

Andy chuckled. 'Really?' He looked at Manny. 'C'mon, harder, harder!' Andy spat at him. 'HARDER—!'

Manny smacked Andy's face.

Andy cackled. 'HELL YEAH!' He bucked his hips, bouncing off Manny like a trampoline.

I cleared my throat. 'I'm so glad I got the chance to talk to you while you're getting *railed*, but I really should—'

'Oh, you're done for the night?'

'Yeah.'

Andy frowned. 'I'm sorry if this makes you uncomfortable.'

It took the strength of my entire body not to burst out laughing. 'Don't worry about me. I've been in worse.' I turned to leave.

'Hey!' Andy called. 'Be a pal and close the door? I don't want to keep anyone up.'

I chuckled. 'Good night.' I shut the door.

A half-hour after we closed, I sat at the bar to add to my diary while Denny wiped down the glasses.

'What do you keep writing in there?' he asked me.

I snorted. 'I think you're the first person to notice.' I flipped the book around.

Denny hopped over and read. 'Oh wow!' he cried. 'That's filthy. You really did that?'

'People pay for the strangest things.'

'Don't I know it.' Denny flipped back a few pages. 'You write about everyone, huh?'

'Have for years. There's three more volumes upstairs.'

Denny cooed sensually at a passage. 'I like this one. Steamy.'

I read the heading. 'Viscount Franners? I haven't seen him in a while. He was quite the freak back in the day.'

Denny turned the page, engrossed. 'Quite the catalogue.'

'I got some of everything. Seduction, fetish fantasies, public encounters, daring escapes.'

'Why do you do it?'

I shrugged. 'They fascinate me. They talk about their wives. Why

they pay for me. How they feel. I'm the only one gets to see who they really are. No lies or secrets. Just people being people.'

'The prostitute philosopher.'

'No. Just a lonely whore writing smut to feel better about himself.'

Denny closed the book. 'Pity. Damn good writing for something no one's gonna read.'

I frowned, an idea brewing. 'You got a point there.'

Denny was right. It was a pity. My life. My story. My achievements. They would all be forgotten if I didn't write them down. I needed to prove I existed. That we all existed.

Andy was an exile in a foreign land, just like me, but he found this place without the years of doubt or loneliness. We were his haven, the community he was told didn't exist. His arrival stirred something in me. I wanted to give the other Andys out there what I never had. Something to help them make the great leap in a single bound. Something to give them hope of a better world. Something to tell them they weren't alone. The brothel could only do so much.

Ultimately, I wrote this novel to show the normal world what it didn't want to talk about, what it refused to remember. If you people knew our pain, what we have to live with, all the ways we're being punished for something we're born with, you'd want to help us. Then the world would truly be a better place.

1. François's Redemption

On the morning of 28 October, I asked François to tell me his life story.

François stared at me, a freshly lit fag burning in his hand.

'Don't think too much into it,' I added, pen at the ready.

François finally took a drag and looked out at Montgomery Street. No one in sight. 'I'm black.'

'More than that. Where'd you grow up? How'd you know you were homosexual?'

'What's it to you?'

'I want to put your story in my novel.'

François snorted out smoke. 'Leave me be, will you?'

'Why?'

François ignored me. His pose was strangely graceful, like a marble statue in a museum.

I stood in awkward silence. 'How did you meet Oliver?'

'Stop.'

I huffed. 'You still don't trust me? After all this time?'

'I don't trust anyone. Don't take it personally.'

I jotted that into my book. 'And why is that?'

François rolled his eyes. 'If I tell you, will you stop pestering me?'

'Where were you born?'

François laughed bitterly. 'Paris.' He paused with brief reluctance. 'My parents were chefs. Brilliant ones, of course. Taught me everything I knew.' He flicked ash over the edge of the porch. 'They ran a neighbourhood café. That made them local celebrities. So many friends. A whole network of artists and bohemians. They liked me too. I had a feeling that once my parents gave me the café, I'd get the friends too. That was nice to think about.'

I scribbled everything down. 'How did you find out you were homosexual?'

'It's Paris, darling. Doesn't take long. I didn't think it mattered, telling my parents. They had so many friends, I thought they were open to everyone.' François sighed. 'Turns out, they weren't. Asked me to leave the next day. They didn't want to lose their friends, I suppose.'

'How old were you?'

'Sixteen.'

I shook my head. 'That's awful, François.'

François shrugged. 'Wouldn't be so bad if that were the end of it.' He sucked a long drag. 'Lived on the street for a few years, looking for a job. Chimney sweep, some kind of servant. The ones who said no didn't hire Negros. The ones who said yes had conditions.' He grimaced. 'I'd have to suck them. Sometimes more. What could I do? I needed a job.' He flicked ash from his nails. 'They smelled bad. Tasted bad. I was so pathetic.' He coughed. 'None of them gave me the job, of course. They just... threw a couple francs and laughed. Porc malade.' He snuffed his fag.

'Why did you come to London?'

'I needed to get away.'

'What happened?'

François swallowed, unusually nervous. 'I was sleeping on the Rue Saint-Denis when I met a man.' A warm smile crept onto François's face. 'Jérémy,' he whispered sweetly. 'He had a suit. That mattered to me in those days. He let me stay with him. Fed me. Sometimes I cooked for him. I hadn't in so long.' He sniffed. 'I didn't

realise how much I missed it. He held me at night. Kissed me awake.' He nodded. 'It was nice.'

I smiled, remembering my night with Oliver. 'How long were you there?'

François bobbed his head. 'Couple of months. Woke up one morning and he wasn't there. He took everything. My clothes. My money. I never heard from him again.' He sighed and lit another fag. 'I met Charlie a year after I came to London, when I was working the corner in Stepney. He tried to be generous, but I didn't care. No more fooling this bitch.'

'What did he do?'

'The usual offers. Food. Money. A place to stay. I told him to get lost.' François raised a brow, thinking. 'Pretty sure I spit on him.'

I chuckled. 'Charlie didn't like that, did he?'

'He ran off, the pansy. I was sure I'd never see him again, but he came back with Oliver. Thought they were gonna jump me, but... They offered me a job. Oliver needed an overseer.' François smiled, unusually sweet. 'He saw something in me I didn't know I had. Sterner stuff.'

I smiled. 'Bet you loved the idea of telling white people what to do.'

François frowned. 'Not everything's about being black, honey. I'm more than just a topic of conversation.'

I groaned. 'My God, isn't that the worst?! How they always have to say something?'

'Mmm-hmm.' François took a drag. 'Someone once asked me if I cried when Lincoln got shot.'

I paused. 'Which one was he again?'

'He painted the Mona Lisa.'

'I thought that was George Washington.'

'He was the Mona Lisa.'

I laughed. 'You know what I get all the time?'

'Sing it, honey.'

'How does an entire country run out of potatoes?'

François winced. 'Merde!'

'And the way they say it too. Like it's up for dispute.'

François furrowed his brow. 'How *did* you run out of potatoes?'

I scoffed. 'The same way Africa ran out of Negros.'

François smirked.

'I've never seen you smile this much,' I said.

François looked off. 'I admit. It does feel good to talk about it.'

'I realised that when I was writing the book. It's like... Knowledge builds progress and silence stops it.'

François nodded. 'That's a good way to phrase it.'

I took a deep breath. 'I forgive you, by the way. For not trusting me when I first came here. After what you've been through, I wouldn't blame you.'

'Don't get soft on me, honey. Jury's still out.' François pointed at my jacket. 'You know I hate the wool.'

I looked at the ribbon tied around François's shaved head. 'Nice hair.'

François pointed dismissively. 'This old thing?'

'Not you. The ribbon.'

François squinted. 'Touché.'

I smiled and walked back inside. I could hear François chuckling behind me.

2. When Mary Met Louise...

'I swear to God, slow down,' Louise muttered.

Mary frantically scrubbed a dirty dish. 'I can stack them next to you.'

'You're rushing. I'm drying off soap.'

'You use crummy lipstick. Thought you'd be used to smelly paste.'

Louise pointed at Mary's soap-soaked apron. 'Love the dress, dirty whore.'

'You wish you had this look.'

I rubbed my forehead. 'Can we get back on topic, please?'

'Which was?' Louise muttered, smacking Mary's hand.

'How did you find out you liked cross-dressing?'

'The same way everyone does,' Mary replied. 'My sister's knickers.'

'Speak for yourself!' Louise cried. 'It was my sister's brassiere.'

'No wonder. Her breasts were as big as yours.'

'Yeah, almost as big as your sis's cunt.'

'HUSH UP ABOUT HER CUNT!'

I stopped writing. 'Hold on. You two knew each other?'

Louise furrowed his brow. 'We went to school in Liverpool. What'd you think we were? Strangers?'

'We pass as brothers,' Mary teased.

'Shut it, Belcher!' Louise barked.

'Oh, wow!' Mary said with a laugh. 'That brings me back.'

'What's a Belcher?' I asked.

'It's my name,' Mary explained. 'My real name. *Georgie Belcher*.' (Mary seamlessly slipped into his real voice, a butch Liverpudlian accent. It made me flinch.)

'Mine's much less nauseating,' Louise said. '*Corey Kehoe*.' (Same accent, much coarser.)

I jotted down the names. 'You two were friends?'

'Absolutely not!' Louise said with revolted insistence. 'I was his bully.'

I stopped. 'What.'

'He was younger, I had a gang. What else was there to do?'

'I dunno, read a book?'

'That's what I did!' Mary declared.

Louise rolled his eyes.

'What did your parents say?' I asked.

'They didn't care,' Louise retorted. '"Boys will be boys." Once throwing rocks at abandoned buildings lost its edge, we started throwing rocks at the younger kids.'

I winced. 'That's awful.'

'Not as awful as his aim,' Mary chimed in.

'I hit you plenty,' Louise chided.

'Fifty per cent, tops.'

'Five out of ten's still five in the face.'

I cringed. 'The face?!'

'No one was worse than Kehoe,' Mary said. 'I hated him.'

'I hated me too,' Louise added. 'Hated my life. Hated Liverpool. Hated my parents, but they hated me first. My gang didn't hate me,

but only because they wanted to see what I did to the other kids. I couldn't tell them I liked dressing like a girl. I'd lose the only friends I was lucky enough to get.'

Mary dashed to the pantry to grab a new bar of soap. 'I wish I had fake friends. Anything's better than being alone.'

'How did you find out about each other?' I asked.

'I was sitting in the outdoor privy,' Mary answered from inside the pantry. 'Trousers down, knickers around my ankles. I was crying, so I couldn't hear anyone walking up, and I didn't know the lock was broken. Suddenly the door opens, and there's Corey bloody Kehoe.'

'And I saw everything,' Louise added. 'His face, his cock... but I kept staring at his knickers.'

'I was screaming my head off,' Mary continued, 'scared to death of what Kehoe was going to do with me.'

'But you know what I did?' Louise asked. 'I lifted my shirt, showed my brassiere.' He snapped his fingers. 'Best mates. Just like that.'

I grinned. 'Wow.'

Louise smiled proudly. 'We dropped out of school, told our parents to piss off, and we've been travelling the world ever since.'

'Where did you go?'

Mary returned to the sink and scrubbed away. 'Paris, Rome, Vienna, Dublin, dozens of places, all over the Continent.'

'We'd get some work here or there,' Louise said. 'But we never stay long. We like to roam. We were in London when Oliver found

us. He bought us a couple pints, told us about the job, and now we're part of this adventure.'

I scribbled everything down as fast as I could. 'I have one more question, Louise.'

'Name it.'

'You're equals now. Why do you keep bullying Mary?'

'I wanted to stop,' Louise insisted. 'Mary said no.'

I looked at Mary. 'But... Why do you want to be insulted like that?'

Mary sighed. 'I'm a homosexual who dresses like a woman,' he said with queer maturity. 'I won't last long without a backbone.' He smiled at Louise. 'Corey keeps me tough. I wouldn't be the man I am without him.'

Louise smiled back, and they shared a touching silence. Ten seconds later, they were squawking at each other like nothing happened.

3. Denny's Fizz

'Stay still,' Denny murmured. 'They're not going anywhere.'

I laid the sketches back in the box. 'They're really good.'

'Look at the window, please.'

I grunted and resumed my pose. 'I'm starting to regret this.'

Denny drew slowly on the piece of paper. 'The price you pay for an interview.'

'How long do I stay like this?'

'Could be ten minutes, could be an hour.'

I looked at Denny. 'You can sketch for an hour?'

'Window.'

I turned back with a huff.

'What do you think I do all day?' Denny said. 'You have a good face. This'll take a while.'

'I don't have an hour. I really should be writing. I promised Charlie I'd finish the addendum by the end of the week.'

'Then why aren't you asking questions?'

'It's hard to take notes when I can't look down.'

'It's called listening.'

I smirked. 'Okay. How did you first find out you were homosexual?'

'Don't be a dandy. Ask about the leg.'

'I don't need to know.'

'Why not?' Denny lifted his stump. 'Look! Look at it! Aren't you curious?'

'I don't want to be rude.'

Denny frowned and kept on drawing. 'That's what everyone says, but no one talks about it. I don't mind. It won't grow back, the least you could do is acknowledge it.'

I sighed. 'I'm sorry, Denny. I don't know what I'm supposed to say.'

'Well, saying nothing ain't a solution. It's just a fizz.'

'A what?'

Denny shrugged. 'A fizz, you know.'

'What are you saying, *fizz*? F-I-Z-Z?'

'You ever drink a shot? Vodka, tequila, anything neat?'

I grimaced. 'Why would anyone want to?'

'You'd be surprised. Soft people, like you, wash it down with fizzy drink to make the burn easier to handle.'

'So that's what fizz is? A fancy bartender word for coping mechanism?'

Denny shook his head. 'Coping mechanisms work. Fizz feels good, but you still get drunk.'

I nodded, impressed. 'Did you make that up?'

'My uncle did. My whole family loved to fizz, especially Mum.'

'Literally or metaphorically?'

'Mum never drank. She had a bad home growing up. Lots of hate, abuse. She didn't know who my father was, so she raised me herself. I don't think she ever grew up. Anytime there was a problem, she pretended it didn't exist. Cockroach in the tub? No more baths. Hated them anyway. Then our roof would leak. Great metronome. Helped me sleep. But when she couldn't ignore them anymore, we packed our things and moved to a different part of Cardiff. I liked the variety, new friends, new neighbourhoods.'

I squinted. 'Do you hear how silly you sound right now?'

'Window.'

I snorted and looked back. 'How did she ignore you being homosexual?'

'Predictably.'

'How so?'

Denny stopped scribbling. Sighed. Put down his pencil. 'Bear in mind, I didn't know it was a "bad thing" until after I told her. I was only ten.'

My blood went cold. 'Denny. What did she do?'

Denny flicked through a box of coloured pencils. 'Where is the—? Ah, here it is!' He picked up a cool blue pencil. 'You have great eyes.'

'Denny.'

'I heard you,' Denny mumbled. 'She hit my head with a brick, and I woke up a few hours later on a railroad track. Because a train was coming.'

I gasped. 'Oh, Denny—!'

'Please stop moving. I don't want to mess this up.'

'Why are you so calm about it?!'

'About what?'

'YOUR MOTHER TRIED TO KILL YOU!'

Denny sighed. 'Please. Don't make me ask again.'

I frowned apologetically and resumed my pose.

Denny smiled. 'Thank you.' He returned to the sketch. 'That's how she fizzed. She was a horrible mother, of course, but it made sense. She couldn't handle me being homosexual, so she tried to make me go away.'

I sighed. 'At least you only lost your leg.'

'A decent consolation.'

'You told me what happened with the Nurse, but what happened to your mother?'

'Never saw her again. After I was discharged from the hospital, I moved in with my Uncle. He owned a fisherman's bar by the docks. Lots of crusty fellows went there, but he was the saltiest of them all. His father abused him too, apparently. Touching, or... something in that realm.'

'Jesus Ch—'

'I liked being at the bar. Have you ever been the only sober man in a pub of drunks? It's exciting, like an opera. There's music in their movements, their camaraderie, their sad stories.'

'Speaking of sad stories...'

'My Uncle pushed me to help out when I got older, but only so he could get drunk while I did all the work. I didn't care. I wanted the independence, to feel useful, and he wasn't in his right mind anyway.'

'Of course he wasn't.'

'He always wanted to be a sailor, but he never had money for a boat. Booze helped him forget how miserable he was, but it didn't change anything. He tried to hang himself when I was nineteen, but I saved him in time. Two days later, he waited till I was asleep and shot himself in the head.' Denny blew shavings off the paper.

I blinked. 'You almost done?'

'The story or the sketch?'

I chuckled bitterly. 'You're so bloody happy all the time! Who knew your life was so depressing?'

'Do you want the short version of the rest?'

'What didn't make the cut, I wonder?'

Denny chuckled. 'My Uncle left me a lot of money, but not the bar. Nope. Gave it to my stupid cousin instead. He never wanted it, of course, so he moved me out and let it default. That was his fizz. Running away.'

'Where did you go?'

'We stayed with his bohemian mates in Liverpool. They had this adorable terrier named Sunshine. I loved that dog.'

'Oh, come on!' I exclaimed. 'A dog named Sunshine?! What did he do, run away?'

'No.' Denny paused, carefully sketching a detail. 'The flat burnt down.'

I gaped. 'Sunshine died in a fire?!'

'No!' Denny said with a smirk. 'The *bohemians* died in the fire! Sunshine was fine. Popped his little head out of the ashes like they were clouds.'

I raised a cautious hand. 'So, you're telling me... Sunshine *didn't* die?'

Denny burst out laughing. 'Of course he did!' he wheezed. 'The stupid thing ran into the street and got squashed by a carriage!'

I cackled. 'You're making this up!'

'No, believe me.' Denny took a deep breath. 'I wish I was.'

I took deep breaths to calm myself down.

Denny stared off into space with a strange frown. 'My cousin ran off after that,' he whispered. 'He said he was getting us tickets. But I never saw him again.' He held that vacant gaze for a few moments and resumed sketching in silence.

I double-taked with just my eyes. 'That's it? You ran out of family members?'

'You said you wanted the short version.'

I smirked. 'If you told me a witch cursed you when you were a baby, I'd have less questions.'

Denny smirked. 'I was working in a pub in Liverpool when I met Charlie. I made him one of my mean martinis, and he was so impressed he offered me the job. I was the first one aboard.'

I bobbed my head. 'Fizz, huh?'

'Great word, right?'

I hesitated. 'You... do see the irony in all this?'

Denny looked at me, matter of fact. 'I force a bright side into everything to fizz what my family did to me.'

I closed my lips.

Denny snorted. 'I do have some self-awareness, you know.'

'I thought fizz was supposed to be bad.'

'It's not bad!' Denny cried with unusual seriousness. 'It's human. Do you know how long I hated them for what they did to me? Years. But if I didn't lose that leg, I wouldn't have met the Nurse. And if my uncle didn't kill himself, I wouldn't be living with my cousin. And if my cousin didn't leave me at that train station, I wouldn't have been in Liverpool to make Charlie's martini and get this job. The world is full of people, not monsters. They fizz because it feels good, not to hurt anyone. No one does horrible things unless they have a damn good reason, so why is it strange for me to be happy all the time? Why should I give up because of what they did to me?' Denny signed his sketch with a flourish and handed it to me. 'Life's too short to waste on hating life.'

I gasped. The sketch was stunning. Perfectly detailed, like I was looking in a mirror. Denny only used colour for my blue eyes, and he shaded it in a way that made my entire expression sensitive. He captured my soul.

'That's unbelievable, Denny!'

'Fair trade,' Denny said with a smile. 'You get your story. I get my best work.'

I handed the sketch back. Denny added it to his collection.

4. The Revenge of Andrew Baxter, American Runaway

At quarter eight, I was transcribing Denny's story into the addendum when I heard a knock on my door. Before I could speak, Andy bounced in. 'Hey there. I know I've been here for three months, but I don't think we've been officially introduced.' He grabbed my hand and shook it. 'I'm Andy.'

I nodded, overwhelmed by the intrusion. 'You're quite popular.'

'Not as popular as you, I'm sure!' Andy sighed dramatically. 'I love Irish boys. So attractive, and much better accents than the English, I say.'

I forced a smile.

Andy awkwardly bobbed his head.

I cleared my throat. 'What was it that you want—?'

'You're writing a book, right?' Andy blurted. 'About your life, I mean. What it's like to be homosexual.'

I hesitated. 'You're quite—'

'Loud? Fast? *Handsome*?'

'Personal.'

Andy stared blankly. Burst out laughing. 'You're really funny!'

I furrowed my brow.

'Anyway,' Andy continued, 'François told me you interviewed him this morning. That's fantastic!'

I blinked. 'You're friends with François?'

'Not really. We just fuck a lot.'

I nodded broadly. *Americans love that word.* 'Is that so?'

'He loves dominating, I love taking it, and... Oh, have you been in his room?! You really should! He's got all this equipment. Whips and paddles and this thing called Hercules and rope to tie me up with and—'

I coughed. 'Heavens.'

Andy frowned. 'You dislike me, don't you?'

'Why would I dislike you, Andy?'

'You didn't ask for my story.'

I gaped. 'Oh, I didn't... think you—'

'You asked François. And Mary. And Louise. And Denny. Why didn't you ask me?'

I shrugged. 'I don't know you very well.'

Andy groaned. 'Isn't that the whole point?! To get to know me?!'

Before I could say anything, Andy plopped onto my bed. *Didn't even ask me if he could. He's bloody adorable, but he didn't even ask.*

I sighed. 'One more won't hurt, I suppose.' I grabbed a piece of paper and opened a new bottle of ink.

Andy's eyes wandered around my room. He pointed at my cigar box. 'Do you smoke?'

'No.'

Andy grinned devilishly. 'You got money in there, don't you?'

'What's it to you?'

Andy laughed heartily. 'You're so funny!'

I pursed my lips. 'Apparently.'

Andy spotted the fake telegram above my bed. 'Oliver Haw—? Oh! I didn't know Oliver was your boyfriend.'

'He's not.'

Andy snorted. 'You love him, though. I can tell. Does he know you keep that above your bed?'

I closed my eyes.

Andy grabbed the telegram. 'What's in it anyway?'

I snatched it out of his hands. 'Why do you Yanks keep sticking your noses where they don't belong?'

Andy smirked. 'Why do you Anglos waste so much time dodging questions?' He raised his eyebrows in a flirtatious challenge.

I squinted. 'You're quite loud, you know.'

'Everyone's loud back home. It's the only way we can hear each other.'

I reluctantly put my pen to the paper. 'Where's home?'

'Chicago.'

I jotted that down. 'And your family?'

'Rich. New money, you know, the annoying kind.'

I stopped writing and stared at Andy. 'You're rich?'

Andy snorted. 'Yeah. I'm a Baxter.'

I blinked, confused. 'That's your name? Andy Baxter?'

Andy gasped sharply. 'You've never heard of the Chicago Baxters?!'

I hesitated and shook my head.

Andy stomped his feet in a rapid gallop. 'I LOVE THIS PLACE! Nobody knows anything out here!'

I pursed my lips. 'Thanks.'

Andy chuckled. 'No, no, I'm sorry. My Daddy is Darryl Baxter. Big name in coal. He's got the second-biggest refinery in America,

factories in Philly, New York, Richmond, Detroit, Atlanta. An empire of soot. You have no idea how hard it is to escape that. Everyone's heard of me. They love me. They hate me. They assume they know my life because of what they read in the paper, but I can't do anything about it because they're too damn stubborn. They actually get insulted when I tell them I want to be treated like a normal person!' Andy sighed. 'I don't have to worry about that out here. I can finally be me.'

I half-smiled. 'I see the appeal.'

'Because you're Irish? Or because you're a famous whore?'

'More than that.' I pointed to my window. 'What do you see?'

Andy looked out at Montgomery Street. 'I dunno. Street lamps. Lots of stars. Why? What do you see?'

'Memories,' I whispered. 'Mistakes I made, who I used to be. Every shop, every sign, every intersection haunting me like spirits.' I frowned. 'This place is tarnished for me, Andy. I can only stretch my legs so far.'

Andy craned his head, straining to see what I did.

'I'd love to go to America,' I murmured. 'Miles away from every person I ever met. A whole world of fresh faces and no questions. The ultimate clean slate.'

'You're crazy!' Andy cried. 'A thousand years of culture here and you wanna go to a place barely over a hundred.'

'What about you? Why did you leave?'

'Same reason you're writing that book. I was powerless.'

I grabbed my pen. 'Was your father strict or abusive?'

Andy snorted. 'Are you kidding? Daddy loved me! He gave me

everything. Vacations. Christmas presents. Boats. Nice suits. My own horse and carriage, driver included. Servants everywhere I went, waiting on me hand and foot. But if I wanted to do things myself, without the servants, he was okay with that too. I could do anything I wanted.'

I chuckled. 'Doesn't sound very powerless.'

'But it was! He never said it, but the only thing he wanted was my loyalty. An obedient heir to the Baxter empire.'

'And you didn't want that?'

'No, I did, but...' Andy smirked. 'I love men. When I told my parents they looked at each other, shrugged, and never mentioned it again. They didn't treat me any different, but I knew. If they acknowledged what I was, I'd become a liability. No grandchildren. Open to blackmail. An empire ruined in scandal. So they played it safe, like it was a business decision.

'A year goes by, right, and I'm getting really sick of their denial. I wasn't a child anymore. I wanted the respect Daddy had. So I brought it up again at dinner. Nothing. So when school started up again, I decided to raise the stakes. I fucked my history teacher. Daddy didn't say anything at first. Then the next day he tells me, "Something's come up, Andrew. We're home-schooling you now."'

'Oh no,' I mumbled. 'The bastard.'

Andy smiled devilishly. 'Oh, I got back at him! I waited until his business partner came by the house. Seduced him. Led him into my father's office. Five minutes later, Daddy walks in and sees his best friend fucking me on his desk!' Andy chuckled. 'Oh, you should have seen him! He was humiliated. Face all red. Screaming at me. And he

finally admits what I am. But he hates losing, so he threw me out of the house. But I didn't care. I went to New York. I was thrilled. I had so much fun. I was fucking everyone. I was finally free. But Daddy sent spies after me to gather evidence so one day he could blackmail me back into the company. So I stowed-away onto a boat headed for Europe, the only market he never conquered.' Andy grinned. 'I know he's sitting in his study right now. Smoking his pipe. Swirling his snifter. Screaming to the heavens, "Damn you Andrew Baxter, the only man who ever beat me!"' Andy cackled triumphantly.

I put down my pen, rubbing my eyes. 'I think I have enough.'

Andy eyed me up and down. 'You're very handsome.'

'Thank you.'

'Wanna fuck?'

I chuckled. 'I'm flattered, Andy, but no. Thank you.'

Andy licked his lips. 'Too bad. Oliver's a lucky man.'

'I told you, we're not together.'

'Why not? You wanna be.'

I rubbed my temple. 'I... It's complicated.'

'Why? What's his story?'

'What do you mean?'

'What do you think? Where's he from? How did he get here?'

I shrugged. 'I dunno.'

Andy wrinkled his upper lip. 'How do you not know?'

'I never knew.'

Andy scoffed. 'Well, now's your chance! You're writing a damn novel!'

'It's not that simple.'

'Why not?'

I struggled to speak. 'Even if he *wanted* to tell me... He's always in his office!'

Andy shook his head. 'I don't understand you people. You control half the world, but you're too soft to tell anyone what you're really thinking. How are WE the weird ones?!'

'I can't just knock on the door and ask about his life.'

'Why not? It's our night off. Ask if he wants some coffee or dessert. Everyone needs a break.' Fast as he came, Andy breezed out of my room.

The silence of my bedroom felt like a void.

I huffed. *Perhaps Oliver feels the same.*

Oliver's office door was ajar. I knocked softly and pushed in.

Oliver looked up from his desk and smiled. 'Hey. Everything okay?'

I took a deep breath. 'Do you wanna get some food?'

Oliver thought for a moment. He looked down at maths in his ledger.

5. Dreaming of a Better World

'Two Délice de Mousse, please,' I told the Waiter.

Oliver raised his eyebrows. 'What is that?'

'Mousse Delight. The best dessert ever made.'

Oliver looked around Dubeau Frères. Every booth was empty. 'We had this one last time.'

'I think so.'

'How does this place stay in business?'

I snorted. 'Been wondering that for years. Sometimes, I don't even think this place is real.' I looked out the windows with a perplexed frown. 'This place is bloody strange at night.'

Oliver chuckled. 'I know. You can't see anything. It's like the rest of the world doesn't exist.'

'It's comforting, though, isn't it? Being the last ones left?'

Oliver's smile faded. He looked down at his tea. 'I remember this blend. Good stuff.'

I forced a smile. 'That it is.'

Oliver pointed at my cup. 'What's that, Darjeeling?'

'Always.'

'Aren't you tired of it?'

I shook my head. 'Had it the first time I came here.'

'There's hundreds of other blends. You might like one better.'

'When I like something, I don't replace it unless I have to.'

Oliver and I looked at each other in awkward silence. The Waiter arrived just in time and placed two Délice de Mousse on the table. I thanked the Waiter, and he left with a polite nod.

Oliver stared at his Délice de Mousse like it was a venomous creature. 'How am I supposed to eat that?'

'With a spoon.'

Oliver chuckled nervously. He scooped a little off the top and tasted it. 'Mmm! You weren't kidding! That's the best thing I ever tasted!'

'Thank God. I thought I was the only one.'

Oliver ate another scoop. 'Why is this place always empty?!'

I fiddled with my spoon, my Délice de Mousse unpenetrated. 'Life isn't fair.'

Oliver hacked away at his, each pass a bigger scoop.

I watched him eat with a small smile. 'Did Charlie tell you about my novel?'

Oliver hummed, mouth full of ice cream. 'It's very brave of you. I couldn't be prouder.'

My heart warmed. 'Thank you, Oliver.' I cleared my throat. 'I'm meeting him on the fifth to talk about it.'

'Is he going to publish it?'

'If he likes it. I hope he does.'

'I do too.' Oliver pointed at my bowl. 'You haven't touched your Mousse Delight.'

I put my spoon down, sighing nervously. 'I spent the day interviewing everyone.'

'François told me.' Oliver wiped his mouth with a napkin. 'But I thought you finished the book weeks ago.'

'I did. The interviews are for the addendum.'

'What's an addendum?'

I rubbed the back of my head, grasping at words. 'Do you know what an appendix is?'

Oliver shook his head.

I sighed. 'Well, when a writer finishes a book, sometimes there's a bit more he wants to say.'

'Like what?'

'A lot of things. Some add a timeline so people can keep track of the chronology. Others want to say why they wrote the book. The

story behind the story.'

'Is that what you're doing?'

I bobbed my head. 'There's a little bit of that. But after I finished my story, I realised I wanted everyone else's.'

'Hence the interviews.'

'Yeah. I was thinking small origin narratives, self-contained, one after another. Like Chaucer, *Canterbury Tales*.'

'But why is it important?'

I chuckled. 'It's not, it's optional, but...' I paused. 'It supports my theme.'

Oliver swallowed, strangely nervous. 'What is your theme?'

'Everything you told me in this booth four years ago.'

Oliver stared at me for a long time. 'I don't want to talk about that.'

'We should.'

Oliver put his spoon down. 'You should've told me this was what you wanted.'

'What makes you think—?'

'I'm not stupid.'

I sighed. 'I didn't want you to say no.'

'My life is my business.'

'Please.'

'Why does it matter?' Oliver whined.

I took Oliver's hand and looked deep into his eyes. 'I love you.'

Oliver whipped his hand away. 'Look, I'm sorry for how I treated you before. All those horrible things I said.'

'Good, I'm glad—'

'Good, because I don't owe you anything, least of all my life story.'

'I'm not forcing. I'm just asking.'

Oliver stared at me, his green eyes getting puffy.

I nodded softly. 'I won't put it in the book if you don't want me to. But you'll feel better if you tell me.'

Oliver wetted his lips, softening by the second. 'I'm not so sure.'

I glanced out the window at the black void enveloping the tea-room. 'I told François something this morning. "Knowledge builds progress and silence stops it." That's why you started the brothel in the first place, right? Once they know we're not afraid, they'd change for us.'

Oliver nodded.

I shrugged. 'I didn't believe that at first, but I do now. Thanks to you.'

Oliver smiled weakly.

'But it has another meaning,' I whispered. 'The book was a way for me to stop being silent to myself. I put everything that happened in there, warts and all, and I'm publishing it for the masses. I never could've done that without you.'

Oliver scratched his cheek. 'I'm not ashamed of myself.'

'I just think you're lost. You worked so hard to make your dream real, you haven't had a chance to enjoy it. You gave me the happiness I have today. So I'm returning the favour.'

Oliver took a deep breath. 'Fine. What do you want to know?'

I finally scooped into my Délice de Mousse. 'Where were you born?'

'London.'

I swallowed my scoop and moaned. Oliver cackled.

I attacked my Délice de Mousse, shovelling ice cream into my mouth. 'Wha wazz your fammery like?'

'Stop!' Oliver covered my mouth with his hand. 'I'll talk, just eat.'

I nodded and swallowed, my next spoonful already loaded.

Oliver softened. 'My parents died in a tenement fire when I was six. I didn't have anyone else, so they put me in the orphanage. I don't know what was wrong with them. They hated children, I guess. Spinsters. None of them under sixty. I couldn't do anything right, they had so many rules. No talking during prayer. No playing during chores. I didn't understand what I was doing wrong, being six years old and all, but they were ruthless. They scolded me in front of the others, and when they got tired of the fuss, they just hit me. That was how it was for a while. Everything was an accident in the beginning, but the more they punished me, the more I wanted to disobey.'

Oliver stopped himself and finished his Délice de Mousse. I watched him cautiously, expecting a deluge of emotion, but he simply gazed out the window.

'Did you ever read *Oliver Twist*?' Oliver asked randomly.

I finished my Délice de Mousse and wiped my mouth. 'Of course.'

'The orphanage had plenty of patrons. Most of the donations were useless. Clothes too big, food half-eaten. But I loved the books, anything that made me forget where I was. *Arabian Nights*. *Count of Monte Cristo*. Then one day, I found a beat-up copy of *Oliver Twist*.' Oliver snorted. 'A book about an orphan, I never heard of such a thing. He was all alone, yet he could look the overseer in the

eye and ask for more food. That changed my life.' He shook his head. 'I can't explain it.'

'You found someone just like you,' I whispered.

Oliver's eyes softened with understanding. 'Liberating, isn't it?'

I sighed. 'Absolutely.'

Oliver crunched into a biscuit. 'I wanted to be just like him, so I started calling myself Oliver.'

'What do you mean?'

'I changed my name to Oliver.'

My jaw dropped. 'Oliver's not your real name?!'

'I don't have a real name. That's my name. Oliver's my name.'

I pushed my tongue against my cheek. 'I don't—'

'The name on my file, the one I was born with, they didn't call me that out of kindness. They used it to control me, to pin demerits to. I became Oliver Hawkett to take that power away from them.'

I nodded, impressed. 'Where did you get Hawkett?'

Oliver smiled bashfully. 'I like hawks.'

I smiled. 'Of course you do.'

Oliver finished his tea. 'The other orphans noticed what I did, and a few sought me out. They changed their names too, followed me around. They were my friends. More than friends, actually. It was more like a brotherhood. I always wanted a family.' He grinned. 'They called me Oliver.'

'You were their hero.'

Oliver grunted. 'His name didn't make me brave. I wanted to run away, but I didn't have the nerve. No, someone else was the hero. An older boy, sixteen. He could've left on his own when he turned

eighteen, but he helped us escape. He planned everything. And it worked! He led us to freedom.' He shook his head. 'He's the greatest man I ever met, even now.'

I tilted my head. 'Who was he?'

Oliver smiled. 'Charlie Smith, of course.'

I gaped. 'CHARLIE?!'

'Can you believe it?'

I shook my head. 'Charlie couldn't have been an orphan. His mum only died eight years ago.'

'He's a bastard. She gave him up.'

'I can't believe that. He seems so well off.'

'He wants people to think like that. In reality, Charlie built his empire from nothing. Made his own name. He might even be the richest homosexual in Britain, outside the aristocracy at least.'

I smirked. 'Wow!'

Oliver nodded. 'We lived on the street after that, all of us, pick-pocketing like Oliver did. It was exciting. We nabbed food, ran from police, shared our spoils. We got more ambitious as we grew. Stealing buggies, pinching silver—'

'Breaking into flats?'

Oliver smirked. 'We ruled the world, thanks to Charlie. And it was nice. While it lasted.' He let out a long, mournful sigh. 'Years went by. The little birdies left the nest, moving on to better things, until it was just me and Charlie.'

'Do you still keep in touch with the others?'

Oliver shrugged dismissively. 'Christmas cards.' He stared off with a gloomy expression. 'Charlie knew I was a homosexual before I

did. He told me the night I turned eighteen. We were on a roof somewhere, drinking beer. It was raining. We hid under a tarp, the drops loud as bullets, but we were safe. Charlie looked out at the city, pensive, solemn, and I asked him what was wrong.

'"I want to tell you something," Charlie said. "Something I never told anyone."

'"What is it?" I asked him.

'"I like men. And I think you do too."'

'Wow,' I whispered.

'He's very perceptive,' Oliver said proudly. 'Like an older brother. I saw a different side of him that night. Sensitive, sad, and yet... optimistic. He told me a lot of things. What they did to people like us. I was scared, but Charlie didn't want me to be. He needed my help.'

'To change the world.'

Oliver bobbed his hair. 'He was tired of being punished for things he had no control over. That's how simple it was for him. Just another jail break.' He suddenly grinned. 'Oh, you should've seen him! The way he talked, the glow in his eyes. He wanted to scream to the world, "We're here, get used to it!"'

I smirked.

Oliver's golden smile melted away. 'I never saw such passion,' he whispered.

'He still has it, doesn't he?'

Oliver shook his head. 'Not the way he used to.'

I frowned. The way he said that made me really sad.

'I was too afraid to say yes,' Oliver murmured. 'He knew it too,

but he said he would wait for me. That's when he gave me my birthday present: *Les Misérables* by Victor Hugo.'

'Great book.'

'It was the copy he read in the orphanage. It inspired everything. Enjolras fought for the world he wanted, why not him?'

'That makes you Marius.'

Oliver rolled his eyes. 'I sure wanted to be. I read it cover to cover, but I knew what I was going to say before I started. I had complete faith in Charlie. We made a plan, him and me. No more stealing, no more hiding from bobbies. We had to think bigger. He started his publishing house, made it a success, and after a year he decided to track down his mother. I was with him the whole way.' He let out a cold sigh. 'A few months after he found her, she got sick. And I was by his side when it happened.' He shook his head. 'I'll never know what that's like.'

I took Oliver's hand. 'I take it she missed him?'

Oliver smiled weakly. 'Every second of every day.'

I laughed, tears forming in my eyes. 'Moms are the best, aren't they?'

Oliver's lip quivered. 'Yeah.'

I sensed the Waiter approaching and whipped my hand away. He collected our dishes and gave me the bill.

'She left him everything,' Oliver continued. 'She came from an old family with lots of money. Charlie was eligible to inherit the lot. But her parents were the executors, and they said no. Every letter he sent, they refused. We stood on their doorstep and they shooed us

away. Two years later, they finally gave it to him. The money. The house. Everything.'

'How?'

'He never gave up. I still can't believe he did it. A bastard with an inheritance?' Oliver chuckled. 'When he asked me to run the brothel myself, I didn't hesitate that time. It was gonna work. Charlie said so.'

The Waiter took our bill and walked away.

Oliver deflated before my eyes. 'After we found the others—Mary, Louise, Denny, François—I started feeling small. I had been following Charlie since I was eleven years old. I couldn't do anything on my own. I spent my whole life copying people, better people. I had no idea who I was.'

I swallowed. 'Then you met me.'

Oliver suddenly beamed. 'The best night of my life. You were so amazing. Beautiful. Confident. The aristocracy in the palm of your hand.' Oliver smiled. 'But you were still a child. All alone. Lost in a fog. Pretending to be someone you weren't, like I was. But you saw the real me. And you're the only one who has.'

I lowered my head in shame.

Oliver chuckled bitterly. 'You didn't even say goodbye.' He shook his head. 'The last thing you ever said to me was that we were all alone, and there was nothing we could do about it. And that hurt me. I started to lose hope.'

'I was wrong!' I cried. 'You knew I was.'

'But *you* didn't. That's what scared me.'

I closed my eyes.

Oliver scratched his nose with a soft frown. 'I tried to stay positive. You'll think about what I said. You'll come back. You'll admit you're wrong. But you didn't. You left me behind.'

I covered my face and sobbed.

Oliver grabbed my hands. 'No, don't,' he whispered. 'Don't cry. Please, don't cry.'

I took deep breaths and wiped my eyes. 'I'm sorry.'

Oliver's face hardened. 'I'm the one who should apologise.'

'Don't be silly.'

Oliver shook his head, eyes swelling with shame. 'I don't know what I'm doing!' he whined. 'I'm not a leader!'

I was taken aback. I never saw Oliver cry before. 'Of course you are.'

'You know I'm not!' Oliver snickered through his tears. 'You know what I do in my office all day, hm? Nothing. Lots of paperwork, lots of breaks. Some days I'm just numb. Or I panic. I can spend an entire afternoon crying, but I can't tell anyone. Not even Charlie. Leaders are supposed to be impersonal and strong, without any doubts. But I'm not like that.'

'I'm sure they all think that way. Even Charlie.'

Oliver wiped his eyes and looked out the window. 'I wanna ask you something.'

'Anything.'

'But you need to tell me the truth.'

I hesitated. 'What is it?'

Oliver smiled weakly. 'Do you think it'll really happen? That one day, we'll be just like them?'

My heart pounded inside my chest. 'We won't be alive to see it.'

Oliver's smile faded.

I lowered my eyes.

Oliver rolled his lips together, too stunned to speak.

I shrugged.

Oliver puffed his cheeks absentmindedly. 'Thank you.'

'Anytime,' I whispered.

Oliver scratched the top of his head. 'The reason I... Ever since I last saw you here, when you passed on the offer, I've been having this reoccurring dream. And it's the most beautiful dream I ever had.'

I readjusted my posture. 'What is it?'

'You and I are in this wooden room, like a cabin. We're lying next to each other under a fur blanket, completely naked, and we hold each other. Shag all day. Just... stay together.'

The hairs on the back of my neck stood up.

Oliver smiled. 'I'm so happy every time, and when I wake up, all I wanna do is go back. It's what keeps me going. Every night I'll be back in that cabin, under the blanket with you.'

I rubbed my temple. 'I can't believe it!'

Oliver snorted. 'I know, isn't that the saddest—?'

'No, I—' I chuckled abruptly. 'I have those dreams too!'

Oliver stared, a bit freaked out.

'Not the cabin part!' I added. 'In mine we're in a white room, on a satin bed, and I can hear the ocean, but otherwise...' I shook my head. 'Exactly the same.'

Oliver's lips fluttered. 'How is that even possible?'

'Do think it means something? Like a sign?'

Oliver shook his head. 'I don't think God gives us signs.' He looked at me, expecting a quick reply.

I gazed at Oliver's beautiful green eyes. His auburn hair. The faint freckles on his cheeks. His strong jaw. I couldn't help but smile. In that moment, I realised just how perfect Oliver was.

'He gave me you.'

Oliver melted at my words. His dimples pushed up, dribbles of tears falling from his eyes. Warmth radiated from him. I felt it in my heart. It wasn't just a compliment. I spoke his thoughts.

Oliver felt the same way about me.

6. Two Children Have Left Dunderrow

'Oh God!' I moaned, 'Oh God, I'm so close!'

'Cum for me, baby,' Oliver muttered, thrusting into me.

A rush of ecstasy travelled up my body, slamming into my head as I ejaculated across my abdomen. Oliver grunted, jutting into me one last time, his body seizing with a loud exhale.

I pulled Oliver down and kissed him. He slid out of me, rolling onto his back as I lowered my legs. The two of us laid on my bed, staring up at the ceiling, savouring every breath.

Oliver touched the semen on my chest. 'What's that now? Two each?'

I took quick, deep breaths. 'Three for me. Sometimes it happens when I don't touch it.'

Oliver wrapped an arm around my shoulder. 'François probably heard us.' He paused. 'No, he would've said something by now.'

I burst out laughing. 'I can't believe this is actually happening!'

Oliver hugged me tight. 'Why didn't we do this before? I wasted so much time.'

'It's okay. You're here now.'

Oliver hummed sweetly and kissed my lips. He rested his head on my chest.

I grinned hard enough to hurt my cheeks. 'I'm so happy!' I whined. 'I can't believe it!'

'I love hearing you say that.'

I looked down at Oliver's head against my breast. Chuckled with disbelief.

'You were right, by the way,' Oliver murmured. 'Saying it out loud, I do feel better.'

'You carried it for so long.' I shook my head. 'I just can't believe you told me. I'm so honoured.'

Oliver kissed my lips and each of my eyelids. 'I love you,' he whispered. 'I've loved you for a long time, even when it didn't make sense anymore. You're the only person I would've told.'

I hugged him tightly. 'You'd tell me your birth name?'

'If I still remembered it, I would.'

'Thank you.'

Oliver kissed me one more time and returned his head to my breast.

I looked down at his beautiful face and took a deep breath. 'You know what I'm gonna do now?' I whispered.

'What?'

'I'm gonna tell you something I never told anyone. It's not even in the book.'

'You don't have to.'

'I want to. You've entrusted me with your deepest secrets. You should have mine.'

Oliver kissed my chest and sucked one of my nipples. 'I'd be honoured.'

I smiled. 'When I was growing up in Dunderrow, I had four mates I did everything with. Seamus Costigan, Kerrigan Mullaly, Bayrd Walsh, and Gregory O'Brien.'

'Seamus sounds familiar.'

'He got me the Footman job in Mulhussey, the one who left to get married. He was my best mate since I was a lad. I met Kerry on our school's cricket team, and I knew Bayrd through him.'

'What about Gregory?'

'I've always known Greg. The O'Briens had the farm next door for three hundred years.'

'Bloody hell!'

'I'm telling you! In Dunderrow, a good neighbour's worth more than ten years of harvests. We did everything together. Susan O'Brien was the head of Mother's bridge club, and the two of them ran the church bazaar. Daniel O'Brien was one of Father's drinking buddies, and they helped on each other's farms during the busier seasons. We went to mass together, birthday parties, Christmases. They had our back and we had theirs. Daniel's father and my Grandfather were drinking buddies, their wives were friends, and so on. That's how it always was.'

'A dynasty of companions. Must've been nice.'

'I dunno. I was forced to be friends with Greg. We had nothing in common, but we did everything together. Seamus, Kerry, and Bayrd were his mates just as much as mine. I actually think they liked him more.'

'Why?'

'Greg was better at cricket and followed the teams. Kerry liked that. And Bayrd had the same sense of humour.'

'At least you had Seamus.'

'Yeah, but he was a lady's man like Greg. And I don't mean they had girlfriends in school, I mean Don Juan, Casanova types. Both of em.'

'They couldn't have been that bad.'

'They had lists of girls when they were sixteen. When we went out to the pubs, they'd go on and on about what they did and where.'

Oliver chuckled. 'That's ridiculous! Who shags at that age?'

'Greg had his first kiss at ten and lost his virginity at thirteen.'

Oliver grimaced. 'Is he attractive?'

I laughed. 'No! But that's the power of attitude, I suppose. He had plenty of that.'

'You sound jealous,' Oliver teased.

I frowned. 'No, I'm really not.'

'Oh no?'

'I hated being compared to him. He kept getting all those girls, and I kept telling myself I'd understand one day. Some boys take longer than others, right? So I waited. Before I knew it, I was twenty-one and never lusted for a woman.'

'You didn't know until you were twenty-one?'

'No, I knew.' I paused. 'I had been in love with Seamus since I was sixteen.'

'Aww!' Oliver cooed. 'That's so sweet!'

I rolled my eyes. 'Wasn't at the time.'

'Tell me about him.'

I smiled. 'He had the best body, so toned, and smooth. And I loved the way his hair fell across his forehead when we roughed around. I didn't know what it was, of course. I just thought I was smitten by his charisma. Then I thought I was jealous of his clothes. And his hair. And his muscles. But as the years went by, Greg's stories started making sense.'

'How did you feel about it?'

'Everyone said it was wrong. Father Dominic called it a cruel temptation of the Devil, the same as lusting for animals or children.'

'Father Dominic shouldn't be thinking about sex during mass.'

'The worst part, he said, was that it would feel normal. That's how Satan worked, apparently. No signing contracts. No mirages. No chances to say no. Not according to Father Dominic.' I frowned. 'Satan's so clever. Even if you didn't want it, it's still your fault.'

'That's rubbish.'

I shrugged. 'It's what we were told. I got scared when I found out what was happening to me, but I couldn't tell anyone.'

'Not even your parents?'

'If I did, the whole town would find out. It's so slow out there. Gossip's as viral as a blight. Any strange business would be the sole topic of conversation for a month.'

'So you didn't tell anyone?'

'I thought it would go away on its own, but it only got worse. After I graduated, I worked on our farm while my brother finished school. I pretended to have crushes on women to look normal for my friends. But every night I touched myself thinking about Seamus, followed by seven Hail Marys just in case.'

Oliver sat up suddenly. 'This is the Incident, isn't it?'

I nodded. 'I never said it out loud before.'

Oliver smiled. 'Thank you.'

I kissed him for strength and took a deep breath.

'It happened on 6 April 1881,' I murmured. 'But the trouble really began New Year's Day. The five of us were out late, drunk, running around town, jumping on benches, walloping, acting rambunctious. We woke a lot of people up, and the whole town was talking about it the next day. My parents forgave me, but they said I couldn't drink with my mates again.'

'That makes sense.'

'No it doesn't. We were just having fun. I didn't want to stop, and neither did Greg, so we made a plan. I'd stay over every Friday night on O'Brien Farm, and when his parents went to sleep, we'd drink beer in Greg's room.'

'Your parents let you sleep over every Friday?'

'It's just next door. And Mother talked to Susan about it. They felt it was normal for us to want independence.'

'And why Greg's place?'

'He was an only child. More privacy. And I liked eating dinner with the O'Briens. Susan wasn't clever, but she made good food, and

Daniel was always very polite. He kept asking about my work on the farm, how Seamus and the others were doing—'

'He knew them too?'

'He drank with their fathers too. I always liked Daniel growing up. He smiled when he talked to me. Laughed at everything I said.'

'Do you think he knew about the beer?'

'If he did, he never said anything. I respected that, you know? Last thing we needed was another adult spoiling our fun.'

Oliver nodded.

'Normally, I'd go home on Saturday morning,' I continued. 'But every once in a while, I stayed the whole weekend, like I did after my birthday. Greg was with Susan at the market, Daniel was in the field, and I was in the house by myself. I slept in, read a book, took a bath, enjoyed the peace and quiet away from my brother, who had just turned seventeen and annoyed the hell out of me. It was unseasonably hot for March, so I didn't bother putting a shirt on after the bath. I just sat in a chair and continued my book.'

'But what if Susan walked in?'

'She shopped slow. Wouldn't be back for hours.'

'Okay, what happened then?'

I stared at the ceiling, my mind wandering back. 'I didn't hear Daniel until he walked past my room. His shirt was off, and he was a big guy. Strong arms, thick beard, hair on every inch of his body. Completely covered in sweat. I could smell him across the room.

'"All by yourself?" he asked me, smiling as always.

'And I said something like, "Finally get a chance to read in peace." I noticed Daniel was staring at my chest, a bit too long.

'"I'm starved," he said. "Want a sandwich?"

'And I said, "If you're making one, sure." His eyes kept looking at me, up and down. I got flustered and asked, "Should I put on a shirt, Mr O'Brien?"

'He snapped from his trance. "Please, call me Danny." Then he walked off. I heard Danny rummaging through the kitchen cupboards. And I had this strange feeling, like I was nervous but also really flattered. I walked to the kitchen. No real reason. I just wanted Danny to look at me again.'

Oliver put a hand to his mouth. 'Oh no...'

I nodded grimly. 'He made sandwiches for both of us. Opened a couple of beers. We sat on the porch, in the sun, and he kept looking at me. I felt all fuzzy inside, the same way I did for Seamus. Danny knew me my whole life, I grew up with his son, but the way he looked at me... It was like he was surprised.

'He said to me, "You must be working hard on the farm."

'And I said, "I try my best."

'"You look it. Must get a lot of attention from girls."

'"Not really. I'm not looking, at least."

'That made Danny laugh. "Gregory doesn't know how to stop. I'm worried I'll be short for the summer." He sipped his beer and looked at me.

'I played coy. "If you need help on your farm, you can ask me."

'"Really? You sure?"

'And I said, "Just ask. Really." I stared back at him, a bit too long.

'Danny smirked. "You want to help me dig out the old pine stump tomorrow?"

'And I said, "Sure." I heard Susan and Greg walk up the house, so I stood and said, "Thanks for the beer, Danny."

'He smiled and gave me a hug. His sweat stuck to my chest. His embrace was tight, like he was saying goodbye, even though I was staying the night. He squeezed. I squeezed back. As he let go, I felt something brush across my thigh. He had an erection. So did I. We both noticed. He hurried off to greet Susan, and I put my shirt back on.

'Danny had some errands that night, so we ate dinner without him. I was relieved. And disappointed.'

'Did you help him with the stump?' Oliver asked.

'Yeah. It was incredibly old and tough to dig out. Danny did most of the work. Every time I bent down to pick out the roots, I kept catching his eye. We didn't say much. I didn't know what was happening, didn't even think long enough to realise Danny was homosexual. I just liked the attention.

'When the job was done, I stood next to the hole where the stump used to be and waited. There wasn't anything more to do. I just kept waiting.

'Danny took off his gloves and looked at me, his eyes squinting in the sun. "You ready to go inside?"

'I didn't say anything. I just stood there.

'He laughed and walked over to me. "What are you doing?"

'I look into the hole and said, "I think we did a good job."

'He looked down. "I couldn't have done it without you."

'And we just stood there, a foot apart from each other, sweaty, covered with dirt. Just staring into that hole in the ground. Both of

us breathing fast. You couldn't tell if you stood far enough away.

'I turned to him and opened my arms. Danny gave me the biggest grin I ever saw, perhaps the first real smile he had in a long time. He hugged me tight, almost oppressive. A truly masculine embrace. I rested my head on his shoulder. He ran a callused hand down my back, all the way down, low as he could. I didn't protest. I had never been touched there before. I looked up, and...'

My lip trembled. My eyes never left the ceiling. 'He kissed me. Danny O'Brien, my neighbour's father... kissed me. No one around for miles.'

Oliver looked at my waist. 'You're hard.'

I sighed. 'I know.'

Oliver rubbed my chest. 'What happened after that?'

'Our relationship evolved. I wanted to visit Danny every chance I could. I told Father I was helping him on his farm. He was fine with that. Danny gave Greg permission to sleep at Seamus's.' I snorted. 'That got him out. Susan made lunch for me as a thank you. When she left for bridge club, Danny and I made love in their bed.

'He loved teaching me about sex. How to suck better, how to maintain stamina during penetration. He asked me what I wanted to know, what I wanted to try. It was fantastic! I never once felt inferior to him. We were truly equals. Being with Danny was the first time I ever felt normal. I was infatuated with him. He had so many hobbies, and he was so smart. I couldn't believe it, a homosexual with a personality. I loved every second I was with him. We tried so hard to make up for lost time.

'On 3 April, Susan took Greg to visit her mother in Killarney for

the week, and Danny and I decided to have a holiday of our own. My parents didn't know they were out of town. I told them I was working with Danny during the day and staying with Greg at night.'

'What did you do instead?'

I smiled warmly. 'Lived a fantasy life. We had rules. First, no clothing, which only applied to me of course.'

'Of course.'

'Second, Danny decided when to have sex. I could tease and beg, but Danny said when. Besides that, we did whatever we wanted. On the first day, I made him breakfast. We shagged in the living room. Slept during the afternoon. He woke me up with more sex. We drank beer in the evening and went to bed together. After more sex.'

Oliver chuckled. 'When did it get boring?'

'Day three. We tossed the rules and spent the whole day cuddling in bed.'

'No more sex?'

'We still did. But we mostly talked.' I sighed. 'Danny said he cared for me. That he never had someone like me before. He kept thanking me for saving him from a sad, lonely life. And that he really wanted to be with me. He told me, "If Susan walked through that door right now and saw us together, I'd take you away. We'll go and live the life we always dreamt of. Together."'

'That's very...' Oliver furrowed his brow. 'Bold.'

'It scared me. It was so desperate and final. A part of me thought Danny was joking, the way romantics do, but he wasn't. I didn't let it bother me, though. I was just happy to be there. In my own skin.'

I stayed silent for a long time, my eyes fixed on the ceiling.

'It happened the next day,' I whispered at long last. 'My brother was fooling around with his friends and twisted his ankle. Mother put some ice on it, and she started getting worried about him missing school. She wanted me to go pick up his homework. Father came in from the fields to look after him while Mother walked next door to get me.'

Oliver closed his eyes. 'Jesus.'

My muscles seized. My chin started trembling. 'Danny and I were... He was on top of me, and... She noticed Susan wasn't there, and she heard noises, and...'

I closed my eyes and cried. Oliver held me, petting my hair, shushing.

'My muh... My mother's eyes...' I sobbed. 'I-I can still hear her scream!'

Oliver kissed my head. 'It's okay, baby. I got you.'

I took deep breaths. 'She didn't run away. She just stood there. Staring at us.'

Oliver got out of bed, grabbed a cloth, moistened it, and handed it to me. I pressed it to my eyes.

Oliver sat back down and gently rubbed my back. 'What did Danny do?'

'He just lay there, frozen in bed. When I put my clothes on, I felt dirty.' I handed the cloth back to Oliver. 'Thank you.'

'No problem.'

'I didn't say anything to her. She didn't either. I guess we thought that was best, but... It wasn't. I didn't say goodbye to Danny. I never got my brother's homework. When we got home, she told my Father

to do it instead. Didn't say why. Not at first. None of us told my brother, but he knew something happened the day he twisted his ankle.'

Oliver kissed my cheek.

I swallowed. 'Three days later, when they got back, Greg invited me over. I asked Father if it was okay, but he said, "No," out of nowhere. He couldn't even look at me.

'I didn't want to disobey Father, but I wanted to see Danny, so I walked over to refuse Greg in person. I could hear Susan and Danny yelling from outside. I don't know why, but I knocked anyway. Susan answered. Her face was covered in tears. She didn't say anything. She just stared at my innocent, confused face. Not with anger or hate. Just pity. Before I could say anything, she slammed the door.

'The rumours spread faster than even I anticipated. I went to play cricket with my mates, but Greg wasn't there. Seamus and Bayrd didn't say anything to me the whole time. Kerry wasn't that subtle. As soon as he saw me, he ran away.

'Our parents were worse. Mother kept hearing my name in her knitting circle gossip. Apparently, the O'Briens stopped going to church, and Susan hadn't left the house in weeks. One of the ladies heard from her son, who heard from his friend, who heard from the O'Briens' farmhands that Danny had seduced me. Father told her to ignore it, but then his drinking buddies started asking him what happened between me and Danny. They kept giving him advice, how he should've raised me, what he should do with me. They recommended priests like they were plumbers.

'None of us talked to anyone. It was just gossip. We knew the

longer we avoided confirming anything, the faster the rumours would die. And I didn't want to lose Danny. I knew if I kept powering through, we'd be together again. He promised to protect me, and I believed him. I trusted him because of how he made me feel.' I let out a melancholic sigh. 'And he was my first. That was supposed to mean something.'

Oliver caressed my cheek, frowning with pity.

I shook my head. 'But even after everything that happened, no one expected the O'Briens to move away. No family had left Dunderrow since the Famine, and that was the only good reason. The narrative changed after that. Daniel O'Brien wasn't the deviant anymore, hiding behind his gullible, dim-witted wife. Suddenly, they were the victims, forced to flee their village to escape the aggressive, homewrecking sodomite next door.'

'Why? What happened?'

'I don't know. I didn't do anything. I was just the one still around.'

Oliver rested his head against my shoulder. 'Maybe Susan forced Danny to—'

'He knew what he was doing,' I hissed. 'He left me behind. I meant nothing to him. He lied to me. He lied to his wife. To his son. To his community. He made fools of all of us. Thanks to him, my own village, the only world I ever knew, the people who watched me grow my whole life... They didn't want me to be happy anymore.

'A few days after the O'Briens left, I heard my parents talking in their room with the door locked, and I started getting scared. "It's not possible," I kept saying. "They'll never do it." But sure enough,

when my brother left for school the next morning, they confronted me. Father tried to be practical at first. I was never to act on my impulses again, and if I did, they'd disown me. No money. No inheritance. I'd be banished forever. When I refused both options, Father started screaming.

'I pleaded with him. Cried my little heart out. Babbled my side of the case. That it felt right. That I hated Danny for leaving, for putting us through that. That I needed my parents to protect me. But Father said no. I even offered to leave in a year, just enough to make it look natural. But Father said no. I told him I wanted to come back, to have my inheritance, but he wouldn't listen. He said if I stayed another minute, he'd call the police.'

Oliver licked his cracked lips. 'What about your mother?'

'She didn't say anything. Just sat in the corner, staring at the floor. I begged for help, but she didn't listen. Then I stopped. I was tired. Tired of crying. Tired of trying to convince those people to let me stay. I agreed to leave and never return. I grabbed as much as I could and walked out.'

I shook my head. 'The last thing I ever said to them... I wanted to hurt them. I wanted them to feel the way I felt. I wanted it to haunt them. So I screamed the cruellest thing I could think of: "If they find me dead, it's your fault."'

Oliver caressed my face. 'I don't blame you.'

'It was wrong,' I whispered. 'I didn't get anything out of it. It just made me sick. I left Dunderrow a child, just like Danny.'

Oliver frowned.

I furrowed my brow slightly. 'It never made sense to me before.'

Oliver hugged me. 'Do you feel better?'

I blinked. 'I actually do.'

'Like the past doesn't have power anymore.'

I smirked. 'That's exactly what it feels like.' I looked at Oliver, his green eyes shining in the moonlight. I took a deep breath. 'I'll put it in the book. In the addendum, right after you.'

'Are you sure?'

I nodded. 'If you can do it, so can I.'

Oliver beamed. 'In that case...' He straddled on top of me. 'I'm gonna suck you this time.'

I chuckled. 'No one's ever done that before.'

'Good. I get to be your first.' Oliver winked.

My heart skipped a beat. I pulled Oliver down. Kissed all over his face. He giggled his lungs out. Pushed himself away. Scooted down my body. Went to town.

An hour later, Oliver slept in my arms. I looked down at him and smiled before falling asleep.

We dreamt of beauty together.

Epilogue: Why It All Matters

I had a special client on 3 November 1888 who reminded me what I was fighting for, a Tory running for political office next year. For obvious reasons, I won't reveal his identity.

I woke from my afternoon nap too late, finally coming downstairs ten minutes after we opened. No one was around, not even Denny or François. The house sounded completely empty.

I found Oliver in the Barroom, sipping a cocktail. 'There you are!' he teased.

I looked around. 'How long have I been asleep?'

'Everyone's in their room. We're a one-client house tonight. You-know-who paid for strict privacy.'

'I didn't think we had a price for that.'

'We don't. You've no idea how much he wants you.'

I grinned, strangely aroused.

Oliver's expression turned serious. 'Be careful, baby. You know what you're doing, but I met the man. He's different.'

'I've seen a lot, you know.'

'What he's paying will set us up a long time. We can't afford to lose him, so don't get him angry.'

I furrowed my brow. 'Why would I?'

BAM! BAM! BAM! BAM! Pounding on the front door, the stomps of a giant.

Oliver downed his drink. 'Good luck.' He kissed me and raced upstairs. I hurried back to the Great Hall, opened the door, and froze.

The Tory was easily the most physically disgusting man I've ever met in my life. He was fat, which was bad enough, but he had scars that made my skin crawl, all over his face and (I'd soon find out) his entire body, like he had been burnt years before. His face didn't help matters. He objectively looked like a pig.

'Evening,' the Tory oinked.

'You must be Mr—' I said his name as I removed his coat.

'Shut the door!' he hissed. I slammed the door, genuinely scared.

The Tory's eyes scanned the balcony.

'Anything wrong?' I asked politely.

The Tory studied the silence. 'No one else is here?'

'It's just us.'

The Tory spun around, grabbed me by the throat, and pinned me against the door. 'Do everything I say, boy,' he snarled. 'Don't question. Don't fight. Obey.'

I was terrified. I never get handled like that without permission. But I felt something else, something stronger that kept the fear at bay.

Lust.

'Yes, sir,' I growled suggestively.

The Tory rushed me upstairs. Forced me into my room. Slammed the door. Before I could turn on the lights, he ripped off my clothes, exposed my arse, and smacked it. No care for my body, just a primal urge to use me. Ravenously. Selfishly. Like a true politician.

The Tory took off his shoes, rolled off those smelly socks I'd grow to hate, and stuck his toe deep inside my

* * *

'That's nice,' Charlie murmured. He plopped the manuscript onto his desk. Rubbed his eyes.

Jack tenderly sat up. 'There's so much left. Is something wrong?'

'I don't want to read anymore.'

Jack chuckled nervously. 'But you didn't even get to the best part. Edgar made me do everything! And at the end, when he bent me over the—'

'Jack.'

'Yeah?'

'There's nothing wrong with it.' Charlie smiled. 'You know what you're doing. I trust you.'

'Oh,' Jack mumbled. 'You liked it?'

Charlie flipped through the pages casually. 'I do, actually.'

'You sound surprised.'

Charlie chuckled. 'I admit, I expected it to be more vulgar, but it's good. Quite good. Daring. Sensual. Tasteful. The sex is more real than gratuitous. And there's intelligence in the descriptions, philosophy even.'

Jack snorted. 'I'm no Plato.'

'Philosophy's more than the meaning to life. It's how you see the world. You want homosexuals to have a place in society, you believe we're being mistreated, and you want your book to inspire change. The story reflects that. It's a perfect manifesto for the cause.'

Jack nodded slowly. Bit his lip. 'It's not too much?'

'I think it's fine.'

'I was worried that... if I said too much, I'd be confessing to a crime.'

Charlie shook his head. 'Books aren't people, Jack. If you wrote in a novel that you murdered someone, no one's gonna think you're confessing. But if you go into heavy detail where you buried the body, and someone goes to that location and finds a dead body, that's a different story. But even then, the novel's just evidence. They still have to prove you did it.'

'So everything I said about the Collins Affair—?'

'You'll be fine. Your facts and fiction are indistinguishable, even to me.'

Jack blinked. 'Fiction?'

'The parts you made up.'

'I know what fiction is. I didn't make anything up.'

Charlie chuckled. 'You're having me on.'

'No. I'm not.'

Charlie's face softened. 'All that actually happened?'

'Of course it did. That's the whole point, to tell the truth. Why would I make anything up?'

Charlie hesitated. 'So this isn't a retelling of Homer's *Odyssey*?'

Jack laughed. 'What?! Where did that come from?'

'The allusions are so obvious, so I just assumed—'

'What allusions?'

Charlie stared blankly. 'Are you serious?'

'Charlie, what are you talking about?!'

Charlie frantically flipped through the manuscript. 'You have the same themes. Redemption. Homecoming. All the plot parallels: the brothel is Ithaca, Vic is the Cyclops, Barrington Place is the land of the Lotus-eaters, Davie is a Siren, Oliver is Penelope, your clients are the Suitors—'

Jack laughed. 'Hey, that's all you!'

Charlie jabbed a page with a finger. 'You even name *The Odyssey* in Chapter Eight!'

'Charlie!' Jack exclaimed. 'Everything. Actually. Happened.'

Charlie leaned back, stunned. 'Who was Lord Barrington?'

'The Earl of Havredom, Robert Harrington.'

Charlie raised a brow. 'Lord Barrington is Lord Harrington? That's the best you could do?'

Jack shrugged. 'It worked, didn't it?'

'It's lazy.' Charlie paused briefly. 'But I suppose it's okay.' He aimlessly flipped the pages. 'Did the others give you permission to use their real names? '

'Yup.'

'François, Denny, Andy—?'

'Everyone.'

'Even Mr Munce?' Charlie asked sceptically.

Jack smirked. 'I didn't expect him to say yes, but he did.'

Charlie crossed his arms. 'You didn't ask me.'

Jack frowned. 'Oh. Can I—?'

'Absolutely not.'

Jack furrowed his brow. 'Don't you wanna take credit for the brothel, or breaking out of the orphanage?'

'Not when it says Charlie Smith Publishing House on the spine.' Charlie flashed a disappointed smirk. 'I'd love to, believe me. But I can't.'

Jack nodded uneasily. 'I guess you're right. I'll give you a good alias, I swear.'

'And a different job. I can't be a publisher.'

'Woah, wait a minute, you have to be in books! I'd have no reason to know who you were.'

'Change the job.' Charlie flipped to a different page. 'And while we're on the subject, remove everything with Morty.'

'Why?' Jack cried. 'He has a good alias! No one's gonna read Marty Williams and think Morty Blasmyth!'

Charlie peered up. 'A Superintendent at Scotland Yard with "a moustache the size of a new-born puppy"? Who else could it be?'

Jack held his breath. 'Okay, you're right about the moustache, but the story won't make sense without him.'

'Jack!' Charlie snapped. 'You named the actual, specific terms of our immunity. That raises a flag, not to mention you went out of your way to say I bought *The North London Press* to advertise the brothel!'

'But you just said it wouldn't be a confession unless they prove it!'

'I'm not taking any chances. It's gone.'

Jack scowled. 'It's supposed to be what happened!'

'I'm publishing your book, Jack. It's not negotiable.'

Jack rubbed his temple. 'What about Edgar Withers? Did I screw that up too?'

'No, you did good,' Charlie mumbled, flipping a page. 'You didn't specify he was running for Parliament, and it's vague enough for people to assume you made the whole thing up.'

Jack slammed a fist on Charlie's desk. 'I don't want people to think I made anything up! I've compromised enough, Charlie. I tacked on that stupid ending you wanted, with all that sentimental rubbish about humanity and how important the brothel is, even though I said in Chapter One that it isn't a bloody advertisement. I understand you want me to change your name and the name of the paper, but this is my book. I didn't write it to protect your Publishing House! I wrote it for the cause!'

Charlie stood, fuming. 'THERE WON'T *BE* A CAUSE IF I DON'T PAY FOR IT!' he roared.

Jack froze with shock.

Charlie scoffed. 'Do you have any idea how expensive it is to change the world? My taxes have to be in good standing for anyone to take me seriously. On top of that, I have utility bills, and payrolls, and bribes, and an entire distribution network that has to keep the pace so I can pay back my lawyers and investors. And I can't keep anything for myself because I give it all to foundations and petitions and lobbyists because I'm fighting for something that's completely illegal! AND I'M THE ONLY ONE! NO ONE GIVES A SHIT!'

Jack softened.

Charlie rubbed his throat. 'The calvary's not coming, Jack. We have to be in this for the long haul, and if telling the whole truth is gonna jeopardise that...' He threw his hands in the air. 'It doesn't matter.'

Jack rubbed his eyes. 'Fine,' he whispered. 'I'll be vague about the deal with Morty. I'll take out the moustache.' He took a deep breath. 'And everything with you.'

Charlie lowered his head. 'I'm sorry for yelling.'

'It's okay. I wouldn't have believed you otherwise.'

Charlie sat down. 'You don't have to make the changes yourself. I'll give it to my editors. Besides that, it's ready to publish. I'll start with a thousand copies next month, just in time for Christmas, and another batch in the New Year if it sells.'

'Do you think it will?'

Charlie shrugged coyly. 'Hard to say.'

'Why? Because it's erotica?'

'No, there's a surprisingly strong market for erotica. But I'm not too sure about erotica for homosexuals.'

'I'm sure there's not that many.'

Charlie folded his hands. 'There's no such thing as erotica for homosexuals, Jack. Until now.'

Jack froze. 'I'm sorry, what?'

'You just wrote the first homosexual erotica in history.'

Jack blinked. 'It's not really erotica.'

'Doesn't matter. It's close enough.'

Jack laughed nervously. 'Since when is that a big deal?'

'The literary world takes its milestones very seriously, Jack. There aren't many firsts left. Your book is making history, whether you want it to or not.'

Jack cleared his throat. 'So... what? People a hundred years from now are gonna read my book and talk about who I was, what I did, just because it's the first of its kind?'

'Much sooner than that, thanks to the subject matter.'

Jack leaned back in shock. He glanced over at a large painting on the wall, a Mediterranean landscape at dawn, a thick blanket of dark grey fog obscuring a potentially breath-taking horizon. As Jack stared into it, he imagined himself sailing across the sky, into the mist, toward that invisible end. What was there, beyond the grey? A silver sand beach? A calming woodland valley of green and gold? Perhaps a hurricane. A mountainside.

'Jack?' Charlie murmured. 'What's wrong?'

Jack swallowed. 'Publish it anonymously.'

Charlie blinked. 'What?'

'That's possible, isn't it?'

Charlie looked down at the manuscript, struggling to speak. 'I-I don't... You'll be famous, Jack! History will remember you. It's what you always wanted.'

'It's my story. It doesn't need my name.' Jack paused. 'If I change my mind in a few years, I'll put it back.'

Charlie bit his lip. 'Actually, in lieu of an author, I would assume the copyright, which you'd have to buy it back after it expires.'

'When will that be?'

Charlie paused for mental calculations. 'Decades.'

Jack blinked rapidly. 'Can't you just give it back?'

Charlie shook his head. 'You'd be relinquishing your rights as its author.'

Jack sighed and looked back at the painting. 'My name would only be asking for trouble.' He paused. 'It might even be better off without it. Mysterious. Like it could be anyone, you know?'

Charlie sat up. 'Can I ask you a personal question?'

'Sure.'

'Are you still ashamed to be homosexual?'

Jack snorted. 'Don't be ridiculous! If I wasn't proud, I-I wouldn't have written it!'

Charlie sighed. 'I noticed something while I was reading it.' He turned the manuscript toward Jack. 'You never actually wrote your name. Not once.'

Jack stared at Charlie in shock. He flipped through the pages, scouring for refutable evidence.

Charlie licked his dry lips. 'You didn't name your parents or your brother either. I checked.'

Jack got to the last page and closed the manuscript. 'I can't believe I did that.'

'I don't think you meant to. I think you did because...' Charlie paused. 'You don't want to get hurt again.'

Jack closed his eyes, sighing softly.

'This is an achievement you earned!' Charlie pleaded in a soft whisper. 'Think of what it'll mean, what good it'll do for the world, for men like us, if they see your name on that by-line!'

Jack shook his head. 'It wouldn't help.'

Charlie frowned. 'Please believe me, Jack. You're going to regret this for the rest of your life.'

'You're telling me to be vulnerable?!' Jack asked incredulously. 'You won't even take credit for your own brothel!'

'I know,' Charlie whispered. 'I'm speaking from experience.'

Jack's blood ran cold. After a deep breath, he muttered, 'I'm not a narcissist, Charlie. I'm sacrificing for the greater good, same as you.'

Charlie nodded reluctantly. 'Okay. As long as you're sure.'

Jack forced a smile. 'The brothel is my home. I would do anything to keep it safe.'

PART II

Jack Branson

CHAPTER TEN

Figleaves in Eden

19 Montgomery Street, Marylebone, Two Months Later...

Jack stood before his mirror, naked head to toe, and studied his body. 'I was at the Summer Exhibition last year,' he whispered. 'They had this painting of Adam and Eve in Eden. Before God evicted them, obviously. Adam's sitting on a rock, looking down at the grass. Handsome. Chiselled jaw. Muscles. Eve's looking up at the sky. Slim. Milky white skin. They had figleaves covering their genitals. Not on a vine or anything, just... *there.*'

Jack flicked his soft brown fringe across his forehead. 'That got me thinking. You know what it says in Genesis? They were naked. It wasn't until after they ate from the Tree of Knowledge that they became ashamed of their nudity, losing Eden in the process.'

Jack pivoted his hips to admire his plump arse. 'They actually censored the painting. Even though it wasn't what happened, even though it doesn't make sense... no penises or cunts in the gallery.'

Jack stared into his blue eyes, a sudden wave of sadness rushing over him. 'But they don't censor books, do they? It's the only medium you can get away with anything.'

Jack turned to his bed. 'Why is that? Does that make any sense?'

Superintendent Morty Blasmyth smiled back, completely naked, head propped by the elbow. 'They don't have a figleaf big enough for you.'

'I'm serious, Morty.'

'So am I.' Morty winked.

Jack smiled. 'Are you staying for the party?'

'Don't think so. Lots to do.'

'I bet.'

Morty pursed his lips. 'Don't remind me.'

'How many interrogations are up to?'

'Almost two thousand.'

'And how many did he kill?'

'Five.'

Jack gasped. 'No! That's it?'

'If it weren't for his bloody letters, nobody would care.' Morty smiled. 'And while we're on the subject of famous Jacks—'

'You couldn't resist, could you?'

'How many copies have you sold so far?'

'Three thousand.'

Morty whistled. 'I can't believe you're allowed to publish something like that.'

'Charlie said, if they can publish Giacomo Casanova's autobiography, they can publish anything.'

Morty laughed. He grabbed his trousers off the floor and pulled a book from the pocket.

Jack snorted. 'Seriously?'

Morty nodded with a simple grin.

Jack turned back to the mirror. 'I'm not signing it.'

'You're my favourite author.'

'I'm not an author. Technically, that's not my book.'

Morty half-smiled, his egregious moustache half-curling. He opened the book to Chapter Three and read:

> '"I lost myself in that moment, my senses finally returning a half-hour later. I was sprawled out on the floor, my arse burning from his scruffy beard, aching and wet in all the right places. Marty looked down at me as he dressed, admiring my spent naked body. I gulped up the air, too stunned to move.
>
> *So that's—*"'

'"That's how he made Sergeant,"' Jack whispered, reciting from memory.

Morty laughed heartily. 'Bloody Hell, Jack! I've must've touched myself to that, I dunno, three times now. You are a fantastic writer!'

Jack nodded with a glum frown.

Morty closed the book. 'Has it really been four years?'

'More than that. That was before Collins, and that'll be four years on Friday.'

Morty furrowed his brow. 'I thought it was the twenty-fifth.'

'23 January 1885. *The Times* printed it late.'

Morty walked over to Jack and hugged him from behind. They stared at their naked reflections.

'You didn't mention my moustache,' Morty whispered in Jack's ear.

Jack smirked. 'There was some contention with that. Gave you a beard instead.'

'Contention with whom?'

'Whom do you think?'

Morty rubbed Jack's smooth chest. 'I thought you liked Charlie.'

'I do, it's just...' Jack shrugged. 'I used to think he was a wizard who could shoot fireworks out of his fingertips. Now he's just a man holding sparklers.'

Morty studied Jack's mirrored body with loving eyes. 'You're so beautiful.'

Jack blushed, resting his head against Morty's breast. Morty closed his eyes with a smile.

Jack stepped away slowly. 'Kensington's anniversary got me thinking.' He opened a dresser drawer and rummaged through his undergarments. 'How long have we been here? Two years?'

Morty crossed his arms, showcasing his tight biceps. 'June of '87, right?'

'July, but still, almost two. And we've never been raided—'

'You're welcome.'

Jack chuckled. 'Thank you.' He stepped into his underwear. 'We haven't been stormed by a mob. No one's lynched us. We really haven't been in any danger.' He tapped his foot, hands on his hips, wearing just his briefs. 'Why couldn't I do it, Morty? It's not like my family would've found out. No one reads out there. And Mother had to walk five miles just to find a bookstore with anything new. And Charlie's only based in London anyway, so the chances of it getting out there—'

'Jack—'

'And I named Dunderrow, and Mr Huxley, and Seamus, even Danny, so why couldn't I—?'

'Jack! It's still a crime. No one's calling you a coward.'

Jack slid into his trousers. 'Aren't they?'

'I'm not.'

'But you know I wrote it!' Jack huffed. 'Just once I want someone to, I dunno, give it to me straight.'

Morty frowned. He reached for his underwear.

Jack stepped forward. 'Morty,' he whispered apologetically.

Morty softened. He tossed his underwear back on the floor. 'What does Oliver think?'

'He says I did the right thing. As usual.'

'He wouldn't lie to you.'

'He just wants me to be happy. I know he doesn't understand. He never had to pretend to be normal.' Jack paused. 'I thought I was better than this, you know? How is this different from Mulhussey? I'm still hiding.'

Morty frowned.

'I neutered myself this time,' Jack whispered with a scowl. 'Guess that makes me a hypocrite, like the rest of them.'

'Stop that,' Morty muttered. 'You want me to give it to you straight? Okay. Your authorship is irrelevant.'

Jack looked at Morty, confused.

Morty chuckled. 'That's what you wanted, right?' He held up his copy of *The Sins of an Irishman in London*. 'I've never been so happy in my life, and it's all because of this book.' Morty sat on the

bed. 'Listen to how it ends.'

'I know how it—!'

'Just listen.' Morty flipped to the last page and read:

> '"That's why it all matters. For men like that Tory, twisted up inside, hiding in plain sight, selling their souls for a chance to be normal, there is another way. Happiness is an option now. Religious beliefs, sexual science, that's merely detail.
>
> The Montgomery Street Brothel is a haven for those silent few who have to choose. Who want a brighter world. Who want just one night in their own skin.
>
> Isn't that more important than anything?"'

Morty clapped the book shut. 'That's perfect!'

Jack rolled his eyes. 'Charlie made me put that in.'

'And he was right to.' Morty grinned. 'You know me, Jack Branson, more than anyone I've ever known. These words right here, no one's ever said them to me. I know you know what that's like. The only reason you feel like a hypocrite is because you forgot how special this is for even existing. You've done the one thing no one's ever done. You're miles ahead of all of us and you're holding the door open.'

Jack frowned. 'I haven't forgotten, Morty. That's why I'm upset.'

Morty's smile faded.

Jack sat beside Morty. 'We're a lot like the abolitionists, aren't we? They banded together, staying strong for decades, until the ones

in charge cared enough to free those slaves. Everyone knows Abraham Lincoln, and I had my chance to be... Well, not exactly, but... Maybe I could've been something. But when you're gone, and Mr Munce, and Oliver... No one's gonna know what I did.'

Morty put his arm around Jack. 'Don't think of it like that. Look at Charlie. He made this place. His dream found you. He knows he'll never get the credit he deserves, but he doesn't let it bother him. In fact, I think that makes him more altruistic—'

'But I'm not like that!' Jack cried. 'I want people to tell me that I'm good and brave and smart, but because it's the truth and not because they get something in return because, I dunno, it means *more*!'

Morty awkwardly moved his arm away.

Jack cleared his throat. 'Listen to me go.' He grabbed his shirt and buttoned it on. 'Not like me to gab when I'm with a client.'

Morty frowned, hurt.

Jack looked at Morty. Instantly softened.

Morty picked his underwear off the floor and put them on. 'I should get back. Don't want Monro thinking I killed those whores in Whitechapel.'

Jack shifted his stance. 'We have to be reasonable about this, Morty. You're letting us go if something happens. That was the deal.'

Morty put on his undershirt. 'Yeah.'

'And it makes sense. Just like my anonymity makes sense.'

Morty slid into his trousers. 'Yeah.'

Jack slammed his eyes shut. 'Christ, Morty. I shouldn't have called you that.'

'Like you said.' Morty buttoned his uniform. 'We have to be reasonable.'

Jack gave Morty a tight hug. Morty squeezed back and closed his eyes.

'I don't want to be like Charlie,' Jack whispered. 'I don't want to forget why I'm doing this. Thank you.'

Morty petted Jack's hair. 'Thank *you.*'

Jack kissed Morty on the lips. Morty caressed Jack's cheek as he grabbed his wallet.

'What're you doing?' Jack asked.

'Paying for my session.'

'You don't have to. It's on the house.'

Morty held up £100 note. 'I know.'

Jack gasped. He looked at Morty with a loving smile, reluctantly taking the note. Morty donned his Superintendent cap. Left the room. Marched down the hallway.

'Morty, wait!' Jack raced down the hallway, a pen in his hand. 'Give it here.'

Morty smirked. Pulled the book from his pocket. Flipped to the title page. Handed it over.

Jack signed extravagantly. Snapped it shut. Handed it back. 'There. The only signed copy in existence.'

Morty kissed Jack one last time and watched the handsome lad return to his room. With great reluctance, Superintendent Blasmyth made his way down the stairs and out the door.

The rain-soaked Montgomery Street was completely silent except for the ice-cold breeze. Morty sat on the porch steps, arms wrapped

around his knees, and sighed at the overcast landscape before him. He opened his copy of *The Sins of an Irishman in London*. Chuckled with surprise.

On the title page, in the most pretentious hand possible, Jack had signed:

Anonymous

Four Hours Later...

POP! Charlie caught the cork with a towel.

Mary clapped frantically. 'It's not time yet,' Louise scolded.

'I never had champagne before!' Mary hissed. 'Stop being so dour about everything.'

Louise leaned towards Denny and whispered, 'Would if I could, tramp.'

'WHAT DID YOU CALL ME?!'

Oliver whistled sharply. 'Okay everyone, settle down and grab a glass.'

François snapped his fingers. Andy obediently fetched a pair of glasses. Mary handed one to Denny, grabbing two more for Louise and himself.

Jack, adorned with a handmade paper crown, stayed in his chair at the end of the table. Oliver carried over two glasses. 'Your highness,' he harrumphed, handing Jack his champagne.

Jack smiled warmly and gave Oliver a big kiss.

Charlie stood and raised a glass. 'To say *The Sins of an Irishman in London* was a success would be an understatement. His name

may not on the cover, but that only makes his accomplishment all the greater: an exceptionally brilliant, exquisitely brave debut novel. Not to mention a damn good read.'

'Hear! Hear!' Denny cheered. The others laughed.

Charlie paused, a self-deprecating frown growing on his face. 'It's because of Jack Branson, not Charlie Smith, that we're celebrating tonight. I merely published. He made it a bestseller.'

Jack looked up at Charlie with humble sympathy. Their eyes met, and for the briefest of moments, they shared a profound moment of mutual understanding.

Charlie smiled warmly. 'I'm so proud of you.'

Jack's heart fluttered. He smiled back.

'To Jack Branson!' Oliver declared.

Everyone raised their glasses. '*To Jack Branson*!'

After a hearty dinner of roasted pig and baked carrots, the whores of the Montgomery Street Brothel segregated themselves along the table. Andy, Mary, and Louise huddled at one end, shuffling through a box of reviews Charlie had clipped from various publications. Oliver, Jack, and Charlie sat opposite, smoking cigars and sipping brandy like true gentlemen. François and Denny sat along the middle, jointly perusing Denny's personal copy of *The Sins of an Irishman in London*.

'I got a good one!' Andy declared. 'It's from *The London News*:

> "The anonymously confessed *Sins of an Irishman in London* is a revelation, a critique on the modern man, an intelligent erotica with themes rivalling high literature. With sardonic wit and unashamed

> honesty, the nameless author (by all indications a true deviant of the night) takes us through a world of perilous secrets and scandals, but more than that, he explores his own pain. I admit, this novel made me empathise with an idea-man, a symbolic figure with just as much authenticity and humanity as any named author today."'

Jack grinned around his cigar. 'Can't ask for more than that.'

'Let's find a nasty one!' Louise exclaimed. 'I wanna hear them squirm!'

Oliver looked over at Denny. 'What part are you reading?'

'Edgar Withers, the Tory MP Jack slept with.'

'He's not an MP yet,' Jack corrected. 'I sure hope he doesn't win.'

'Not a chance,' Charlie said. 'Grant's held that seat for thirty years. He's not gonna lose to some solicitor with no experience.'

'YUCK!' Denny cried, dropping the book. 'You really did that with his feet?'

Jack squirmed. 'Washed my mouth for hours.'

Denny cringed.

'Oh, this is good!' Louise cried. '*The National*:

> "I condemn *The Sins of an Irishman in London* for disgracing my Christian eyes with a sympathetic glorification of heinous acts. I hope the unnamed author is not what he claims, that his so-called 'confession' is nothing more than an elaborately marketed piece of fiction, but I truly doubt this novel is anything less

> than authentic. Such a thought makes my stomach turn."'

Jack sighed, the cheer slowly draining from his face.

Oliver recognised Jack's discomfort. Forced a smile. 'Are you going to tell your mum about the book?'

Jack shook his head. 'Don't think so.'

François leaned in. 'Don't waste your time, Jack. If she hasn't written back by now, she's not going to.'

'I'm not expecting a reply.'

'Then why are you holding on? You're wasting five pounds a day.'

Jack shrugged. 'They're my parents.'

'So were mine. So were Denny's, so were Andy's. When they moved on, we moved on, and you'd be better off.'

'Maybe I don't want to be better off. My family made me who I am.'

'They stopped being your family the moment they decided to forget about you.'

Jack frowned. A chord had been struck.

'That's enough, François!' Oliver scolded.

François pursed his lips and turned back to Denny.

Oliver rubbed Jack's shoulders. 'He shouldn't have said that.'

Jack sighed. 'We're all thinking it.'

'This one ain't bad,' Andy called. 'It's from *The Times*:

> "The controversially erotic (and erotically controversial) *Sins of an Irishman in London* has the literary world divided. The notorious novel, anon-

ymously released through the Charlie Smith Publishing House, is shrouded in mystery. Humourists deem it a satire on the desperation of the poor. Academics praise its commentary on the intelligence of sex and the business of prostitution. Cynics call it an exposé on the corrupt aristocracy. Whether you agree with its argument is up to you, but it is thoroughly convincing nonetheless, selling three thousand copies in its first two months with no sign of stopping. Dozens of bookshops have pulled the novel from their shelves for its explicit content, so grab a copy while you still can and see just what all the fuss is about."'

Jack stood abruptly and strode away.

'Jack, what's wrong?' Charlie asked.

'I'm tired,' Jack mumbled. 'Good night everybody.'

'I'll come with you,' Oliver said, racing after Jack.

Upstairs, Jack collapsed on his bed. Oliver sat beside him and petted his back.

'Are you okay?'

Jack smushed his face into the pillow. Oliver leaned in and kissed Jack's cheeks. Jack swatted him away.

Oliver blinked, confused. 'What's wrong?'

Jack sat up, his lip trembling. 'They love it, baby. Even the bigots thought it was convincing.'

Oliver swallowed. 'You did the right thing—'

'I don't care, I shouldn't have done it. I wish I didn't!'

'You were just being cautious.'

'I'm a bloody coward! I wrote the whole thing, but I couldn't do it. I couldn't just...'

Oliver closed his eyes, trying not to cry. 'Don't blame yourself, baby.' He forced a smile. 'It's still your story. The fact that you've come this far is enough.'

Jack shook his head. 'No, it's not.'

Three Weeks Later...

In the Dining Room, Andy watched François and Mary bicker over eggs and toast.

'No one wants anything to do with whores,' François insisted. 'Not while Jack's in every paper.'

'There's no such thing as bad publicity!' Mary retorted. 'People are thinking about whores every day now. Besides, Jack's killing women! How's that hurting business?'

'What did I do?' Jack asked, walking in with Oliver.

'Not you,' Andy groaned, suffering from debate fatigue. 'Jack the Ripper.'

Jack smirked. 'You never know. I had a flat in Whitechapel.'

'I wanna hear what Oliver thinks,' Mary declared.

Oliver snorted. 'I'm afraid to ask.'

'Is Jack the Ripper hurting business?' Andy mumbled.

'Of course he is!' François exclaimed. 'He's killing people!'

'Only the whores!' Mary retorted. 'The papers make them look like victims anyway, and that's practically condoning prostitution.'

François gaped. 'That doesn't make any sense!'

'What do you think, Andy?' Jack asked with a smirk.

Andy blew on his coffee. 'Just happy to be here.'

Louise crept in with a horrified look on his face.

'Louise!' Mary pleaded. 'Thank God! I need an ally!

'Not now, Mary,' Louise whispered, holding the door open.

Mary scowled. 'Stingy bitch!'

A grim-faced Mr Munce walked in, a letter in his hand.

The room went silent. One by one, the others looked at Jack.

Jack put a hand to his heart, eyes wide with shock.

Mr Munce held out the letter.

Jack ripped it from Munce's hand, ready to tear it open, but he stopped when he recognised the envelope.

His handwriting. Addressed to his mother. Postmarked the day before. A big red stamp across its face:

UNDELIVERABLE

Jack's hands trembled with fear. 'What does it mean?'

Munce shook his head. 'I don't know.'

Jack scowled. 'What do you mean *you don't know*?! You're supposed to have all the answers!'

'There's, um...' Munce cleared his throat. 'Plenty of reasons, Jack. She could've refused it, or they moved, or she's—'

'Dead?' Jack whispered.

Munce stopped talking, his breath audibly wavering.

Jack's entire body froze.

Munce wetted his lips and answered, 'Or incapacitated.'

Jack immediately sprinted out of the Dining Room. Dashed up

the stairs. Into his bedroom. Ruffled through his drawers. Haphazardly threw shirts onto the bed.

Oliver strode in, already in crisis mode. 'What do you need?'

'I need to go home,' Jack tossed a handful of socks onto the pile.

'Jack, just because one came back doesn't mean anything's wrong—'

'I don't care if Father calls the police. I'm seeing my Mother.'

Oliver swallowed. 'It's okay to be worried, but you need to calm down and think this—'

'She could be dead!' Jack cried, tears running down his cheeks. 'I don't care anymore! I'm done waiting! I need to know what's going on!' He collapsed onto the floor, sobbing wildly. 'I don't want her to go!'

Oliver crouched down and held Jack. 'Don't think like that, baby.'

'How can I not?'

Oliver kissed Jack's head. 'I'll come with you.'

Jack sniffed. 'You will? Really?'

Oliver smiled, wiping away Jack's tears. 'Of course I will.' He kissed Jack and ran to his bedroom.

One Hour Later...

Jack and Oliver loaded onto a growler headed for King's Cross, where they caught the boat train to Southampton Dock. They boarded the last ship to Queenstown with five minutes to spare.

That night, Jack and Oliver sat on the deck, blankets around their shoulders, the wind buffeting them mercilessly. They would have held each other if they were not in public. As a consolation, Oliver

took Jack's hand under their blankets, squeezing tight when Jack got scared, stroking his palm when he was sad. They did not speak the whole night. They simply looked up at the stars.

Jack woke at dawn. Oliver was asleep, his hand still clutched onto Jack's. Jack smiled and watched the sunrise.

They landed at Queenstown two hours later. Oliver hailed a growler outside the station and tied their luggage to the back.

'Dunderrow, please,' he told the Driver. 'Branson Farm.'

Somewhere in County Cork, One Hour Later...

Jack and Oliver sat across from each other in the growler and looked out at the rolling hills.

'It's so green,' Oliver marvelled. 'Must've rained yesterday.'

'This is nothing,' Jack whispered. 'My parents took us to the Cliffs of Moher when I was nine. The grass was so vibrant it hurt your eyes. The wind made it breathe. There were rocks miles beneath us, sharp as daggers, like a drop at the edge of the world. I remember the four of us standing there. Mother and Father behind me. Harold to my left. We just stared out at the sea. It stretched beyond our sight, so big, so chaotic it was frightening. But the horizon! So perfect and comforting. A straight line every way we looked. I can still hear the silence. The hush of the breeze. Harold chuckling, the way all toddlers do. Mother had her hand on my shoulder. Father smiled. He never smiled. The air was cold, but I wasn't. Not really.' Jack frowned. 'Memories are all I have now.'

The growler turned with the road. Oliver gasped.

Just beyond the road was a majestic valley, spanning all the way

to the mountainous horizon. Soft green grass in every direction, yellow and pink flowers scattered about. Something in the way the sunshine broke through the clouds made everything sparkle.

'It's so beautiful!' Oliver cried.

Jack looked at Oliver, a sweet smile growing on his face. He reached over and took Oliver's hand. 'I can't believe I'm bringing back a man. Wish it were under better circumstances.'

Oliver whipped his hand away to point out the window. 'There's the sign!'

Jack looked out the window. On the side of the road was a large headstone with DUNDERROW carved into it.

'This doesn't feel right,' Jack said with a frown. 'I feel like a child breaking curfew.'

Oliver shook his head. 'You're older and wiser.'

Jack snorted. 'Not enough. It's not just a village. It's as old as the hills. The earth soaked with sun and bad memories. Its people ruthless like the wind. Grudges strong as trees. Their values, heavy boulders.'

Oliver smirked. 'You just made that up, didn't you?'

'I never stop writing.'

'You could make it sound a bit more pleasant.'

Jack sighed. 'Not when it's the truth.'

Oliver studied Jack's blank gaze, the way his beautiful blue eyes looked *past* the majestic landscape, and a wave of pity rushed over him. 'What about your friends?' he asked with forced joviality. 'Will I get to meet them?'

Jack's face softened, his eyes drooping, lips forming a vulnerable pout. 'I didn't have friends in Dunderrow. Just family.'

Branson Farm, Dunderrow, Twenty Minutes Later...

The growler stopped in front of a stone cottage encircled by a brown wooden fence. A cattle barn stood in the distance, surrounded by acres of farmland.

Oliver hopped out and approached the box seat. 'We'll get the bags in a moment, Driver. Won't be long.'

The Driver nodded. Whipped out a sandwich.

Jack wandered toward the post-box, entranced. He reached out and caressed it. 'Nothing's changed. Thank God.'

Oliver unlocked the fence gate and held it open. 'Why do you say that?'

Jack plodded in with a hefty sigh. 'Because it looks like they waited for me.'

Oliver closed the gate slowly, his eyes fixed on the cottage. A sudden chill ran up his spine.

Jack stopped walking and looked back at Oliver with a smirk. 'You're more nervous than I am.'

Oliver snapped out of his daze and kept walking. 'I'm sure I'm not.'

Jack moseyed his way toward the cottage, gazing out at the farmland surrounding them. 'We're too late, you know,' he said definitively. 'She's already dead.'

'Don't say that.'

'I've accepted it. Nothing's worse than that.'

They stopped before the old pine door. Jack could hear soft voices chattering over a crackling fire. He smelled breakfast sausage.

'It's been eight years,' Jack whispered. 'What if they don't want to talk to me?'

Oliver placed a gentle hand on Jack's shoulder. 'They still love you, baby.'

Jack nodded softly. He raised a fist, primed to knock.

The door whipped open. A young man with messy brown hair stood at the threshold, blue eyes wide with surprise.

Jack froze. 'Harold.' He smiled awkwardly. 'Hey, it's been a while.'

Harold turned away. 'Pa, it's for you.'

'Wait! Harold!' Jack pleaded.

Harold walked into his bedroom. Closed the door.

Jack poked his head inside the cottage. The curtains were slightly drawn, light enough to see, dark enough to forget the time. The corner bedroom door was open, and Jack could see a priest kneeling beside the bed. A woman lay under the sheets, her hands folded atop her abdomen, rising and falling as she breathed.

'She's still alive!' Jack whispered. 'She's ill, but she's alive!'

Donald Branson suddenly appeared, a burly grouch with snow-white hair. 'What are you doing here?' he grumbled with spite.

Jack's nostrils flared. 'What happened to Mother?'

Donald stepped out and slammed the door. His icy eyes did a double take at Oliver.

Oliver gulped. He stepped back to a safe distance.

'What's wrong with her?' Jack asked sternly.

'Pneumonia,' Donald mumbled. 'Won't last the night.'

Jack swallowed. 'I want to speak to her.'

Donald scowled. 'I told you never to come back here!'

'Let me speak to her, Father!'

'She's had her last rites. I won't let you ruin that for her.'

Jack's lip quivered. 'But I'm your son!'

'Leave now or I'm calling the police.'

'He came all this way!' Oliver snapped. 'Just let him say goodbye!'

'Stay out of this, boy!' Donald growled.

'His name is Oliver!' Jack cried.

'I don't care who he is! You're not—' Donald suddenly turned away and coughed deep, phlegm-drenched hacks into his arm. He softened with exhaustion. 'Why can't you leave us alone, Jack? Have you no pity? First the letters, and now this?'

Jack gasped. 'She got my letters? Why didn't she write back?'

Donald frowned. He looked to the ground. 'We burnt them.' He closed his eyes. 'All of them.'

Jack blinked rapidly. 'You burnt...?' His voice fizzled away.

'We thought you'd stop on your own,' Donald explained with a hint of regret. 'What you did was bad enough. Couldn't you let her move on?'

'She didn't read any...?'

Donald shook his head. He stepped back into the cottage. 'You're not welcome, Jack.'

'NO!' Jack held the door open. 'Please, Father! I want to see her!'

Donald gently pushed Jack's arm off the door. 'She doesn't want to see you.'

Jack gasped, his eyes filling with tears.

Donald bowed his head. Shut the door. Locked it.

Jack covered his eyes, his breath hardening.

Oliver stepped forward. 'Jack.'

Jack re-donned his paddy cap with trembling hands.

Oliver swallowed. 'Jack?'

'Let's go,' Jack croaked, inching back to the growler. Oliver stood his ground, too weak to move, eyes full of tears.

Jack suddenly stopped. Backed against the side of the house. Hunched over. Wailed his heart out. Sharp screeches echoing throughout the town. Tears falling like rain. He didn't care how loud he was. He didn't care if his Father heard him. He didn't care about anything.

Through his babbles, Jack cried, 'I want my mummy!'

Oliver grimaced at the traumatic sight before him. He looked through the window of the cottage.

Inside, Donald sat by the fireplace, face buried in his hands, trying his best to ignore Jack's cries. After a few moments, he stood from his chair, faltered into his wife's bedroom, and closed the door.

Oliver kept staring through the window, scowling, waiting for someone to emerge. Nothing. He stepped back from the window. Took a deep breath. Wiped the tears from his eyes. Crouched down to Jack.

'Let's go home.'

Oliver struggled to help Jack to his feet. Jack's eyes were beet red, tears and snot running down his face. Oliver practically carried Jack past the fence-gate and into the growler.

'Driver!' Oliver barked. 'Queenstown! Now!'

The Driver looked back with concern, nodding softly. After Oliver closed the door, the Driver flicked the reins and drove away.

Jack rested his head in Oliver's lap. Oliver petted Jack's hair, shushing gently, his heart broken.

Beyond the creaking of the wheels, Oliver suddenly heard a loud voice on the wind. He whipped his head around, but it was too late. The cottage was obscured by trees.

Jack opened his eyes with concern. 'What's wrong?'

Oliver kept staring. Another chill raced up his spine. He looked down at Jack and forced a smile. 'Nothing. Don't worry about it.'

Jack closed his eyes, falling asleep in seconds.

As the growler crossed the border of Dunderrow, Oliver frowned at that majestic valley, his eyes red and emotionally spent.

19 Montgomery Street, Marylebone, Three Days Later...

Oliver unlocked Jack's bedroom door with the master key. He treaded lightly across the sea of dirty clothes and shook Jack awake. Jack dropped the empty whisky bottle in his hand, his eyes fluttering open. 'What time is it?'

'Almost eight,' Oliver whispered. 'You've been in here for two days.'

Jack swallowed. 'I'm drunk.'

'I know you are.'

'Of course. I'm Irish.'

'That's not what I—'

'You like my accent?' Jack slurred. 'Ask me about the famine and my not-red hair!'

'Baby—'

'Mock me while I can hear you! I'm not one of you! Who cares what I think?!'

Oliver closed his eyes. 'Oh Jack, I'm so sorry.'

Jack sat up, stopping from dizziness. 'I loved her. I loved her so much.'

'I know.'

'I don't under... Why, why would she burn...?'

'Please don't think about that, baby.'

Jack shrugged slowly. 'She never loved me.'

Oliver's lip quivered. 'That's not true.'

'I've been thinking about the... All that money. She didn't know, I guess. She would've if she opened one. Just one. Even by accident.'

Oliver stood. 'I'll get you some water.'

Jack twisted the whisky bottle by the neck, the thick corners hitting the floor. THUMP. THUMP. THUMP.

'I wanted to tell her I... I could've. I had so much time, I *could've*. But I can't now. It's too late. She's gone. And she'll never know that I... After everything...'

Oliver swallowed. 'I'm sure she—'

'NOT A SINGLE ONE!'

Jack threw the bottle at the wall. CRASH! Glass flew everywhere. Oliver flinched.

In the silence that followed, Jack burst into tears. 'It's all my fault! She didn't love me. She used to, before I...' He shook his head.

'But she didn't anymore.'

Oliver sat back down and held Jack. 'She—'

'Why didn't she write back if she still cared?'

Oliver kissed Jack's head and stood again. 'I'll get you something to eat.'

'I'm not hungry.'

'Yes, you are.'

Jack rolled over. 'I'll get it later.'

Oliver stopped at the threshold, sighing helplessly. 'Just... Just carry on, baby.'

'What for?'

Oliver frowned. He closed his eyes and shut the door.

Downstairs, François, Andy, Louise, Denny, Mary, and Charlie sat in silence around the Dining Room table.

Oliver lumbered in. 'The same.'

'He couldn't even see her,' Andy murmured.

'Could she still be alive?' Denny suggested.

Oliver shook his head rapidly. 'No.'

'Who knows, maybe she got better. Plenty of people—'

'Maggie Branson died of pneumonia on Branson Farm, Dunderrow on the fifteenth of February,' Oliver recited from memory. 'Three hours after we left.'

Denny deflated.

Oliver shrugged. 'I asked Munce to check. He told me this morning.' He scratched his head. 'I don't know what else I can do.'

François clenched a fist and stood. 'Alright everyone, get up.'

Oliver furrowed his brow.

François scowled at the others. 'Up, I say!'

The others stood, looking at each other curiously.

'What're you thinking, François?' Oliver asked.

François snapped and pointed at Mary and Louise. 'Wash your hands!'

Mary looked at Louise. 'How did he know?'

'We're baking, you morons!'

Andy grinned. 'A surprise for Jack?'

François smirked. 'You bet, honey. We got a lot of work to do.'

Four Hours Later...

Oliver kissed Jack awake.

Jack jolted up. 'What is it? What time is it?'

'Late,' Oliver whispered, holding up a glass of water.

Jack glugged it down, gasping for air.

Oliver chuckled, rubbing Jack's back. 'You must be hungry too.'

'Starved.'

'Good. Follow me.' Oliver helped Jack to his feet, wrapping an arm around his shoulder.

'Where are we going?' Jack asked.

Oliver smiled. 'Trust me.'

Oliver led Jack into the Dining Room. On the table was a silver lidded tray. Charlie, François, Andy, Mary, Louise, and Denny stood by with cheery, exhausted expressions.

Jack snorted. 'What is this?'

Oliver pulled out a chair and Jack sat down. François lifted the lid.

'*SURPRISE*!' everyone cried.

On the tray was a homemade Délice de Mousse. It had a bit of a posture problem, but was technically accurate nonetheless.

Jack's jaw dropped at the rustic beauty before him. 'You made this?!'

'We all did,' Denny said. 'We heard about your mum and wanted to cheer you up.'

Jack smiled. 'Thank you. I...' He chuckled gleefully. 'I love it!'

'It was François's idea,' Andy blurted.

Jack gaped at François, his eyes fluttering.

François snorted. 'Don't go soft on me!' Mary elbowed François in the chest. François grunted. 'Sorry.' He gave Jack a soft smile. 'I knew how much you liked it from your book. And nothing helps grief more than food, take it from me.'

Jack grinned. 'Thank you.'

François nodded respectfully.

Jack studied the Délice de Mousse up close. 'How did you do it?'

Louise blew his lips. 'It wasn't easy. Oliver and Charlie had to break into Dubeau Frères just to swipe the recipe.'

'In and out, two minutes,' Charlie reported proudly. 'Forgot how much fun it was.'

'François ran the kitchen,' Mary added. 'But *some of us* couldn't keep up.' He glared at Louise.

Louise frowned back. 'Why are you looking at me? I tried my best.'

'Tried your best?! You burnt the mousse! Who burns mousse?!'

'You kept distracting me, you clumsy bitch!'

'Hush up!'

'Who the hell wears heels in a bloody kitchen?!'

'I looked good!'

'QUIET!' Andy roared.

Mary and Louise widened their eyes and cowered away.

François petted Andy's blond head. 'Good boy.' He looked at Jack. 'Bad enough I had to deal with amateurs. We would've finished an hour ago if Andy here hadn't knocked the first one on the floor.'

'It was trash anyway!' Andy insisted. 'You should be thanking me! I did you all a favor!'

François raised a finger. 'Bad boy.'

Oliver shook his head. 'No, François, Andy's right. It *was* trash.'

Andy rolled his eyes.

Jack shook his head. 'I can't believe you went through all that trouble, just for me.'

'Of course we did, Jack.' Denny smiled warmly. 'You're our brother. We love you.'

Jack's lip quivered, his eyes suddenly filled with tears. 'Thank you.'

'Thank us all by eating it!' François cried. Everyone laughed with audible exhaustion.

Oliver handed Jack his spoon and kissed his cheek. Jack scooped the top of the Délice de Mousse. Put it in his mouth. Savoured the taste. A moment later he pounced, picking off generous scoops, ice cream rolling down his chin. François handed him a napkin. Jack quickly wiped his face and resumed his vicious attack until the

Délice de Mousse was mercifully defeated. He left the spoon in the bowl and leaned back to rest.

Mary stared in horror. 'Four hours. Four damn hours, and he finished it in thirty seconds.'

Louise guided the traumatised Mary to Jack for one last bedtime hug. He followed suit, then Denny, Charlie, and Andy, one by one.

François, the last in the queue, held Jack tenderly. 'I'm sorry about your mum,' he whispered. Jack nodded respectfully and watched François stagger to bed.

Oliver and Jack washed the dirty mixing bowls and utensils in the kitchen sink. After they finished, Jack gave Oliver a big hug. 'Thank you for coming with me.'

Oliver smiled. 'I never got to say goodbye to my mum. Wanted you to have the chance.'

Soon as the words left his mouth, Oliver's mind coasted back to Branson Farm, to that loud voice on the wind.

His blood went cold.

At that moment, Jack kissed him. Soft lips pressing sweetly. Warm tongue roaming around.

Oliver closed his eyes and surrendered. His body warmed up. His mind went blank. And he could taste Délice de Mousse.

CHAPTER ELEVEN

A Dangerous Cave

19 Montgomery Street, Marylebone, Three Days Later...

'Charlie!' Jack stormed into the Barroom. Andy followed, an issue of *The North London Press* in his hand.

Jack met eyes with Denny, standing behind the counter with a polish-drenched cloth. 'Where is he? Have you seen him?'

'He's upstairs,' Denny murmured, puzzled.

Jack huffed. 'I'll get him, Andy. Wait here.' He sprinted out of the room.

Denny furrowed his brow at Andy. 'What was that about?'

Andy sat at the bar and showed Denny the magazine. 'Came out this morning.'

Denny took one look at the headline. 'Oh hell.'

'I thought the immunity was supposed to prevent something like this.'

'You would think.'

Jack ran back in with Charlie and Oliver, snapping his fingers at the magazine. Andy held it out. Charlie bugged his eyes at the cover.

'What does it say?' Oliver asked.

Charlie flipped to Page Four and read aloud:

'"A WOLF IN SHEEP'S CLOTHING:
EDGAR WITHERS'S IMMORAL SECRET
by August Hammersworth

Edgar Withers has never been a politician. He has never managed a staff, balanced his own figures, maintained his own practice, or kept a client longer than two years. He is a meek man, with suits too tight and hats too big, like a child pretending to be his father, or perhaps an actor miscast in a role beyond his ability. It is understandable that the Tories want an amateur on their side in the House of Commons, someone to vote yes on everything they want, a clean slate they can corrupt with their posh elitism."'

('No wonder they lost their sponsors,' Jack mumbled.)

'"If only they knew just how unclean Withers was, how corrupt. There is a blight in this city. A boil on the face of the empire. A den of sin. A new Sodom for lustful perverts to engage with male prostitutes, destitute boys forced to degrade themselves, their lives besmirched with abuse and despair. The Tories have never seen this world of poverty, yet they want it to linger with selfish policies that solely benefit the aristocracy.

Like his right-wing brethren, Edgar the solicitor will keep this world alive if he defeats incumbent Geoffrey Grant MP this September, but not because

> the Tories expect him to do so. Because it would be his pleasure.
>
> My anonymous source, a man deep in Edger's inner circle, revealed to me his immoral secret: Mr Withers frequently visits this revolting underworld, but not for legal matters. Personal, base ones. For long hours into the night, he fulfils his carnal needs. Edgar Withers is a sodomite, plain and simple."'

Charlie lowered the magazine, eyes staring off in a trance.

Denny bobbed his head. 'Subtle.'

'You didn't know about this?' Jack asked Charlie.

'They don't need my permission,' Charlie answered. 'Actually, it's a good thing I *didn't* know about it.'

'How's so?'

'It means Morty's doing his job. Whoever the source is, he doesn't have a connection to the police. And I've heard of August Hammersworth. He's notorious for not checking his facts.'

Oliver took a deep breath. 'So we have nothing to worry about?'

'They run smear pieces all the time,' Charlie explained. 'It's what they're famous for, getting a rise out of people. I doubt they can prove Edgar was even here.'

'But what if someone reads it and assumes it's true?'

'The only ones who read *The North London Press* are radical liberals and secret homosexuals. No one takes it seriously.'

Centre of Belgrave Square, Four Hours Later...

Geoffrey Grant MP stood on a makeshift stage before a large crowd. He was quite fit for his age. Cold grey eyes. Thick head of snow-white hair. Ivory beard circling his face like a mane.

'Edgar Withers will never step foot in Parliament!' Grant roared from his podium. 'He is an immoral, disgusting cretin. And not just because he's a solicitor.'

The crowd laughed on cue.

Grant held up a magazine. 'Here is this week's edition of *The North London Press*. On page four, renowned journalist August Hammersworth reveals that Edgar Withers, the scourge of the common man, is in fact a sodomite!'

The audience shouted in anger.

'I am not surprised to learn of Edgar's secret life. I suspected it myself. Before last month's debate, when Edgar and I were backstage, I asked him a simple question. "Do you like brandy?" He said no.' Grant shrugged. 'Okay. It's an acquired taste. So I asked him if he preferred cigars. He denied that too. Again, strange but not unusual. The great Lord Byron once wrote, "Gentlemen have only three vices: brandy, cigars, and women." Edgar has never mentioned a wife in any of his speeches, so I asked him, "Edgar, do you have relations with women?" And guess what? He didn't answer!'

The crowd booed.

'He doesn't like brandy! He doesn't like cigars! He doesn't like women! What does it make him if he hates all three?'

'*A SODOMITE!*' the audience screamed back.

'That's right!' Grant sipped from a glass of water. 'Like many of

you, I know August Hammersworth has a reputation of stretching facts. I admit, even I hesitated to believe his source. But I know for a fact Hammersworth wrote the truth. I can prove Edgar Withers visited a homosexual brothel last November.'

The crowd murmured uneasily.

Grant held up a book. 'You might recognise this. The bestselling novel, *The Sins of an Irishman in London*. If you go to the epilogue at the end of the addendum, you'll find a detailed encounter of the writer, an authentic male prostitute, having sexual relations with "a Tory who's running for political office next year," a man he describes as "fat" with scars "all over his face." Does that not sound familiar to you?'

'*YES*!'

'Who does it sound like?'

'*EDGAR*!'

'You're damn right it does!' Grant roared victoriously. 'My staff has scoured that chapter and studied every sentence, and we have found seventeen similarities between the Tory in this book and the wicked Edgar Withers. That proves that he is what he always was. A degenerate. A liar. And a man who does not deserve my seat!'

The crowd erupted in applause.

17 Old Gloucester Street, Hoborn, Two Hours Later...

Edgar Withers smashed a vase against the wall. 'Bastard!'

Simmons (Edgar's personal solicitor) casually flipped through *The Times*. 'I hope you plan on paying for that.'

'How dare he say that shit about me in Belgrave Square!'

Simmons folded the newspaper. 'Polls have switched. Grant has a double-digit lead now.'

Edgar kicked his desk angrily. He winced, nursing his toes. 'Damn!'

'Maybe it was a lucky guess.'

Edgar sat on his desk. 'Don't be naive, Simmons. Grant had me followed. I know it.'

'Then don't say anything. Denying allegations this big will only hurt your chances.'

Edgar huffed. 'There has to be something we can use to discredit him.'

'I've had two men on that since day one. Everything's coming back clean.'

Edgar rolled his eyes. 'A lifelong politician with no secrets. How's that even possible?'

Simmons chuckled. 'Lots of money. Friends in high places.'

Edgar scowled. 'He thinks he's so noble. If they only knew the truth.'

'Even if you could prove Grant's a two-faced phony, no one would believe you.'

Edgar looked up, suddenly struck with inspiration. 'No. But they'd believe him.'

'What do you mean?'

Edgar smiled impishly. 'I know what to do.'

Simmons snorted. 'You do.'

'Yeah.'

'Okay. Sure.'

'You ready?'

'Christ, Edgar, just say it.'

Edgar folded his hands. 'We'll sue him for libel.'

Simmons laughed. 'Libel? He's telling the truth.'

Edgar raised a finger. 'In a criminal libel case, the burden of proof is on the defendant. How can Grant prove I was at that brothel without confessing to surveillance?'

Simmons opened his mouth to retort. Froze. Widened his eyes. 'Bloody hell.'

Edgar cackled. 'I know! He'll never do it! It would cost him the election! I did it, Simmons! I sacked the bloody captain!'

'Possibly. Let's not get ahead of ourselves.' Simmons stopped to think. 'Hammersworth's source. Do you have any clue?'

Edgar paced back and forth. 'I'm not worried about that.'

'Why not? If he's in the campaign—'

'If he knew anything worth a damn he would've gone to *The Times*, not *The North London Press* and definitely not August Hammersworth. What else?'

Simmons scratched his head. 'What about Branson? We can't sue him.'

Edgar hummed. 'You got a point there.' He stopped pacing. 'Sue the publisher. He won't be able to prove anything, whoever he is, without revealing Jack's identity.'

'He wouldn't tell Grant? Edgar, if Jack testifies—'

'Jack wouldn't even sign his own book. Do you really think he'd put himself in danger to save his publisher?'

Simmons snorted. 'Can't say I know him very well.'

'Well, I do. He won't.'

Simmons nodded. 'Edgar, I can't believe I'm saying it, but you might've found a way out of this.'

'Get the courthouse and...' Edgar checked his watch. 'Damn. Okay, go tomorrow and file the charges. In the meantime, send a statement to *The Times*. We need to make this as public as we can. Light a fire under his arse!'

Scotland Yard, The Next Morning...

Superintendent Morty Blasmyth knocked on the door. 'You wanted to see me, Commissioner?'

Commissioner James Monro, a cross old man sitting at a massive oak desk, looked up from a memo. 'Sit down, Morty.'

Morty removed his hat, closing the door behind him. 'Something the matter, sir?'

Monro handed Morty the memo. 'It's from *The Times*. Edgar Withers is suing Geoffrey Grant and Charlie Smith for criminal libel. It'll be in tomorrow's paper.'

Morty's stomach dropped. He forced a naive look as he sat down. 'I'm sorry, Charlie...?'

'Smith, the publisher.'

Morty nodded absentmindedly. Looked down at the memo.

Monro tilted his head. 'Are you okay, Superintendent?'

'Yes sir, I was just...' Morty cleared his throat and handed the memo back. 'Thinking of someone.'

'Think later.' Monro tossed the memo aside and folded his hands. 'Grant told his supporters last night that Withers visited a sodomite

brothel on Montgomery Street last November. Now, why would he say that?'

Morty hesitated. 'There aren't any brothels on Montgomery Street, sir. Not even a normal one.'

The Commissioner squinted. 'Is that really how you want to play this, Morty?'

Morty inhaled sharply.

Monro raised his brows knowingly. 'I got curious, so I had my secretary look through your archives.' He dropped a large stack of papers on his desk. THUD!

Morty's heart raced. 'Sir...'

Monro frowned. 'One hundred and fifty, Superintendent. One hundred and fifty. How the bloody hell does that happen?! Sodomy. Prostitution. *Both*. For two years? And all at the same house? I'm not irrational. I can see one or two, maybe even ten. Carelessness. Laziness. Sure, it adds up. But one hundred and fifty?' He shook his head. 'You better have a damn good explanation for this, Morty.'

Morty forced a chuckle. 'Sir, I don't know what you're implying—'

'Why did you ignore them, Superintendent? Answer the bloody question.'

Morty's heart raced. He looked at the memo. Skimmed.

Charlie Smith

Publisher

Libel

A smile grew below Morty's moustache. 'Yes. I have been meaning to tell you, sir—'

'Tell me what?'

Morty feigned shame. 'You see, well... I've been building a case for two years, so for the sake of confidentiality I kept it within my department.' He nodded. 'You're right. There was a sodomite brothel at 19 Montgomery Street.'

Monro blinked. 'Was? What do you mean?'

'I think it's abandoned, sir. I had all intentions of raiding it, but obviously—'

'You should've told me when you first learnt of its existence.'

'I'm sorry, sir, I wanted to.' Morty sighed. 'I was advised not to bother you with it until I was ready to raid.'

'Who would tell you such a silly thing?'

'I know he was below me in rank, sir, but he had more experience, so I assumed you'd be—'

'Just say it.'

'Vic Wainwright.'

The Commissioner's face hardened. He absentmindedly rubbed his cheek. 'Figures. That freak had no respect for authority.'

Morty nodded.

Monro chuckled. 'Did I ever tell you how that oaf lost his nightstick?'

Morty inhaled sharply. 'Many times, sir.'

Monro furrowed his brow. 'Oh.' He looked off, tapping his fingers. 'Did...? Did you say you *think* it's abandoned?'

Morty's face went numb. 'Oh, uh... You're right. I-I never confirmed it sir. But I am pretty certain.'

Monro rubbed the bridge of his nose. 'Even still... We shouldn't

take any chances. Can you raid it by day's end?'

Morty froze. 'What.'

'Can you, or can't you?'

Morty licked his lips. 'Um... Yes, sir.'

Monro nodded. 'Gut the place. Gather as much as you can. I'm sending everything to *The Times*. If we're quick about it, it'll be in tomorrow's paper.'

'Everything, sir?'

'Jack the Ripper made a mockery of us with those damned letters of his. If Withers really is a sodomite, we can't afford to look complacent. The press would kill us.' Monro placed a hand on the stack of reports. 'I'm sending these over as well.'

'But sir,' Morty objected. 'You can't send all of them. They haven't been properly vetted.'

'So?'

'What if there are false accusations in there?'

'Truth isn't our field, Superintendent. If we don't get ahead of this, *The Times* might accuse us of taking bribes, and we can't have that.'

Morty frowned. 'No, sir.'

'Good,' Commissioner Monro mumbled. 'Dismissed.'

Morty slowly stood, donned his cap, and scurried out of the office. Commissioner Monro watched him leave, a moment of doubt fluttering across his brain. He looked down at the memo, his eyes swelling with shame.

'Wainwright, you piece of shit,' Monro whispered. 'Why can't I be rid of you?'

19 Montgomery Street, Marylebone, Ten Minutes Later...

Jack yawned as he slid out of bed. He stumbled to his desk with an airy smile. Grabbed a piece of paper. Wrote the date on the top left corner. Dipped his pen for more ink.

Stopped.

Closed his eyes, snorting harshly. 'Goddamnit.' Jack bowed his head, an irate scowl on his face. He smacked himself in the head. Again. Again. Ripped up the paper, wet ink running down his fingers.

'DAMNIT!' Jack screamed, memories flooding back. Trembling, he wiped his ink-stained hands on a towel, collapsed on the bed, and cried himself back to sleep.

34 Cherry Street, Camden Town, Thirty Minutes Later...

Mr Munce scribbled onto a piece of paper and handed it to Morty. 'How's that?'

Morty silently read the telegram draft:

> Enjolras
>
> Times told Monro about EW. Files audited. Forced to confirm its existence but nothing else. Repeat: he knows nothing. We're raiding a clean house in twelve hours. Good luck.
>
> Williams
>
> P.S. Make sure J understands.

Morty handed back the paper. 'On second thought, change it back to eight hours. Don't want Monro to get suspicious.'

Mr Munce nodded and edited the message. 'Don't you worry, Superintendent. I'll make sure Charlie has this in his hand.'

'I'm sorry for putting you in this position, Mr Munce.'

'It's what he pays me for.'

'Very well.' Morty swallowed. 'When will he get it?'

'Within the hour.'

'Will they have enough time to get out?'

'They'll be fine. It's just down the street, you know?'

Morty sighed. 'Get me a coffee, will ya?'

Mr Munce grabbed a mug from under the counter. 'Can I ask you something personal, Superintendent?'

'Morty. And of course you can.'

Mr Munce poured a cup of coffee and handed it over. 'Two questions, actually. Sugar?'

Morty chuckled. 'No, thank you.'

Mr Munce grabbed his own cup. 'When the Commissioner found out about the brothel, why did you change your mind? I thought turning them in was part of the deal.'

'It was.' Morty took a sip and winced. 'YOW! Bloody hell!'

Mr Munce blinked. 'What? Too hot?'

'Burnt my bloody mouth.'

'Oh, I do apologise,' Mr Munce said with a chuckle. 'I can't seem to taste it anymore unless it's boiling. Must've built up a tolerance.'

'Why were you drinking boiling water in the first place?'

'Mixes the gin better.'

'What?'

'Nothing. You were saying?'

Morty rolled his tongue across his gums. 'I knew it was only a matter of time before they found out and that I'd have to come clean. But now that it's actually happened...' He shrugged helplessly. 'I don't want it to go.'

Mr Munce smirked. 'Jack has that effect on people.'

Morty nodded. 'That he does.'

Mr Munce laughed. 'I mean, I can't believe he actually roped me into a sodomite prostitution scheme *twice*!'

Morty blew on his coffee. 'Considering you carried over the clients, isn't this just a continuation of the first one?'

Mr Munce flashed a snide smirk. 'Drink your coffee.'

'Wish I could.'

Mr Munce scoffed. 'Now, I don't understand the way you people—'

Morty raised his brows.

Mr Munce pursed his lips. 'How *people like you* work. And I don't wanna know, personally. But I do want to know, if it's not impertinent of me, Superintendent—'

'Oh no, don't stop now.'

'Why that place?' Mr Munce shrugged. 'What's the deal? Why everyone's so drawn to it? Is it the sex?'

Morty cautiously took a sip. 'It's not just physical.'

'Oh?'

Morty sighed wistfully. 'It's the warmth.'

Mr Munce nodded broadly.

Morty smirked. 'You have no idea what I'm talking about, do you?'

'Not a clue.' Mr Munce laughed.

Morty sipped some more coffee, his expression more serious. 'How is Jack?'

Mr Munce dropped his smile. 'Oliver told you?'

Morty nodded mournfully.

Mr Munce frowned. 'He's hasn't been the same, and can you blame him? Breaks my heart to see him like that. There ain't much that can do that, I've seen a lot. That kid does not deserve this. He'll think he does.' Munce shook his head. 'And there's nothing I can bloody do about it.'

'He must've known they wouldn't let him back.'

'Even still,' Mr Munce whispered. 'Jack held on for so long.'

Morty sighed. 'Now it's like they never existed.'

Mr Munce's upper lip coiled in disgust. 'Old bastard! How could he do that to him? How can any man treat their son like...?' His eyes unfocused, a great wave of shame passing through him. 'Like that. It's not right.'

Morty recognised Mr Munce's melancholy. Forced a smile. 'Jack speaks very highly of you, Mr Munce.'

Mr Munce snapped back to the present. 'We go way back,' he said with a smirk. 'I taught him everything he knows.'

Morty tried not to laugh.

'About the post office, you sewer-minded—!' Munce snorted. 'Oh, if you weren't a Superintendent, I swear I'd—!'

Morty held up a calm hand. 'You're a good man, Mr Munce. I've seen a lot of people in my line of work, and you have more decency than you get credit for.'

Mr Munce blinked. 'You mean that?'

'Jack does too.'

Mr Munce licked his lips. 'He...' He paused. 'Jack said that, he really did?'

Morty nodded.

Mr Munce gasped softly. 'Wow, I...' His lips fluttered into a smile. 'How bout that.'

Morty finally finished his coffee. 'He's lucky. I wish I had a grandfather like you when I was his age.'

Mr Munce snorted. '*Grandfather*?!' He crossed his arms. 'How old are you anyway?'

'Fifty-six.'

Mr Munce's eyes bugged.

Morty furrowed his brow. 'Why? How old are you?'

'Fifty-four.'

Morty cringed at Mr Munce's thinning hair and wrinkles. Mr Munce gaped at Morty's muscles and tight skin.

Morty thumbed behind him. 'I think I should—'

'Yeah,' Mr Munce said with a nod. 'And I'll make sure Charlie gets the—'

'Good. And thanks for the—'

'Of course. Anytime. Anytime.'

They stared awkwardly. Walked away from each other.

31 Newman Street, Marylebone, Thirty Minutes Later...

'Can Edgar do this?' Charlie yelled. 'It's absolutely absurd!'

Lemmy (Charlie's personal solicitor) folded the memo from

Simmons's office. 'Since Grant used the book to support his accusations, it's considered evidence for libel, which means you're gonna have to prove—'

'I don't care. I'm not getting Jack involved.'

'It's more than just the book, Charlie. He was there! With Edgar!'

'Do you have any clue what you're asking?' Charlie grimaced. 'That man put his heart and soul into that book. He made the brothel what it is today. His mother just died!'

'Cut the melodrama,' Lemmy mumbled.

'But most of all, he trusts me.' Charlie shook his head. 'If you had any idea how valuable that is—'

'Then you must settle,' Lemmy insisted. 'You won't win without his testimony.'

'It would be a very poor return after everything he's done for us. There has to be another way.'

'Good luck finding one.'

'I've never met Grant in my life! Can't I just prove we're not in cahoots?'

Lemmy sighed uneasily. 'How are you gonna prove you don't own *The North London Press*?'

Charlie covered his face with one hand, leaning back in his chair. 'I can't believe this.'

Lemmy chuckled. 'I know! The fact that he used both—'

'THAT BASTARD!' Charlie screamed, his face beet red.

Lemmy blinked. 'Who? Edgar?'

'Both of them! BLOODY POLITICIANS!'

Charlie's secretary opened the door, an envelope in his hand. 'Charlie?'

'Not now, I'm in a meeting.'

'Mr Munce dropped off a telegram. He said it was urgent.'

Charlie snatched the envelope. Ripped it open. 'Dammit, Morty turned.' He softened as he read, sighing with relief. 'Oh, thank God!'

'What?' Lemmy asked.

'Morty didn't turn. But he's raiding the brothel in eight hours. We need to evacuate everyone.'

'He didn't tell Monro?'

'He's keeping the deal alive. He's doing it for Jack.'

Lemmy shook his head. 'He can't wait out a scandal this big.'

'He can if we beat Edgar.'

'And that's a big if!'

'It's still worth a shot. As long as no one finds out I own the brothel, we still have a chance.' Charlie pointed at his secretary. 'Shut down the factory indefinitely,' he ordered. 'Get some mattresses down there. Is Mr Munce still in the lobby?'

'Yes, Charlie,' the Secretary replied.

'Tell him to wait. I need him to run a telegram to Mum's house.'

Lemmy stood grimly. 'Charlie. If you want to fight Edgar on this, I'll support you as much as I can, but I'm afraid I must be blunt.'

'Why start now?'

'If you lose, the damages alone will ruin you. And as for your reputation...' Lemmy chuckled. 'Even bookshops don't hire convicted slanderers.'

Charlie hesitated, his tenacity wavering. 'Then we won't lose.'

19 Montgomery Street, Marylebone, One Hour Later...

Jack wandered downstairs, in a trance. Denny waddled after him. 'Jack, wait up!'

Jack stopped mid-step, huffing with annoyance.

'What's wrong?' Denny asked, inching down the stairs.

'I almost wrote to her again,' Jack whispered.

'I'm not surprised. It's only been a week.'

'Can you hurry up?!' Jack snapped.

Denny frowned. 'Jack, I know I can only speak from my own experience—'

'If you start another lecture, I'm leaving without you.'

'In times like this, it helps to have someone to talk to—'

'I don't wanna talk about it!' Jack cried. 'I wanna move on!'

Denny halted, visibly hurt. Jack grunted and stormed down the stairs.

'There's no shame in it!' Denny called after him. 'I lost a mum too, you know!'

'I lost her a long time ago,' Jack mumbled to himself. He grabbed a cup of coffee from the kitchen and sat in the dining room with François and Mary.

'How's business?' Jack asked.

François and Mary glanced at each other knowingly.

'Good,' Mary answered. 'Bit of a lull.'

'There's no lull,' François retorted.

'There has been since Jack took off.'

'He's not that integral!'

'They're his clients!'

Jack crunched into a piece of toast. 'We'll find out tonight.'

François's face went blank. 'What?'

'You don't have to come back yet,' Mary insisted. 'I'm sure there isn't a lull. Really, you can always—'

'Yes, Mary,' Jack insisted. 'I'm coming back.'

Mary sighed, picking at his eggs.

François swallowed. 'Jack?'

'What, François?!' Jack snapped. 'What now?!'

François hesitated. 'Do you want me to make you some eggs?'

Jack softened. 'Thank you, François,' he whispered. 'I'd love some.'

Oliver raced in, a telegram in his hand. 'François! Jack! Mary! Pack your things! We're leaving in an hour!'

Mary shot up. 'What?! Why?!'

Oliver handed Jack the telegram. 'Burn it when you're done.' He dashed out of the room.

François, Mary, and Jack huddled to read the telegram:

MARIUS

> CLOSE DOWN NOW -(STOP)- RAID AT FOUR -(STOP)- GET TO FACTORY BEFORE TWO -(STOP)- LEAVE NOTHING -(STOP)- WILL EXPLAIN ALL -(STOP)- WILLIAMS DID NOT TURN -(STOP)- IMMUNITY INTACT - (STOP)-
>
> ENJOLRAS

'So that's what they look like,' Jack whispered.

'I better go pack.' François downed his coffee and raced upstairs. 'I'll tell Andy and Denny.'

'I'll get Louise,' Mary said, dashing out.

Jack tossed the telegram into the fireplace and ran up to his room. He emptied out his drawers, stuffing his clothes, his cigar box, Oliver's fake telegram, his books, and his diaries into his suitcase until it stretched in every direction.

Everyone was packed and ready to go by quarter two. François breezed through the rooms to make sure everything was gone. After a final headcount, Oliver locked the door and led the parade down Montgomery Street toward Charlie's office.

A half-mile down, Jack turned for one last look. Despite the sun shining with unseasonable brilliance, the house was a cold shell, devoid of life.

A chill ran through Jack's body. It was really happening. That scared him more than anything.

31 Newman Street, Marylebone, Fifteen Minutes Later...

The ground floor of Charlie's office building was a large factory with five printing presses, each the size of a carriage. Oliver ushered the others into the vendor's entrance, where Charlie was waiting for them.

'My secretary brought down some mattresses,' Charlie told the caravan, parading them between the presses like Moses. 'The kitchen's upstairs, bathroom's in corner.'

'How long will we be here?' Andy asked.

'A fortnight at most. Morty's men won't find anything, but they'll be thorough.'

'What's the hell's going on, Charlie?' Oliver murmured.

Charlie handed him Simmons's memo. 'I suppose that's a start.'

For the next twenty-five minutes, standing before the others in a field of mattresses, Charlie summarised everything that had happened. August Hammersworth's article. Geoffrey Grant's speech in Belgrave Square. Edgar's libel suit. What Morty told Commissioner Monro. Both telegrams.

'What happens now?' Denny asked.

Charlie took a deep breath. 'Tomorrow morning, *The Times* will formally announce the brothel's existence. Morty's files were audited, which means the article will most likely include a list of our suspected clients. This won't stop until the raid is over, and I'm warning you now: the next two weeks will not be easy. Given the prestige of the accused, this will be a bigger scandal than Collins ever was, and that's saying something.'

Jack closed his eyes. Oliver placed a hand on his shoulder. Jack shrugged it off.

'There is still hope, however,' Charlie insisted. 'Morty had every right to end the immunity and turn me in for prostitution and bribery, but he didn't. Edgar's lawsuit started this whole thing, and Morty knew we'd be able to continue our arrangement once the Montgomery Street Scandal is old news.'

'Question!' Louise raised his hand. 'Isn't it a bad thing that the Commissioner knows about us?'

'Because we evacuated in time, Scotland Yard will have no choice but to believe the brothel once existed, but not anymore. That means they won't be looking for us after Edgar's trial—'

'Question!'

Charlie chuckled. 'Yes, Louise?'

'Who's to say that the scandal will end after Edgar's trial? Won't it make us more notorious?'

'Well, the papers will care more about the election than the brothel itself, so—'

'Question!'

Charlie groaned. 'What?'

'Won't Edgar's barrister ask you about the brothel?'

'No one knows I own the brothel. If he asks anything, it'll be regarding Jack's book—'

'I wanna ask a question now!' Mary called.

'This isn't a hearing!' Louise snapped.

Mary gaped. 'But—! You got—! I don't—!' His face turned red. 'UGH!'

Louise grinned devilishly.

'What is it, Mary?' Charlie asked.

Mary took a deep breath. 'So let me get this straight. Edgar accused you and Grant of lying about him sleeping with Jack, but not only did he actually sleep with Jack, he's lying about not sleeping with Jack, but you have to prove you didn't conspire with Grant to lie about Edgar sleeping with Jack, not because you own the brothel, but because you own *The North London Press* and published Jack's book, both of which Grant used to hurt Edgar and win the election, but Grant didn't know you were attached to both when he did that, but Edgar did, which is why he sued you and Grant at the same time, but Edgar does know he slept with Jack, and that you're not lying about him sleeping with Jack, and that you have to prove that you

weren't lying about the truth, which is that he slept with Jack, but Edgar thinks that's something you can't prove, being just the guy who published Jack's book, but he doesn't know that you actually can prove he slept with Jack because you also own the brothel, which is something no one knows about.' Mary paused. 'Except Morty.'

Silence. Brain-dead expressions all around.

Louise scowled at Mary.

Mary smirked back. 'Read a book, bitch.'

Charlie furrowed his brow. '*What* was your question, Mary?'

Mary cleared his throat. 'Since no one knows you own the brothel, and since the papers only care about how the trial will affect the election, does that mean we'll be safe regardless of the verdict?'

Charlie blinked. 'That's... actually a really good question.'

Mary stuck his tongue at Louise.

Charlie swallowed nervously. 'If we lose, two things happen. First, I'll have a liar's reputation, which will significantly damage my business. And second, in order for me to pay the damages...' He hesitated. 'I'd have to sell the house.'

Jack gasped.

Oliver covered his mouth.

Andy looked at François. François gaped back.

Denny lowered himself to the floor.

Louise closed his eyes.

Mary blinked, a stupid grin on his face. 'Oh.'

'I say again,' Charlie insisted. 'We still have a chance. If we win, the press will tear Edgar apart, as a liar, as a sodomite, and he will

certainly lose the election, which means Grant will owe us big time.'

Jack scratched his nose. 'How are we going to win?'

Charlie looked at Jack, agape.

Jack furrowed his brow.

Charlie scanned the desperate faces of the others. Forced a smile. 'Grant's barrister will represent the both of us, so... I'll keep everyone updated.' He checked his pocket watch. 'I'll be in my office in you need me.' He nodded politely. Shuffled away.

Jack's eyes followed Charlie as he climbed the staircase.

Louise sidled over. 'Now there's a man shaken to the core.'

'This is gonna get worse,' Jack whispered ominously.

Louise paused, taken aback. 'How do you know?'

'Just a hunch.'

'You've never been good at those.'

Jack sighed. 'I know when I've had one before.'

Mary plopped onto a mattress. 'I won't be able to sleep on these things.'

'It could be worse,' Denny said.

Mary huffed. 'I thought you're supposed to be the pirate, not the parrot.'

'What does that make you?' Louise mumbled. 'The plank?'

'Hush up, you scurvy—!'

'He's the poop deck!' Andy quipped.

Louise and Denny cackled. Mary sobbed hysterically. 'No! Not you too!'

François spanked Andy proudly. 'I'll make us lunch.'

'Thank you, François,' Oliver said, unpacking his bag.

Andy whipped out a deck of cards. 'Poker, anyone?'

Mary stopped crying instantly. 'Sure, I love games!'

Denny scooted over. 'I'll play if Mary's playing.'

'Wouldn't be so eager if I were you,' Louise warned. 'Mary's a card sharp. He played his way out of a German prison.'

Denny rolled his eyes. 'We'll see about that.'

Oliver sat next to Jack. 'You wanna play?'

'Not right now, thanks,' Jack whispered.

Oliver petted his head. 'We'll be back to normal soon.'

'This wouldn't be happening if I didn't write that book.'

'You didn't know this would happen.'

'The world wasn't ready for it. We're gonna lose the brothel because of me.'

Oliver smiled weakly. 'Promise me you won't give up hope.'

Jack glared back. 'When I woke up today, I was happier than I've been in a long time. Since then, I stopped myself from writing a letter to my dead mother, who'd just burn it anyway, acted like a bloody jerk to the only friends I got left, and I had to pack everything I ever owned so I could go hide in a factory for the next two weeks because of a scandal I created. And I didn't even have time to eat my goddamn breakfast! So how the hell do you expect me to promise anything?'

Oliver frowned.

Jack huffed. 'Okay. How about this?' He scratched his cheek. 'I promise not to lose hope if you promise not to believe a word I say when I'm like this.'

Oliver shrugged. 'Deal.'

Jack and Oliver stared at each other for five long seconds before simultaneously bursting into laughter.

The Next Morning...

The Times broke the dyke:

MONTGOMERY STREET BROTHEL EXPOSED

The article named over a hundred Lords as alleged regulars. Jack knew dozens of them from the beginning, but a great many names were unrecognisable.

'They're false tips,' François realised over breakfast. 'Jealous mistresses or business rivals tried to get them in trouble with the police.'

'That doesn't make sense,' Mary said. 'Why would *The Times* print their names if they didn't do it?'

'That's what they did to me,' Jack said.

'But you did do it.'

'They didn't know that. I was never charged with anything.'

Mary frowned. 'That's not fair.'

Jack smirked. 'First sodomy scandal?'

Two Weeks Later...

The Montgomery Street Scandal was a nightmare for England but a bacchanal for the tabloids. Doubling down on the first sensation to match Jack the Ripper's profitability, *The Times* released new developments every day. Describing the brothel's rooms. Speculat-

ing what happened in them. Even the American newspapers got wind of it; *The Washington Post* suggested Prince Albert Victor was a regular patron, wondering why his name was conspicuously absent from *The Times. The North London* Press, in their typically radical fashion, outright accused the British government of covering-up evidence that protected aristocratic sodomites.

At half eight in the morning, Charlie came downstairs with a telegram from Morty. The raid had finally ended, the brothel officially 'abandoned.' Thanks to Lemmy's careful planning, the Metropolitan Police could not find any records of Charlie or his mother owning the property.

The return journey started at noon. Oliver escorted two at a time to avoid suspicion. Jack, in no hurry to return, volunteered to take the last trip.

Oliver, Jack, and Denny were about to leave when Charlie came downstairs with an uneasy expression. 'Jack, can you stay behind? I need to speak with you in my office.'

'Sure,' Jack responded. 'Just a second.'

'We can wait,' Oliver suggested.

'No, you go ahead.' Jack kissed Oliver goodbye and followed Charlie upstairs.

Charlie avoided looking at Jack as they approached the office. 'What's wrong?' Jack asked.

Charlie silently held the door open. Jack walked in. Froze.

Geoffrey Grant stood from Charlie's desk, wearing a spotless three-piece suit and a delightful smile. 'Jack Branson!' He marvelled, holding out his hand. 'Glad you could finally join us.'

Charlie rolled his eyes.

Jack looked at Charlie. Back to Grant. 'Who are you?'

Grant looked down at his hand, hovering in mid-air.

Jack crossed his arms.

Grant chuckled awkwardly. 'Aren't you going to introduce me, Charlie?'

'Introduce yourself,' Charlie mumbled.

Grant flashed a cold smile. Dropped his hand. 'Mr Branson, my name is Geoffrey Grant. I believe you are familiar with my *good friend* Edgar Withers.'

Jack scowled at Charlie. 'You told him?!'

Charlie opened his mouth.

'Give me some credit, surely!' Grant interrupted. 'I guessed and got it right.'

Jack glared at Charlie. 'You didn't have to confirm it.'

Charlie pointed to a chair. 'Take a seat, Jack. Please.'

Jack stared at Grant as he sat down. 'What is this? A threat?'

Grant laughed heartily. 'What kind of man do you think I am?'

'A politician.'

Grant shook his head. 'Charlie said you were feisty.'

'I also said it was my desk,' Charlie grumbled.

Grant flashed a fake smile and hopped onto a different chair. Charlie sat down with a groan.

'Jack,' Grant started. 'We have a favour to ask.'

'I didn't want you to get involved, Jack!' Charlie blurted. 'He made me!'

Grant spun around. 'We talked about this.'

'He said he was going to—!'

'Quit being a child!' Grant snapped.

'He needs to know this wasn't my idea!'

'It is now!' Grant turned back to Jack, resuming his phony smile. 'I'm sure you know Edgar's suing your friend. And me, as it happens.'

Jack hesitated. 'I am aware.'

'Now, I don't know about you,' Grant muttered, flashing Charlie a stern look, 'but *I'm* certainly facing the reality of the situation.'

'Which is?'

Grant folded his hands. 'Edgar Withers might be a weak, spineless piece of filth—!' He swallowed spitefully. 'But he knew what he was doing.'

Jack inhaled sharply, a grimace forming.

Grant drew his brows together. 'I wasn't expecting you to be this young. It's throwing me off.'

'You want me to testify against Edgar, don't you?'

Charlie closed his eyes.

Grant held up a cautious hand. 'Jack, hear us out.'

'No!' Jack cried. 'I won't do it!'

'Jack,' Charlie whispered. 'Believe me, there is no other way.'

'I don't care! Find another way!'

'It's a libel suit, Jack,' Grant explained. 'Telling the truth is the only chance we have to win.'

'There has to be others ways you can prove Edgar's a homosexual without getting me involved.'

'Not in England! Juries full of fools, corrupt judges...' Grant

laughed. 'The fact that *we* have the burden of proof is just ridi—!'

'Jack,' Charlie pleaded. 'We can't save the brothel if you don't testify. That's a fact, and you have to accept that.

Jack shook his head. 'How could you do this to me?'

'Jack—'

'Let me speak!'

Charlie nodded apologetically.

Jack cleared his throat. 'I was only suspect with Collins and I lost everything. Now you want me to take the stand and just *confess* to being homosexual?! Why would I ever do that?'

Charlie sighed desperately. 'It's the brothel, Jack.'

Jack scoffed. 'Do you really think I'm stupid? If I testify and you win, the press won't just go after Withers. They'll go after me. I might even go to jail. So don't you dare put this on me, Charlie. It's my choice, and I will not compromise my safety.'

'I'm on your side, Jack,' Charlie insisted. 'I am the only one on your side!'

Grant raised a hand. 'Will you let me—?'

'SHUT UP!'

Grant looked away, huffing.

'It's still your choice, Jack,' Charlie whispered. 'It always has been. But I need you to remember the big picture, and that's keeping the cause alive. I won't mince words with you. It is not looking good. We only have a chance of winning with you, but we will lose without you. I know it's a lot to ask. There might be repercussions, but it's nothing you can't handle. I promise you, Jack, I would do anything to keep you out of prison.'

Jack raised his brows. 'Anything?'

'Anything.'

'Would you confess to owning the brothel?'

Charlie sighed. 'Be reasonable, Jack.'

'No, Charlie, tell me. If it came down to you going to jail to save me, would you do it?'

Charlie hesitated.

Jack frowned. 'That's what I thought.'

'I have to pay for everything!' Charlie cried. 'How am I supposed to do that in prison?'

Jack shook his head.

Charlie looked down in shame.

Grant clapped his hands. 'May I speak now?'

'What about you?!' Jack snapped. 'Why do you care what happens to me?'

Grant grinned. 'I've been your MP for thirty years.'

'You don't care about our cause. You just want to win the election.'

'I care about all Londoners.'

'I'm not a Londoner and you know it.'

Grant smiled politely. 'You're no fool, Jack Branson.' He nodded eagerly. 'You're right. I am thinking about my campaign. But Edgar Withers is a bully, and I don't want a brilliant establishment like yours to founder because of a slimy Tory runt.'

Jack squinted. 'You knew about me and Edgar when you mentioned my book, didn't you?'

Charlie sat up, brow furrowed.

Grant laughed. 'Don't be ridiculous. It was a lucky guess!'

'And the article in *The North London Press*, the one August Hammersworth just so happened to print that morning?' Jack pointed at Grant. 'You were the source.'

Grant grimaced. 'I was not!'

'DON'T LIE TO ME!' Jack snarled.

Grant looked at Charlie. Charlie glared back.

Grant's sophisticated charm deflated in real time. 'Fine,' he spat. 'No more games.' He folded his hands and sighed. 'Augie's one of mine.'

Charlie shot up. 'You son of bitch! Why didn't you tell me?!'

'One of your what?' Jack asked.

'He's my professional blackmailer,' Grant explained. 'He's had a file on you ever since Collins. He's quite exceptional. I've been using him for thirty-five years.'

'So ALL this?!' Charlie cried, waving his hands in big circles. 'The lawsuit. The raid. The whole scandal started because of YOU?!'

'I AM NOT YOUR ENEMY!' Grant roared. 'Nor am I yours, Jack! I told Augie to put the article in *The North London Press* because I knew Edgar read it, NOT because I wanted any of this to happen! The only people who read *The North London Press* are radical liberals and secret homosexuals! Everyone knows that! If anyone told me Charlie Smith OWNED the bloody rag, I never would've used your book in the first place!'

Grant angrily adjusted his tie. 'Edgar started it! He's your enemy, making everything public. A real man would've ignored it, or better yet played the game, but NO! He got scared and played dirty!' Grant

gagged. 'Criminal libel. What I did wasn't a crime, it's POLITICS!'

'You made a bad bet and Edgar called your bluff.' Jack shrugged. 'Maybe you deserve to lose your honour.'

Grant stuck out an accusing finger. 'Don't you get virtuous with me, Branson! I've read your book. You know what this world is like, just as well as I do. Sure, I'm a scoundrel. And if we lived in a fair world, I would not be victorious in this. But we don't, do we Jack? We tell others to be honest and charitable, yet we reward cheaters and blackmailers. You of all people know this. The same men who call you evil and perverted, the ones who say you'll go to Hell for being what you are, they pay you in secret! If there is a right and wrong, we do not know the difference.'

Jack softened.

Grant crossed his arms. 'What about your honour, Jack? Edgar paid you to sleep with him, but when the truth comes out, he denies ever knowing you. And those people, those *good Christians* who hate you, and hunt you, and imprison you, and lynch you, and make the rules that rob you of a normal life, they will reward him for LYING! How is that fair? Why should he win because he got caught? Why should your brothel be destroyed because of him? You wrote that book for a reason, didn't you? You're done being afraid. You hate being the victim. You want this world to change? Here's your chance! Edgar doesn't think you're brave enough to challenge him, so prove him wrong! Call him a liar! Take credit for your book! Defend who you are! Look out at the purest members of our society and tell them what they really are: bloody hypocrites!'

A silence filled the room.

Jack took a deep breath.

Grant waited anxiously.

Jack swallowed. 'I think you're mistaking me for someone else, Mr Grant.'

Grant gasped with genuine surprise. Jack stood and headed for the door.

Charlie stood. 'Jack. Don't.'

Jack looked back. Frowned with shame. Closed the door.

19 Montgomery Street, Marylebone, Thirty Minutes Later...

Jack's blood chilled when he saw the front door lying on the ground. Boot marks covering the floor. The windows broken, a cool breeze wafting throughout. Utensils and dishes confiscated from the Kitchen. No liquor at the bar. The air felt different. The house had been violated.

Jack climbed the stairs, dropped his suitcase on his bedroom floor, and collapsed on the bed.

Oliver wandered into Jack's room with a smile. 'I missed you, baby.' He kissed Jack. Sat beside him. 'What did Charlie want?'

Jack removed his paddy cap. 'I don't wanna talk about it.'

'What happened? Tell me.'

'Just leave me alone, okay?'

'Was it about the trial?'

Jack hesitated. 'Maybe.'

'What about?'

Jack stared into Oliver's green eyes and softened. 'They want me to testify against Edgar.'

Oliver furrowed his brow. 'Oh.'

Jack nodded. 'Yeah.'

Oliver looked away, stunned.

'Grant was there too,' Jack said with a grimace. 'Charlie told him. The bastard led me into a bloody ambush.'

'That doesn't sound like Charlie.'

'Does to me.' Jack looked at Oliver, squinting. 'You didn't know, did you?'

Oliver stared back, visibly offended. 'How could you ask me that?'

'Was that why you offered to wait for me?'

'If I knew, I would've told you.'

Jack hesitated. 'Would you?'

Oliver scowled. 'I would never lie to you! Don't you trust me?'

'I do, but—'

'But what?'

Jack took a deep breath. 'I know you tend to... *hold back* to keep me happy.'

Oliver blinked. 'Why...?' He licked his lips. 'Why-why would you say that?'

Jack hesitated. 'Am I wrong?'

'Yes,' Oliver lied.

Jack studied Oliver's face. He nodded. 'Okay. I'm sorry.'

Oliver's gaze lingered on Jack. He slowly looked away. Forced normalcy. 'What's Grant like?'

Jack snorted. 'A phony who's proud to be a phony. Charlie hates him.'

'What do you think?'

'The jury's still out, pardon the pun.' Jack paused. 'But he knows how the world works, I'll give him that.'

'I'm sure Charlie wouldn't have told him unless he had no choice. They must be pretty desperate.'

Jack stood. 'Not as desperate as they are now.'

'What do you mean?'

Jack crouched to the floor and opened his suitcase. 'What do you think? I said no.'

'To what?'

Jack froze.

Oliver lifted his brows.

Jack stood back up. 'Forget I said anything.'

'Aren't you gonna think about it?'

'No.'

'Why not?'

'Please, just... *don't*, okay? Not today.'

'Tell me! Why won't you do it?'

Jack closed his eyes. 'I knew it, I bloody *knew* you wouldn't understand.'

'Then I must be missing something. You would never let the brothel die. Not you, anyone but *you*!'

Jack rubbed his hat-hair. 'It's my choice, Oliver, so just... take my side, alright? Make me happy. That's what you're good at.'

Oliver chuckled. 'Oh, I get it now. You're giving up.'

'I don't want to confess to being homosexual! How is that giving up?!'

'You're letting Edgar win.'

Jack scrunched his face. 'Do you want me to go to prison? Is that it?'

Oliver gaped. 'How could you be thinking about yourself at a time like this?!'

'Because it's gonna happen!'

'You don't know that!'

'I'm the only one who seems to know that!'

'But what about the cause? This place? What it represents?'

'This place doesn't mean anything!'

Oliver's eyes widened. 'Doesn't mean anything?! You wrote a whole bloody book about it!'

'And look what happened!' Jack cried. 'The only reason I'm still here right now is because I didn't sign my name!'

Oliver shook his head. 'That's not—'

'No, let's just be honest, okay?! This place is nothing but a fantasy world. We're just hiding in a cave, telling each other stories about how great we are, how we made the world such a better place, but that's not true! It's the same cruel, vicious world it was two years ago. I wouldn't have written the damn thing if I knew that, if I didn't bloody believe it was safe out there. That makes it more dangerous in here!'

Oliver pointed an angry finger in Jack's face. 'Don't you dare justify what you're doing by saying *it doesn't work*! It has! You know it has!'

'Are you calling me a liar?!'

'Absolutely!'

'Well, you're wrong.' Jack chuckled bitterly. 'Wouldn't be the first time!'

Oliver swallowed hard. 'I know everything about you, Jack Branson. I know how you get. You say things you don't mean because it makes you feel better about yourself.'

Jack blew his lips. 'Guess you don't know me then.'

'You don't want to testify because you're too afraid of what's going to happen to you.'

'I'm being cautious! I thought that was your thing!'

'You're nothing but a bloody coward!'

Jack grimaced.

Oliver cackled. 'See?! I KNEW that would piss you off!'

Jack's lip trembled furiously.

Oliver shook his head slowly. 'You can't lie to me, baby. If you wanna finagle your way out of this one, you'll have to try a lot harder than that—'

'HOW?!' Jack roared. 'How can I possibly make you understand? It's happening again, baby! I'm losing everything AGAIN, and you'll NEVER know what that's like! You wasted your life reading books and sitting on your arse! Without this place, you have nothing!'

Oliver's heart skipped a beat. He looked down at the floor.

'NOTHING!' Jack screamed, tears in his eyes. 'You'd say anything to make me happy, to keep me here, because you can't be alone! You didn't know you were homosexual until Charlie *told you* you were! You doubt the cause every five minutes! You can't even remember your own name!'

Oliver closed his eyes.

Jack snorted. 'That hard enough for you?'

Oliver swallowed bitterly. 'I know you're trying to hurt me because you blame yourself for what happened in Dunderrow, but I don't care. I love you! I love every bloody part of you!'

Jack grimaced. 'Why can't you be on my side?'

'Because I know you can do it.'

'No, I can't!'

Oliver scrunched his face. 'Why don't you believe me?!'

'How do I know you're not lying?!'

'YOU BELIEVED DANNY!' Oliver cried. 'HOW COULD YOU BELIEVE HIM BUT NOT ME?!'

Jack gasped.

Oliver folded his legs, hugging them.

Jack scowled. 'Take that back, you son of a bitch.'

'NO! You deserve that!' Oliver frowned bitterly. Helplessly. 'What more could I have done, huh? Do you know how hard it was for me to see you cry that day? Do you have any idea how much I *hate myself* right now because of what you just said to me?! Hm?!' Oliver shook his head, his eyes watering. 'DO YOU EVEN CARE?!'

Jack swallowed, hurt.

'Just let me help you, baby!' Oliver whined, wiping his eyes. 'I know I'll never understand what it's like to be banished, or to get arrested in a raid, or to pretend to be normal to keep a job, but I know what it's like to lose a mother.'

'You didn't even know her!' Jack snapped. 'What were you, four?!'

Tears fell from Oliver's eyes. 'That was cruel.'

Jack's lip wanted to tremble. He hardened his face instead.

'Well...' he said with a shrug, 'You made me think I was worth something. That was cruel.'

Oliver glowered. 'Fine. You win. You don't want to save this place?' He shrugged. 'Get out.'

Jack hesitated. 'I will.'

Oliver chuckled. 'I'll believe it when I see it.'

'Don't you trust me?' Jack jeered.

Oliver smirked. 'You'll do what you always do. You'll calm down, you'll realise I'm right, you'll crawl back, and you'll beg for my forgiveness. So why don't you save yourself the trouble and start acting like a bloody adult for once in your goddamn life?'

Jack scowled. Reached into his suitcase. Pulled out Oliver's fake telegram. 'I don't want this anymore.' He threw the envelope at Oliver's face.

Oliver glared back, swallowing nervously.

Jack's lip trembled. He closed the suitcase and carried it out of the room, his footsteps fading down the hall.

Oliver picked up the telegram. Stared at it, his breath picking up. He wept mercilessly.

No one saw Jack leave the house. As he stormed down Montgomery Street, his muscles relaxed, his breath returned, and he suddenly understood the reality of what he was doing. His pace slowed to a stop.

Jack sat on the ground. Leaned against his suitcase. Wept. Face flushed. Snot dribbling into his hands. A breeze whipped by. Jack shivered. He could still see the house a half-mile behind him. The fight replayed itself in his mind. Everything felt raw at the time.

Emotional. Pure reaction. Second-hand, everything was stale. He couldn't remember what he had been reacting to. Just his cruel words. His senseless actions.

Jack stood with weak legs. He looked behind him, then back to the brothel. He knew once he made his choice, he'd have to follow it through to the end.

Jack took one step toward the brothel when he realised... he already made his choice.

With a heavy heart, Jack readjusted his grip on the suitcase and walked away from the Montgomery Street Brothel.

CHAPTER TWELVE

The Hydra and the Phoenix

Eaton Square Gardens, Belgravia, Eight Days Later...

Jack leaned back on the bench. Closed his eyes. Took a deep breath. Smiled. Savoured the sun on his face.

Lords and Ladies strolled past him, chattering peacefully to each other. Somewhere children laughed.

Jack's smile faded. He opened his eyes. Looked around. Sighed. 'Happy Birthday.'

Returned to his book. Kept reading.

95M Eaton Square, Belgravia, Six Days Later...

Jack opened his eyes. Beautifully crisp white ceiling. His new flat. He huffed. Rolled back to bed.

Two hours later. Jack woke again. Finally got up. Inched to the cooker. Filled a kettle with water. Put it on the cooker. Turned it on.

Jack sat by his window. The afternoon light shined brilliant. He sipped his Camomile. The sweetness made him gag. Forced himself to finish the cup. Sighed. Looked over at the 5lb bag of leaves, barely dug into. Cringed.

55 Elizabeth Street, Belgravia, Three Days Later...

Jack sat across from Mr Belling, the manager of the local tea shop. 'Mulhussey,' Mr Belling mumbled, reading Jack's application. 'Where is that? Ireland?'

'It is, sir,' Jack answered politely. 'Near Dublin, actually. I was First Footman for Lord Harrington, the Earl of Havredom. A very respectable household.'

Mr Belling nodded, impressed. 'May I see a reference?'

Jack forced a smile. 'I'm sorry. I must've misplaced it.'

Mr Belling nodded slowly. He handed back the application. 'We'll let you know.'

370 Commercial Road, Stepney Green, Late That Night...

Jack sipped his glass of whisky at the Rusty Spit, the third-seediest pub in the East End.

'You want another, boyo?' the bartender asked in a silly Irish accent.

'Not funny, Max,' Jack slurred.

'You need to loosen up, mate,' Max said in his native Cockney tongue. 'It's just a tea shop.'

'Yeah, that's what I'm upset about. The tea shop.'

Max snorted. 'Bloody Micks,' he muttered, lumbering away.

Jack closed his eyes. Slammed his head on the counter. 'Ow.'

'You really shouldn't be doing that.'

Jack rubbed his temple. Looked at the Pale Man sitting next to him. Shaved head. Pudgy body.

'You'll feel awful in the morning,' the Pale Man said, sipping a beer. 'Whisky's a bitch on its own.'

'I know I just hit my head,' Jack mumbled. 'And I'm drunk. But you look really familiar.'

The Pale Man smirked. 'Hit yourself again, Jack. Maybe you'll remember.'

Jack blinked. 'Did...?' He pointed. 'Did you just say my name?'

The Pale Man shrugged.

Jack squinted. 'Have we met before?'

'In a past life.' The Pale Man double-tapped his nose. Red burns around the nostrils.

Jack gasped. 'Wyatt?'

Wyatt rolled his eyes. 'What's left of him.'

'I thought they sent you to the workhouses.'

'Yeah, I'm still there. Thanks for reminding me.'

Jack looked down at Wyatt's trousers. 'Is it really gone?'

'Let's not talk about me.' Wyatt forced a smile.

Two Hours Later...

Wyatt and Jack sipped their fifth round.

'Does it get any easier?' Jack whispered. 'Not living the life?'

Wyatt shook his head slowly. 'The void doesn't go away. Find something else to obsess over. Opera. Art.'

'I did all that already. I saw all the museums, read books in libraries, cafés, tea rooms. I finally have money. A whole city at my fingertips. But none of it means anything.'

'What about that nice new flat of yours? Perfect for a hermit.'

'I can't waste my life in there. I need a job. Something to do.'

Wyatt thought for a moment. 'Actually, I was at a pub last week on Montgomery Street that needed a—'

'No. Can't go there.'

Wyatt chuckled. 'Not the whole city, then.'

'Can't work in a pub anyway. They don't hire Irishmen. Too political. Or we drink on the job.'

Wyatt smirked.

Jack shook his head. 'I hate this city. I just want to rebuild my life. Why won't it let me?'

'Because you can't. It's not possible.'

'No. It's not too late. Nothing's too late.'

Wyatt snorted. 'It's not some hobby you always wanted to try.'

'Why not? I always wanted to be a different person.'

'Rubbish.'

'I just need to know how to start over.'

'Rubbish!' Wyatt slurred. 'No one starts over. You can avoid Montgomery Street, and Dubeau Frères, and drink all the horrible tea you want, but that's not moving on. That's pretending the past didn't happen.'

'I can have another life. People change all the time.'

'People don't change, Jack. Enough time goes by and they stop trying to be what they're not and accept what they are.'

'But I don't want to be like this.'

'Doesn't matter. It's the hand you're dealt. That's not gonna change. Just like being homosexual ain't gonna change. You think I

can just move on and pretend Collins didn't happen? I'm reminded every time I piss.'

Jack sighed uneasily. 'I'm sorry.'

'The trial's three weeks away. You can still make up for what you did.'

Jack shook his head, eyes staring off. 'They needed me. I abandoned them. I shouldn't get to come back from that. I deserve to be punished. It should fit the crime, I say. My clients can come up to my new flat. I'll spend the rest of my life in bed. Naked. Door unlocked. One by one, they'll come in. Ravage me all they want. That'll be my fate. A mindless receptacle. Strangers abusing my body. Ripping me open. Mashing me to shreds. And I'd beg for more. Like an animal. No friends. No family. No purpose. Just a pathetic wretch who ruined his own life. Dying of tuberculosis in his forties. All alone...' Jack lowered his head, sobbing mercilessly.

Wyatt rolled his eyes. Checked his pocketwatch. 'On that cheery note...'

Jack wiped his eyes. 'I'm sorry, Wyatt. I just want it to stop.'

'Then stop fantasising like Dante Alighieri. You are being punished. You punished yourself. Running away was the worst thing you could've done.'

Jack frowned helplessly.

Wyatt pulled out his wallet. Paid both tabs. 'By the way...' he added, clapping Jack on the shoulder. 'Loved the book.'

12 Edward Avenue, Westminster, The Next Day...

Jack wandered into Barnum's Books with a splitting headache

three coffees couldn't fix. He stood before the new releases shelf. Dragged his finger down the line. Stopped.

The Sins of an Irishman in London
by Anonymous

Jack let out a gentle sigh. Caressed the spine with his finger, back and forth between the covers. After a brief hesitation, he pulled it out. Studied its face.

A young blond woman with glasses eagerly walked up. 'Have you read it yet?'

Jack removed his paddy cap, smiling politely. 'A long time ago. You?'

'Twice.' She tentatively held out her hand. 'I'm Claire.'

Jack shook it. 'Pleasure to meet you, I'm...' He paused. 'Jack.'

'Pleasure to meet you too.' Claire smiled flirtatiously. 'Jack.'

Jack looked around awkwardly. 'Do you, um... work in this shop?'

'My mum does. I just like being here.'

Jack bobbed his head. Looked down at the book. 'What an ugly name, Anonymous.'

'I know. Sounds like a Greek playwright.'

Jack laughed. 'Yeah. Yeah, it does.' He casually flipped through the pages. 'You liked it, huh?'

Claire nodded eagerly. 'I don't read many books twice, and that's saying something.'

Jack sighed. 'And do you like... him? As a person?'

'He's very charming. And quite funny.'

Jack smirked. 'So I keep hearing.' He licked his lips. 'Do you...'

He scratched his nose. 'Do think he and Oliver are still together?'

Claire thought for a moment. Shook her head. 'No.'

Jack frowned.

Claire shrugged. 'Pains me to say it, being a romantic and all. I just don't see it lasting.'

'Why not?'

Claire pointed to the book's by-line. 'That's why. He certainly didn't write like he was publishing anonymously. I think he backed out at the last minute. That's a sign of distrust.'

Jack struggled to suppress his discomfort. 'I dunno. Maybe he was being cautious.'

'That's rubbish. He didn't really believe what he was writing. Maybe he wanted to believe it, but that's not the same.'

Jack mussed his hat-hair. 'Maybe he did truly believe it, but he didn't want to put his name on it because, um, he opened himself up before. Or rather, he tried to be himself, but maybe he... Maybe by doing that, he let himself be vulnerable. And people he loved and trusted hurt him when he did that. And something always went wrong when he did that, so... So he wanted to not lose anything anymore.'

Claire blinked, puzzled. 'Why would he lose anything?'

Jack pursed his lips. 'I don't know, he... He doesn't know who or what every time. He doesn't see it coming, and... Maybe by putting his name on the book, people he knew could... No, people he *didn't* know could... They would know everything. And people who would read it and say, "Oh, he's the worst," or "Oh, he deserves to have bad things happen to him," and... Maybe he didn't want any of that

because his life was already unpredictable, or at least unstable, as it was. And taking the name off was the only thing he could do.'

Claire nodded slowly. 'So you think he believed what he said, but he didn't want to give the world the power to hurt him.'

Jack squinted. 'I think so.'

Claire mused. 'That's an interesting interpretation. Makes sense, considering what happened with Danny. Every time he opens up to someone, he gets hurt. That fear of the unknown keeps getting in the way.'

Jack huffed. 'So he is a coward.'

'On the contrary, I think he's very brave. He just confuses stubbornness for pride.'

Jack furrowed his brow. 'There's a difference?'

'It's a fine line. If you're stubborn, you want control over your life and who you are as a person. You don't want to change, not because you're right or wrong, but for the principle of not changing. You don't want to give the people who disagree with you the satisfaction.'

'And what's pride?'

'Pride's the same thing, but you wouldn't care what people think of you. In a way, it's a test of faith.'

Jack snorted. 'How can I not care what people think of me?'

Claire softened, suddenly understanding.

Jack's heart raced. 'I-I mean—'

'Because you love yourself more,' Claire whispered.

Jack nervously looked into Claire's eyes.

Claire smiled with recognition.

'Claire!' an older lady called from behind the counter.

Claire turned her head. 'Coming, Mum!' She looked at Jack, suddenly nervous. 'It was nice meeting you.'

Jack smirked. 'You've given me a lot to think about.'

Claire nodded. 'Good luck, Jack.' She waved politely and walked to the counter.

Jack took a deep breath. 'Jack Branson.'

Claire looked back. Smiled. 'I like it. It's better than nothing.' She waved again and followed her Mum.

Jack frowned. Replaced the book on the shelf.

14 Varden Street, Whitechapel, Two Hours Later...

Jack removed his cap and wandered into the flat. Gazed up at the mouldy ceiling. Contemplated. Looked over at the amber-crusted window.

'What a dump!' François cried, stepping through the door.

Jack whipped around. 'What are you doing here?'

François held up a sack. 'I was getting truffles down the street. Saw you walk in.' He cringed at the ceiling. 'This is where you live?'

'Used to.'

'Explains a lot.' François wiped dust off a chair and sat down.

'It was the best I could get. I hated it when I was here, but I was just walking by, and...' Jack smirked. 'I gave the Landlord a shilling just to see it again.'

François squirmed. 'Not surprised it's still vacant.'

'You see that hole?' Jack pointed at the floorboards. 'That's where I kept my cigar box. I used this table to write to Mother.'

'How long has it been? Since you left?'

'Collins.' Jack sat down. 'Feels like a million years ago.'

François frowned at Jack with unusually soft eyes. 'Please come back. We need you.'

Jack shook his head. 'I can't.'

'Don't you want to save the brothel?'

'It doesn't matter what I want.'

'Why not?'

'Because I don't get what I want.'

'What do you want?'

'To be different. Better. Someone who doesn't care what people think.'

François laughed. 'If you cared what people thought of you, you wouldn't have run in the first place!'

Jack lowered his head. 'Oliver hates me, doesn't he?'

'I don't know. He hasn't left his office since you left. Won't stop staring at that envelope with his name on it.'

Jack took a deep breath. 'I want to save it, François. I just don't think I can.'

François sighed. 'You don't need to be better, Jack. You're exactly who you need to be.'

'I couldn't put my name on the book.'

'You wanted to.' François bit his lip, suddenly nervous. 'But that wasn't what I was talking about.'

Jack looked up. 'What?'

François swallowed. 'I'm falling in love with Andy.'

Jack blinked. 'I don't believe it.'

François snorted. 'What else is new?' He shrugged. 'He's so full of

life. And adorable. And funny. Not to mention a hungry sex slave.'

'Does he feel the same way about you?'

François rolled his eyes. 'Hard to say. I know he'd love to tell his father he's got a black boyfriend.'

Jack chuckled. 'I can hear him now. "Hey Daddy, I'm fucking a ni—"'

'Never mind,' François interrupted slyly. 'But I will say this. We enjoy being with each other, even if we don't know why.'

'Sounds like me and Oliver.'

François smiled sweetly. 'Where do you think I got the idea?'

Jack looked into François's eyes. 'You really think I should do it, huh.'

'The way I see it, honey... You wasted so many years getting it wrong. Now you have a chance to get it right. Get up there. Look that pig in the eye. Make him scared. Tell those old ladies in the gallery what scum they are. Get the praise you bloody deserve.'

Jack squinted. 'Charlie told you to find me, didn't he?'

François frowned. 'François Brion doesn't *take* orders.' He softened. 'I did it for the brothel. You know what that place means to me.'

Jack shrugged. 'I'll think about it.'

'Well, hurry up!' François snapped.

Jack smirked.

François gracefully stood. 'I almost forgot. Munce is looking for you. Make time and see him, okay?'

Jack nodded.

François nodded back and strutted out of the flat.

34 Cherry Street, Camden Town, One Hour Later...

DING DING DING! Mr Munce smiled from the counter. 'Jack!'

Jack moseyed inside. 'Mr Munce.'

'I've been looking for you for a while. You haven't been with the others.'

Jack removed his cap with a huff. 'Did Charlie tell you what happened?'

Mr Munce hummed. 'Not surprised you ran.'

'Well, I changed my mind. I'm gonna do it after all.'

'Excited?'

Jack rolled his lips. 'Terrified.'

Mr Munce laughed. 'I've been in court before. Nothing too bad. Just answering questions.'

Jack swallowed. 'I don't think that's what I meant.'

Munce sighed, understanding.

Jack shook his head. 'I can't face him, Mr Munce. I said such awful things.'

Mr Munce removed his spectacles. 'I know I don't know the lad very well. And I still don't forgive him for starting that row.'

'You threw a broom at him.'

'Nevertheless.' Mr Munce smiled warmly. 'Oliver must be a truly special person to love you unconditionally. Most people can't do that. They let fear and doubt get in the way.'

Jack flashed a crooked smile. 'Do you think he'll forgive me?'

'I'm sure he already has.'

Jack beamed. 'I love hearing you speak so highly of him.'

'He treats you with respect. That's enough for me.'

'He respects me more than I respect myself.'

'The best ones always do.'

Jack tightened his face, his eyes watering. 'I ran away, Mr Munce. I know I'll talk my way out of it, but... I don't like that I did it at all.'

Mr Munce put a hand on Jack's shoulder. 'You didn't run away because you were too afraid to fail. You ran because you didn't trust your instincts.'

Jack wiped his cheeks. 'I thought I had it all figured out when I wrote that book. Maybe I didn't put my name on it because...' He sighed. 'I didn't want to be wrong.'

'There's nothing wrong with making mistakes.'

'But I don't want to make mistakes.'

'So, you want to be perfect?'

'No, I just want to know what I'm doing.'

Mr Munce chortled. 'No one knows what they're doing! You young people never seem to understand that.'

Jack furrowed his brow. 'Then how does anything get done?'

'Don't ask me. I'm a postman.'

Jack chuckled. 'But what about those great people throughout history? What were they, average people who got lucky?'

Mr Munce shook his head. 'They knew exactly what they needed to do in the right place at the right time.'

'And you think I'll know what to do when the time comes?'

'I know you can.'

'How can you be sure?'

'When you went to Morty on opening night, you had the choice to save yourself or buy immunity for the brothel. You made the right

call then, didn't you?'

'That was a very lucky night,' Jack muttered. 'I don't think I can do that again.'

Munce smiled enigmatically. 'You already did, Jack. You didn't even know it.'

Jack stared at Munce. 'What... What are you talking about?'

Munce rubbed his hands together. 'Now it's *my* turn to tell a story.' He cleared his throat. 'A couple months ago, the manager of the Southampton Post Office, Mr Dowe, received a letter from Dublin's export office addressed for London. As per normal procedure, Mr Dowe sent the letter to the city's distribution centre. Before it could be delivered to its destination, however, the London manager, Mr Salsbury, discovered the recipient no longer resided at the address written. Again, as per normal procedure, Mr Salsbury stamped it "Undeliverable" and rerouted the letter back to its sender. Two days later, Mr Dowe received the letter a second time, heading in the same direction it was the first time. Apparently, the sender died the day she sent it.'

Jack's lip started quivering.

Munce raised a silent finger. 'Mr Dowe then argued with Mr Salsbury via many telegrams over what to do next. Should it go to the flat anyway? Should they send it back to her family? Neither wanted to take the blame if someone complained, so as a matter of last resort, Messrs Dowe and Salsbury agreed on a half-solution: dumping the letter to the recipient's former landlord, an oafish fellow who subsequently tossed it on a pile and left it there... for three weeks. Two days ago, for absolutely no reason whatsoever, the

landlord decided to clean his office and send every letter he had stockpiled to his local branch.' Munce pulled a wooden box from under the counter. 'Me.' He lifted the lid, revealing a letter addressed to Jack's flat in Whitechapel.

Jack's hand trembled as he picked it up. The return address made him dizzy.

Munce smirked. 'I hate this job,' he said with a chuckle.

Jack stared at the envelope, his heart ready to burst.

Mr Munce nodded. 'I'll give you a moment.' He ducked under the counter, whipped out a pack of fags, and walked outside.

Jack tenderly opened the envelope.

Pulled out the letter.

Read:

> My dear son,
>
> I'm sorry if this letter seems rushed. I am very sick, and the doctor says I don't have much time left. Just a moment ago, your father informed me that you were outside asking to see me, and that he sent you away. I know he was angry at you and your friend, and I do apologise for his behaviour. He refused to let you in because he thought it was what I wanted. He was wrong. As soon as he told me, against the advice of the physician, I yelled at him to go out and bring you inside. But it was too late. Your growler was driving away. Your father called after you to turn around, but you must've been too far away to hear him. There

was so much I wanted to say to you, Jack, so I asked your father to transcribe this letter on my behalf. Forgive the horrid handwriting.

I never wrote to you before now because I was angry at you. What you did. What you said. But more than anything, I was angry at myself. Your father and I are ashamed of what we did to you. We burnt your letters and tried to carry on, convincing ourselves we did the right thing. But we felt no joy without you. I stopped reading. Your father hasn't enjoyed nature the way he used to. We blamed you for everything, even things that happened long after the Incident. Because it was easy. Because it made us feel better about ourselves. At first, it made us sick to think of you like that, but we got used to it over time.

Five years ago, your father took Harold to Dublin to visit your grandparents. I stayed behind, alone in the house for the first time since you left. It was your birthday. Your twenty-seventh birthday. Your daily letter had just arrived, and out of lonely curiosity I opened it. I gasped when I saw the £5 note, and after reading the letter I realised it wasn't the only time. Every time. Imagine my reaction when I discovered what else you put in those envelopes. Forgiveness. Kindness. Beauty. Love.

I never told your father what I did. I was too ashamed, and I feared what would happen if he

found out we had been burning free money all this time. I was never great at maths, but you sent us a fortune over the years. To hide what I did, I burnt your letter and the £5 note, and after your father returned, I watched as he continued to burn your letters, never objecting. Worst of all, I never replied, even when you needed my words the most, my comfort and love when you had none.

Why? Was the shame and guilt I bore to keep my pride worth it? Why did I refuse to admit we were wrong in banishing you? Was I worried what our friends would think if they found out, or the church? Why were their opinions so important in our lives? I suppose none of that matters now.

I gave excuses. I kept telling myself I had more time to postpone the pain of writing this letter, but I wasted the few precious years I had left. Once your father told me you came all the way from London, without a single reply in eight years, just to see me, I knew I couldn't wait another second.

I'm sorry, Jack. I failed to look past your sins and recognise my son, the boy I loved, the man you've become. I am so proud of you. You see beauty in the world and forgive selflessly. We all have our sins, yet we foolishly judge characters because of them. Your sins were not out of malice, but of love. Just not the way I was told people were supposed to love.

> Even if your sins are as terrible as they say, no sin on earth is more despicable than mine. I humbly ask you to forgive me the way you always did, love the way you always have, and live the best life you can with all the joy and splendour in the world. Nothing is more important than that.
>
> If the Lord holds me accountable for what I did to you, so be it. But even if it is too late for me, may it not be too late for you.
>
> I love you, Jack. God bless you.
>
> Your mother,
> Maggie Branson

Jack held the letter tightly against his chest and wept.

Ten Minutes Later...

The setting sun shone off the wet cobblestones, giving Cherry Street a golden glow. Mr Munce watched, puffing away with a contemplative frown. Jack wandered out, letter in hand, and stood alongside Mr Munce. They didn't look at each other. They simply shared the silence.

'Mr Munce,' Jack whispered.

'Jack.'

'What happened to my bike?'

Mr Munce raised a brow. 'What bike? The one you left outside, overnight, without a lock, four years ago?' He took a drag. Thumbed behind him. 'It's in the back.'

Jack furrowed his brow. 'You never said.'

'Honestly, I forgot.'

Jack sighed. 'All this time I thought someone stole it.'

'That piece of shit? Not a chance.'

Jack burst out laughing.

Munce chuckled. Squished his fag. 'I'll be back.'

Five minutes later, Munce walked out the back entrance with Jack's bike. Jack crouched down and inspected the frame. Just the way he left it. Cleaner, actually. Jack looked up, moved to tears. Mr Munce smiled back. They embraced.

Jack hopped on the bike, gave Munce a final nod, and kicked off, racing away, weaving around pedestrians with ease. He held out his arms, the wind blowing past him. Laughed.

He was flying.

19 Montgomery Street, Marylebone, Ten Minutes Later…

Jack parked his bike out front. Pounded on the door.

'Who is it?' Andy asked meekly.

'It's Jack. Let me in.'

The door whipped open. Andy pounced. 'You're back!'

Jack hugged back, startled. 'Where's Oliver?'

'His office, where else?' Andy cupped his hands. 'JACK'S BACK!'

Jack tried to make it upstairs, but Andy had summoned the entire congregation. Mary. Louise. Denny. François. One by one, they greeted him with hugs and kisses. No one asked why he left or if he changed his mind about the trial. They just smiled and laughed.

Jack finally broke free. Raced upstairs. Turned the corner. Burst into Oliver's office.

Oliver looked up from his ledger, his eyes fluttering with casual recognition.

'Oliver,' Jack muttered, already out of breath. 'I was wrong. I insulted you because everything you said was right. I hated my flaws. I wanted to hurt you for calling them out. I'm so sorry I ran away. I wanna help now. I'll do everything I can to keep this place open. I'm not letting that piece of filth call me a liar.'

Oliver stared blankly.

Jack dropped his letter, catching it in mid-air. 'Mother sent me this, can you believe it? She sent it the day we were there. Before she died, obviously. She knew about the letters. She apologised for everything, baby. For banishing me. For not writing me back. And Father wrote it all down for her.'

Oliver kept staring.

Jack swallowed. 'I don't think I'm doing it justice. It's a lot more natural than that. You can read it. Later, if you want.'

Oliver didn't move.

Tears filled Jack's eyes. 'Oh baby, I missed you! I want you back in my bed! I want to hold you! And kiss you! I was so wrong, baby! Please, please forgive me! You are the best person in the world! You're so brave, and smart, and I can't bear to live without you! Please let me back! I love you! I don't care who knows it! I love you, Oliver Hawkett, and I want to spend the rest of my life with you!'

Oliver blinked, his expression unchanged.

Jack's lip quivered. 'Say something.'

Oliver smiled. 'You're so adorable when you're like this.'

Jack gasped. 'Wait-wait-wait, what do you... You forgive me?'

Oliver blew his lips. 'I forgave you twenty seconds after you left.' He checked his pocketwatch. 'Ooh, dinner! Let's go.' He jumped up, beelining for the door.

'Why?'

Oliver raised a brow. 'It's six o'clock.'

'No, why did you forgive me so soon?'

Oliver's smile vanished. He sighed. 'You were right too.'

Jack scrunched his face. 'I was?'

Oliver nodded. 'I have forgotten what it's like out there, in the real world. People change a lot slower than they do in novels. And it's not nearly as obvious.' He hesitated, building himself up for a confession. 'So much good could've happened if I just... If I was just a bit more patient.'

'What do you mean?' Jack asked.

Oliver looked down at the letter in Jack's hand. A warm realisation rushed over him, a sense of comfort. Could it have been fate, the way everything happened? Perhaps the *what* was inevitable but the *how* had to be corrected. Or maybe it was all a warning, one of those miraculous punishments Jack wrote about. Oliver did not know for sure, but he received the message just the same.

'I shouldn't have pressured you to do something you didn't want to do,' Oliver answered. 'And for that, I'm sorry.'

Jack chuckled. 'I thought I was going to relive what happened the last time I apologised in this room.'

Oliver shook his head. 'I understand you now. You're not selfish.

You're beautiful. And all you ever wanted was a home that stays put. That doesn't change. Filled with people who will always love you, the real you, no matter what. So that's what I'll be. Your home. I'll be there. And I'll forgive.'

Jack grinned so hard his cheek muscles started twitching.

Oliver flashed a smirk. 'Now kiss me before I change my—'

Jack pulled Oliver in and kissed him. They held each other close. Breath mingling. Bodies warming up. Cocks growing in sync.

For the first time in his life, Jack Branson was in the right bloody place at the right bloody time.

CHAPTER THIRTEEN

Pride Incarnate

Old Bailey, City of London, Three Weeks Later...

The Times declared *Withers v Grant* the Trial of the Century before the date was even announced. The fate of an MP election hanging in the balance. A controversial bestseller the key piece of evidence. The melodramatic climax of a scandal combining sodomy, prostitution, and corruption. Everything the public wanted on paper alone.

At last, 17 April 1889 had arrived. Crowds outside the Old Bailey. Gallery filled to maximum capacity with eager spectators. Dozens of reporters (some from America and the Continent) forced to stand in the back, their pens cocked and ready to fire. All eyes were on London that morning. The world waited with bated breath.

A half-hour before the trial started, Jack sat in the Witness room with Oliver by his side. 'It's so quiet here,' Jack whispered. 'Hope we didn't miss it.'

Oliver smiled. 'François said they're like sardines in there.'

'Then you better go in before someone takes your seat.'

'I just don't want you to be nervous.'

Jack kissed Oliver. 'I'm done being nervous.'

The door opened, a rush of noise pouring in from the Lobby. Charlie walked in with a smile. 'How are you doing, Jack?'

'Holding up.' Jack looked at Oliver. 'Go, I'll be fine.'

Oliver kissed Jack again and left, closing the door behind him.

Jack took a deep breath and stood. 'It's mad out there.'

'That's the least of our problems, unfortunately,' Charlie mumbled. 'Our barrister vanished ten minutes ago.'

'He's coming back, right?'

Charlie shook his head. 'Grant's panicking.'

'You don't sound worried.'

'If there's one thing Grant's good at, it's pretending he knows what he's talking about.'

Jack chuckled.

Charlie rubbed across his jaw. 'Jack, before we go in...'

Jack's face softened.

Charlie swallowed, visibly hurt. 'I am so... *so* sorry for ambushing you like that. I told myself I wouldn't, I tried not to, but I did. And I put all that pressure on you, and...'

Jack shook his head. 'I'm not perfect, Charlie. I'll never be perfect. But the one I can say with complete sincerity is that I do really bloody well under pressure. You knew that. You were right. About this, about everything. I just wish I believed you sooner.'

Charlie smiled weakly. 'You've grown so much, Jack. I couldn't be prouder.' He paused. 'You remind me so much of myself. In another life. Nothing else mattered but truth, justice. The greater good always came first. I could do anything.'

'What changed?'

'Mum dying,' Charlie whispered. 'Suddenly I had money, a house, solicitors, trusts, a business front. Everything got so complicated. I was so focused on trying to keep the brothel alive, I forgot why I built it in the first place.'

Jack nodded respectfully.

Charlie stuffed his hands in his pockets. 'I just wanted you to know that... Even before all that, I never would've had the courage to do what you're about to do. I just hope that one day I can be as great as you are.'

Jack's hair stood up on end. He forced a self-deprecating smile. 'I dunno. Fighting your grandparents for your inheritance seems pretty brave to me.'

Charlie smirked, visibly confused. 'What did Oliver tell you?'

'Not much. He made it seem like you went to court and fought them in a blaze of glory.'

Charlie laughed. 'I swear, that boy reads too many novels.'

Jack crossed his arms. 'What happened, then?'

'My grandmother was the one who sent me to the orphanage. She was an old soul, more ashamed of her daughter than she was of me. But I took it personally. I had no legal right to inherit anything, but I didn't care. I hated her for what she did to me. After Mum died, I kept sending my solicitor to her estate in the Highlands with subpoenas and demands. They got into rows over me, real nasty ones, borderline harassment. I kept hurting her because I needed someone to blame, even though I wasn't going to win. No matter how much I yelled at her, or cried about fairness, or what Mum would've wanted... I did it because it felt good.'

Jack sighed, a familiar pain rushing over him.

Charlie nodded. 'She got a bad case of influenza a couple months after that. I dropped everything, took a train to Scotland, and stayed by her side. I brought her fever down. Changed her bedpan. Kept her company. I stayed up with her. And we talked about Mum. I lost a mother, and she lost a daughter. Just being there in her time of need, getting her back to good health, that was enough. She admitted she was wrong about me and gave me everything.' Charlie shrugged. 'It was just a small victory, but it won the war.'

'That's not nothing,' Jack insisted. 'Forgiveness goes a long way.'

'Yeah, but it's not the same.'

'You're right. It's better.'

Charlie looked at the floor. 'You have no idea how much that means to me, coming from you.'

Jack grinned. 'You are the bravest man I ever met.'

Charlie inhaled sharply. 'Thank...' He held a hand to his mouth.

Jack walked over and hugged him, shushing softly. 'We'll get through this. We'll go home and we'll pick up where we left off. I promise.'

Charlie nodded, trying not to cry. 'You have always been so kind to me.'

'You were kind to me first,' Jack whispered.

Charlie cleared his throat, pulled out a handkerchief, and wiped his eyes. 'I'm sorry, I...' He sniffed. 'I'm not used to getting compliments.'

'I'm the same way.' Jack chuckled. 'Christ, I'm saying that a lot lately.'

'I know I seem intelligent, even psychic at times,' Charlie said, pocketing his handkerchief. 'But it's only because I know something a lot of people don't realise until they're much older: There's only so many kinds of people in the world.'

Jack nodded. 'I think I'm figuring that out.' He paused. 'Makes me wonder why I was so afraid. We all have the same problems, the same insecurities... but we all think we're the only ones.'

'You just summed up the entire human race.'

Jack smirked. 'That must've been it. Sounded too good to be true.'

The door whipped open. Mary stormed in, tears streaming down his face, barely recognisable without makeup or a wig. 'It's a zoo out there! I can't even get a moment alone!' He raced to the window, footsteps light as a bunny's, hands flapping like pigeon wings. Quick as the wind, he whipped out a fag and lit it. After a few puffs, he finally noticed Jack and Charlie, staring back with serious expressions. 'I'm sorry,' Mary whined, his lip trembling. 'I just... I need a moment.' He fanned himself like a debutante. 'Louise is such a BITCH!'

Jack studied Mary's flamboyant posture, suddenly inspired.

Mary blew smoke out the window, hip jutting out, toes tapping impatiently. Jack stood behind Mary and imitated the pose, chuckling to himself.

Mary scowled at Jack. 'Don't mock me!' he cried, flailing his hands with each word.

'*Don't mock me*!' Jack parroted in a feminine voice, moving his hands the same way.

'Stop it!'

'*Stop it*!'

'Char-lie!' Mary pleaded, a child calling for mother.

'*Char-lie*!' Jack mimicked.

Mary fluttered towards Charlie. Jack chased after him like the bogeyman.

Mary hid behind Charlie. 'Jack's so mean!'

Charlie struggled to contain his laughter. 'Jack, what the hell are you doing?'

Jack moved his arms through the air, settling into Mary's mannerisms like a new gown. 'Practising.'

'*Practising*!' Mary spat in a butch Irish accent.

Charlie raised his brows. 'Practising for what?'

Jack strutted around the room. 'I'm pulling a Charlie Smith. Small victories win the war, right?'

Charlie grinned. 'Of course.'

'I'll never have an audience like this again.' Jack flapped his hands. 'So I'll give them a performance they won't forget. Even if they wanted to.'

Twenty-Five Minutes Later...

Hundreds of spectators watched the Jury enter the courtroom, unusually silent with suspense.

Charlie Smith stood beside Geoffrey Grant at the Defence's desk; a third chair, reserved for Grant's barrister, was vacant.

Standing at the Prosecution's desk was Edgar Withers, Simmons, and Sir Philip Tennant, the skeleton of a man Simmons chose to act

as Withers's barrister.

In the last row of the gallery, Oliver stood beside Denny, Mary, Louise (also in masculine attire), François, Andy, and Mr Munce.

The moment the last Juror took his seat, the Judge burst into the courtroom, a bumbling gorilla with pounds of fat under his chin and eyes too small for his face. His powdered wig bounced with every step. 'The court is now in session,' he slurred through crooked teeth.

BLAM! quoth the gavel. The entire congregation sat in unison.

'Prosecution,' the Judge mumbled impatiently. 'Opening statement.'

Tennant stood and faced the Jury. 'Edgar Withers is a decent man,' he declared, his prestigious birth showing through his dialect. 'An unorthodox candidate for Parliament? Perhaps. But not a deviant. A man of honour. A lifelong solicitor dedicated to upholding the law and all that is good on God's green earth. One who respects moral standards. A decent fellow, without enemies or grudges. He is unmarried, but only because of his dedication to his career.'

Edgar smirked at Grant from across the room.

Grant rolled his eyes.

Tennant pointed to the Defence's desk. 'Geoffrey Grant, on the other hand, has held a seat in the House of Commons for thirty years. His entire way of life hinges on the preservation of that position. His allies in the House of Lords. His aristocratic donors. The dependence of his middle-class supporters. Without his role in Parliament, Mr Grant has nothing else. He is a widower with no children. He would do anything to keep his power, even something

as common and dishonest as lying about his opponent on the campaign trail. Before his speech in Belgrave square, when he questioned the purity of my client, Mr Grant was ten points behind Mr Withers in the polls. To prevent loss of favour among the voters of this great city, Mr Grant decided to attack, and out of desperation, resorted to slander.'

Tennant took a sip of water. 'Charlie Smith is the owner of a reputable and financially successful publishing company, the Charlie Smith Publishing House in Marylebone. As a businessman, his priority first and foremost is keeping profits high. His industry does not make money from prestige, investments, or foundations. Mr Smith makes his money from sales alone.'

Tennant reached into his briefcase and held up a book. 'Four months ago, Charlie Smith published this memoir, *The Sins of an Irishman in London*, credited to an anonymous author, a potentially fictional male prostitute. In the epilogue of the addendum, the alleged deviant writes that he had sexual relations with a Tory politician bearing Mr Withers's description. Because the author was never identified, Mr Smith receives the entire net profit instead of the typical 40 to 50 per cent. He was well aware of the legal implications of publishing the slanderous contents of the novel, so he took advantage of a loophole in our society: If you remove the name, you say whatever you want about anybody.'

Charlie rubbed his temple.

Tennant pulled out a magazine. 'The accusations in Mr Smith's book were cited by Mr Grant to supplement a rumour published in this magazine, *The North London Press*, a publication already

infamous for its radical political coverage and the unhealthy relationship with its former sponsors. The article in question, titled "A Wolf in Sheep's Clothing: Edgar Withers's Immoral Secret", was written by August Hammersworth, a journalist with his own reputation of exaggeration and unreliable sources, a man Mr Grant personally complimented during his defamatory speech in Belgrave Square. Mr Hammersworth, however, does not profit from the sales of the magazine he wrote for. The owner of the paper, the man who controls its advertising, profits from its sales. And who is the owner of *The North London Press*?' Tennant pointed to the Defence's table. 'Charlie Smith.'

The audience murmured anxiously. Charlie glared at Grant. Grant looked away.

'Falsely accusing my client with sodomy would benefit both Mr Grant and Mr Smith,' Tennant continued. 'The former would guarantee a win in September's election, maintaining the long-standing influence he so depends on. And his accomplice, the latter, sells the book that accuses the man and the magazine that keeps the story alive. These two tricksters represent everything wrong with an unchecked press. They can cheat and lie and warp the minds of the public. No evidence necessary, just implication. To protect the sanctity of truth, as well a good man's reputation, the defendants must be held accountable. Thank you.' Tennant bowed and sat down.

Edgar looked over at Grant. Winked.

'Defence,' the Judge declared. 'Your opening statement.'

Grant looked at the empty chair next to him. Turned his head to the door.

'Does the Defence have representation?' the Judge asked.

'It's too late,' Charlie mumbled to Grant. 'We're on our own.'

Grant nodded. Reluctantly stood. 'We do not, m'lord. In lieu of a barrister, I ask permission to defend myself and Mr Smith.'

The Judge rolled his eyes. 'Fine. Your opening statement.'

Grant raised a finger. 'M'lord?'

'What?'

Grant smiled bashfully. 'We do not have a prepared statement, m'lord.'

A mist of whispers filled the room.

The Judge folded his hands, donning a patronising smile. 'Mr Grant, are you not a politician?'

'I am, m'lord.'

'Can't you make one up?'

Grant smiled with realisation. Looked at Edgar. Winked.

Edgar furrowed his brow.

'I cannot, m'lord,' Grant replied. 'However, I would like to state for the record that we did have a barrister this morning, one Mr Patrick T Lowe.'

The Judge squinted at the empty chair. 'Then why is he not present, Mr Grant?'

'He vanished about an hour ago.'

Edgar gasped, his eyes wide with fear. He frantically whispered to Simmons.

The Judge peered over his glasses. 'Your barrister *vanished*?'

Grant shrugged theatrically. 'I can't explain it either, m'lord. But I did find it strange that he left so soon after speaking to Mr Withers.'

'How is that strange, Mr Grant?'

Simmons turned away from Edgar. Whispered into Tennant's ear.

'I have since learnt,' Grant stated calmly, 'that Mr Lowe and Mr Withers went to law school together.'

'M'lord!' Tennant called, standing up. 'Strike that from the record!'

Grant gaped. 'No, m'lord! Mr Withers—'

'Strike it, m'lord!'

Quoth the gavel, BLAM! BLAM! BLAM!

'Quiet, all of you!' the Judge yelled.

Grant and Tennant slowly sat down.

The Judge adjusted his wig, snorting harshly. 'I will not let this courtroom turn into a pigpen. If the Defence does not have an opening statement, sit down and move on!' He paused. 'DOES the Defence have an opening statement?!'

Grant stood, scowling. 'No, m'lord.'

The Judge turned to the transcriber. 'Let the record show the Defence does not have an opening statement and strike all other comments.'

Grant plopped back down, defeated.

'What do we do now?' Charlie whispered.

'Defence,' the Judge grumbled. 'Call your first witness.'

Charlie swallowed nervously. 'Should we call Jack?'

Grant glared at Edgar's smug face staring back at him.

'Mr Grant!' the Judge called impatiently.

Grant shot up. 'M'lord, the Defence calls Edgar Withers to the stand.'

Edgar dropped his smile. He whispered anxiously to Simmons and Tennant.

'What are you doing?!' Charlie hissed.

'I shared a stage with the louse,' Grant muttered back. 'If there's a man who can buckle under his own stupidity, it's Edgar bloody Withers.'

Five Minutes Later...

A clerk carried a Bible to the Witness Stand. Edgar placed his right hand on the cover. 'I swear by Almighty God,' he rattled from memory, 'that the evidence I shall give shall be the truth, the whole truth, and nothing but the truth.'

Grant sipped from a glass of water and stood, beaming with confidence. 'Mr Withers, how are you today?'

'I'm doing fine, Mr Grant. How about yourself?'

'I'm on trial at the moment, I could be better.'

The gallery laughed. A couple of Jurors smiled.

'The questions, Mr Grant,' the Judge whined.

Grant cleared his throat. 'Mr Withers, what is a lie?'

Edgar blinked. 'What is it?'

'The definition. What is a lie?'

'Something that isn't true.'

Grant nodded. 'Can you give us an example?'

'No. I don't lie.'

Grant smiled at Jury. 'Neither do I.'

'The point, Mr Grant?!' the Judge cried.

'I have one, m'lord.' Grant looked at Edgar. 'Lie about me then. What colour's my beard?'

Edgar studied Grant's ivory mane. 'White.'

'I asked you to lie.'

Tennant stood. 'M'lord, the Defence is trying to trick my client into committing perjury.'

Grant grimaced. 'I am not!'

'Strike this line of questioning,' the Judge ordered the transcriber.

'M'lord, I—!' Grant stopped himself. Took a deep breath. 'Fine. Mr Withers, if you said I didn't have a beard, that would be a lie, correct?'

'It would,' Edgar answered.

'Because it is obviously very large and very white.'

'I'd be surprised if anyone didn't know that.'

Grant flashed a bitter smirk. 'Next question, Mr Withers.' He paused. 'Where did I go for lunch yesterday?'

Edgar raised an eyebrow. 'Lunch?'

'Yes.'

'I don't know.'

'Can't you guess?'

'No.'

'It's not a lie if it's just a guess.'

Edgar hesitated. 'I dunno... The Criterion in Piccadilly.'

'And what did I eat?'

'Steak.'

'And my drink?'

'Brandy.'

'And my waiter's name?'

Edgar chuckled. 'Why is that important?'

'Guess my waiter's name, Mr Withers.'

'I cannot.'

'And what did Charlie eat?'

'I suppose the same thing you did.'

Grant raised his eyebrows. 'Really? Charlie was eating with me?'

Edgar rolled his eyes. 'I don't know.'

'What did he drink?'

'I have no idea.'

'Why, Mr Withers? Why don't you know where I ate lunch yesterday, or what I ate, or what I drank, or what my waiter's name was, or what Charlie ate, or what he drank, or whether or not he was even there?'

'Because *I* wasn't there!'

Grant shrugged. 'How can it be so difficult to guess, Mr Withers?'

Edgar grunted. 'For starters, there are hundreds of places to eat in London alone, if you even ate in London, not to mention thousands of drinks and millions of waiters!'

'You can't guess because there are too many variables.'

'Yes.'

'But what if you guessed everything right? The restaurant, the food, the drink, my waiter's name, whether or not Charlie was even there? You might be so lucky.'

'No one's that lucky,' Edgar grumbled. 'That would be a miracle.'

'You would've had to have been there.'

'Yes.'

Grant nodded. 'I see.' He turned to the Prosecution's desk. 'May I borrow your copy of Mr Smith's book, Sir Philip?'

Tennant opened his briefcase and handed the book to Grant.

'Thank you.' Grant held the book up. 'Mr Withers, do you recognise this novel?'

'Of course.'

'This is *The Sins of an Irishman in London* by Anonymous, published by the Charlie Smith Publishing House, correct?'

'Yes.'

'Has your barrister confirmed that this copy has never been edited or tarnished?'

'He has.'

'And he's confirmed that it had been purchased three days ago by an unrelated third party?'

'He has.'

'Can he also confirm that this copy has never come in contact with myself or Mr Smith before this moment?'

Edgar looked at Tennant. Tennant nodded back.

'He does,' Edgar answered.

Grant opened the book, flipping to the back. 'In addendum, under the section "Epilogue: Why It All Matters", does the author claim that a Tory politician who's up for election visited the Montgomery Street Brothel on 3 November 1888?'

'That's what it says.'

'I assume by your tone that you weren't there that day?'

Edgar raised his hands incredulously. 'That's why we're here!'

'Can you verify where you were on that day?'

'I'm not the one on trial, Mr Grant.'

Grant pursed his lips. 'You don't have to answer that if you don't want to.' He flipped a few pages, reading silently. He looked up at Edgar. 'Are you five-foot-eight?'

Edgar hesitated. 'Yes.'

Grant hummed. He looked down at the page, tracing a sentence with his finger. 'What about your arm? Do you have a large birth-mark on your left bicep?'

Edgar shifted awkwardly. 'P-possibly, I don't... I dunno.'

Grant tilted his head. 'You don't know? Will you please roll up your sleeve and show the jury?'

Edgar inhaled sharply. 'Fine, I do. What of it?'

'On your left foot do you have...' Grant read from the book. '"A patch of hair in the shape of a whale?"'

Edgar gulped. 'I do.'

Grant flipped a page and smirked. 'And is your penis four and a half—?'

Edgar squeezed his eyes shut with shame. BLAM! BLAM! BLAM! The gallery gasped with revulsion, except Andy, who cackled and stomped his feet.

'That vulgarity is not allowed!' the Judge decreed.

'Answer me, Edgar,' Grant ordered.

Edgar shook his head rapidly. 'I won't.'

'Answer the question!'

Tennant shot up. 'M'lord!' he cried incredulously.

'One more minute, m'lord!' Grant pleaded. 'I'm almost done.'

The Judge glared at Grant. 'Thirty seconds. And keep it decent.'

Grant looked back Edgar. 'Do you have corns on the index and middle toes of your right foot?'

Edgar swallowed. 'Yes.'

'Do you have knife scars across your abdomen?'

'Yes.'

'Do you have burns across the right half of your chest?'

'Yes.'

'Does the physical description of the Tory in this book match your own?'

Sweat dripped down Edgar's forehead. 'It does.'

'Including the areas under your clothes?'

'Yes.'

Grant snapped the book shut. 'Mr Withers, you say you weren't at 19 Montgomery Street on 3 November but you can't prove it. You say you've never had relations with a male prostitute, yet the author of this book knows what you look like under your clothes. And you just said a minute ago it would be a miracle for someone to guess all those variables correctly without actually being there. So tell us, Mr Withers: HOW DOES THE PROSTITUTE WHO WROTE THIS BOOK KNOW THE DETAILS OF YOUR NAKED BODY?!'

Edgar gulped in horror.

The audience gaped.

Grant smirked.

Edgar looked at Charlie. A cruel victor's grin grew on his face. 'I

don't know, Mr Grant,' he answered with a coy shrug. 'Who can say a prostitute even wrote the book?'

Grant's smile instantly vanished.

Edgar tilted his head curiously. 'Why would you of all people believe such speculation? You know how blackmail works, surely you do. If my enemies wanted to intimidate me with indecent details, all they'd have to do is bribe my physician.'

Charlie gasped. The gallery murmured. BLAM! BLAM! BLAM! went the gavel.

Grant swallowed. 'You don't think a homosexual wrote this book?'

Edgar pursed his lips. 'I wouldn't go that far. I know a prostitute didn't write the book because I've never met such a fallen creature. But any man who'd go to such lengths to slander my Christian reputation is a greedy degenerate, one without morals or decency. Anyone can blackmail, but an entire novel? Only a sexual deviant could write such perverted imagery.' Edgar smiled at Charlie. 'You write from what you know, don't you, Mr Smith?'

The audience erupted with gasps.

Charlie scowled back at Edgar.

Quoth the gavel, BLAM! BLAM! BLAM! 'Order!' roared the Judge.

Grant grimaced at Edgar. 'Have you no shame?'

Edgar smiled back devilishly.

The Judge cleared his throat impatiently. 'Are you finished, Mr Grant?'

Grant looked away. 'You may step down, Mr Withers.'

Edgar nodded and sauntered back to the Prosecution's desk.

The Judge rubbed his eyes. 'Defence. Call your next witness.'

Grant looked at Charlie with a knowing smirk.

Charlie smiled. Nodded back.

'M'lord!' Grant declared triumphantly. 'The Defence calls *Jack Branson*!'

The gallery chattered with confusion. The Judge slammed his gavel, BLAM! BLAM! BLAM!

Edgar stared forward, turned to stone by Medusa's head. He slowly closed his eyes, the only proof he was still alive.

Five Minutes Later...

The doors swung open, Jack Branson strutting down the aisle like the belle of the ball.

A tsunami of revulsion rushed across the gallery. Every thrusting hip. Every airy hand. Every feminine sigh. Every flamboyant move evoked a reaction. Gasps. Gags. Angry grunts. Jack smiled through it all, his posture erect and immovable.

The Judge cringed at the sight, ready to vomit.

Jack smirked at Edgar as he sashayed past the Prosecution's desk. Edgar glared back.

Jack sat at the Witness Stand, crossing his legs with a flourish. The clerk tentatively approached with a Bible. Jack placed his right hand on it.

'Mr Branson,' Grant said. 'Do you swear by Almighty God that the evidence you shall give shall be the truth, the whole truth, and nothing but the truth?'

Jack made direct eye contact with Edgar. 'Absolutely.'

Oliver smiled proudly from the gallery. Mary and Louise squealed in unison.

Grant forced down a smile. 'Can you tell the court your full name and place of birth?'

'My name is Jack Donald Branson, and I was born in Dunderrow, County Cork, Ireland.'

'And what do you do for a living, Mr Branson?'

Jack sighed, moaning a little.

The Old Lady sitting next to Oliver squirmed with disgust.

'I am a professional sodomite,' Jack answered.

The audience erupted in a mass of cries and screams. BLAM! BLAM! BLAM!

'Order!' cried the Judge.

'I'm not familiar with that term,' Grant asked with feigned ignorance. 'Professional sodomite?'

'I shag men for money.'

The Old Lady fainted in her seat. Oliver chuckled with surprise. Andy galloped in place.

'How did you meet these men?' Grant asked.

'Eagerly.'

'No, I meant in what way.'

'Open mouth and open legs.'

Quoth the gavel, BLAM! BLAM! BLAM!

The Judge yelled, 'I will not have such levity in this courtroom!'

Grant chuckled. 'I apologise for being vague. By what means did these encounters take place?'

Jack nodded. 'From November of 1881 to January of 1884, I pretended to deliver telegrams to many powerful people, who would then take advantage of me inside their own homes.'

'And why did that stop in January of '84, Mr Branson?'

'I was implicated in the Collins Affair.'

'To what extent?'

'Scotland Yard released me for lack of evidence, but *The Times* published my name anyway.'

'Why did they do that?'

'Because the police found me at Kensington, naked, among the rest of them. They just couldn't prove why.'

Mr Munce scanned the other people in the gallery, their faces frozen in shock, hands covering their mouths. He chuckled.

'What happened after the police let you go?' Grant asked.

'I fled to Ireland to wait out the scandal,' Jack replied. 'I worked as a Footman in Mulhussey.'

'And when did you return to London?'

'June of 1887.'

'For what reason?'

'I had graduated to the world of brothels. I worked at the one on Montgomery Street. You might've heard of it.'

Grant nodded and pointed to Charlie. 'Do you know this man?'

'Of course I know Charlie Smith. He published my novel.'

The gallery hushed among themselves. Edgar rubbed his temple furiously. Simmons glared at him.

Grant tilted his head. 'You're a published author as well?'

Jack flapped his hand. 'Anything to pay the bills, am I right?'

'Don't be modest, Mr Branson. What is its title?'

'*The Sins of an Irishman in London*.'

The entire courtroom gasped at once, the Judge included.

Grant faked surprise. 'You wrote *The Sins in an Irishman in London*?'

'Pretty good, huh?'

'I agree, but I can't speak for everyone.'

Jack smiled proudly.

Grant cleared his throat. 'I know this is a silly question...' He threw a nasty look at Edgar. 'But is everything you wrote in your novel true?'

'I used aliases to protect my clients, but yes. Everything really happened.'

'So why did you publish anonymously?' Grant asked.

'I had enough fan letters.'

One person laughed. BLAM!

Grant smirked. 'You've had the quite the roster of customers, haven't you, Mr Branson?

'Enough for another book.'

'Are any of them sitting in this courtroom today?'

Jack theatrically scanned the gallery. Stopped. Chuckled with shock. 'How honest do you want me to be, Mr Grant?'

BLAM! BLAM! BLAM!

Grant forced his lips shut to stop from laughing.

Jack shrugged apologetically and resumed his search. His eyes stopped at the Prosecution's desk. 'There,' he said, pointing at Edgar. 'I definitely spent a night with him.'

A Juror gasped. Edgar looked down in shame.

'You've had sexual relations with Edgar Withers?' Grant asked.

Jack squirmed in his seat. 'Unfortunately.'

'And how did you arrange the encounter?'

'I didn't. He came to us. Paid a lot for privacy.'

'Will you tell the jury what happened that night?'

Jack huffed anxiously. 'I apologise, Mr Grant, but I wrote it into the addendum so I'd never have to recount it again.'

'Everything you did with Edgar is written in the epilogue of the addendum?'

'Yes, except one thing I forgot to add.'

'What?'

'He didn't tip.'

Grant laughed heartily. 'Your witness, Sir Philip.'

Tennant took a deep breath and stood.

Jack batted his eyes flirtatiously.

'Mr Branson,' Tennant mumbled. 'Do you admit to being a sodomite?'

'I prefer homosexual, but who's asking?'

Tennant frowned. 'Sir Philip Tennant.'

Jack snorted. 'Take a joke, darling!'

François smirked with pride.

Tennant grumbled. 'Have you ever been a victim of sexual abuse?'

'Does a fat Lord with a hernia count?' Jack asked.

'No.'

'Then no, I haven't.'

'Have you ever been molested?'

'No.'

'Sodomised?'

Jack blinked. 'Uh, yeah. It's the best.'

Tennant stared back, unamused.

Jack gasped. 'Oh, you mean *raped*! Oh, no, no, I haven't, no.'

'Have you suffered any physical abuse in your childhood, perhaps at the hands of your parents?'

Jack held up a confused hand. 'Why are you asking me that?'

'I want to gauge your state of mind.'

'Why? Because I'm a whore, I must be batty?' Jack laughed. 'Nothing made me this way. I love doing this. It's the only way I'm allowed to be the real me.'

Simmons waved Tennant over and whispered into his ear. Tennant nodded. Returned to Jack. 'What do you gain from testifying against my client, Mr Branson?'

'I get to take credit for my book.'

'Let me rephrase the question.' Tennant paused. 'How are you being compensated by the Defence?'

'Free publicity.'

'Anything else?'

Jack hesitated. 'Satisfaction in performing my civic duty.'

'Anything else?'

Jack chuckled. 'Are you asking me if I'm being bribed, Sir Philip?'

'I'm asking how you're being compensated.'

Jack shook his head in disgust. 'I don't understand you people. I'm not here because I'm getting paid, and I'm not here because I'm

insane. I'm here because I believe in something so strongly that I am breaking my anonymity to defend it.'

'And what is that, Mr Branson?'

Jack shrugged coyly. 'Something you can't find in a courtroom, Sir Philip.'

Tennant furrowed his brow.

Jack leaned forward. 'Truth.'

Grant beamed from his seat.

Jack pointed to the four walls. 'You know what this is? A doll's house. Gentle, clean, flawless, everything the perfect size with nice bright colours, but that's not what real homes are like. Where's the mould? Where's the rot? Where's Mum and Dad screaming at each other? You made a system to judge the real world, but there's nothing realistic about it. Out there, no one talks with perfect grammar. No one quotes Latin on a regular basis. No one stands where they're told. No one waits their turn. They don't memorise lines and strut around a stage with fancy suits, shined shoes, and bloody powdered wigs. You've got lots of rules, but anything middle ground is forbidden. There isn't any room for justification or redemption because you're so obsessed with absolutes. Good or bad. Innocent or guilty. Nothing's indecent or inconsistent or complicated because, I dunno, that would be too much for a jury to understand. It might not be what society wants to hear, but it's the truth.'

Jack looked out at the gallery. 'Isn't that why we're here? To stop lying about ourselves? How are we supposed to get better if no one tells the truth, the whole damn truth? I am here because Edgar

Withers is a liar. That's the truth, but it's not the whole truth. I am here on behalf of every homosexual you disowned and exiled. Every sodomite you lynched. Every mother's son you castrated and institutionalised. Every life you ruined. Every Incident you want to forget because it hurts. It's SUPPOSED to hurt! I'm not gonna be your gentleman anymore. I don't give a damn about your rules, or your phony etiquette, or your delicate feelings. I'M NOT AFRAID OF YOU PEOPLE ANYMORE!'

Edgar and Simmons looked at each other uncomfortably.

Charlie grinned with wonderment.

Denny and Louise fanned Mary, who had fainted in his chair.

Mr Munce nodded with respect.

The Judge gaped.

Jack took a deep breath. Folded his hands. Smiled politely at Tennant.

Tennant hesitated. 'Why should anyone believe you, Mr Branson?' he asked tenderly. 'What good is the word of a homosexual over a man like Edgar Withers?'

Jack shrugged. 'I can't make any of this up if I tried. It's my life. I've been doing this for almost ten years, and I don't regret a single minute of it. I've met some amazing people, men I never would've known if I stayed in Ireland. And I'm more than a homosexual, Sir Philip. I'm just like you.' He looked at the gallery. 'All of you. I have friends. A family. I ride my bike. I read books in the park. I drink Darjeeling with lemon. I eat Délice de Mousse. I am no different because of what I do.'

Jack met eyes with Oliver. 'Or who I love.' He winked.

Oliver smiled warmly.

Jack grinned back. 'The strange thing is many of you already know that. Because you know someone like me. Or you read my book. Or you feel the same way and you're too ashamed to admit it. If you want to live like me, go ahead. I won't judge. Live like me. But don't call me a monster and then pay me to suck your cock, you don't get both.'

Jack stared blankly at the Prosecution's desk. 'Edgar Withers is trying to get both. He is nothing but scum.'

Edgar looked up, frowning with shame.

Jack softened with pity. He looked at the Jury. 'If you believe Edgar Withers, if you take the word of a selfish, cowardly, lying hypocrite over mine...' He sighed. 'Then you're scum too.'

The Jury shifted in their seats.

Jack gazed out at the hundreds of silent, shocked faces staring back at him. He smiled. Leaned back in his chair. Closed his eyes. Took a deep breath. Savoured it.

Jack looked back at Tennant. Smirked. 'Any other questions?'

CHAPTER FOURTEEN

Strangers in a Strange Land

Old Bailey, City of London, One Hour Later...

Jack sat on the windowsill of the Witness Room, arms wrapped around his knees, his blues eyes gazing out at the London skyline. He replayed the testimony in his mind with a soft smile.

Oliver let himself in, closing the door behind him.

Jack jumped up. 'BABY!' He raced over and hugged Oliver.

Oliver sighed, stepping away. 'Jack.'

'I can't believe it, baby! I did it! I—'

'Jack!' Oliver exclaimed. 'The Jury came back.'

The joy evaporated from Jack's face. 'They can't have.' He forced a chuckle. 'Hasn't even been twenty minutes.'

Oliver looked to the floor.

Jack gasped. 'Oh God, please tell me I didn't miss—'

'They just said it.' Oliver's lip quivered, tears rolling down his face. 'I'm so sorry, baby.'

Jack shook his head. 'No, no, that's not...'

Oliver hugged Jack, crying into his shoulder.

Jack squeezed his eyes shut. 'It can't be true. You're having me on.'

Oliver shook his head against Jack's breast.

Jack grimaced. He ripped away from Oliver, grabbed a table lamp, and SMASHED it on the floor. A tense silence followed, echoes of the crash vibrating throughout the room.

Jack looked at Oliver with shameful frown.

Oliver scowled back. Grabbed a stack of books. Threw them against the wall. CRASH!

Jack burst out in a nervous fit of laughter. Oliver chuckled along, his body trembling with shock. They let it all out, light chitters morphing into dense, cathartic cackles. As their energy dried out, the men lowered themselves to the floor, lying on their backs and gazing up at the dusty ceiling.

Jack scooted over and held Oliver. 'How did Edgar react?' he whispered.

'Last I saw? Sobbing with joy.'

Jack groaned, chuckling slightly. 'Just when I thought he couldn't get more pathetic.'

Oliver frowned. 'Charlie's mortified.'

Jack sighed. Closed his eyes. 'When's the sentencing?'

'Right now.'

Jack hesitated. 'I can't hear anything.'

'Me neither.'

Jack squeezed Oliver and kissed his cheek. Oliver smiled. They closed their eyes.

The two of them stayed on the floor, enjoying the magic of that room where the rest of the world didn't exist.

The Next Day...

Geoffrey Grant MP relinquished his seat in the House of Commons, officially dropping out of the election, leaving Edgar to run unopposed.

Charlie Smith spent the entire day at Lemmy's office, liquidating his assets and officially dissolving the Charlie Smith Publishing House. Despite his best efforts to pay the damages from his own pocket, Charlie had no choice but to sell his mother's house as an extension of the Middlesex Hospital. With the flourish of a pen and a notary's stamp, the golden days of the Montgomery Street Brothel were over.

The Times dissected the verdict on page seven, immortalising in great detail the conspiracy of desperate incumbent Geoffrey Grant MP and the once-esteemed Charlie Smith to slander Tory underdog Edgar Withers. The front page, however, focused on a different matter:

THE SINS OF JACK BRANSON
by Dr Haywood Goldsborough,
Reader in English Legal History,
University of Cambridge

> I do not believe in fate. The world is too large and chaotic, and human beings are burdened with too much weakness to achieve anything resembling a destiny. But every so often, by complete accident, the stage is set for something magnificent. The once-in-two-hundred-years kind of magnificent. The perfect

moment. History being made. Legends being born.

Such a moment occurred at Old Bailey on Friday when Jack Branson, a male prostitute from Dublin, took the stand for the Defence and delivered a testimony so infamous, so sensational, that the transcriber stopped recording from pure shock. Such a moment deserves to be louder than words. No description could properly recapture how Mr Branson affected the courtroom. His brazen effrontery reduced the gallery to utter silence, and several elderly women fainted at his words.

However, his power was not as simple as his use of explicit language. Mr Branson was also sharp and witty. His defiance, already highlighted in his best-seller *The Sins of an Irishman in London* (his secret authorship just one of many surprises that morning), was one of strength and pride, with no fear toward the society that sought to oppress him. His commentary on truth, in which he deconstructed the hypocritical nature of our justice system and the wishful thinking of our laws, was nothing less than a revelation.

At the risk of sounding maudlin, I predict that Jack Branson's testimony will one day be studied in every major school of law in the world. Just as significant as his words is the man himself. Without exaggeration, 'Dublin Jack' just made himself the

most famous male prostitute in history, a distinction both well-earned and incredibly disgusting.

It's also the truth.

19 Montgomery Street, Marylebone, Two Days Later...

Sitting on the porch, Jack folded the newspaper with a smile. 'I couldn't ask for a better reputation.'

François puffed his fag. 'You're really gonna let them call you Dublin Jack?'

Jack shrugged. 'It is catchy.'

François checked his pocketwatch. 'We better get in.'

Jack reluctantly stood. He gazed out at Montgomery Street, lit only by streetlamps and the millions of stars in the sky.

'I don't want to go,' he whispered.

François snuffed his fag. 'We had a good run.'

'They were the best years of my life. Why couldn't I savour it?'

'You did, darling.'

Jack shook his head. 'I didn't realise how special it was until now.'

François smirked. 'None of us expected it to end. That's what made it special.'

Jack gave François a big hug and kissed his cheek.

François clapped Jack's shoulder. 'Come on. Let's go out like kings.'

That night, the whores of the Montgomery Street Brothel had one final party. François cooked the best steak they ever tasted, and Denny made everyone cocktails. After dinner, they moved to the

Barroom for a celebration of art and drink. One by one, they stood upon a makeshift stage and performed acts for the others. Denny went first. He grabbed three snifters from the bar, dropped his crutch, and juggled as he hopped on one leg.

A few minutes later, as Denny performed feats of flexibility, someone knocked on the front door. Jack made his way to the Great Hall, opened the door and gasped. 'Morty!'

Morty held his hat with a bashful smile. 'I shouldn't stay long. I just wanted to pay my respects.'

Jack let Morty inside and gave him a huge hug. 'I never got a chance to thank you.'

'For what?'

'For not turning us in. That was so brave of you.'

Morty pursed his lips. 'It wasn't enough.'

'On the contrary,' Jack said with a smile. 'It meant a great deal.'

Tears formed in Morty's eyes. 'You don't have to go,' he whimpered. 'The Commissioner said he wasn't going to arrest you.'

Jack blinked with surprise, but he shook his head anyway. 'It's time for me to move on. But I'll miss you.'

Morty frowned. 'Please don't lie. I know I'm just a client to you.'

Jack took Morty's hand. 'I never lied to you, Morty,' he whispered. 'You are a beautiful man, inside and out, and I am so lucky to have known you. I will miss you, because out of all those men I've been with, you're the only one who truly cared for me. And for that...' He smiled warmly. 'I love you.'

Morty smiled, his moustache curling in a truly genuine grin.

Jack nodded. 'You'll be a great Commissioner one day, Morty Blasmyth. I know it.'

Morty wiped his tears. 'I'll never forget you, Jack Branson.'

Jack and Morty kissed one last time, slow and with plenty of care. The perfect send-of. With a tip of his cap, Superintendent Blasmyth stepped out and made his way back home.

As Jack watched Morty fade into the night, he felt a queer sense of familiarity, as if a scene from his past had just repeated itself. Differently. Better. The way it was supposed to. Jack could not remember what it was, if it actually happened at all, but there was still satisfaction in accidentally getting it right.

Ten Minutes Later...

Oliver grabbed another cocktail from the bar. 'Amsterdam? What made you pick that?'

'It was always the next stop of our world tour,' Louise said. 'Mary likes the beer, and I like the bikes.'

'Not to mention the red-light district,' Mary added. 'We might stay if we like it too much.'

Denny finished his act to hearty applause. Charlie handed him his crutch and the two moved to the bar.

'What's next for you?' Charlie asked, sitting at the counter.

Denny scooped ice into a cocktail shaker. 'Rome. Mary says it's beautiful over there. I can sketch full-time. Maybe even start a studio.'

'You'll do great.'

Denny poured gin into the shaker. 'Of course I will.'

Charlie looked off in deep, morose thought.

Denny sprinkled a couple drops of vermouth, softening. 'Where will you go?' he whispered.

Charlie sighed. 'I'll stay with my grandparents until I figure something out. Maybe I'll reach out to one of my mates from the orphanage. Start something new.'

Denny shook the shaker. 'Don't your folks have a castle in Highlands?'

'Yeah. Why?'

'You should take a holiday.' Denny strained the martini and slid it towards Charlie. 'You've done so much to deserve it.'

Charlie smiled. 'The one that started it all.'

'Best drink I ever made.' Denny raised his glass. 'Thanks for everything, boss.'

Charlie lifted his martini. They clinked their glasses.

Oliver wandered in from the Great Hall, confused. 'Where's Jack?'

Louise sat on the floor, squeezing his feet into tap shoes. 'I think he went upstairs.'

Oliver nodded slowly. 'Okay. I'll get him.'

'Don't miss our act!' Mary called. 'They loved it in Paris.'

'I'll hurry back. I promise.'

Andy watched Oliver leave the Barroom. 'I hope he makes it back for our scene.'

'Focus, honey,' François murmured, his nose in a script. 'We have to finish this.'

'Why do I have to be Juliet?'

'Because you do what you do best.' François flipped a page. 'Lie there while I do all the work.'

Andy stared at François. 'I love you.'

François froze. Lowered the book. Slowly turned his head toward Andy.

Andy smiled warmly. He caressed François's chin, leaned in, and kissed him.

François pulled away, laughing. 'Stop, cheeky devil, or I'll hit you!'

Andy growled suggestively.

Louise and Mary stepped up to the stage, clapping their hands twice in perfect unison.

'Ladies and gentlemen!' Mary declared.

'Lords and Ladies!' Louise added.

'Her Majesty the Queen!'

'Her guest of honour, Jack the Ripper!'

'Children of all ages! We have a special show for you tonight!'

'Our horrible parents proudly present...!'

Mary pointed to Louise. 'Liverpool's own Corey Kehoe...!'

Louise pointed back. 'And Georgie Belcher!'

'Better known as the iconic...!'

'The incomparable...!'

'The legendary double act of...'

'MARY AND LOUISE!' they cried in unison. The two instantly broke into a frenzied, perfectly synchronised tap dance routine. Denny, Charlie, Andy, and François cheered.

Upstairs, Jack sat on his bed, hunched over the front page of *The*

Times. The muffled mirth of the Barroom below floated up through the floorboards.

Oliver knocked on the door. 'Why are you up here by yourself?'

Jack folded the newspaper. 'I could've done more.'

Oliver sat next to Jack. 'You did enough, baby.'

'No, there had to have been something more.'

'You made old ladies faint!' Oliver chuckled. 'You did your best.'

'But Edgar won! Charlie lost everything. The brothel's closed down. Everyone's splitting up.' Jack scoffed. 'Why are we even having a bloody party?! We lost, Oliver!'

Oliver stroked Jack's hair. 'It's the last day we'll be together. They'll always be our family. You of all people know how to love your family from afar.'

Jack frowned. He rested his head on Oliver's shoulder. 'Morty said they're not gonna arrest me.'

'I'm not surprised.'

'But they know everything about this place, what we did here. I was in two different sodomy scandals! Why would they let me go?'

'Because you impressed them.'

Jack looked up, confused.

Oliver shrugged. 'They'll never admit it, of course. But after what you said? Wouldn't be right.'

Jack sighed. 'We were never going to win, were we?'

Oliver shook his head. 'World's not ready for that yet. But now they know we're not afraid.'

Jack grinned. 'They don't want to test me. I know too much.'

Oliver laughed, shaking Jack playfully. 'That's the spirit.'

Five Minutes Later...

Jack and Oliver returned to Barroom and joined the groundlings. François (the dead Romeo) lay on stage while Andy (Juliet) stood over him with a prop dagger.

'Yea, noise?' Andy cried. 'Then I'll be brief. O happy dagger! This is thy sheath!' He stabbed himself with the fake weapon, moaning in pain. 'There rust and let me die!' He fell onto François.

'YOW!' François yelled.

'Oh! I'm sorry, baby!' Andy straddled François, kissing him deeply. Louise and Mary walloped suggestively.

'Now we're talking!' Denny catcalled. 'My kind of show!'

François blew raspberries. Andy helped him up, and the two started clearing the stage.

Jack smiled at Charlie. 'What will you do? Sleight of hand?'

Charlie sighed. 'I'm sitting it out.'

Jack frowned. Looked off. Thought of something.

'Okay,' François mumbled, stepping off the stage. 'Who's next?'

Jack stood, swiped a cocktail from the bar, and walked on stage. 'Attention, everyone! Get a drink. I want to say a few words.'

Charlie looked up at Jack, agape. Oliver, Andy, and the others grabbed their glasses.

Jack took a deep breath. 'Before I do my act, I want to raise a toast to a great man.' He looked Charlie in the eye. 'It was his vision that changed our lives, and he's an inspiration to everyone he's ever met.'

Charlie's eyes started to water.

Jack nodded. 'Charlie Smith broke himself, Oliver, and many

other boys out of an orphanage two years before he was able to leave on his own, and he led that band of pickpockets for many years, ruling the alleyways with sympathy, love, and courage. He dreamt of a world where we could be like everyone else. He's a legend for bastards and homosexuals, and he earned his inheritance with love, not hate.'

Denny nodded, moved.

Jack's breath wavered. 'He gave a lonely orphan a hero. An amputee his purpose. A French Negro his power. A pair of cross-dressers a new adventure. An American runaway a new home. And...' His voice caught in his throat.

Oliver put a hand to his heart.

Jack fought through his sobs. 'You gave an Irishman, a man who thought he meant nothing to the world...' His lip quivered. 'You gave me a family.'

Charlie closed his eyes, tears falling down his face.

Jack forced a smile. 'Charlie gave us hope, a place for ourselves, and pride in who we are. But the best thing he ever did, just one of his many unrecognised accomplishments, was bringing us all together.'

Charlie wept into his hands. Mary and Louise scooted over and hugged him.

Jack wiped his eyes. 'For my act, I wanted to pay tribute to the home Charlie made for us, but also to the memory of the woman to whom it originally belonged. I never met her. I don't even know her name. But I don't need to. In a way, she's all our mothers.'

Jack closed his eyes. Took a deep breath. Sang:

'The water is wide, I cannot get over
And neither have I wings to fly
Give me a boat that'll carry two
And both shall row, my love and I

Where love is planted, oh there it grows
It grows and blossoms like a rose
It has a sweet and pleasant smell
No flower on earth can it excel

A ship there is, and she sails the sea
She's loaded deep, as deep can be
But not so deep as the love I'm in
I know not if I sink or swim...'

Jack's voice faded away. He opened his eyes.

The light was warm, the air warmer. Andy and François resting against the wall, holding each other in a loving embrace. Oliver and Denny at the bar, cocktails in their hands. Charlie on the floor with rapt, shimmering eyes. Mary and Louise on either side, tears streaming rouge down their cheeks. Every one of them looking back with sweet, loving smiles. Jack's heart fluttered as he scanned the faces of his friends, preserving that beautiful scene in his memory.

He held up his glass. 'To Charlie.'

Everyone raised theirs. '*To Charlie.*'

The Next Day...

The farewells started early. François and Andy rushed to catch

the eight o'clock boat train to Paris, where they planned to start a brothel of their own. Jack, Oliver, and the others hugged them and wished them well.

The relentless onslaught of goodbyes continued in the afternoon. Mary and Louise departed for Southampton Dock at two. Denny caught the train to Portsmouth only one hour later.

Jack and Oliver, their red eyes depleted of tears, wished Charlie a final goodbye. They hailed a growler and left for Jack's flat in Eaton Square.

With a final sigh (and a bit of a smile), Charlie Smith locked the doors of that old house on Montgomery Street and handed the keys to his solicitor.

95M Eaton Square, Belgravia, Six Weeks Later...

Jack and Oliver spent their last weeks in London living the fantasy life they had been dreaming about. They slept in every day. Held each other in bed. Made love all they wanted. Ate lunch together. Strolled through the Eaton Square Gardens. Toured the Summer Exhibition. Watched a couple operas. Danced beside the River Thames under the moonlight.

Fourteen days before their lease expired, the two men stayed up and had a serious discussion about their future. After deliberate consideration, with little resistance from both parties, Jack Branson and Oliver Hawkett agreed to pool their savings and sail west for New York City.

34 Cherry Street, Camden Town, Two Weeks Later...

On the morning of 12 June 1889, Jack and Oliver's growler pulled up to the Cherry Street Post Office. As Jack hopped out, memories of Tommy Munce wafted through his head before vanishing like smoke.

DING DING DING! Oliver held the door open as Jack wheeled his bicycle inside.

'Oh no,' Mr Munce whimpered, stepping out of his office. 'Is it the day already?'

Jack nodded. 'Afraid so.'

Mr Munce leaned his behind against the counter. 'You must be glad to see the back of this place.'

Jack slowly shook his head. 'I'm surprised myself.'

Mr Munce scoffed. 'Don't be daft! Think of America. This city had its time. You deserve something new.'

'I know,' Jack said. 'But one morning I'll wake up and miss the cobble streets. And the wet lampposts. And the grand houses. And I won't remember the smell, or the rubbish, or the horrid flat with the mouldy ceiling.' He looked at Oliver with a loving smile. 'London made me a man.'

Oliver took Jack's hand, beaming.

Mr Munce wagged a stern finger. 'No flirting in my lobby.'

Oliver laughed. He gave Mr Munce a big hug.

Mr Munce rubbed Oliver's back. 'Take good care of him.'

'I will.' Oliver let go and stepped aside.

Mr Munce and Jack stared at each other. Devastated frowns on their faces. Their eyes filling with tears.

Jack raced over. Clapped his arms around Munce. Squeezed as hard as he could. Mr Munce closed his eyes as he held Jack.

'Thank you for everything,' Jack whispered.

Mr Munce nodded. He tilted Jack's head down and kissed his forehead.

Jack wiped his eyes and wheeled the bike toward the counter. 'You're gonna need this to deliver those telegrams.'

Mr Munce chuckled, sniffing a bit. 'It's so small. My back's gonna hurt for weeks.'

Jack smiled. 'Something to remember me by.'

Mr Munce held the door for Jack and Oliver, watched them step into the growler, and waved goodbye it drove away.

On their way to King's Cross, Jack and Oliver stopped at Dubeau Frères and shared one last Délice de Mousse.

Somewhere on the Atlantic Ocean, Five Hours Later...

The ship sliced across the sea, no sign of land on the perfectly straight horizon. Oliver and Jack stood at the bow, gazing out at the limitless water.

'Can you believe it's out there somewhere?' Oliver asked.

Jack looked behind him, double-checking for witnesses. All clear. He reached out. Lifted Oliver's chin with a finger. Kissed him. Slowly. Softly. Deeply.

They stopped. Stared into each other's eyes. Warm sun on their face. Soft breeze rolling past. Ocean waves crashing around them. It was all so familiar. They did it. They were finally there. But it was real. It was never real before. And they always woke up before...

Before. Before what?

A profound chill ran down Jack's arms. Oliver nodded. He felt it too. They turned back to the horizon.

'This must've been how the explorers felt,' Jack murmured, hugging Oliver from behind. 'Always the same thing. Only so many places to go, so many people to meet, so many stories to tell. Everything found, everything done, everything known... and then something truly different.'

Oliver shook his head with wonder. 'How brave they must've been, going out there. Making new cities that never existed. New nations to do whatever they want. No idea what they were doing. What was to come.'

Jack nodded. 'Spain. Britain. France. Turkey. Great empires with greater armies, sacking the same cities over and over for centuries. They suddenly knew nothing. No maps. No territorial advantages. No precedents. No mistakes to learn from. Only what they had on them.'

Oliver smiled. 'Civilisations thousands of years old didn't know what was beyond the bend for the first time. Like the whole world started over. Everyone was equal. No borders. No traditions. Nothing but strangers in a strange land.'

'We still are,' Jack whispered, his eyes shimmering like the sea. 'No land is stranger than our future.'

POSTSCRIPT

This novel is inspired by real people and events. While creative liberties have been taken with linguistics, historical accuracy, and a modern interpretation of homosexuality, the most unbelievable parts of *The Sins of Jack Branson* actually happened.

Jack Branson is based on John Saul, aka Jack Saul or Dublin Jack. Saul was born in a Dublin tenement slum on 29 October 1857, the eldest son of eight children. He moved to London in 1879 to work as a prostitute, sending money home to his impoverished mother, Eliza Revington Saul.

Jack Branson's memoir *The Sins of an Irishman in London* is based on *The Sins of the Cities of the Plain*, an anonymously published erotica from 1881. It was one of the first exclusively homosexual works of pornographic literature published in English, as well as an early form of the nonfiction novel. Its authorship is commonly attributed to John Saul.

Mary and Louise are based on Thomas Ernest Boulton and Frederick William Park, aka Stella and Fanny, who were frequently arrested for sodomy and public cross-dressing in the 1870s. They are prominently featured in John Saul's novel.

The Collins Affair is based on the Dublin Castle Scandal of 1884,

in which Irish nationalists accused the staff of Dublin Castle (the seat of the British government's administration in Ireland at the time) of having homosexual orgies. Among those charged was Captain Martin Oranmore Kirwan, one of John Saul's sexual partners when Kirwan was a lieutenant. Saul was questioned by the police and released for reasons unknown.

The Montgomery Street Scandal is based on the Cleveland Street Scandal of 1889, in which a homosexual brothel was discovered at 19 Cleveland Street in London. The government was accused of covering up the scandal to protect its aristocratic patrons, most notably Prince Albert Victor, Queen Victoria's grandson and second-in-line to the British throne.

Ernest Parke, editor of the obscure, politically radical weekly *The North London Press,* discovered that the arrested prostitutes, many of them pretending to be telegram boys, had been naming their aristocratic clients in exchange for lighter sentences, but those accused were never charged. In November 1889, Parke published a story publicly accusing Henry James Fitzroy, the Earl of Euston and eldest son of the 7th Duke of Grafton, of being a patron of the infamous Cleveland Street Brothel. Euston immediately sued Parke for libel.

The final defence witness at Parke's trial was John Saul, a resident of the Cleveland Street Brothel since 1887, and he delivered a brazen testimony so explicit that it shocked the courtroom to silence. In January 1890, the jury found Ernest Parke guilty of libel. John Saul was not arrested for reasons unknown. Historians now believe Saul was telling the truth and that Euston was well known in

the homosexual underworld.

Charlie Smith is a composite of William Lazenby, the publisher of Saul's novel, and Charles Hammond, the straight (and married) owner and operator of the Cleveland Street Brothel. The house at 19 Cleveland Street was demolished in the 1890s for an extension of the Middlesex Hospital, which itself was bulldozed in 2006.

On 28 August 1904, John Saul died of tuberculosis at Our Lady's Hospice in Harold's Cross, Ireland. He was forty-six years old.

King Henry VIII officially made sodomy (used synonymously with anal sex) a capital offence in 1533. The punishment changed from execution by hanging to life in prison in 1861. The Criminal Law Amendment Act of 1885 added the vague charge of 'gross indecency', used broadly to prosecute all male homosexuals, including consensual adults in private settings, when actual sodomy could not be proven. It was punishable by two years of hard labour. Almost 65,000 men were convicted of gross indecency over the next eighty-two years.

Male homosexuality in England and Wales was decriminalised in 1967, Scotland in 1980, Northern Ireland in 1982, and Ireland in 1993. Female homosexuality was never a crime.

On 31 January 2017, the United Kingdom issued automatic posthumous pardons to 49,000 men convicted for homosexual acts and started accepting expungement applications from the other 15,000 still alive.

Same-sex marriage has been legal in England, Scotland, and Wales since 2014, Ireland since 2015, and Northern Ireland since 2020.

ABOUT THE AUTHOR

David Schulze (né Stehman) was born and raised in Phoenixville, Pennsylvania. A lifelong admirer of movies, mythology, and classic literature, David loves stories across all mediums. He wrote his first novella as a senior in high school, a "literary opera" that combined prose, an original Shakespearean tragedy, and an unusual structure simulating a real-time opera house performance.

In 2017, David graduated Cum Laude from Emerson College with a BA in Writing for Film and Television and a Minor in Literature. He has written nine feature screenplays and four shorts, many of them placing in screenwriting competitions. Falling back on his love of prose, David adapted his ninth feature, *The Sins of Jack Branson* (2018 Final Draft Big Break Contest Quarterfinalist), to be his debut novel.

David lives in Marlton, New Jersey with his husband Howie.

Want exclusive stories, in-depth analyses, and updates on future projects? Go to davidschulzebooks.com

---

C000172729